UNDYING VENGEANCE

UNDYING VENGEANCE

A Novel

K.L. BURNHAM

This novel is dedicated to

My dad, who always believed in me and encouraged me to shoot

for the stars.

My daughters, Enya and Kaitlynn, who are my world.

My mom, sisters and many nieces and nephews for your continued

inspiration and love.

Dr. Gary Humphries for his advice, guidance, support and belief in me

and my accomplishment.

And to all my close friends for your words of support.

"The tragedy of life is what dies inside a man while he lives."

—Albert Einstein.

CHAPTER ONE

"SIMONE! SIMONE!" ARMANI screamed. The left side of his face burned like the fires of Hell. He stared at the ceiling and tried to sit up but a jolt of pain like lightning stopped him.

"Where the hell am I?" Armani asked, staring at the IV needles in both his arms. He slammed them against the bedrails like an animal ramming itself against the thick wire of a trapper's cage. Seconds later he heard faint steps getting louder.

Two nurses in pink scrubs ran in followed by a man in white.

"Relax. Lay your head on the pillow." A jolly nurse ordered.

"Check his vitals!" The man in white, whom Armani presumed to be the doctor said. "We're going to need to sedate him."

The nurse put a cuff on his arm, checked her watch, and counted his respirations. Armani thought it was a pretty stupid thing to do at this time. His blood pressure would be sky rocketing. His breaths were labored, as it was. No one seemed to want to tell him what was going on and why he woke to find himself in this hospital bed. The doctor and nurses were talking as if he weren't in the room.

"Doctor, his blood pressure is 186/101. Shall we give him another dose of morphine for pain?" The jolly nurse asked.

Armani rolled his eyes. Of course his blood pressure was high. No one seemed to give a damn about him and offer an explanation. Armani looked at the nurse. "Don't sedate me." He ordered and shifted his gaze at the doctor. "Excuse me, Doctor, but what is going on here? How did I end up here? I have no memory of admitting myself into this hospital or of what happened to land me here. It's my right to get an explanation right now. And where's my attorney? I want to call him."

The doctor nodded and looked Armani in the eye. "Mr. Belvedere, three months ago a tragedy occurred that the police are still investigating." The doctor said and paused like he was searching for how to say what needed to be said.

Armani was losing his patience. 'Why doesn't the doctor just get to the point?' he thought. Beating around the bush was for shallow people who were afraid of the truth. Shades of gray didn't work for Armani. He wanted to hear things in black or white, simple as that.

The doctor cleared his throat, looking Armani in the eyes. "You were brought here by ambulance three months ago. A housekeeper found you unconscious on your hotel room floor. Your heart rate was deathly low. The medics thought they would lose you on the way to the hospital. The police believe it was either an insider with a vendetta against you or a crazy fan gone mad who may have been stalking you for some time." The doctor paused and rubbed his chin. "The people or person who did this must have taken you by surprise. The police believe when you opened the hotel room door they hit you with a hammer or blunt object hard enough to knock you out. You hit your head hard on something sharp when you fell. The gash on the side of your head was large and deep causing you to lose a lot of blood."

"That wouldn't put me here for three months, Doctor." Armani stated. "It's Impossible."

The doctor sympathized with Armani because he knew the worst news was about to be dealt. He sat and folded his small hands in his lap and nervously licked his lips. "Armani, after you collapsed, the person or people who did this, injected you with a drug to keep you passed out. You were unaware of what was going on. Armani, the left side of your face was severely burned with third degree burns. You were near death when the medics arrived here with you. We immediately took you to the burn unit where we sedated you and worked on you for hours."

Armani's brows creased with worry. "What procedures were done, Doctor? I don't remember any of it. Please explain to me what happened the past three months that I've been here." He touched the left side of his face expecting to feel scabby skin but instead felt a large cotton wrap. "I want to see my face."

The doctor cleared his throat. "No, not yet, Armani, one thing at a time. Let me first explain to you what we did to help you heal as you asked first."

Armani nodded for the doctor to continue, trying hard to be patient and understanding. After all, these people had saved his life, and hopefully Simone's as well.

"As you can see, we have you hooked up to IV's which are still transporting fluids into your body. Most of it right now is saline. We had to secure additional venous and arterial access, so I inserted a flexible plastic catheter into your femoral vessels, entering near your groin, a necessity because of the risk of death due to shock. The continuous flow of fluids entering your body kept this at bay. This needed to go on for months once we started, and we constantly drew blood to test the carboxyhemoglobin level which is an indicator of how much deadly carbon monoxide is circulating in the blood."

"Why can't I remember?" Armani interrupted.

"Burn unit patients all spend a long period of time heavily sedated so that they don't remember anything of the horrible time spent in the hospital during operations and the healing process. It is for the sake of the patients and their loved ones." The doctor paused, noticing Armani looking at the IV line in his arm puzzled. "That IV was first used to deliver morphine and Versed into your body the past three months. The morphine was for pain, the Versed was to quell anxiety and induce amnesia." He smiled. "The IV's are delivering antibiotics and saline into your body now."

Armani looked at the doctor's face. "Thank you for reading my mind." Armani hated drugs of any kind. He was a rock star but never succumbed to the lifestyle of sex, drugs, and rock-n-roll. His music was the only drug he needed to get high.

"It was all a necessity, Armani," the doctor said. "Our next procedures were healing the burns on your face. We used what is called Bair Huggers. We would heat a solution called Ringers Solution to 102 degrees, dip the Bair Huggers into it and spread them on your face. Up until a week ago, you had a nasogastric tube inserted through your nostril and into your stomach to vent gas and carry liquid nutrition to feed you as well as your hungry wounds and to keep your bowels from shutting down. The foley catheter will be removed later this afternoon." The doctor stood up and placed his hand on Armani's shoulder. "I'm sorry, I know this is a lot to take in and understand."

"I want to see my face now." Armani said.

"You will later. We did reconstructive work and skin graphs on your face. Why don't you wait until after dinner? A nurse and I will remove the bandages and allow you to see your face. Tonight, I suggest taking ambien for sleep and getting a solid nights rest."

Armani grabbed the Doctors arm and read the name on his tag. "Dr. Weaver, who did this? Where is Simone? Was she as badly injured as I was?"

"Armani, nobody knows who did this. We notified the police department that you were out of sedation and available for questioning. An officer should be here shortly to speak with you. They will have more answers than I do." The Doctor's heart went out to Armani. "I'm sorry for everything that has happened to you." Dr. Weaver said, his eyes misting over. He turned and walked toward the door, the nurses close behind.

"But what about Simone? Is she . . . . ." Armani asked, but before he could finish Dr. Weaver had closed the door. His heart ached and a sinking feeling of loss punched him in the gut. He looked at the white tile ceiling. A tear trickled down his cheek and landed on the pillow. Armani was alone in the cold empty hospital room, his body a soulless hollow shell.

A knock on the door startled him. The same jolly nurse he had seen before entered the room and smiled warmly at Armani. "Hello Armani. I'm going to give you more morphine per Doctors orders."

Armani cringed. Thinking about more meds in his body made him feel sick. "How about Ibuprofen or Motrin? I'd prefer over the counter meds, please." 'How about something for severe depression?' Armani thought. He was trying his best to be compliant and with the staff while he was stuck in this dreary hospital room wanting answers.

"I'll have to ask the doctor about that." The nurse studied Armani's face, noticing the sadness in his eyes. "Armani, would you like to talk with me about your feelings?"

"That's fine," he stated. "By the way, what is your name?"

"Louise," the jolly nurse said. Her gray hair was slicked back in a tight bun. When she smiled, her brown eyes sparkled like stars in the sky on a clear night. "I know this is probably a terrible time to ask you a favor," she began, her cheeks tinged red. "I wondered if I could get your autograph. I've been a fan of yours for a long time. I love your music and your voice is divine, mesmerizing, in fact. Your voice sounds so much like Chad Krueger, the lead singer of Nickelback. Are you brothers?" Louise asked, sitting in the chair beside the bed.

Armani smiled. His first real smile since he awoke to find himself lying in a hospital bed. "Thank you for your gracious compliments. No, Chad and I are not brothers. When our band started touring we were the opening act for Nickelback. He coached me in many areas of vocalization and taught me to sing as he does. That's why we sound so familiar," he said and put his finger to his mouth. "Don't tell the press."

Louise handed him a photograph of Armani and his band. "Would you autograph this for me? It would make my day."

Armani took the photograph, trying not to look too closely. "What would you like me to write?" He looked at Louise and smiled.

"Write anything that comes to your creative mind."

"Ok, simple enough." He said, took the pen from Louise and wrote a quick note. *'Louise, thanks for being a dedicated fan of ours. Keep rockin' to our beat. Sincerely, Armani Belvedere.'* He tried to smile and handed the photo to her.

"Thank you so much," Louise said a grin the size of Texas on her face.

Armani extended his hand and shook hers. "No, thank you. Without our fans, we wouldn't be where we are today."

Her chubby cheeks turned bright red. "Sorry to change the subject, but I've got to ask Dr. Weaver about the meds and see if he'll let you have something other than morphine. I'll be right back." Louise said and left the room.

She was back a few minutes later. "I'm sorry, Armani. Dr. Weaver wants you to have morphine. He said the other pain meds haven't fully worn off yet, but when they do, you will be in extreme pain. He wants you to rest before the police and detectives arrive."

Armani sighed. "So be it, then. You're just doing your job."

Louise injected a vial of morphine into Armani's IV. "This is a fairly large dose. Rest well, Armani." She said and squeezed his hand.

Armani felt the effects of the morphine take effect right away and felt like he was floating on a cloud soaring to the Heavens. In the

Heavens he saw Simone surrounded by angels singing a beautiful chorus. "Where's Simone?" Armani asked Louise, his eyes pleading for an answer.

Louise wrapped her chubby hand around his and squeezed. "I'm not allowed to say anything about that. I'm so sorry. I wish I could. The detectives will be here in a few hours to talk with you. Please get some rest now." She said and placed his hand on his chest. "I've got to go do my rounds, but I will check on you in a bit." Louise pulled the blankets up to his neck before leaving the room.

He knew the detectives would have answers for him. He held onto the hope that Simone was in the hospital recovering as he was. Armani could no longer fight sleep and drifted into complete darkness hoping to dream of Simone.

CHAPTER TWO

FIVE HOURS LATER, Armani awoke, his face burning and throbbing with pain. He slowly opened his eyes and saw two detectives standing at the foot of the bed. "Who are you people?" He asked, confused.

The short bald man with a no-nonsense look on his face spoke first, "Armani Belvedere, I'm Detective Mitchell." Armani nodded, switching his gaze to the other detective. He was a dark haired man in his thirties with a kind smile.

"Hello Armani. I'm Detective Phil Cooper. You can call me Coop, if you wish. I'm a huge fan of yours. Your music kicks ass." He said and shook Armani's hand.

"Pay no attention to 'Coop'. He's a rookie," Detective Mitchell said crossing his arms. "Professionalism, Cooper. This is business." He spat and shot a warning glare at Detective Cooper.

"Damn it." Armani said frustrated. "Will one of you tell me what the hell happened? Who did this? Where's my Simone?" Armani asked. His temper was going to flare if they didn't get right to the point.

"I'm sorry, Mr. Belvedere to bring you this news. You and Simone were both drugged, attacked and beat. There is no easy way to say what needs to be said next. I'm sorry but Simone is dead. She was dead when the medics arrived. This is the worst part and I don't leave details out." He paused a moment and continued, "Simone was raped before she was shot in the chest twice. I'm so sorry."

Armani cried out pulling his hair. "MY GOD! NO!" Tears streamed down his face. He felt like his heart had been torn from his chest. His face turned ashen, the blood flowing through his veins felt cold as ice. "Can I see my Simone? I don't believe what you're telling me. Who would do this to her? You're lying." He spat.

Detective Mitchell clasped Armani's hand trying to calm him down and ease the pain. "No, it's not possible to see her. She was buried three months ago. I'm sorry."

Armani picked up a glass of water and threw it across the room. "I want to see Simone NOW! Where is she?" He yelled.

Detective Mitchell squeezed his hand harder. "Please try to calm down. I know the news we delivered is horrible but we need your cooperation in order to begin putting the pieces of the puzzle together and figure out who did this to you and Simone. Believe me we want to catch whoever is responsible for this horrific crime."

Louise and another nurse ran into the room, concerned looks on their faces. "Is everything OK? We heard yelling in here." Louise asked. She realized the detectives had delivered the news to Armani about Simone. Her heart went out to him. "Oh, I'm sorry. We didn't mean to interrupt, but it's protocol to check on these types of situations." Louise made eye contact with Armani and gave him a sympathetic smile.

"We are the detectives working on this case and would appreciate privacy. Close the door on your way out." Detective Mitchell ordered, not even bothering to look at the nurses.

Armani felt like an empty vessel. Life now was meaningless and he wished the detectives would leave. He already had his fill of both of them with their 'acting'. They didn't know him, only that he was in a successful rock band. How could they possibly empathize with him and his situation? They couldn't. Acting must come with the job and you either learn to numb yourself or go find another career. "I need the nurse to come back. I want more pain meds," Armani said. The burnt side of his face intensified with every tick of the clock.

"We will send her in a few moments." Detective Cooper said. "I'm not going to ask you the typical 'Do you have any enemies or know anyone who would do this to you?' Because of course you do. You are the lead singer of a famous rock band and no doubt you have a lot of fans. Some with disturbing mental issues, fans jealous of your success. I've seen many fans obsessed to the point of craziness. Then, there are other people or fans who just want to hurt someone, knowing when they get caught they will get publicity for it." Coop paused. "Unfortunately, we live in a world where many people are crazy, to the point of madness." He finished and shook his head in disgust.

"Excuse me, let me interject," Detective Mitchell said. "Do you know of anyone you recently pissed off that would destroy your life like this as a result?"

Armani rolled his eyes. "Of course, I've pissed off a lot of people. Several I know, and more than likely a few I don't know. You're the experts. Do your job and let me know. Believe me, if I knew who did this, they wouldn't be breathing right now." Anger erupted like a volcano inside him. He didn't particularly care for Detective Mitchell with his stony expression and emotionless eyes. "I want to go home now."

"You are going to be here for a few more days, Mr. Belvedere. The medical staff has informed me that you will undergo a few more treatments on your face." Detective Mitchell handed Armani his business card. "If you think of anything I should know, give me a call. We will do our best to solve this case as quickly as possible."

'Yeah, sure.' Armani thought. 'Just like they have the past few months. Assholes.' "Believe me, when I'm out of here, I'll be doing some detective work myself." Armani sneered at Detective Mitchell.

"Use your last few days here to get some rest," Detective Cooper said with a half smile. "I want to see you on stage soon." He handed him his business card, patted Armani's shoulder and both detectives walked out of the hospital room.

Armani wanted the bandages off his face and wished he could leave this place of gloom. He used the remote, put the bed in the upright position and stared out the window. The emptiness of life without Simone hit him with an awful blow. "Simone, Simone, my love. I will find who did this to you." His heart ached and the damn holding back his tears broke. He hung his head and wept for what seemed like hours, his whole body wracking with emotion and pain. "Why!" He screamed. "Why!" The emotional pain was too much to bear. He picked up the vase of flowers placed on the tray table and threw them against the wall. The glass shattered sending pieces flying across the room. His heart, soul and body ached with pain. A pain he knew would never go away.

The next three days in the hospital were the longest days of Armani's life. Louise came into his room often on her shift and tried her hardest to cheer him up. He appreciated her support but nothing could make him happy. His attorney made regular visits discussing things with him. Armani had no family. Simone was his family and his life and now she was gone forever. Emptiness and sadness overwhelmed him. He wept more the past few days than he had his entire life. There was a large gaping hole in his heart that only Simone could fill and losing her was a burden he didn't know he could live with. Thoughts of suicide entertained him, but he wanted revenge and was going to kill the people responsible for taking his reason for living. When he found them, he would turn his sorrow into anger and avenge his Simone's death. "God have mercy on their souls," Armani said. "May they burn in hell for what they did."

A knock on the door startled him. "Armani, it's Louise and Dr. Weaver." Louise said. They entered the room and walked up to the hospital bed. Dr. Weaver took off his glasses and stuck them in the pocket of his bleach white lab coat. "It's time to remove the bandages from the left side of your face. You get to go home today, Armani. Do you feel you're ready?"

"Yes, I am more than ready to go home. I'm a bit worried about seeing my face," Armani said and gazed at Louise, grateful she was there. "My attorney made arrangements for my friend, Rex to pick me up. He should be here by now." He peered past Louise and Dr. Weaver, hoping to see Rex waiting for him. No sign of him yet.

"He called and is running a bit late. He's stuck in rush hour traffic. We all know how that is,." Dr. Weaver stated. "I am going to write you some scripts for pain medicine as well as a script for 60mg of Prozac. It's the highest dose, but I believe you need it at this time." Dr. Weaver said. "Not permanently, but for awhile and I would advise you to take it daily. It's in your best interest."

Louise nodded in agreement, took Armani's hand in hers and smiled at him. "We are going to remove the bandages now. So, lie down and try to relax."

Armani did as told. Anxiety lines etched his face. His palms were sweaty. He knew it wouldn't be pretty. The right side of his face was still gorgeous. God had blessed him with good looks with his jet-black hair, piercing green eyes, high cheekbones, large perfect lips, and a physique toned to perfection. If Simone were alive, she would love him no matter how mangled the left side of his face was. Thinking about Simone stung his eyes with fresh tears.

Louise saw this and comforted him. "It will be Ok, Armani. You will still be gorgeous."

He turned his head. "It's not about that. I hurt for Simone. I miss her. She was and will always be the love of my life. My tears are for her, not me. I don't care what my face looks like. I wish I would've died instead of her." He regained composure, swallowed back tears and turned to face Dr. Weaver and Louise so they could do what had to be done.

Dr. Weaver removed the bandages with ease and threw them in the wastebasket. "I'm going to send a couple months worth of bandages and antibiotic ointment home with you. You will need to apply the cream and bandages every night and leave them on while you sleep. It will prevent infection and continue the healing process. Your face looks much better than when you first arrived, but I must warn you that the left side of your face will have permanent visible scarring." The doctor stated and rubbed ointment on Armani's burnt face.

Armani flinched. "Is it supposed to be this sensitive?"

"Yes, I'm afraid so. Your face will be tender for quite awhile," Dr. Weaver said. He reached into his white lab coat and pulled out a business card. "Here's my home number, cell number, and office number. Please call if you have any questions." Dr. Weaver smiled, handing it to Armani.

"Thank you Dr. Weaver. I'm sure I'll be fine, but I appreciate your concern and graciousness." Armani set the card on the nightstand.

Louise exited the bathroom with a black hand held mirror in her pudgy hand. She bit down on her lip. Armani noticed her hand shaking. "Are you ready for this, Armani?" She asked sympathy in her eyes.

"Probably more than you are. I just want to get out of here and go to my home." Armani said. He held out his hand and took the mirror.

Armani held the mirror to his face and gasped. The left side of his face was a patchwork of red, pink, black, and brown, the skin shiny and taut. The tip of his left ear was singed off. The eyebrow and eyelash were swept away. "Oh my God, this is horrible. Louise, I thought my face would look more human than this." He said, pointing at his face. A tear threatened to escape but anger held it back. "This side of my face is hideous!" Armani gripped the mirror so hard his hand turned red. "Dr. Weaver, is there some sort of mask I can wear that will conceal the left side of my face? How long will it look this way?"

Louise loosened the mirror from Armani's grip, and placed her hand in Armani's.

Dr. Weaver studied Armani's face. "We have prosthetic masks, but in my opinion, they make the face look worse and draw more attention to oneself. You're free to check them out, but your face must heal first before you can wear one."

"And just how long do I get to walk around looking like a circus freak?" Armani asked. He liked Dr. Weaver, but the man had a tendency to answer questions vaguely instead of getting straight to the point. Armani was doing his best to keep his temper under control. 'If only Rex would appear in the room and get me the hell out of here.' Armani thought.

"Four to six months," Dr. Weaver responded. A shrill beep came from the doctor's waist. He glanced at his pager. "I've got to go and make a call, Armani. I wish you the best of luck. I have your discharge papers ready for you to sign." He smiled. "Louise will take care of everything from here and get you packed up and ready to go home." He shook Armani's hand before exiting the room.

"I'm sorry about everything that has happened to you the past few months," Louise said. "I wish things were easier. If it makes you feel any better, you are still gorgeous." Her cheeks tinged red.

Armani saw her eyes twinkle and forced a smile for her. "I want to thank you for being so kind to me while I was here. You're a wonderful, caring nurse. I'll learn to accept my appearance. Justice will be served to the ones who are responsible for this. I promise that."

Louise packed Armani's things into a hospital bag. "Do you want this?" She asked.

Armani nodded. It was the hand held mirror. "I may as well take it home. Spare someone else using it, only to see how ugly they have become." His looks were a small matter compared to the heartbreak he felt when he imagined what these monsters did to Simone. He wondered if they mutilated any part of her face while torturing her.

Was she alert? Did she feel pain? Was she dead before they raped her? These thoughts filled him with rage.

"I'm almost finished packing." Louise said and looked at Armani. She gasped and shuddered. Goose bumps spread over her body like a disease. "Armani, your eyes are black as soil. Are you alright?" Louise swore she saw the devil in his eyes.

"I'm fine, Louise," He assured her. "Rex should be here any minute."

Two minutes later, Rex walked into the hospital room. He was tall and lean with long wavy blonde hair and sky blue eyes. Today he wore a black leather jacket, white t-shirt, blue jeans, and snakeskin cowboy boots. "Armani, I have missed you, man," he said and walked to the bed and hugged his best friend hard.

"Thanks for coming," Armani said. "Rex, this is Louise, the nicest nurse here. She kept me going."

Louise blushed when Rex shook her hand. "It's a pleasure to meet you, Louise." Rex said.

"Same to you," she smiled. "Well, Armani is ready to go home. I know that for sure. Here's his bag. I'll get a wheelchair so you can get him out of here easily. We just have to make one stop at the nurse's station to get his signature on the discharge papers."

Armani waved his hand. "No need for a wheelchair, Louise. I'll walk. Thanks for thinking of it, though." He swung his legs over the side of the bed and looked at his legs. "Guess I better put some pants on, huh?"

"I brought you these," Rex said. He threw a pair of black sweats on the bed. "I'm looking out for you, brother."

Armani slipped his feet into the sweats, stood, and pulled them up. "Let's go." He nodded at Rex.

They left the room and twenty minutes later the paperwork was signed and Rex, Armani and Louise stood waiting for the elevator. Louise hugged Armani and wished him well. "Feel free to visit me anytime." She said and forced a smile.

Armani noticed how sad Louise seemed that he was leaving. He assumed she probably got more attention from him the last couple of weeks than she had ever gotten from any man in her lifetime. His heart went out to her. How he wished that were his only problem. His heart was torn to shreds. Simone, how would he ever live without his beautiful angel?

"Thanks for all you've done for me, Louise." Armani kissed her cheek. "You aren't just a nurse, you're an angel." He meant that, too. The elevator doors opened and Rex and Armani stepped inside. As the doors closed Armani glanced at Louise one last time and saw a tear roll down her cheek.

CHAPTER THREE

REX AND ARMANI were on Highway 21, two miles from Armani's exit. "I am so sorry about all that has happened," Rex said, hands on the wheel. "I don't know what else to say, honestly. This must be the most painful thing you will ever go through in your life."

Armani knew Rex was trying hard to be sympathetic. As long as he had known Rex, emotions were never easy for him to show. Rex was the type of guy who ran from his own pain as well as the pain of others. "I appreciate your concern. I'll be fine." Armani lied. 'Once I get revenge,' he thought.

Armani looked out the window. The trees were blanketed in white snow. The last time he was on this highway was with Simone and the trees were beautiful colors of red, green, orange, and yellow. Everything reminded him of Simone. Simone loved fall. How would he ever live without her?

Rex interrupted his thoughts. "Do you want to stop somewhere and grab a bite to eat?" He lit a cigarette and rolled down the window an inch. "You have to eat, ya know."

"No thanks. I want to get to my home." Armani's heart broke. He knew he'd be faced with the memories of Simone the minute he walked in the door.

"Here's the exit. Are you sure you're ready to go home?" Rex asked. "I can stay with you for awhile, if you want company."

Armani touched his face desperation filling his heart, soul, and mind. "No, Rex. Please don't ask me any more questions. I'm a grown man and you know as well as I do, that I need 'alone' time." He stated. "I appreciate the concern. I really do." He laid his head back, closed his eyes and tried to rest for the next ten minutes it would take to get to his house.

Rex turned onto the entrance of the half-mile long driveway that led to Armani's home, which resembled a castle like Sir Dracula's. He stopped the car at the gated entry. "I forgot the code to unlock and open the gate. It's been awhile since I've been here." Rex said. He dangled his arm out the window and fidgeted with the buttons.

Armani lifted his head and winced in pain. "My face is burning. Guess I have to accept that. But Simone being gone, I will never come to terms with that." He placed his hand on the left side of his face and recited the code. Rex punched it in and the gate opened. The driveway needed plowing, but the car managed to make its way through the deep snow.

The driveway was lined with trees covered in snow. It was beautiful in the Spring and Summer. Wildflowers of different colors grew in the woods and Armani had his gardener plant a variety of bright gorgeous plants and flowers of red, blue, yellow, orange, and auburn.

Armani's home came into view after the first twist in the driveway. It was three floors with two large towers at the ends of the mansion. It was built with poly-chromed brick, which was a whitish gray stone with specks of black. The roof was flat with ornamental stone walls waist high around the entire roof, which Armani and Simone had used as a patio to view the gardens, park, and large ponds which surrounded the majestic home. Armani had hired Jacob McIntire, an architect and generation relative of Samuel McIntire to design the home with a castle theme. His home was a 19th century European Gothic Style mansion. Armani had seen a picture of the renovated Old Louisiana State Capital, fell in love with its appearance and had Jacob design it almost exactly the same. His mansion was beautiful, yet dark, which fit Simone and his personalities perfectly. Now, Armani viewed his home as a dark place. He and Simone were going to be married in their home, raise a family, and grow old together. That reality was gone and was now just a dream of the past, a dream that would forever be a nightmare to him and in time would awaken the monster within.

"Here we are," Rex said. A large hawk flew overhead, circling the house. "Hey Armani, check out that hawk." He pointed at the metallic black hawk with a white spot on its chest. "It sure is beautiful. I've never seen anything like it. That would be a great picture for one of our future album covers."

Armani pulled himself out of the car and gazed at the bird. "I've seen him around before. One day when Simone was on the patio she took a picture of it flying over the house and had it enlarged and framed." He paused lines of pain etched the right side of his face. "It looks like a professional photographer did the work." Armani said and hung his head. He fought back the tears. "We just never got around to hanging it up in the living room."

Rex continued to stare at the hawk and watched it land in a nearby tree. "It looks like it's watching every move you make, man." Rex said. A chill ran down his spine. Something about the hawk made it seem almost human, yet its gaze held an evil aura. Rex walked toward the door. "Come on. Let's get you settled in." Rex waited in front of the heavy, black door made of steel and turned the knob.

"Here are the keys," Armani said and placed them in Rex's hand.

"Guess we don't need them. Your door was unlocked." Rex stated a concerned look on his face.

Armani shrugged, pushed the door open and walked into his home. "I'm sure it was a simple mistake by one of my employees. I have surveillance cameras if I think something isn't right or looks amiss." Armani walked to the black plush couch in the living room and lay down, not bothering to look around.

Rex was worried about his best friend and band mate. The depressed state he was in was obvious. Who wouldn't be after what he had gone through? To wake up in a hospital, three months of your life gone forever, one side of your face disfigured, and the love of your life murdered and not even a chance to say a final goodbye. Plans for the future changed in the blink of an eye. Rex realized how much people take for granted with their live in the moment attitudes. There is no guarantee for tomorrow. Not for anyone, no matter how famous you are or how much money you have. None of that would save you from fate, whether good or bad.

Rex picked up the leopard print blanket that was draped over the back of the couch and placed it on Armani. His friend was already asleep, or he was a great actor. Armani stated he wanted to be alone, and Rex would respect his wishes, but he couldn't help but wonder if the events that had happened to Armani would be the end of him. "Sleep well, my friend. Know that you're not alone." Rex whispered. He walked to the door and turned around watching Armani sleep. His heart ached for his best friend.

Armani opened his eyes when the door closed. He needed his space and time alone to mourn the loss of Simone and the many dreams they had. Exhaustion plagued him but he had too many things on his mind to take it easy. Life was no longer easy and every day was going to be hell for him. The sooner he accepted this the better off he knew he would be. But, Armani wasn't willing to accept what happened to Simone or himself. That would be like asking a poor man for a loan of an outrageous amount, which was more than impossible. It was unimaginable.

Armani threw the blanket off of him and slowly sat up. His head hurt and the left side of his face burned. The doctor wanted him to take the bandages off several times a day so the skin could get oxygen as part of the healing process. For what, Armani had no answer. His face was forever deformed and scarred. He stood and walked to the winding staircase.

The walls lining the staircase were decorated with black gothic light fixtures and candles spaced apart every three feet. He looked up at the beautiful stained glass dome built into the ceiling. Not even that made him smile. It served as a reminder of Simone. She was the one who had requested it and of course he said yes. He could count on one hand the number of times he said no to her.

There were six bedrooms and bathrooms upstairs. One bedroom was Armani and Simone's. The other five were for the children they had talked about having once they were married. Simone wanted a large family and the two of them agreed that five children would be perfect. Only God knew how many children they would've been blessed to have. These thoughts raced through his mind as he climbed the stairs. When Armani reached the top of the stairs, he ripped his shirt off and threw it over the stairway railing and screamed a dreadful piercing scream. Agony, heartbreak, loss, and anger swirled inside him like a hurricane. Armani fell to his knees, placed his head in his hands and cried. The loss was unbearable and the tears wouldn't stop streaming down his face. If only he could hold Simone one last time. "Why did you let her be taken from me?" Armani screamed. He lay down on the floor and curled up in the fetal position.

He felt like an abandoned newborn. The one thing he lived for was gone forever. Life was meaningless and death was a welcome guest to him.

Armani raised his head, wiped his eyes, stood up, and stared down the hallway that lead to Simone and his bedroom. The only thing keeping him alive was the revenge he would have on the ones who killed Simone and left him damaged physically, mentally, and emotionally. His face was a hideous reminder of what these people took from him that he would never get back. Only upon his death would he see Simone's beautiful face and smile that lit up a room. Death would be his end after he made the people who did this pay with their own lives. He felt like an empty shell and for Armani, the darkness had just begun.

He walked with heavy footsteps toward the bedroom he and his love had once shared. A cold draft blew through the window, the curtains dancing like ghosts in the wind. The smell of her perfume still lingered in the air. God, how his heart ached as he wished she would be in the bedroom waiting for him. When he reached the bedroom he paused and took a deep breath before opening the door. Simone was so beautiful, long brown hair, brown eyes, and a smile that melted your heart.

But, there was no Simone. She was gone forever, but he could feel her presence in the bedroom. He walked in and sat on the king sized bed sinking into the soft, white down comforter. "Simone, I'm so sorry. If you hadn't met me you would still be alive. Someone had a vendetta against me for a reason I have no knowledge of. It caused you to die, and my sprit to die forever." Armani said. It felt peaceful to talk to her even though he knew she didn't hear him. He vowed to catch the murderers and get revenge. Only then could he let Simone's spirit rest in peace and allow himself to let go and rest in peace as well. Happiness was a thing of the past for him. "Simone, I love you and only you, and always will. I hope you can hear me and feel my devotion to you." Armani closed his eyes and lay on the bed remembering when they first met.

Chapter Four

THEY MET AT Armani's birthday bash. Rex had planned the party and held back no expenses to make sure it was the best day for his best friend. It took place on Rex's large yacht with over two hundred people in attendance.

Rex knew how to throw a party. Balloons, a dance floor brought in onto the yacht, a DJ, a bar staffed with ten people, and a cake that looked like it could feed a city. The cake was a personal favorite of Armani's. It was decorated with his face and those of his band mates and on top was a mini stage with instruments made of candy. That alone must have cost a fortune. Armani was happy he had so many friends and family who loved him and thought he was as happy as he could ever be. He had his band, a lot of friends, fans, wealth, success, and beauty. Maybe a bit too proud at times, but Armani knew he was attractive and could have anyone he wanted. He enjoyed being single but his mind changed when he first saw her at this birthday party. Something inside him told him that Simone was the woman he had been waiting a lifetime for and that he would spend the rest of his life with her. Who had she come with? He wondered. A woman this beautiful had to be here with a date.

Armani walked around and found Rex at the bar talking to a young woman with red hair. He wasn't drunk yet, lucky for the woman sitting next to him. Rex had a tendency to act like an idiot when he consumed too much alcohol.

"Excuse me ma'am, I hate to interrupt, but I have to ask Rex a quick question." Armani said and smiled at the young woman. Her eyes were emerald green and sparkled like diamonds. No wonder Rex was smitten with her.

"Not a problem," she said with a wave of her hand.

Rex seemed irritated, but he would get over it. He turned to look at Armani.

"This will be quick, don't worry. You see that woman over there," Armani said pointing at Simone. "Who is she?"

Rex turned to look. "Oh, that's Simone. Her father owns some big computer company. I don't remember the name, but he's a very powerful man." Rex smiled at Armani. "Interested, buddy?" He asked.

Armani shrugged. "Maybe, but I haven't even met her yet. Is she here with someone?"

"Yeah, she was invited here by a girlfriend. From what I gathered, Simone came with a girlfriend of hers who won tickets to the party. Not that she couldn't have pulled some strings and came anyway."

Armani smiled. "Well, that's a good start. No guy in my way." He chuckled. "Why didn't I hear about the tickets people were winning?"

"Our manager raffled off about ten of them with the proceeds going to charity. It's a good cause. Lighten up. After all, it makes us look better to the public. Good publicity is always better than bad publicity." Rex slapped Armani's shoulder. "Go ahead and talk to Simone. I'm a little busy myself with this beauty." Rex said and flashed a grin at the red head. Clearly she loved the attention from Rex, the rock star.

Armani laughed. "Thanks. Enjoy yourselves." He put a piece of gum in his mouth and thought about how to approach Simone and what to say.

"Hey, just ask her to dance." Rex said as if reading Armani's mind.

Armani turned to look at his friend who was already lost in conversation with the pretty red head.

Simone stood in the distance watching people dance while she sipped red wine. Armani walked in her direction unable to take his eyes off her. She saw him coming and smiled. Her smile lit up his heart, which was crazy because he didn't even know her. Her face and smile showed she had inner beauty as well.

"Hi, I'm Armani Belvedere." He said and extended his hand.

Simone blushed. "Hi Armani, I'm Simone." She said taking his hand. "This may sound stupid, but I want you to know I love your music. Your voice is so wonderful." She let go of his hand and fidgeted with her hair, "and happy birthday."

"Thank you, Simone." Armani said. His heart raced. He felt like a school boy with a crush. "Would you like to dance with me?"

Simone held her hand out. "I'd love to," she gushed. "Dancing is one of my favorite hobbies."

They danced to many upbeat songs and held each other tight during the slow sets. Armani felt the connection between the two of them immediately.

Simone stopped dancing and wiped her brow. "I'm thirsty, how about a drink?" She asked. "I haven't had this much fun in a long time."

"Sounds wonderful," Armani said and led her through the crowd of people who were busy dancing, laughing, and talking.

Rex approached them, staggering and laughing and wrapped his arms around Armani.

"Happy birthday to you, my best friend!" He exclaimed.

"Rex, what the hell are you doing?" Armani asked, handing Simone a fifty-dollar bill. "Simone, go ahead and order whatever you want, and I'll have whatever you have." Simone smiled and walked toward the bar.

"There's nothing wrong, dude. Happy fucking birthday!" Rex exclaimed.

A short Spanish man handed Rex a microphone and pulled out a chair for him. Armani wished he could hide. He swallowed hard when Rex jumped onto the chair.

"Hello, party people!" Rex's voice boomed through the speakers. "My best friend turned 33 today and deserves a birthday serenade." Rex shouted and waved his arms back and forth as he led the crowd in a chorus of happy birthday. People raised their glasses and sang along. Rex, being the humorous guy he was, held his lighter in the air and swayed.

Armani smiled. It was a sweet gesture and he loved everyone singing to him, but he was ready to throw himself overboard. Being a musician for two years, he was used to performing in front of tens of thousands of people, but he hated surprises when he wasn't ready for the attention.

Rex jumped off the chair and handed the microphone to Armani. Armani stood on the chair and cleared his throat. He was a tall handsome man with chiseled features, high cheekbones, shoulder length black hair, big lips, and piercing green eyes. His days at the gym had paid off and the women never failed to show their appreciation.

"Thank-you, Rex for that surprise and thank you everyone who came out tonight to celebrate me getting another year older." The crowd applauded and hollered. "But, in all honesty, I think birthdays should stop being celebrated after your twenty first birthday. I feel like an old man." He laughed and gazed at Simone. "I want everyone to know that the best gift I received today was the opportunity to meet Simone, the beautiful brunette standing over there." He pointed in her direction and winked. "Thank you everyone and let's keep this party rocking and rolling."

Armani jumped off the chair and hugged Rex. Simone tapped Armani's shoulder. "Thanks for acknowledging me. That was sweet but embarrassing." She handed him a cosmopolitan and gulped hers down quickly.

"I'm sorry, but I meant what I said. One thing you should know about me is that I'm always honest, about everything." He said and clasped her hand in his. "Let's find a quiet place and talk."

Simone followed Armani to a table overlooking the ocean. "What a beautiful night. You couldn't have asked for better weather for an outdoor party."

The blue-green waves of the ocean rolled, licking the sides of the yacht. It was a peaceful evening. They could see the city lights in the distance. Overhead a hawk circled in the sky.

"Now, that's odd. I've never seen a hawk hunting near the ocean," Simone said, her gaze on the hawk. "And its eyes seem to be glowing red." She stared a moment longer and chuckled. "I guess I drank my cosmopolitan too fast."

Armani looked at the hawk. "That is strange. Maybe it got into the punchbowl." He chuckled.

"Maybe, but it's still a bit spooky to me. Do you have a jacket or something I can put on? I feel cold." She said rubbing her long, lean arms.

Armani slipped his black leather jacket off and helped Simone put it on. "That should help." He sat down and put her hands in his. "Forget about the bird. Now, tell me all about you."

Two men standing across the dock stared at them through binoculars. One of the men threw his down and pounded his fist on the rail.

"We've got to get her away from him. Simone is to be with me, father. That is and always has been the plan, even from the time I was young and she and I were playmates." Adam said. He was a short bald man, his face like a lions with uneven eyes. "Being with her will increase my wealth and our popularity in the community. There's no such thing as love, you and I know that. All that matters is money, power, and status."

Alex looked at his son and placed his hands on his shoulders. "We will, my son. Money talks and you know I have many people I can pay to get rid of him and possibly her if need be. Did I mention Gabe Davis is paying us top dollar to inflict pain on Armani?" He asked an evil smile on his lips. "As you see, Simone made it to the party and naturally caught Armani's eye. This is working out better for us than I thought. You understand how the mafia works. What belongs to us, we always get at any price and Gabe is paying us a handsome sum and in the future will get us access to their hotel floor and room. Gabe gets what he wants and we get what we want." He threw the binoculars overboard and walked to the yacht's exit. "Come on son, let's get the ball rolling."

Adam took one last look at Armani and Simone, his round face turned red and hatred filled his heart. He wanted them both dead. Armani, because he was the beautiful rock star all women wanted, and Simone because time and time again she turned down his offers to date him and be his. She always told him it was better if they remained friends and yet she was never available to do things that friends did together. He wouldn't force her to be with him, like his dad wanted. He would kill her and make sure his face was the last one she ever saw.

Armani loved listening to Simone talk about her family, her career and her future plans. Her voice was like sweet music to his ears. This was Heaven.

The black hawk they had seen earlier shrieked and flew around the yacht. Armani watched the bird as it flew in circles seeming to want him to pay attention to what it was doing. It dove up and down in the dark night sky aiming toward a yacht a few hundred yards away.

Armani saw two men standing on the deck of the yacht the hawk was obsessed with and wondered why they were focused on Simone and him.

He nodded his head toward the yacht. "Looks like the paparazzi spotted us," Armani said.

"More like they spotted you and want to start some rumors about us," Simone laughed. "Can't wait to see what stories they come up with." She rolled her eyes.

Armani smiled at Simone dismissing the men and the hawk with a slight wave. "Back to you," He said. "I could listen to you talk forever."

Armani remembered that special day as if it happened yesterday. His eyes filled with tears. He should have seen it coming. Someone as beautiful, perfect, and wonderful as Simone was bound to be too good to be true. A woman who loved him for who he was, not what he was and that made her even more special.

He thought of the hawk he had seen over the years since meeting Simone. Was this bird some sort of messenger or a mere coincidence? The black hawk acted like a guardian angel watching him incessantly. Puzzled, Armani got off the bed wishing he would die. There would never be an end to the pain he felt. It ate him up inside. His soul was empty. Falling to his knees, he put his face in his hands, looked up at the ceiling and screamed.

CHAPTER FIVE

DONOVAN PACED BACK and forth across the living room floor. Watching Armani through the eyes of his faithful black hawk, he felt the pain as if it were his own. He had once been a man and knew what it was like to feel the anguish and pain of losing someone you loved more than life itself and to have them taken from you without even a good-bye. It crushed your soul, sucking the will to live out of your body like a vacuum.

Donovan's shackles were loosened by his savior and father, Victor who saved him from eternal damnation. He stopped pacing, remembering their first meeting and shuddered.

The experience was horrifying when Victor came to him in his darkest despair. Victor's appearance was like that of a raven with his jet black hair, black eyes, pointy sharp nose to his long black cape which danced around him like the wings of a bird.

"Who the hell are you?" Donovan asked.

Victor studied him with unblinking eyes. "I am Victor, Master of the Dark Ones. I'm here to rescue you from your anguish and pain." He walked a circle around Donovan daring him to say no or look away. "Trust me and do as I say. You will not avenge the ones who killed your loved one as a human. I know this because I have witnessed this group of powerful people. You will avenge your lovers death only to have them kill you soon after."

Donovan shook his head bewildered. Was Victor reading his mind? Questions he had for Victor were being answered before the words had a chance to leave his mouth.

Victor poked Donovan with his long bony finger. "And you were going to take the easy way out and kill yourself. You coward! These men who hurt you would get away with murder and without justice being served." A mocking smile played on his lips. "What then?"

Donovan shook with fear. Goosebumps prickled over his body. Licking his lips he said, "I honestly don't know. Why are you here?" He asked feeling like a mouse cornered by a cat.

"Don't be scared, Donovan. I'm here to help you, to offer you a better life, a way to make this group of people pay for what they did to you and your soul." He seethed and smiled, fangs glistening.

Donovan winced. Was it his imagination? Did Victor have fangs or were the drugs and alcohol he consumed making him hallucinate?

"I have been watching you for a long time. Your torment and pain has reached me and I want to help. Also, yes, I am a vampire. A good one, I might add. I'm in the business of righting the wrongs done to people." Victor bared his fangs again. "And I'm wonderful at reading people's minds as you have already figured out."

"Please, just leave me alone," Donovan begged. "I don't need your help."

Victor laughed. "It seems you do. Do I need to remind you that you were about to hang yourself until I showed up?"

"Yes, but so what? It's not your business. Be gone, I command you." Donovan said and did the Hail Mary.

Loud laughter erupted from Victor. "Please, don't try to entertain me. You have no choice in this matter. You are going to cross over."

Donovan tried to escape. He leapt toward the door, only to be blocked by Victor. "Sit down and prepare yourself." Victor said and shoved him into a chair.

The rest was history. Donovan had become an immortal and his revenge was sweet. The people who killed his beloved and caused him needless pain were forever erased from earth. He was thankful for Victor and always would be. Victor saved him from himself and his plan for suicide, a death that would have made the enemies victorious.

Lost in thoughts Donovan jumped when he heard a tap on the window followed by a loud shriek. Donovan craned his neck and saw the hawk perched on the window ledge. Without touching the floor, he glided across the room and opened the window. The jet black hawk lowered its head in submission and Donovan rubbed the hawk's head and body.

"You have been a wonderful seeing eye for me. Our work is not complete and you will continue to watch over Armani during the day while I slumber as I feel he needs more time to heal." He said and handed the hawk a cracker. Its razor sharp beak gently took it from Donovan's hand. The hawk's eyes were on the aquarium a few feet away filled with mice scurrying to and fro. "You will get a few of those, don't worry, my friend." Donovan draped the long black cape over his shoulders, his stomach telling him it was time to drink some precious life blood but first his hawk needed its reward. He drifted to the aquarium, the hawk following. "Here you are," he said placing a few mice on the wood floor of his rundown house. The hawk shrieked and dove after the mice.

Donovan exited the house and whistled a tune enjoying the darkness and the light of the half—moon wondering where he would meet his next victim. A few minutes later he heard the hawk, his faithful companion fly overhead. Donovan joined him as they soared high into the sky, eyeing the busy city streets.

Donovan thought about Armani and felt his pain. In time he would show himself to Armani and convince him to join The Dark Ones and forever be immortal and free from his human pain.

CHAPTER SIX

THE BIRDS CHIRPED outside and the sun shone through the bedroom window onto Armani's face making it feel like a piece of meat on the grill. He got up and looked at his yard, once so wonderful now held no beauty to him. Isolation had been his answer to life's problems since arriving home from the hospital. Armani continued to stay behind closed doors, occasionally talking to Rex and his agent on the phone. The full time staff he employed had been told not to show up for work until notified differently. Armani was a sensible man and continued to send them their weekly wage through the mail. It wasn't their fault his life was hell and they shouldn't have to pay for his problems and depression. His heart was numb and cold, but compassion for others still existed.

He sat on the wood chair he had made for Simone and thought about the last person he saw. The mailman had come to the door with a delivery for him. Assuming it was Rex, he answered the door without his mask on. The shocked look on the mailman's face plagued him. The left side of his face was charred and slightly deformed his left eye a little lower than the right due to scarring, the eyebrow gone forever, and his hairline was back three inches from his forehead. Armani rarely if ever looked in a mirror. He prayed his face would return to normal but the doctor gave him little hope.

What was there to hope for anymore? His only hope was avenging the death of Simone, seeing the men who destroyed him served their justice. His depression made him uninterested in his band with all the tours, schedules, screaming fans cheering for him and his band, Faded Cross. Armani smirked. How symbolic the name, Faded Cross was now of his life; a fading dream, a fading life that felt like death on a cross.

Armani walked to his music room, sat at the piano and played numerous songs he had written. The room was a beautiful auburn color, the floor made of black and white checkered marble. Pictures in black and white hung on the walls. Instruments of all kinds filled the room; guitars, drums, bells and numerous instruments most people would be shocked to see in a rock musician's home. He loved to play the cello, harp, and violin, so he had a few of each in the room. The most beautiful instrument was the shiny black grand piano in the center of the room. Armani walked to the piano, placed his hands on top of it and looked up at the black marble ceiling and drummed a tune with his fingers. 'My dearest Simone, I shall play a few songs for you and hope that you hear them in Heaven.' He prayed.

He walked to the chest filled with his sheet music, picked up a few of Simone's favorites he had written for her. That seemed so long ago, but it was only a short time. Simone wasn't musically gifted, but she loved to sit next to Armani when he'd play the piano and they would sing together for hours. Sometimes when she tried to hit a high note, they would both laugh hysterically at her efforts. Armani loved that both of them had the ability to laugh at themselves.

Armani found the songs he wanted to play. Being a ritualistic man by nature, he dimmed the lights as he had done so often when he would serenade Simone. He reached into his pocket, pulled out a lighter and lit two red candles sitting atop the piano. Once lit, he held the lighter to his eyes and stared at the flickering flame. The left side of his face grew warmer. Gritting his teeth, he squeezed the lighter and threw it against the wall shattering it into pieces. "That's what those evil men have done to my heart. They will pay," he seethed.

Armani sat at the piano and placed the sheets of music in front of him. The first song was a melody he wrote for Simone titled, 'My Heart Beats for You.' His fingers moved gracefully along the keyboard, his voice seductive and edgy. Closing his eyes Armani lifted his head to the Heavens seeing visions of Simone dancing. He played this song three more times before stopping to take a breath. He played the next two songs, his heart grieving for her like a mother's for a deceased child. He knew the pain would be with him forever. The last song 'One Look,' he played four times as tears streamed down his cheeks.

Armani was emotionally spent. Lifting himself off the piano bench he caught sight of his reflection in one of the mirrors that lined the walls. He shuddered and cursed at himself. 'So, this is my curse,' he thought. 'It's what I deserve for destroying Simone.' The thought that if she hadn't met him she would still be alive haunted him, the guilt, like a cancer ate him up inside.

He walked up to the mirror and stared at himself. "What a horrible looking monster you've become," Armani said. He turned and focused on the unscarred right side of his face. Armani reasoned that the tormentor's left one side untouched sending him a message every time he looked in the mirror. The message was clear to him now for the first time. They had taken away Simone, his other half, just as they had taken away half his face. He could never look at himself without the physical and emotional wounds being reopened. Forever the scars will remain. 'Indeed the ones responsible will suffer for this.' He thought and slammed the music room door shut.

Dazed, he walked to the top of the stairs and stopped when he heard pacing footsteps like a caged zoo animal. A cold chill blew through the hallway making it feel like the temperature dropped fifteen degrees. The window was closed, so why did he feel cold? He wrapped his arms around himself and continued to listen. The pacing ceased. 'Maybe it was psychosis plaguing him again.' He thought with a shrug.

He stopped, goose bumps rose on his neck. Glass shattered. He assumed he must've left a window open and the breeze knocked over a glass. It was impossible for anyone to break in or step foot on his property. His home was surrounded by a wrought iron gate, surveillance cameras, alarm systems, and two large Rottweiler's imported from Germany and trained as guard dogs and were on alert for intruders. The dogs wouldn't hesitate to attack if someone dare trespass.

Straining his neck he listened. Silence answered him from the main floor. The dogs barked like they had gone mad. He jogged to the nearest bedroom and looked out the window. Both Rottweiler's paced back and forth barking, their eyes fixed on the house. He heard enough. Armani jerked the window open and hollered at the dogs to shut up and go to their kennels. They peered at him and did as told with great reluctance.

Armani was too hungry to let fear keep him caged upstairs. Whatever he had heard was gone now. Cold, empty silence was the only visitor in his house. He walked down the white spiral staircase lined with red carpet holding onto the railing. A sense of fear kept him on alert. The cold chill he had felt earlier was gone. He dismissed the chills with the possibility of having a fever. The doctor had told him that wouldn't be uncommon as he may get infections periodically. "It's nothing to worry about." The doctor had said. "It's just normal fluctuations of your body's temperature as it fights minor infection." Armani planned to call the doctor later and get a prescription for insomnia and psychosis. Lack of sleep was probably the cause of psychosis. Terrible nightmares plagued him every night. He woke up sweating several times a night and it was becoming routine. One he didn't welcome. His dreams were dark and horrifying. In them, he would see Simone being tortured, raped, and killed in the most graphic way as he stood by not able to help her. Always in these nightmares, a man appeared to offer him help and promised him an eternity of living in peace and freedom from pain. But, he wasn't fully man. His face resembled a hawk's with black eyes, long brown hair, stone cold blue eyes, pointed nose, long sharp nails and always dressed in black from head to toe. Armani wished the man existed, but it was just a dream, a recurring nightmare he hoped would end soon.

When he reached the last step Armani looked to the left and right. His home was extraordinary. The room to the left was the large living room furnished with two large black leather couches, a large black chair, and a 72inch flat screen TV. Two dining rooms were in each corner on the main floor, a large library, a sitting room, a porch which overlooked the landscape, and a kitchen the size of an apartment.

He saw nothing out of the ordinary and walked into the kitchen and the lights automatically turned on. He gazed at the front door as he passed. It was still locked. Armani slapped the right side of his face hard. He had to get a grip on reality. When he looked around the kitchen, his heart lurched. Simone had decorated the kitchen. It hurt to look at the walls of mahogany red, the floor consisted of black and white checker tiles and every appliance was tuxedo black.

Disappointment clouded his face when he opened the refrigerator and saw he had very little food left that wasn't already expired. He walked to the cupboard, pulled out a loaf of bread and settled for a peanut butter sandwich. He ate it in seconds but hunger still pained him. He opened the refrigerator again and pulled out a beer. The top popped with a welcoming sound. He guzzled down one and drank two more.

He walked to the window and stared at the yard covered with a blanket of white snow that sparkled like a thousand diamonds in the sunlit. Memories from the previous winter flooded his mind. He smiled remembering when Simone and he made snow angels and a snowman laughing like two giddy children. There was never a dull moment with her. He frowned and a tear slid down his cheek.

Armani retreated back to the refrigerator and pulled out the remaining nine beers and walked into the living room. He set the beers on the coffee table next to the couch and turned on the TV. Flipping through the channels, he finally found back to back episodes of his favorite show 'Law and Order'. Hopefully, this and the beer would keep his mind distracted for a while. It helped until a commercial break. A funeral director was talking about how they can help you through the grieving process while making arrangements as heart and compassion are the focus of their business, the funeral director said with a somber look on his face. Armani rolled his eyes and cracked open another beer. The balding man talked about how his funeral home also helps pick out tombstones, professionally engraved by them.

Armani felt like the funeral director stabbed him through the heart. What kind of man was he? He hadn't been to Simone's grave. Guilt plagued his soul. His beautiful Simone was buried without a gravestone, he was sure. His plans for tomorrow were to get out of the house for the first time in weeks and visit Simone. The commercial came to an end and Armani wrote down the phone number.

Simone was his angel. His world had become a dark, cold, and lonely place since her death. He would visit the funeral home and pay the funeral director to engrave 'My Angel in the Night' on a tombstone of his choice.

Armani lay down and pulled a blanket over himself. Too dizzy to even use the bathroom he closed his eyes hoping for a long peaceful sleep.

CHAPTER SEVEN

R EX BEAT ON Armani's front door. What the hell was he doing in there? He was worried about his friend's lack of interest in life. Armani didn't want to leave the house or even talk about touring. The rare times they talked on the phone it was more like talking to a robot. Today, Rex was determined to get Armani out of the house. Keeping yourself cooped up behind closed doors was not healthy for anyone, especially someone in the grieving process. Any shrink would tell you that.

"Armani, open this door, now!" Rex yelled, banging hard with his fists. The dogs sat at Rex's feet staring wide—eyed. He patted both of their heads. "Maybe you both should stay in the house with Armani and keep him company."

Rex's patience grew thin. He kicked the door with his boot. Trying to reach him on the phone failed. His calls went directly to voice mail.

Armani jumped off the couch, his head pounding. Damn Rex and his persistence.

He opened the door and tried to smile. The red orange sun shone like a ball of fire in the pale blue sky. What a beautiful sight and one

Armani had always treasured. He would never grow tired of seeing the sunrise. They symbolized hope and a fresh start.

Rex frowned. "You look like shit. I've been trying to call you for hours." He pushed Armani aside and walked inside. "Come, sit down. We need to talk and it's not a choice. You're going to hear what I have to say." Rex scanned the living room and picked up an empty can of beer. "Have a party last night, Armani?" He asked, smirking.

Armani stared at the sunrise, savoring the warmth. The dogs whined and waited for Armani to allow them in. He snapped his fingers twice and gestured with his hand. "Go lay down."

Armani glanced at the clock on the wall. "What the hell are you doing here at seven o'clock in the morning?" Armani asked. "Couldn't you have come later in the day?"

Rex shot him a cold look. "I'm here to get your ass out of the house. That's not a choice, neither, in case you think about telling me no or coming up with some excuse."

Armani sat on the recliner and thought about Simone's gravesite. "That's not going to work for me today. Sorry, but I have other arrangements."

Rex laughed. "And what might they be? Sitting on your ass feeling sorry for yourself?" He asked matter of fact and cocked his head.

"I'm going to visit Simone's grave. Is that O.K. with you, Rex?" He asked. "She needs a proper burial site with only the finest tombstone money can buy. So, say what you need to say." Armani leaned back in the chair and stared at the ceiling.

Rex watched Armani. He seemed a thousand miles away, but Rex had things that he needed to address whether Armani wanted to hear it or not.

"I'm here on behalf of the band and myself. We want to work on our new album and we can't do that without you. You write the lyrics and make things happen. I hate to admit it, but you're the backbone behind 'Faded Cross.'" Rex cleared his throat. "Without you, there is no group. It's time to move on with your career and future. Our agent wants to set tour dates. You're the lead vocals and we can't tour without you."

Armani interrupted him. "No shit. Well, tell Mr. Gabe Davis, our wonderful manager to stick it up his ass." He closed his eyes wishing Rex would get the hell out of his house. His wounds would not heal for a long time and until then, the band was something he had no desire to be a part of. "On second thought, tell him to find a new lead singer."

"What the hell is wrong with you, man?" Rex asked pissed off. "The fans miss you, they miss us. You need to think about others instead of yourself. All your buddies need to make a living, too. We have families and lives to lead, which requires making money. We can't just sit at home doing nothing." Rex regretted having to say this, but he was a man of blunt honesty, sometimes to a fault and this was one of those times.

Armani lifted his head and glared at Rex. "I hear you, Rex. I know you have a family. Well, I don't and I'm grieving the loss of the one person who was my family. Don't you dare say anything like that or you'll never see me again." He clenched his fists to keep from hitting Rex. "Do I make myself clear?"

"Sorry, man, that came out wrong." Rex stood up and walked to the window. "It's a beautiful day. Are you sure you don't want company today?" Rex knew he sounded desperate. The words he said about family had cut deep into Armani's heart like a double-edged sword. The worst part about it was that he couldn't take them back. Turning around, he noticed Armani staring at him, an odd look in his eyes. His face was a mess on one side. If he was honest with himself he knew he'd probably hide away too and avoid the stares and gossip. If he wasn't Armani's best friend, Rex would feel repulsed by the left side of his face. "Hey, you know what? We can get a mask for your face if that would make you feel more comfortable going out."

Armani frowned. "What a great idea, Rex. Then I can look like some sort of Erik wannabe."

"Who the hell is Erik?"

"Are you kidding me? You really don't have a clue what I'm talking about." He shook his head. "Erik is the Phantom in 'The Phantom of the Opera.' You know the guy with the appearance of death reincarnate and he wears a mask to hide his face from the world. It's an epic story."

Rex shook his head. "Oh, ok I know who you're talking about. You could at least consider a half mask or some sort of cover so you feel comfortable going out of the house." He offered. "I know someone who can make you one but only if you want to."

"I'll think about it. I think I'd rather go out looking like this instead of hiding behind some mask." He lied, pointing to the left side of his face.

Rex paced from one end of the living room to the next. It was a mess. Trash was scattered around the couch and chair, beer cans laid on the floor and coffee table. The absence of his housekeepers was apparent. "When are your housekeepers coming back to work?" Rex asked. A book on the coffee table caught his eye. He bent over, picked it up and scanned the inside of the cover and back flap. His eyebrows creased a puzzled expression on his face.

"When I call them to come back and work," he shot back. "They are my employees and I'm paying them, even in their absence." He dismissed the conversation with a wave of his hand. "What are you reading? I didn't know I had a book out here," Armani asked staring at the book in Rex's hands. "I only read in the library and that's where the books stay."

It troubled Rex that Armani had this book in his house. "I didn't know you were interested in Vampirism." He tossed the book to Armani.

"I'm not." Armani gazed at the glossy black cover. A man in a flowing red cape stood in the distance with outstretched arms. A creamy full moon hung in the sky, bare trees lined the street and the head of a large black hawk with red eyes encompassed the cover like a snow-globe. Chills ran down his spine. These images were all too familiar to him. "Did you bring this here as some sort of joke?" He asked his eyes glued to the strange book.

Rex crossed his arms. "No. You know better than that. I'm not into gothic worship of the devil and I don't believe in vampires, so why would I even waste my time or money on a book like that?" He asked. "Get real, my friend."

"I'll have to do some research on Donovan, the author." Opening the book, Armani frowned. "No last name. That's odd."

Armani's thoughts raced to the previous night when he heard someone walking through his house. It was impossible. There was no evidence that anyone was inside. But, the eerie feeling of not being alone was too real. He studied the cover as if in a trance. The hawk stared back at him. He held the book up and moved it from right to left. The hawk's red eyes followed staring into his eyes. His hands violently shook and he dropped the book.

"Are you alright?" Rex asked. "You look like you saw a ghost."

Fear gripped his heart and soul. "I'm fine." He said, sat down and placed his head in his hands. "I just need to rest before I visit Simone's grave."

"I'll leave you alone, but give some thought to what I said about the band." Rex patted his friends back. "Call me if you need anything. I'll be in touch and please answer your phone."

"Will do, thanks for stopping."

Rex opened the front door and saw a hawk sitting on a low tree branch one hundred feet from the house. It extended its wings, flapped them, the sound like leather. "Come here, Armani. The black hawk is back and it's staring right at me."

Armani moaned, stood and trudged to the door. "So what, it's been around here since Simone and I had this house built. What's the big deal?" Maybe it was a big deal because this was the same hawk in his dreams. A cold chill ran down his spine. The hawk stared at him like a predator eyeing its prey.

Rex gasped. "You know what? That hawk looks like the same one on the cover of that twisted book you have." He pointed. "I don't know about you, but that thing gives me the creeps."

The hawk screamed, flew off the branch and ascended toward the Heavens.

"It's huge," Rex said staring at the bird. Horrified, he watched the hawk descend toward them, its eyes blood red. Rex pushed Armani into the house, followed and slammed the door. The hawk flew into the door with a loud thud.

"It was trying to attack us!" Rex screamed. The hawk shrieked, beating on the door with its body and long sharp beak.

"What do we do now?" Armani asked. Goosebumps covered his arms.

Rex ran to the gun case. "We shoot the bastard!" He yelled over his shoulder.

Armani walked to the window and looked at the bird. The hawk stopped beating on the door, cocked its head and stared at Armani.

"It's the weirdest thing I've ever seen. It's staring at me. Not just staring, but searching my soul," Armani said.

Rex rolled his eyes. "Oh, come on, Armani. It's a God damn bird gone crazy or rabid." Rex didn't bother hiding his annoyance with Armani. "Help me load this thing." He tossed the bullets to Armani who missed them sending them crashing to the floor.

"Leave it alone, Rex." Armani ordered.

The hawk flew out of sight and reappeared carrying a piece of paper in its razor sharp beak. The hawk dropped the note behind a bush. Armani watched the hawk caw, spread its wings and fly away.

Armani was relieved to see the hawk go. He wanted to retrieve the note, but he'd have to wait until Rex left. He reasoned Rex would assume he was delusional.

Rex opened the door, gun cocked. "Where the hell did it go?" He asked, irritated. It was here a minute ago." He took a few steps and looked at the sky. "Damn. You were supposed to keep your eyes on it." Rex stormed back into the house and handed the gun to Armani.

Armani's patience wore thin. "Oh well, it's gone. Who cares? Now, if you'll excuse me, Rex, I have things to do." He covered his face with his palm, marched to the stairs and stopped. "Thanks for coming over. See you around." He took the stairs two at a time without a backward glance.

"Yeah, see you later, buddy." Rex hollered, walked outside and slammed the door.

Armani looked out the bedroom window and watched Rex leave. He needed to go to the funeral home and have a proper tombstone made for Simone.

He yanked open his drawer and pulled out a black sweater and a pair of jeans. But, there was something he had to do before taking a shower. He slowly walked down the steps.

His heart pounded with every step closer to the front door. He opened the door and looked from left to right and stepped outside. There it was. A simple piece of paper folded into four parts.

Armani reached for the paper. "Ouch!" He flinched. A branch scraped his arm. He grabbed the note, held it tight and dodged into the house.

Armani locked the door and stared at the piece of paper he held with shaking hands. No address or name on the front or back. He unfolded the note and the color drained from his face. It was signed 'Donovan.' How could that be? That was the author of the mysterious book on Vampirism Rex found. He had never heard of anyone named Donovan or cared about Vampirism. Armani walked to the living room and sat on the couch. He leaned over and shuffled trash and cans around until he found the book. "Shit." The hawk looked identical to the one he saw and had been seeing since he met Simone.

Nothing prepared him for what Donovan had written. His heart rate sped up, sweat beaded on his forehead and his blood ran cold. Armani read and re-read the note several times before setting it aside. He laid back and stared into space, unable to move.

Chapter Eight

The highway into downtown Grand Rapids was backed up for miles. Cars were at a stand still. Angry people yelled obscenities out their windows and honked their horns.

"Damn!" Gabe muttered, his face turning red. He was running late for his morning appointment with a prospective band, which appeared to be promising for him to represent. Gabe rolled the window down and drummed his fingers on the door of his sporty silver Lexus.

Gabe was the most popular and successful agent for musicians, mostly consisting of cutting edge rock bands. The famous 'Faded Cross,' with lead singer, Armani Belvedere, was his top moneymaker and they were in high demand. Not only for their musical talent and ability to put on a great show, but since the tragic accident which left Armani scarred physically and his fiancée deceased. If he made money on each call he received about Armani, he'd be a billionaire.

Armani was in demand for radio interviews, photo shoots, live TV interviews, and club appearances. But, when he contacted him about doing some of these Armani's always answered with a resounding 'no.' Gabe didn't blame him, neither. It was sad how the media seemed to delight in tragedy, only to help their ratings go up. Curious people would watch the interviews to look at his face, whether they cared about Armani or not. The story was all over the media. Some true and some false. Guilt washed over Gabe like a waterfall. He was partly to blame for the tragedy and whenever he talked to Armani by phone, it was like talking to a hollow shell. Armani's passion and zest for life was gone.

"Aw, come on," Gabe hollered. "This is ridiculous."

He shifted the rear view mirror and looked at his reflection. He smiled when he saw his shaved bald head shining like the moon at twilight. Gabe was short with large brown eyes and wore glasses that made him look like a professor at a university. He always wore three piece suits and polished black or brown shoes.

Success was his mission since college and that's what his life was. He was greedy, which lead to his growing frustration with Armani. He would get a percentage from all Armani's appearances, but he knew getting Armani to do anything he didn't want to do was like bleeding a turnip. Time was the only thing he could give his star lead singer.

Traffic picked up. He lit a cigarette and focused on the road. His phone was ringing. 'Murphy's Law,' he thought. It didn't ring while sitting idle in traffic.

"Hello, Gabe speaking."

"Hello, Mr. Davis. This is Carl Casper from Dateline. How are you today?"

Gabe rolled his eyes. "I'm doing well. What can I help you with?"

"I was calling in regards to your client, Armani Belvedere, lead singer of 'Faded Cross.'"

"You and every other News network out there. I say yes, but unfortunately my client, Armani says no."

"Sir," Carl sighed. "I wondered if he would appear on our show in one week. We want his side of the story and burn the rumor mill to the ground, no pun intended." He cleared his throat. "We want to set the record straight for the public who are hearing horrible things about the accident. As his manager, you should want the best for him."

Gabe waved to a pretty blonde in a Mercedes convertible next to him.

"The answer is still no. I'm sorry, but Armani wants his privacy at this time and that's all I can say." Gabe was growing irritated.

Carl coughed. "This may change his mind. The network which airs our show is willing to pay him three million dollars for a one hour interview. The contract is written and ready for both your signatures." He finished sounding like a salesman.

"Thanks for the sales pitch, Carl. The answer is still no." Gabe answered. "Let me give you a metaphor to help you understand. The price you'll pay for an interview is gold. The price of privacy is platinum. Hope you understand now."

Carl grunted. "Alright, thanks for your time."

"Damn reporters. It had to be the third time today the pushy news anchor's called about Armani." Gabe said aloud gesturing with his hands. "Leave me alone, assholes!"

The driver one lane over in a blue Toyota Prius stared at him like he was nuts.

Gabe shot him a dirty look. "You got a problem, son?"

The man glared. 'Odd looking fellow,' Gabe thought. Traffic finally moved at the posted speed. Gabe sighed, happy to make progress.

Gabe arrived at his downtown Grand Rapids office twenty minutes later. The office was lined with posters of artists, CD's encased in glass, and old school records. He heard his secretary typing on the computer and answering phone calls.

"Excuse me, Sir I'm going to put you on hold." The secretary said. She slammed the phone onto the receiver and twisted in a half circle to face Gabe. "I am so sick of the calls regarding Armani. I'm going nuts."

She pulled on her hair. "Have you heard from him recently? He won't answer my phone calls."

"Yes, I talked to him a week ago. He's the same and has no interest in 'Faded Cross'." Gabe walked to the counter and poured a cup of coffee. "There's nothing like Starbucks coffee before a meeting."

The secretary waved her hand. "They're in the conference room waiting for you."

"Are we out of sugar?" He asked.

She walked to the cupboard and pulled out a new bag. "Sorry, I haven't had time to refill the bowl."

Gabe smiled, his eyes roaming her body. "That's fine, Katie. Maybe I wanted to admire you and I can see more of you when you stand." He winked.

Katie blushed. "Thanks Gabe." Katie was a thirty-year old single mother of two. She had beautiful black hair, innocent brown eyes, with curves in all the right places.

"You have my permission to be rude to people who keep calling about Armani." Gabe said.

Katie laughed. "Good. I've said no to more people this week than I do to my kids in one week."

Gabe sipped the coffee. "Now, this is Heaven. Well, I better not keep the band waiting. Cross your fingers that they work out." He took a few steps and turned around. "Here, go take your lunch and the rest of the day off."

Katie was shocked. "This isn't necessary." She said and tried to hand the one hundred dollar bill to him.

"Take it or you're fired," he joked. "Seriously, you've put up with a lot of shit lately and deserve it. Good day now, Katie."

Katie watched him walk to the conference room, relieved for the break and economic boost. She wondered what secret Gabe was hiding. He wasn't acting like himself. She picked up her purse and left not realizing it would be the last time she saw Gabe.

Gabe entered the conference room and looked at the men dressed in black. The five men stood to greet him and stared in awe like he was Elvis Presley come back from the dead.

"Hello gentlemen." Gabe smiled. "We have a lot to discuss. I have listened to your demo CD and I believe your band has potential or quite frankly, you wouldn't be here."

The men grinned.

"Sir," one of the men said. "How is Armani?"

Gabe's face turned crimson red. "Let's get this straight. We don't have a relationship yet, and even if we did, that's none of your business." His gaze rested on each of the five band members. "Do I make myself clear?" He paused. "Now, let's get to business."

CHAPTER NINE

A RMANI DROVE TO the funeral home in silence analyzing everything that was happening in his life. 'Donovan, Donovan. Who the hell is he?' Armani wondered. 'And what am I to make of that hawk?'

Armani pulled into the parking lot and parked his black Lincoln Navigator. He took his black ski mask off and stared at the large white brick funeral home with two large pillars at the entrance. The shades were drawn and the lamps dimmed.

Armani walked to the funeral home lost in his thoughts when a noise stopped him. He looked up to see the hawk sitting in a nearby tree. Armani shuddered, picked up his pace and opened the door.

The funeral home was beautiful. A crystal chandelier hung in the entryway. Black, white and burgundy furniture accented the white walls covered in monotone pictures. Armani forgot how distorted the right side of his face was looking at the beauty inside this house of death.

A greeter approached him. "Hello, sir, may I help you?" He asked and extended his hand.

Armani covered the burnt side of his face. "Forgive me. I know my appearance is appalling," he apologized. "I'm here to see Mr. Jenkins.

I informed him that I would be stopping in today."

"No need to apologize," he said and smiled. "Right this way." The man walked ahead of Armani with a purposeful gait.

Armani followed at a slower pace and stopped to look in a room to his left. What heart wrenching agony the parents must be going through at the loss of their child. Armani stared at the small coffin where the child lay, unable to move when he saw a shadow appear behind the coffin.

The dark shadowy figure with red eyes stared at him. Armani shook his head. A chill ran down his spine as he watched the shadow become human, grasp the coffin and stare at the child. The man wore a long black cape. His long brown hair hung over his shoulders. The human lifted his head, red drops of blood trickled down his cheeks and onto the child. He stared at Armani, flashed long sharp fangs and bent over the child.

The man in black turned around. "Sir, are you coming? You look like you've seen a ghost." He stood waiting for a response.

Armani pointed at the coffin. "There's something wrong in here. Come look." His eyes were glued on the man.

The man kissed the child. Armani blinked. The man moved with such swiftness.

"I'll be right there." The greeter said.

Armani's heart pounded. The man by the coffin stood tall, stared at Armani and said, "Justice will be served for you both. I'm watching you, my friend. Don't fear me for I will come for you soon." He said his voice like Darth Vader's.

"Who are you?" Armani asked, his hands shaking.

The funeral director approached Armani and clasped his hands in his. "Are you OK? Are you talking to someone?" He asked. He looked in the room and saw nothing wrong.

Armani looked at the funeral director. "I'm sorry, sir. I've been through a lot lately and haven't been sleeping well. I think I'm getting delusional as a result." He shrugged and looked in the room.

The funeral director had a concerned look on his face and released Armani's hands. "I understand." He turned his gaze to the child. "It's a shame what happened to that sweet little girl. She's only four years old and died so terribly young."

Armani sighed. "Was it cancer?" He and 'Faded Cross' had set up a foundation benefiting cancer research and help for families with children diagnosed with the illness. He had a passion for this.

"No, I'm afraid not. That would've been more of a blessing for her," he sighed and continued. "Her name is Bonnie, Bo for short. Her parents killed her. Police reports said she was beat to the point of barely breathing and drowned her in the bathtub."

"My God, that's horrible. Why would they do this?" Armani asked.

"I wish I knew." He said a sad look in his eyes. "Would you like to view her and pay your respects?"

Before Armani could answer, the funeral director led him to the little girl. His thoughts were scattered everywhere from Simone, to the little girl, and to the creature he saw standing beside the girl's coffin.

"Is it hard to prepare a child for a funeral?" Armani asked.

They stopped in front of the little girl lying in the coffin. The funeral director turned and looked at Armani. "Yes, it is the hardest part of this job. It makes you think of your own children, grandchildren, and this poor little girl . . ." His voice trailed off and he turned away. "This was heartbreaking for me."

"I'm sure justice will be served," Armani said. He pictured the man and the hawk wondering if the creature he saw was Donovan. The creature cried red tears of blood weeping for the little girl.

Armani thought about the hawk, Donovan, the creature, the book. These things couldn't be a coincidence. Someone was trying to tell him something and what did this creature mean when it said it would come for him? Did it mean he was going to die? Well, Armani welcomed that with open arms. Yet, he needed to have his revenge and justice.

The creature did say justice will be served. Did the creature mean for the little girl? So many questions he wanted answers to but he would have to wait until the creature came for him as it promised.

"See how beautiful she is. Doesn't it look like she's sleeping and dreaming fairy tale dreams?" The funeral director asked. "Little girls dream about being fairies, you know. Maybe she's a fairy in Heaven." He said and wiped an escaped tear. He kept his head bowed and his eyes on Bo.

Armani looked at the girl. His heart ached. "She's such a beautiful girl." He choked on his words and tears escaped his eyes. "I bet she's an angel in Heaven right now. Maybe even dancing and singing with my beloved Simone." He wiped away the tears, careful not to rub the burned half of his face too hard. Armani placed his hand on her cold stiff hand. "Your parents will pay for this, sweet angel. I promise you that." He stared at her face. She looked just like a sleeping innocent child with a peaceful expression on her face. The girl's curly hair was a bright blonde and lie around her face.

"Well, let's take you to your appointment. I'm sure Stan is waiting." The funeral director said. "Come this way." He walked toward the hallway his hands folded in front of him.

"Ok, thank you sir." Armani said. He gazed at the pillow the girl's head rested on. There was a red dot. Leaning closer, he saw that there were two and they looked wet. He dabbed his finger in it and rubbed them together. 'My God, it is blood. The tears from the creature he had seen.' He thought shocked. His heart rate sped up. The blood flowing through his veins felt as cold as the little girl's hand.

Armani could sense the funeral directors eyes on him. He quickly turned around and followed him in silence to Stan's office.

"Stan, Armani is here to see you." He gestured for Armani to go in.

Stan looked up from his paperwork and smiled at Armani. He stood and extended his hand. "I'm Stan. We talked briefly on the phone. Please take a seat."

Armani shook Stan's hand. "Nice to meet you," Armani said and sat in a red chair across from Stan.

"Armani, I understand from our brief phone conversation that you would like to pick out a proper tombstone and have it engraved." Stan put his glasses on and handed Armani a magazine with a large tombstone on the cover. "There are over three hundred different types of stones in here. If you have any ideas I'm sure our artists will be able to accommodate your wishes."

He took the magazine and flipped through the pages trying to find the perfect one. "Forgive me, sir for bothering you. My fiancée passed away a few months ago and I was in a coma and never had a chance to say good-bye, let alone have a proper funeral for her. I just feel she needs the best tombstone you can make."

"Why on earth would you think you're bothering me?" Stan asked looking over top of his glasses.

"I'm sure you are a busy man and I drop in at no set time. If you have other things to do, go ahead." Armani said apologizing once again.

Stan stared at Armani with compassion. "How are you doing emotionally and physically?"

Armani knew his face must have shocked him a bit. "Do you want the truth?"

Stan chuckled. "I prefer the truth. Believe me I'm used to it in this place. No one comes in here pretending to be happy like they do in the outside world. It's true raw emotion." He sat back and crossed his arms waiting for a response.

"Horrible. I feel like I'm dead and just trying to live day by day." Armani answered avoiding Stan's gaze. "It's like the world is darkness and the only light I had is gone." He paused and pointed to his face. "This is my curse."

Stan stood, walked to the front of his desk and sat on the edge. "Listen closely to what I have to say." He waited for Armani to look at him. "I know who you are, although I'm not a fan of your music." He chuckled with a wave of his hand. "I know of your fame and fortune. You have numerous fans that love you and will continue to follow you and your music regardless of your appearance. And may I add you are still extremely attractive, as I'm sure the ladies would tell you."

Armani cut in. "I'm done with the band for a long time. When I'm ready to perform, I will." He stated his jaw set like stone.

"I'm not here telling you to perform and be in the band again. That's up to you and it's your business. I presume you have a pushy agent bugging you about that already. The last thing you need is two "dads" giving you their opinion as if it's God's law." He said using his forefinger and middle finger to make parenthesis in the air. "I want to tell you something I'm sure you already know. Time heals all wounds and in time you will heal. Maybe not fully, but life will get easier." Stan finished and walked to his chair.

Armani knew he was trying to help but talk was cheap. "Is that what you're trained to tell people who have lost loved ones when they come in here to make funeral arrangements?"

Stan looked hurt. "Yes and no. Your situation is a lot different than most people who come here. In a sense, your fiancée was taken from you and you didn't know it until you woke up from your induced coma. That in itself is a bitter pill to swallow."

"I apologize for my comment. I know you're trying to help and I thank you, but I just want to get a tombstone and go visit my Simone." Armani said. He gripped the magazine so tightly his knuckles turned white. "I'd like to sketch the tombstone I'd like for her grave."

Stan handed him a piece of paper and a pencil. "Go ahead. I'll be back in about twenty minutes."

Armani nodded. He took the paper and sketched a tombstone he knew Simone would love and appreciate.

He drew a tall rectangular stone and a wide platform seated on top. Next he drew an angel with long flowing hair and big eyes. She wore a robe that was blown by the wind, her wings pointing to the Heavens and in her hand she held a harp close to her chest. Her bare feet were crossed. The inscription at the bottom of the stone read, 'Simone Richards, My Angel in the Night.' He smiled pleased with his work.

Armani jumped when Stan walked in the office.

"Sorry, I didn't mean to scare you," he apologized. "Let's see what you've got."

Armani handed the sketch to him. "This would be perfect if you can do this for me."

Stan took the sketch, studying it. "It's beautiful and yes we can do that for you. I'll send it to our guys and it should be ready in a day or two. I will call you when it's finished and you can come in and pay for it upon delivery." He smiled. "What type of stone would you like?"

"I want shiny black marble." Armani said. "And spare no cost." He smiled, rose to his feet and shook Stan's hand. "Thank you very much for your service, Stan. Here's my number." He handed him a business card.

"Glad to be of help to you," Stan said. "Let me show you to the door."

Armani felt a cold chill as they neared the room where Bo, the little girl lay in her coffin. Fear gripped him and he forced himself to keep his eyes straight ahead willing whatever was in there to go away. His peripheral vision failed him and he saw the dark shadow standing by her coffin. The creature's eyes burned through him like molten lava. A deep raspy voice whispered his name but he kept walking, grateful to pass the viewing room.

Armani cleared his throat. Had he gone mad? "Stan, did you feel a cold draft a minute ago?"

Stan shook his head. "No. Why do you ask?"

"Never mind," Armani dismissed the question with a wave of his hand. "Have a good day and thank you for your time." He pushed the door open grateful to be outdoors.

Stan watched as Armani pulled a black ski mask over his face and walked to his car. He shook his head wondering why Armani asked him about a cold draft. He shrugged. The heater worked fine.

The funeral director walked past the room where the little girl lay and felt an icy draft. He stopped, jerking his head to stare in the room. A dark shadow disappeared into nothingness. He rubbed his eyes. What was going on?

CHAPTER TEN

D ONOVAN STOOD BY the window and watched Armani walk out of the funeral home. He knew he had scared him but he needed to forewarn him of things to come. Donovan was a vampire but he had a heart of compassion and felt a great deal of sympathy for Armani. He hoped he could persuade Armani to crossover of his own free will. God forbid, Victor become involved.

Victor, the Master of the Dark Ones was not a vampire to reckon with and his presence cast an evil aura. Victor, strong and mighty at 491 years old believed in being a vigilante, but he also had a thirst for blood from innocent people. Victor had a heart of stone and Donovan feared that in time what little spark of love left in Victor's heart would vanish forever.

Donovan remembered sitting at Victor's home after he crossed over as Victor told him of his tortured life, his need for revenge and the reason for creating The Dark One's.

"Sit down, son," Victor said, pointing to a high backed black chair.

Donovan sat and looked at Victor's living room. What a dark dreary place. The walls were painted black, all the furniture a shade of black. Pictures hung on the walls, mostly of black, white, and red. One caught Donovan's eye. "What is the meaning of this picture, sir?" Donovan asked, walking toward the picture to get a better look. He cocked his head to the side, scratching his chin.

Victor laughed. "Look closely, and tell me what you see." His beady black eyes never left Donovan's face. He watched him like a hawk. "I'm very interested to know."

Donovan studied the picture and felt a sadness wash over him like a tide at noon. The background of the picture was black. A yellow moon the size of a dime hung in the sky. A porcelain white five year old naked boy sat in a corner cowering like a dog that gets beat, his hands covered his cheeks and his legs were curled close to his body. Maroon blood dripped from the boy's back and neck. Donovan craned his neck and looked closer. His face contorted when he saw the purple and blue bruises on the boy's body. Donovan tried to move but was unable.

Victor was at Donovan's side in a flash. "It's a powerful masterpiece, as you can see and feel. Try to move away from it." Victor paused. "You can't and that's because it's one of my best pieces of art I made with all my heart and soul." Victor said, pride ringing in his voice like a thousand cathedral bells. "You see, I made this picture three hundred ninety one years ago. I was one hundred years old and a young vampire still capable of love."

Donovan turned and looked into Victor's eyes. It was like staring at a cold empty vessel. He didn't understand why Victor would draw a picture like this if he had the capacity of love in his heart. The painting was one of hurt, pain, and loneliness. "I don't understand what you mean. This painting is quite frankly, depressing." Donovan was pointing at the boys wounded arms and legs. "And his tears look like drops of blood. Don't get me wrong, it's amazing, but yet so sad."

"Let me explain the meaning to you, my young vampire." Victor said. "First of all, one thing that I love dearly is the innocent children who are victims of abuse. They are helpless to the devices of their parents or other adults who are heartless. I have no patience for it and I kill these child abusers without hesitation. I lay and wait for them in the shadows like a hungry lion watching a herd of zebra. You see these adults who victimize children are weak and I attack and kill them based on their weakness, just like a lion targets the weakest link in a herd of prey." He laughed his fangs gleamed wickedly in the light.

Donovan walked away and sat feeling uncomfortable standing so close to Victor. Evil permeated off him. He looked at his arms, lined with goose bumps. Donovan watched in shock as Victor sailed across the floor, his feet never touching the floor and sat in his chair with the poise of a ballerina.

Victor pointed his bony finger at Donovan. "Wipe the fear and worry out of your eyes, son. You have nothing to fear from me. I'm not going to attack and kill you, for God's sake. Did you forget that you are now 'one' with me?" He laughed the sarcasm thick. "We are vampires. You are not a mere mortal anymore." His stare penetrated Donovan's face.

"Yes sir. I realize that, but being a vampire is new to me and to be honest with you, all this talk scares the hell out of me." Donovan stammered. "So, what is the meaning of the picture? Do you know the little boy?" Donovan asked changing the subject.

"You fool!" He exclaimed. "The boy in that painting is me."

"I-I-I'm sorry," Donovan stuttered. "I didn't realize this. You must have been through so much pain."

Victor stood and faced the fireplace. "Yes my son, I learned at a young age what living in hell is like. My parents were wicked people who did terrible things to me." He turned and Donovan saw sadness in Victor's eyes. "I hope now you understand what my mission on this earth is." He nodded toward the painting. "It's to help children who are put in that position. My method of help is permanent, however. I kill and have no regrets."

Donovan understood and empathized with him. "I would feel the same, sir, but murder isn't always the best answer."

The words no more than left Donovan's mouth and Victor was in front of him. He grabbed Donovan's head and jerked it back. "You know not what you speak of! Murder is the only answer in these situations." He shoved his head down hard. "Never question my motives, son. That's your first lesson. I am a strong vampire and will not have you doubt me or tell me your petty opinion on a subject." Victor sneered at the painting. "I have love for children and that is all. No other mortal matters to me or ever will."

"Why did you choose me? Why?" Donovan asked.

Victor smiled, but his eyes dark. "Why? Well, because I care about you and I see potential in you. I will train you to be exactly like me. You were going to kill yourself and I won't allow that from a human." He stated matter of fact. "I wanted to help you retrieve justice for the wrong done to you. Men love to take the easy way out and I don't believe in that." Victor poured himself a glass of brandy. "Would you like a glass, my son?"

Donovan was confused. Vampires didn't drink beverages or eat food. Their diet consisted of blood and only blood, according to the tales. "I thought we couldn't drink or eat as humans do," he stated confused.

Victor laughed. "You know how to put a smile on my face, Donovan. I am grateful for that. It's been a long time." He handed Donovan a glass of brandy. "I make the rules as the Master of The Dark One's. Tried, tested, and true and guess what? We can enjoy food and drink as humans do as well as go out during the day. What can be better than that?" Victor smiled. He watched Donovan sip the brandy. "So, we are vampires, who right the wrongs, enjoy all the benefits of humans, and get away with murder." Victor sat losing himself in the brandy.

Donovan had unanswered questions but didn't dare ask them for fear of upsetting Victor. He finished the brandy in minutes and set the glass on the end table with a clang.

"Go ahead and ask your questions, my son," Victor said. "I will be honest with you. No question is too stupid to ask me. I consider this one of your learning sessions. I'm the teacher and you're the pupil. How else will you learn?" He held out his hand waiting for the questions Donovan had for him. Reading minds was also a gift of the Dark Ones.

Donovan chuckled for the first time since arriving at Victor's house. "I do have questions and lots of them, father." He finally felt at peace to talk freely to Victor. Maybe it was the brandy. He didn't know. "O.K., my first question is can we have humans as friends?"

"Yes, of course. But, make sure to be careful because trust is earned and humans are the hardest creatures to trust." He paused and sipped his brandy. "Also, why would you want to be friends with humans anyway? The only reason I see is for the purpose of them having a connection to the people or person you want to kill for the wrong they have committed against you. You do realize that the people who killed your fiancée are two of your best friends." Victor knew this would be a blow to Donovan, but he needed to hear it. The vengeful seed needed to be planted. He knew he was dealing with a man with a soft, loving, and giving heart. Trust was too easy for him and in the end it cost him the one thing he loved the most in the world. That was why Victor was there before Donovan hung himself. The two men who did this deserved to die and Victor would be sure Donovan was the one who made them pay. Sure, he could have done it just as easy, but what fun would that be? He wanted the man who was wronged to take pleasure in making the men pay for their crimes. Justice was always the final answer. Left to the state, justice wouldn't be served properly. "You know, if I didn't rescue you from your own fate, the two people you called 'friends' would have had a wonderful life sentence in prison, providing of course they were ever caught in the first place. You see the problem with America is that people get away with a lot of horrible crimes, never caught. When they are caught, they get to spend a lifetime in prison with all the necessities they need on our tax dollars." Victor said and poured another glass of brandy. "Pass me your glass and have another before I continue my rant." He said. It was more of an order than an offer.

Donovan obeyed, sipped the brandy and nodded for Victor to continue.

Victor cleared his throat. "The two cowards that you called friends who killed your fiancée would have had their lives to work out, eat three meals a day, take educational courses and have a barber to cut their hair instead of their throats . . ." He paused, looked at the ceiling and laughed. "Those clowns would have had a lifetime of medical care for free. What a wonderful punishment for the crime they committed. What do you have to say about that, young Donovan?"

Donovan's throat was dry. He was filled with hate and despair. The news Victor dealt him was a dagger pierced deep into his heart. "I honestly had no idea that my best friends did this. Why?" Tears welled in his eyes.

"Don't cry, son. I hate to see you sad. You need to replace the sadness with anger, hate, and revenge. There is no time for sorrow. Kill the people who you thought were your friends. They are free and roaming the streets. The Bible says, 'Eye for an eye.' Therefore I believe in that."

Silence filled the room for what seemed like hours. Victor and Donovan sat and stared at each other.

Donovan was confused. "Victor, may I rest for awhile? I need some time alone." He asked like a scared child.

"But, of course, my son. Let me show you to your room." Victor said. He stood and extended his hand to Donovan.

Victor's hand was cold but Donovan was grateful for the assistance. He followed him down a long hallway to a spacious room. Victor helped him into bed and bid him farewell until morning when their session would begin again.

Donovan remembered one thing after lying in bed and it was the strangest and most unexpected thing. Victor had leaned over, kissed him on the forehead and told him to sleep well. Was he showing love? Did Victor have feelings and emotions? Was he just a stone cold vampire without feelings? Donovan didn't know the answers. Time would tell him these things and so much more.

Donovan awoke to the aroma of a delicious breakfast being cooked. He sat up and looked out the window. The golden sun rose welcoming a new day. Thoughts of the night before ran through his mind. Confusion, stress, anger, sadness, hopelessness, and despair ambushed him. His thoughts were interrupted by a knock on the door.

"Yes. Come in."

"Good morning Donovan. Breakfast is ready and I'd like you to join me." Victor said.

Donovan rubbed his eyes. "I'll be down soon. Thank you."

"I'm looking forward to your presence at my table."

Donovan got out of bed and dressed. He was going to ask every question he had, damn the consequences to hell. Victor wasn't here to hurt him, only to aid him. Although Victor appeared to have the attitude of a cold-hearted killer, he didn't think Victor would ever hurt him. Well, part of him believed that . . . . .

Chapter Eleven

Armani sped away from the funeral home, relieved that he wouldn't have to go back to that place of heartbreak and sadness. He was visiting Simone's grave for the first time since arriving home from the hospital. He didn't want to think of it as saying good-bye, but in reality this is what it was. He had allowed a flame of hope to flicker within his soul; a hope that maybe the doctors were wrong and any day Simone would show up at their home, alive and well. That somehow she escaped the monsters that did this but his heart told him the truth and he needed the closure once and for all.

The ride to the cemetery was a blur. He saw the sign a block ahead and turned right turn into Blakesly Cemetery, keeping the Navigator at a slow speed so he wouldn't disturb the resting souls. A chill ran down his spine. He turned the heat up a few degrees.

The cemetery was beautiful and well maintained. Tombstones of all sizes and designs rose above the snow marking the final resting place of people's loved ones. Tall trees stood erect, their branches reaching to the Heaven's like they were asking God to resurrect the dead. A white building with two large pillars stood in the center of the cemetery. A sign hanging on the door read, 'Office,' so Armani steered the Navigator in that direction.

He glanced at the passenger seat and saw the two letters he had brought. One of them was from Donovan and the other was a love letter he had written to Simone. Armani managed to talk himself into going to a floral shop earlier, mangled face and all, to pick up a dozen roses for Simone's grave; ten red, one black and one yellow. Being an artist, he picked out the colors with a symbolic meaning. A tear escaped, his ski mask absorbed the moisture. He willed himself to be strong and hold back the tears until he had talked with the management.

"Get a grip on your emotions," Armani instructed himself. He gripped the steering wheel with enough force to break it in two. Turning the Lincolns wheel hard, he pulled into a parking space and shoved the Navigator into park. Armani took off his ski mask and threw it in the backseat, stepped out of the SUV and walked to the front door careful not to slip on the icy patches.

He opened the door and bells jingled. A pleasant looking man with small eyes sat behind the reception desk. He looked at Armani and smiled. "Hello, sir."

Armani noticed the man gawking at his face. He chose to ignore the urge to act violently towards this man. The thought of punching this man in the face was exhilarating. Armani smiled. "Hello. Don't mind my face. Sometimes when I'm bored it's fun to burn myself." He said sarcastically.

The man blushed and stuttered. "I-I-I'm sorry, sir. I hope you can forgive my rudeness." He stood and extended his hand.

Armani took his hand and gripped it hard. "Not a problem. Maybe you assumed I was a dead man come to life," he sneered. "I am here to see my fiancée, Simone Richard's burial site. I've ordered a tombstone for her that will be delivered here in a couple days."

The man sat again facing the computer. The click of the keypad echoed in the silence. "Alright, I found her name. Simone was buried in the far right of the cemetery. We have her burial site marked with a small ground level stone." He looked up at Armani. "Let me print the map out for you." The printer spit out a single sheet of paper. "Here you go." He handed it to Armani.

Armani took the map. "Thank you very much. But, I do have some questions that I'm hoping you can answer." Armani's eyes bore into the small man.

The small man appeared nervous. "I'd be happy to answer any questions you may have." He lowered his eyes from Armani's piercing gaze.

Armani cleared his throat. "I'm sure you've heard the news of the attack on her and I." He waited for the man to nod his head. "Unfortunately, I'm alive and she's dead. I never got to say good-bye." Armani tried hard not to cry. His heart broke in two like a wound that gets re-opened without a chance to heal. "Were there people who attended her funeral and burial ceremony?" He asked his voice cracking.

Sadness clouded the small mans face. "I'm sorry to have to be the one to tell you this, but, no. Not one person attended, except me. Well, a priest from the hospital came and preached a small sermon and said a prayer." The small man wandered into the back room and came back holding a box. "I am deeply sorry for your loss." He held the box out to Armani.

No condolences would mend his broken heart. Armani had to accept the fact that he would live forever a broken man, a crippled bird with no hope of ever flying again. Armani squinted at the box and took it. "What is this?" He asked.

The box was addressed to his home with a 'return to sender' stamped on the front. Armani saw it was dated a few months ago.

"The funeral directors tried to send it to your home, but were unsuccessful. They knew you would eventually come here." The man said. "That is, if you survived what had happened to you. They left it with me until you arrived to visit Simone."

"Well, I thank you for holding onto this for me." Armani said, staring at the small box. "I'm going to go now, and I thank you for your time." A lump formed in his throat.

"You're welcome, sir. Have a good day."

He stepped outside and the dam broke and Armani's tears flowed. He got in his vehicle and slammed the door. His heart and soul ached, longing for Simone. He didn't want to accept the finality of death. Life had no meaning and he would give his life to be able to touch and hold Simone again. Thoughts of suicide raced through his mind. If he ended his life, he would be with his angel. She would be at the Gates of Heaven waiting for him. Oh, how her face would light up when she saw him. Armani envisioned both of them running towards each other, arms wide open with nothing but billowy white clouds of cotton surrounding them. He would have eternal life with Simone in a perfect place with no pain, sorrow or regret. But, suicide was not an option until he avenged Simone's death. Armani laid his arms on the steering wheel, placed his head on his arms and wept bitterly.

Startled, Armani jumped. A pleasant looking couple knocked on the window. He wiped the tears, tried to smile and rolled down the window.

"Sir, are you OK?" The woman asked. "I couldn't help but notice your pain." She said and looked away from his face.

Before Armani had a chance to answer the man spoke up. "Hey, I know you. You're Armani, the lead singer of 'Faded Cross.'"

Armani was baffled. Who the hell cared? My God, they were at a cemetery and obviously he was here to mourn the loss of his only loved one. If this man was a fan, he knew the whole story. It was all over the news and in the tabloids. Play by play, everyone knew of that fateful night and the end results.

"Yes, I am, and to answer your question, madam, no, I am not OK." Armani said, wishing he could share his pain with these people. But, it wasn't any of their business and he knew he had to be careful what he said to anyone. Everyone was out to make a buck, and these two could relay what he said to the papers. Privacy was something he held dear to his heart and that would never change as long as he had breath in his lungs.

"I am so sorry about all that happened to you," the woman said. She was a pretty petite brunette with big blue eyes. "No one should ever have to bare the burden you have."

The man she was with wasn't as respectful as she was about the situation. He was a tall muscular man with sandy blonde hair and probably the high school's prom king.

"Could I get a picture with you? I've been a fan of 'Faded Cross' for as long as you guys have been around." He said with no remorse for Armani's loss.

The woman glared at him. "How dare you!" She exclaimed. "This man is mourning the loss of his lover. Jesus, why else would he be here and you have the nerve to ask for a photo with him." She punched his arm.

Armani gave her a grateful look. "Excuse me I have business to attend to." Averting his gaze to the man, he glared. "Why in God's name would I want you to take a picture of you and I?" Armani said, covering the left side of his face. "Have you no heart? No conscience?" His temper flared. "Good-bye, and have a great day." He fumed and rolled up the window. Armani put the Lincoln in reverse without a second look at the couple, and sped off to Simone's gravesite.

Armani remembered the package the graveyard manager gave him. He picked it up off the passenger seat and set it on his lap as he drove through the loops and turns of the cemetery. He glanced at the map, but he didn't need it to know he was headed in the right direction. The aching in his heart told him he was almost to Simone's grave.

There it was the place where Simone lay six feet under the soil. He stopped the vehicle, stepped out and slowly walked to the grave. He frowned at the small stone that marked her grave. The only thing engraved on it was her name. No flowers, no verse, no mantra.

"This disgusts me!" Armani exclaimed to the Heavens. Armani looked around at the graveyard. Simone's grave was a distance away from the others. A large oak tree stood near and a few large pine trees. Snow covered the ground, but Armani could tell there wasn't much in the way of landscaping in this graveyard. Flowers were few and far between. Rose bushes lined the outer skirts of the graveyard. Surely the rose bushes were beautiful in the spring and summer, but in winter they reminded Armani of lonely lifeless branches weeping the loss of the rose so glorious and bright, just as he wept over the loss of his beautiful flower, Simone. Unlike the rose bushes, the flower in his life would never bloom again. She was gone forever and not for a season. Tears filled Armani's eyes. He wiped them away and walked to his vehicle.

He picked up the box with shaky hands and slowly opened it. Inside was Simone's three-karat diamond engagement ring he had given her and the gold necklace she had always worn. He clutched the ring and gold chain in his hands, held them to his chest and cried. "I love you and miss you so much Simone." He said opened the gold chain's clasp and slipped the ring onto it. He fastened the chain around his neck and let his fingers slide down the gold chain to the ring. Armani tightened his grip around the ring holding it for a moment. He tucked the necklace into his shirt where Simone would be forever close to his heart. He walked back to her grave, leaving the vehicles door open.

Armani kneeled at Simone's grave and sang a love song to her with so much passion it shocked him. He didn't remember singing like this at any time in his musical career. When Armani finished, he held the roses to his nose and inhaled savoring the sweet smell.

"Simone, I am so sorry this happened to you, to us." He said, choking on his tears. "I love you so much. I miss you. Is there a way you can come back to me? I am not complete without you." Armani paused and pulled the poem out of his pocket. "I wrote you a letter, my beautiful soul mate."

Armani unfolded the paper and cleared his throat.

> *My dearest Simone,*
>
> *I cannot begin to convey how much I miss you. Everyday my heart aches for you, longs for you. I am only half a man without you by my side. I know I will never be whole again. You were the sunshine in my heart. The blood that flowed through my veins, the air I breathed. I'm suffocating without you. I love you so much and I always will. There will never be another woman for me, but you. I can't go on without you. I want nothing more than to get revenge on the men that did this to you, to us. Please forgive me as I already plan on taking matters into my own hands. They will pay for what they have done. Please understand what I must do. I want to join you in eternity, and soon I will for I can't bare this world alone. You are always on my mind and in my heart. I love you, my angel.*
>
> *Forever yours,*
> *Armani Belvedere.*

Armani threw himself on her grave, crying, unable to move. "Is there any way I can see her again?" He cried out to God.

A rustling in the distance interrupted his mourning. He looked up and saw the black hawk high atop an oak tree staring at him. When Armani met its gaze, it didn't turn away. It sat still its head slumped as if sympathizing with him.

He felt the same cold chill he had experienced at the funeral home when walking past little Bo's viewing room.

"What do you want? Why are you following me?" He screamed.

The hawk flapped its wings and continued to stare.

"Are you a guardian for my Simone?" Armani asked desperation clouding his voice. "If you are, then I welcome you, my friend. Please guard her as she lay resting in peace." A sudden sense of calm overcame him. Could the hawk really be Simone's guardian? He turned from the hawk.

Armani picked up the dozen roses he had bought for his beloved. "Simone, I brought you some roses. I know how you always loved the beauty and smell of them. I picked each color as a symbol and message from my heart to yours." He held them to his nose, savoring the scent. "Simone, there are ten red roses, one yellow rose, and one black rose." He gathered the ten red roses and held them to his chest. "My love, the red roses symbolize everything beautiful about you, inside and out. You are my first true love and my one and only love. Thank you for bringing the color of love into my life. The first day I met you I knew you were the only woman in the world for me. The red roses show my undying love for you. My heart will always be tied to you. Your beauty, illuminating smile, and all of the tender moments we shared are within the red roses. The yellow rose stands for the sunshine you brought into my life. You brightened my life everyday, never failing to make my heart take flight. The yellow rose also stands for the hope I have that soon you and I will be together again." He paused, wiping tears from his eyes. "The black rose, my dearest Simone stands for two things, death and revenge. Your death has filled my heart with a black hole, emptiness I cannot put into words. I ache for you with every breath I take." Armani's chest felt like someone was jumping on it. "The revenge is something even I can't fathom, but it's going to be closure to your death. Revenge is mine and I plan to make the people responsible for this pay with their lives." He put the roses in a vase he had brought and placed the letter under this.

Armani felt shame in admitting to Simone that he planned to kill the guilty ones. "I hope you can forgive me and understand that this is something that I need to do for you and for me." Armani kneeled, placed his hands on the ground and kissed Simone's tombstone. "I love you, my angel in the night."

Armani stood, reached inside his shirt and pulled out the necklace with Simone's ring attached. He kissed it, tucked it in his shirt close to his heart. The hawk sat in the tree, not once taking its eyes off him.

The north wind picked up, whistling and whirling around him while he walked toward his car. He fastened his coat and walked faster. Armani stopped a few steps from his car door when he heard a whisper in the wind.

He assumed it was his imagination playing tricks on him, took a few more steps opened the car door. This time he heard the voice clearly like someone was whispering in his ear.

"I understand and I love you, Armani." Simone said her voice soft.

Armani fell beside his car, curled up in the fetal position, and wept. Simone's voice so near broke his heart into a million little pieces. Armani was lost in darkness and despair, unaware of anything around him including the black hawk standing a few feet away.

CHAPTER TWELVE

DONOVAN WATCHED ARMANI mourn for Simone and his heart went out to him. He feared he would lose him to the blackness of death soon if he didn't help Armani cross over and become a vampire.

"You incompetent fool!" Victor raged.

Donovan jumped. "Sir, I am busy watching Armani through my friends eyes." Turning his head he glared at Victor. "Can this wait for a few minutes?" He asked. Donovan turned back to his crystal globe. The globe was his connection to his hawk and he used this to see things the hawk saw.

When Victor had mentioned Armani and the need for him to become a member of The Dark One's, Donovan jumped on the opportunity for a number of reasons. The first was that Armani made him feel human again, instead of a vampire. The sad reality was that Donovan wanted to be human again and this enraged Victor. Victor stuck to the belief that once you cross over and join the Dark Ones, your heart becomes black and human feelings such as love should be a thing of the past. For Donovan this wasn't the case. Victor tried to brainwash him, but it was to no avail, because Donovan would always believe in love.

Victor was behind him in seconds. Donovan felt the cold steel blade of a knife on his neck. "I'm starting to think I should have let you die that night." A gut wrenching dark laugh escaped him. "You are worthless as one with me. Do you know why?"

Donovan moved from the cold blade and stood to face Victor. He blocked his thoughts so Victor couldn't read his mind. "I'm sure I can give you an answer." He said his heart racing.

Victor slid his tongue over his protruding fangs like a hungry animal at feeding time. Donovan had never seen him look so evil. It was like staring into the eyes of the Devil.

Victor threw the knife down and stared at Donovan. "You bore me! Answer my question. Do you not remember the rule? When I ask you a question, I expect a direct answer." Victor threw his cloak behind him. "Not in a minute, right now!"

Donovan stared into Victor's eyes. "I know exactly why. It's because I have my own way of handling situations and people." He paused and continued before Victor could interrupt him. "I'm not going to rush into Armani's home and force him to cross over. He needs time to mourn, say good bye to Simone, and be ready for me to help him realize that becoming a vampire is the right choice . . . ."

Victor screamed. It sounded like a high-pitched squelch. "You are to do things the way I see fit for you to do them. Why do you have sympathy on this man? He means nothing to you. All that should matter is that we are building an army of vigilante vampire's called The Dark Ones. We both know Armani is a perfect candidate. The evil is within him. All he needs is for you to release him from his pain."

Victor flew to the ceiling and circled Donovan. "I'm hungry," He seethed through sharp fangs.

Donovan tilted his head, looked at Victor and was met with a blow that threw him on his back. His head hit the wood floor. He opened his eyes and Victor was on top of him staring at him. Donovan tried to move his arms but Victor had them pinned down.

"Let me give you an ultimatum, son," Victor began. "I want you to talk to Armani in two days and convince him to cross over. If you don't, then I will do it myself." A smile played on his lips. "And you know what that means." He laughed, rolling his head back. "If he refuses me, I will take him by force and I'll come back here and kill you. So, the choice is yours, Donovan. You have two days to meet Armani and convince him to join the Dark Ones. I'd really hate to kill you, but I'm sure your blood is sweet." He smiled. "I will drain you dry and then burn you."

Victor stood, extended his hand to Donovan and helped him to his feet. "I know you'll do the right thing." He walked toward the door, stopped halfway turning his head to the side. "You know it's not all about you anymore. Your friend, Armani, is close to death. He has been contemplating suicide for a time now and if you don't act in the next couple of days, it will be too late."

The door closed and Victor was gone. Donovan knew what had to be done. He believed Armani needed more time to mourn, but time was something he had no control over. Victor was a man of his word and if he were to get involved with Armani's cross over, they may as well both be dead. Victor was not one to reckon with.

Donovan's heart raced. How could he do this in a gentle way? How would he convince Armani to cross over of his own free will? He had so many unanswered questions he felt he was going to lose his mind.

Donovan was a fortunate vampire in many ways. Although he was lonely more often than not, he still had a conscience and a heart of compassion. Many of the members of the Dark Ones were emotionless. Their soul desire was vengeance. They thrived on the blood of humans and took delight in tormenting their victims before drinking the blood. Most members of The Dark One's didn't kill the innocent, but a few drained them to near death which was dangerous because it could easily go too far and allow rage and hatred to devour them. Once a vampire took an innocent's life they escalated from vigilante to predator.

Donovan vowed to never do this no matter how strong his desire for human blood was.

Donovan heard a rustling and turned to see his faithful companion perched on the window ledge. The hawk used its sharp beak and pecked the window when it arrived home from a mission Donovan had sent him on.

Donovan opened the window and said, "Hello there, my friend. You did well. Thank you for watching Armani. He is a hurting soul and needs our companionship." Donovan walked to the aquarium filled with white mice. He lifted the cover, caught two of them and placed them on the floor.

The hawk eyed them, swooped down and using his powerful talons grabbed both rats.

"Those poor mice don't have a chance with you. What an awful death to be swooped up by a powerful bird such as you, torn apart and eaten alive." Donovan shuttered. It was an awful death for the little critters.

The hawk tore their flesh apart, its head twisting and turning, white fur flew in the air like a pillow fight gone bad.

Donovan thought about Armani. He had to visit him in the next two days and his plan was to do this tomorrow evening. He hoped Armani would be home, because God have mercy on both their souls if Victor interceded.

Victor sat perched high in a tree beside Donovan's house watching him and reading his mind.

"I'm sorry, Donovan," he said, "but if you don't do this by tomorrow night, I will kill you."

The sun set in the distance, his stomach told him he had sat longer than he expected. Hunger plagued him. Not only hunger for food, but a burning for the blood of a human. Victor knew he was losing the battle with evil. Killing had become an adrenaline rush for him like hunting wild game. In the past he had only drained his victims of blood to the point of unconsciousness and he always erased it from their memory. Not any more. That Victor was gone forever. He enjoyed the look of terror and the smell of fear in his human victims when he ascended upon them. The blood mixed with fear tasted sweeter. There was no turning back once a vampire craved humans that way. The only way to end that compulsion was for a vampire to kill himself, and Victor refused to do that. He'd hide what he really was from Donovan and the others who would join The Dark Ones.

Victor stood on the thick branch and extended his arms, feeling so much freedom. Why wouldn't any human want to be a vampire and possess these powers? He couldn't answer that and didn't care to think about it. It was time to hunt for his next victim.

He swirled his black cloak around him, soared into the sky and scoured the streets listening to people's beating hearts.

"Ah, sweet music to my ears," Victor said blissfully.

Victor decided to hunt at Manhattan Park. It was the perfect place to find an unsuspecting victim. Tall trees lined the park's pathway and benches were scattered throughout. Victor scanned the grounds and admired the beautiful stone sculptures. He loved the statue of a large black horse rearing like the black stallion. Victor smiled. This is the spot where he first saw Armani. A spark ignited within. He knew Armani would one day be a member of The Dark One's. One sniff and he sensed the monster lurking within Armani's soul.

Armani must become one of them. Victor sent for Donovan and the hawk to be the guardians for these two mortals. Victor wanted Armani and he always got what he wanted. Unfortunately, Simone had to be killed by malicious men who would soon meet their own deaths at the hands of Armani. Victor was looking forward to watching Armani kill the two men who did this.

Victor sighed and sat on the bench near the horse statue. A few people were walking through the park; couples holding hands, people walking their beloved dogs, and a few loners.

A grin spread across his face. There she was. He licked his lips, his mouth salivating.

"Perfect," Victor said, his black heart beating wildly with anticipation of the kill. In an instant he was behind her, watching and waiting, like a predator stalking its prey.

The little dog turned and growled, pulling on its leash trying hard to break free and come to Victor.

"Stop it!" The woman exclaimed. She turned to see what the dog was looking at. "I'm sorry, sir. My dog tends to get a bit over excited and growls at people." She bent over and picked up the dog holding it close. "Have I met you before?"

Victor wondered why she would ask such a stupid question. He smiled. 'Pick me up, if you dare, my dear.'

"No, I don't believe we have met." Victor said his eyes flickered. "My name is Victor and you are?" He extended his hand and held hers.

The woman blushed. "I am Katrina. I come here just about every day to walk my dog. It's so beautiful here, even in the cold of winter." She smiled her bright blue eyes sparkling like a glassy sea.

Katrina was a beauty. Maybe he would rethink killing her and just take her to his home to feed on from time to time. Make her his slave of love, to do as he wished. And the steady blood from her would be a godsend when he didn't feel like hunting. 'Well, sweetheart, this may be the last time you see this park for a long time.' He thought. Victor smiled his eyes like ice. Having crossed over from human to vampire at the age of 34, he remained that age although he was hundreds of years older. Would he cross this young beauty over? The thought excited him. He had so many things he could teach her.

"May I interest you in joining me for a cup of coffee?" Victor offered. The anticipation of the hunt excited him, such an adrenaline rush. This was proving to be too easy. 'Stupid, stupid girl, I'm surprised you're not dead already. So naïve,' he thought with a shake of his head.

Katrina blushed and looked at the snow covered ground. "I'd love to, but I need to bring my dog home and freshen up a bit if that's ok?" She stated, meeting Victor's gaze. What a handsome man. This stranger was tall with long raven black hair, mysterious cold green eyes that lit up when he smiled. Looking him up and down she noticed he was decked out in black from head to toe. "Are you in a gothic band or something? What's with the black cape?"

Victor rolled his head back and laughed. "That's funny, but I'll take it as a compliment since you took me up on the offer to go out for coffee." He stopped laughing and put his hands on her shoulders. "No, I'm not in a band, but I guess you could say I am a gothic guy, if that's what you call it nowadays."

A chill ran down Katrina's spine. His touch was cold. "Yes, that's what we call it. You should know that since you dress the part." She stepped away from Victor. "Well, I'll be going now. Where do we meet?" The dog growled.

Victor stared at the dog wanting to kill the half pint rat. It's whining and growling was wearing on his last nerve but people walking and talking as they passed by reminded him to act like a decent man. "Let's meet right here." He stated, pointing at the park bench.

Katrina twirled her hair around her finger. "That sounds great, see you then." She smiled and hurried off with her dog in tow.

Victor watched her walk away listening to her heart beat precious life blood through her veins. The hunger pangs for blood gnawed at him. Victor knew what he must do in the next hour to sustain himself until he got Katrina to his home. "Time to find a victim to feed on," he said, a wicked smile on his lips.

The wind whistled through the trees as the sun set. A few snowflakes danced in the sky. People scurrying through the park made it easy for him to spot his next meal. A short fat girl sat alone on a bench a few feet away. Victor noticed she had been watching Katrina and him with envy and jealousy. Her soul was black and full of hate. He made eye contact with her and she quickly averted her gaze to the ground. 'That one doesn't deserve to live,' Victor thought. In a flash, he was sitting next to her on the wooden park bench.

"Excuse me," the girl said. "I'm waiting for someone."

Victor laughed. "I know. You were waiting for me. Don't bullshit me, girl. You are waiting for no one or you wouldn't have been staring at me while I talked to that lovely lady. I see inside your cold, empty, lonely soul." He grabbed her hand with his icy grip and dug his nails into her flesh. Fresh blood dripped from the wound.

"Ouch!" She exclaimed, trying to pull her hand from his. "Let me go!" Tears streamed down her chubby cheeks.

Victor shot into the sky, holding her hands and scanned the park for a safe desolate spot. The girl kicked and screamed trying desperately to free herself. "Please don't hurt me!"

Victor found the perfect spot, descended and thrust her onto the ground. "Shut up. I have no patience for the likes of you and begging for your life only excites me more." Victor crossed his arms and stood over her. "I am a predator and you are my prey." He swirled his black cloak in front of his face and slowly lowered it exposing his fangs.

The girl screamed and sobbed. Tears fell down and she curled in the fetal position. "Please, let me go. Don't hurt me," she whimpered.

Victor dropped to his knee and held her face in his hands. "I do have a question for you, my dear." His stare shot daggers into her soul.

"W-w-what?" She stuttered. "Just let me go home."

"Too late for that, so stop your begging. I don't like it. It only infuriates me more." He wasn't playing games. "I'm hungry and thirsty. Now, how old are you?"

Victor pinched her cheeks so hard her lips shaped like a fish's. "I'm 31, sir."

Oh, the tears, the endless tears. What drama these humans went through to try to get themselves out of a jam. The human race should win an Emmy Award for their performance to please only to get their way. Victor loathed people like this. He preyed on them. He knew his food supply would never run short.

"Nothing will save you now." Victor threw his cloak aside, grabbed the girl's head, tilted it and sunk his fangs deep into her jugular vein. He sucked, enjoying the bittersweet taste of blood. She fought him, screaming and hitting but after a few minutes she twitched and ceased to move. He knew she was dead and his bloodlust was satisfied.

Victor picked up the girl and threw her aside like yesterday's trash and wiped his mouth with a cloth. It was time for him to wait for his new angel, Katrina.

The park was enveloped in darkness, street lamps illuminated the sidewalks. Victor inhaled, enjoying the sweet smell of the night air mixed with blood. He felt like he was in Heaven, which held no place for him.

His keen sense of hearing made him turn his head. There she was, Katrina, his piece of Heaven walking toward him, a big smile on her beautiful face. For the first time in his long existence Victor felt nervous and happy for a brief second but the rage and hatred returned just as quickly with force.

Katrina was going to be his prisoner forever! If he didn't kill her in time, he would turn her into a vampire. He swallowed hard, his mouth salivating, adrenaline rushed through his veins. Victor stood, his black cape swirling in the wind. He flashed a sexy smile at Katrina and walked toward her.

Katrina smelled like fresh flowers. What a delightful sweet aroma.

"Hello, my dear," Victor said and kissed her hand. "You look stunning." His eyes devoured her from head to toe.

"Thank-you, Victor," Katrina said, smiling. "Well, shall we go?" She took a few steps in front of him and tried to ease the nervous butterflies dancing in her stomach.

Victor watched her walk and yearned to taste her blood. Katrina's hips seductively swayed, her long brown hair cascaded down her back, the petite frame, so fragile. 'My God, her appearance is almost identical to Armani's beloved Simone.' He thought.

Katrina whirled around waiting for Victor to catch up. "Are you coming with me or shall I go by myself?" She joked.

Victor was at her side in a second, taking her hand in his. "I'm ready, my dear. Let's make this a night to remember." He looked into her eyes and smiled, using powers of illusion to put her at ease and bend to her to his will. Who knew he still had it in him to play the part of a romantic.

They walked together in silence for a few city blocks to Victor's relief. Katrina tried to release her hand from his grasp and he tightened his hand around hers.

"I don't think we're going the right way, Victor." The nervousness rose in her voice.

Victor stopped and shifted to face her, mesmerizing her with his gaze. "Yes, this is the right way. You need to trust me. I have many exciting things planned for our first evening together." He smiled wickedly, caressing her cheek with his hand. "Trust me. This is a surprise you will never forget."

Katrina nodded her head staring at Victor in awe and allowed him to guide her down the street.

CHAPTER THIRTEEN

L ONELINESS FILLED THE home once so full of happiness. Armani paced back and forth in the living room thinking, always thinking about Simone. She consumed his thoughts like his music had when he first rose to stardom.

Wood crackled and the heat from the fireplace's flames was comforting. Armani rolled up his sleeve and saw the tattoo he had had done when he and Simone were on a date. It was beautiful, yet simple; a small black circle encasing a red heart with the letters 'A' and 'S' for Armani and Simone forever. They got matching tats to symbolize their undying love for one another. Undying? "Ha, that's a crock of shit!" Armani hollered.

A knock on the door startled him. 'Go away,' he thought.

The knocking got louder. Armani wrapped his hand around the necklace with Simone's ring attached and pressed it to his chest. "I love you, my Simone." He said and walked toward the door. He wondered who would be coming over this late at night.

His two dogs were on the defense, hair raised, growling while they glared at the door.

Armani stopped walking. The chill he felt at the funeral home hit him. He glanced at the book about Vampirism. It remained untouched on the coffee table. Fear shot him like a bullet. What if the shadowy figure he had seen at the funeral home was here? The creature had said it would come for him.

"Stop your nonsense," he commanded. Both dogs cocked their head's to the side. Their focus was on whatever stood behind the door.

Armani gripped the door handle and slowly turned it. "Who is it?" He asked, his hand shaking.

"Open the damn door, Armani," Rex ordered.

Relieved, Armani asked, "Who's with you?" He thought he heard someone talking to Rex.

Rex sighed, irritated. "Gabe is with me. It's time to talk business. Just let us in."

Armani opened the door not hiding his disgust seeing Gabe Davis, their band's manager, standing beside Rex with a smug smile on his face.

"Hello, Armani. It's been a long time since we've seen one another, let alone spoke. You avoid phone calls like the plague." Gabe said, extending his hand to Armani. Armani didn't return the favor. Gabe shoved his hands into his jacket pockets and waited to be invited in.

Rex hugged Armani. "Well, are you going to let us in or force us to stand out here in the cold all night?" He laughed.

Stepping aside, Armani motioned for them to come in. "Make yourself at home. I apologize for the mess." Scattered beer cans, trash, food, and balled up papers covered the floor. He cleared a spot on the couch for each of them to sit. "Have a seat." He said and walked to the mini bar.

Gabe's groaned. "How in the hell can you live like this?" Shaking his head, he asked, "Why don't you have your housekeepers come back and do their job instead of paying them for not working?"

Holding a bottle of wine, he handed Rex and Gabe a glass. "That matter doesn't concern you, Gabe. It's my business what I do with my house, my life, and how I choose to support my employees." He sat and poured wine into each of the glasses. "It's not their fault I want time alone. I don't want to lose them, so I have chosen to pay them during their absence." Armani took a sip of wine and set down the glass hard. "They're too good of workers to lose even one of them, so I've chosen to insure the fact that they will come back." His tone made it clear that the conversation was over.

Rex noticed the dark circles under Armani's eyes. His friend had been to hell and back. A mask of white bandages covered the burned deformed side of his face. "Do you have to wear those bandages all night?" Rex asked.

"Yes, I do, but I don't always." He said and leaned back in the black leather chair and ruffled his hair. "My face still hurts like hell but not half as bad."

"What does it look like? Is it healing?" Gabe asked, concerned.

Rex shot him a venomous look. That was not the way to win Armani over if they ever hoped to convince him to rejoin the band.

Armani tipped his head back. A menacing laugh filled the house. "It looks like a piece of raw charred meat." He scoffed and leaned forward. "I guess you could say I resemble Erik from 'Phantom of the Opera'." He stood and crossed his arms. "Why are you asking about my appearance? Oh, and to answer your question, no, you can't see my face, Gabe."

Rex intervened. "He wasn't asking to see your face. Gabe was simply trying to make conversation."

Armani rolled his eyes. "Come on, Rex. We both know he's only here to talk me into joining the band, touring, producing albums, and perhaps a possible interview or two on national television." His icy gaze returned to Gabe. He pointed at him. "You don't give a damn about me. All you care about is the money you can earn off my hard work. Have you ever stopped to think about the fact that I'm in the process of grieving?" Armani asked, his anger rising like the temperature in the desert. "I'm not a freak show for the world and media to see so you can make money off of my humiliation!" Armani picked up an empty beer bottle and threw it against the wall, shattering it into pieces.

Gabe's face turned crimson red. "I didn't mean to upset you, Armani. To answer your question, yes, I would love to see you in the band again. You have too much talent to just fade away in your dark depression. You are an artist with the skills of a master musician." He paused and cleared his throat. "You can play almost any instrument, sing like an angel from Heaven, compose music and write lyrics." Gabe looked down and kicked an empty beer can. "Armani, you are a gifted man blessed with the ability to reach people through music."

Armani faced Gabe and saw what looked like sincerity in his eyes. What Gabe said was true but he wasn't ready to face the world. Ashamed at having thrown a temper tantrum Armani busied himself picking up the pieces of glass from the beer bottle.

Rex bent down, helping Armani pick up the glass. Rex glanced at Armani and saw tears flowing. Pain shot through Rex's heart like an arrow from a hunter's bow. Rex realized how much pain Armani was in physically, emotionally, and mentally and his heart went out to him. He wished they were alone because he wanted to offer a shoulder for his friend to cry on but he couldn't, not with Gabe present. Armani was a private man and would never forgive him if he did this.

Gabe interrupted the awkward silence in the room. "We should be going now, Rex." Gabe walked toward them stopping near Armani. "I have something I'd like you to at least look at, Armani." He said, pulling a piece of paper out of his pocket.

Rex stood and held out his hand. "I'll give it to him." He stated, taking the contract from Gabe. "Go outside and wait for me in the car," Rex ordered.

Gabe hesitated and sighed. He hoped to be able to talk with Armani about the interview on Dateline, the money, the publicity and the overall closure for the public on what really happened. Selling an idea was his specialty, but it looked as if he wouldn't get his chance. This time, at least. Persistence was his middle name and he wasn't about to give up. The interview on Dateline was a lifetime opportunity for the band but more importantly for himself.

"Please." Rex stated, growing impatient with Gabe. "I have no problem throwing you out if you won't listen to a simple command." His eyes sparked with anger like stars in the darkest night sky.

Gabe turned and walked to the door. "Have a good night, Armani. I will be talking to you soon as you are aware I don't give up easily." He slammed the door.

Armani sighed, relieved and stood. "Thank you for getting him out of here."

"That's what friends are for," Rex said. "Do you want to talk to me about anything?"

Armani glanced at the cathedral ceiling, lines of exhaustion around his dark eyes. "No, I wish to be left alone." He realized his words had slapped his friend across the face. "I'm sorry, Rex. You know me better than anyone and right now isn't the time or place to discuss my feelings, let alone a deal with that madman, Gabe. All he cares about is money and nothing else." Armani grabbed the paper from Rex's hand and read aloud. Disgust creased his brow. "Pathetic!" He screamed. "I will not become a spectator for money." Armani whirled around, spit on the paper and handed it to Rex. "Tell Gabe to take this contract and shove it up his ass as far as it will go."

Rex was concerned. "I feel you falling away, my friend." Rex whispered.

Armani broke down, crying and pointed to his face. "This is my curse that I must live with forever." He put his hand on his chest and continued. "And this is where the scars will forever remain." Wiping tears, he walked away from Rex, extended his arms and spun in a circle. "Now there is only emptiness in this house. Darkness and despair are my only companions."

"I don't know what to say, man. Let me help you." Rex blurted, knowing he sounded foolish.

Armani motioned to the door. "You can help me by leaving." He said without emotion. "I wish to be alone."

Rex walked away, his heart hurt for his friend. He was speechless. Rex turned briefly to look at Armani before leaving. "Good night."

The door shut and Armani was once again alone in darkness, loneliness, and despair.

Gabe's car's engine hummed outside, but Gabe was nowhere to be found. 'Where the hell did he go? It's cold and dark out here.' Rex thought. "Damn it." Rex muttered. He was forced to look for him.

Rex zipped his jacket to his chin and stomped toward the backyard. A piercing scream stopped him.

"Gabe!" He screamed. "Where are you? Answer me!" Rex jogged in the direction of the scream.

He saw a shadow near the entry to the woods and ran towards it. "Gabe!" A tall dark figure hovered over Gabe, who lay helpless on the forest floor.

A large hawk flew in the night sky and shrieked. Rex's heart rate sped up. That was the same hawk he had seen days ago that also looked like the hawk on the cover of the Vampirism book in Armani's house. He stopped one hundred yards from Gabe and the dark figure.

"Who are you?" Rex yelled.

The shadowy figure stood tall, lifting Gabe to his feet and shoved him toward Rex. "That is none of your business. I must advise you that this man, Gabe, is not welcome here or near Armani's property." Donovan's eyes glowed crimson red.

Gabe, face as white as a sheet, ran toward Rex and fell when he reached his feet.

"Be advised that I keep an eye on this property, and if you violate my orders, there will be a price to pay." Donovan boomed, pointing at both men. "Heed my warning." With a swirl of his black cape, he disappeared.

Gabe coughed, stood and shot a backward glance at the forest and ran to his car. Rex ran after him, clenching his chest until they reached the car.

Gabe got in the car faster than Bo jumped into General Lee on the Dukes of Hazard.

"Get in!" Gabe screamed, beads of sweat dripping down his forehead.

Rex slammed the door and Gabe took off like a Nascar driver. Rex glanced at Gabe noticing his hands were clenching the steering wheel so hard his knuckles were white.

"What the hell happened back there?" Rex asked his breath labored.

Gabe punched the window hard. "I don't know, honestly." He cleared his throat, catching his breath. "I was sitting in the car waiting for you when all of a sudden this thing in a black cape with unusually long fingernails tapped the window. I locked the door and tried to get a look at its face, but I couldn't see a damn thing in the dark . . . ." His voice trailed off.

Rex looked in the direction of Armani's house and saw the silhouette of the hawk dance in the night sky against the full moon. He shook his head and stared at the road ahead of them. "What happened after that?" Rex asked not sure he wanted to know.

Gabe sipped the cold coffee sitting in the cup holder. "The doors unlocked themselves, he reached in, grabbed me and we ended up at the entrance of the forest." Shaking his head as if he didn't believe what he was saying, he continued. "We didn't walk. He held me by my arms and we were flying. It's not human, whatever it is."

Rex thought about the book on Vampirism sitting in Armani's house. The hawk on the front, the weird occurrences Armani had been experiencing and this strange creature in the forest. Rex shivered.

"What are you thinking about?" Gabe asked. "You have that look on your face that says you know something, like you're putting the pieces of a puzzle together. You know the missing piece. What the hell is going on, Rex?"

Rex ignored the question while he analyzed the situation.

The highway was a welcome sight. Merging onto the highway, Gabe muttered a slew of cuss words under his breath at the traffic.

"Well, we're almost to your house. I'm heading home after I drop you off." Gabe stated. "Now, tell me what you know." Anger caressed every word. "I nearly lost my life back there. The black caped creature threatened to kill me if I ever made contact with Armani again."

Rex fidgeted with his hands and said, "I believe the creature is a vampire and for what ever reason he wants Armani and will kill anyone who gets in his way." Rex explained why he believed it was a vampire for the next ten minutes. "And that hawk is always around Armani's house. I've even seen that bird around there when Simone was alive." Rex rubbed his chin. "That hawk has the oddest coloring. Have you ever seen a black hawk with a white patch on its chest?"

Irritated, Gabe pulled into Rex's drive. "Not until tonight. That hideous bird was flying above the vampire, so you call it, when he had me pinned down. All I remember is the color and its cold yellow eyes. Watching you like a hawk has new meaning to me now." Gabe laughed for a minute, but became serious just as quick. "I thought it was going to pluck my eyes out with its sharp beak." Gabe patted Rex's shoulder and bid him good night. "I won't let that creature stop me from making money. Believe me I will be contacting Armani again. Since you seem to think what we saw was a vampire I'll approach Armani in the daylight." Toying with his seatbelt, he rolled his head back and laughed. "Vampires sleep during the day, right? Which means no harm can come my way. Legend has it they can't come into the sunlight or come out during the day because they will die."

"Yeah, that's what I've heard." Rex turned his head and made eye contact with Gabe. "But, if I were you, I would leave Armani alone. I may be wrong, but maybe, just maybe this thing isn't a vampire and it's something more powerful," he said in a serious tone.

Gabe dismissed the thought with a wave of his hand. "I guess the truth will come out eventually." Gabe shifted the car into reverse signaling the conversation was over. "Have a good night, Rex."

"Please be careful." Rex said and stepped out of the car.

He watched Gabe drive away and had a sinking feeling in his gut that it may be the last time he saw Gabe alive again. Greed would bury Gabe one day.

Rex pivoted and walked to the steps of his home mumbling to himself. "I suppose the phrase, 'Pride cometh before the fall' should be 'Greed cometh before the fall.'" Rex said to no one. Rex sighed, looked at the full moon and opened the door to his home. "God have mercy on your soul, Gabe."

Rex turned on a few lights and sat on the brown couch. He picked up his phone to call Armani and warn him of what just happened at his house.

"Come on, man. Answer the phone." Rex said, rubbing his forehead.

Armani allowed himself a simple pleasure tonight. Sitting in the hot tub, he slowly sipped wine. The constant interruption of his phone ringing angered him. It had to be Rex or Gabe. He was sure he pissed them both off, but didn't care.

Armani slid down until the hot bubbly water reached his neck. He put his head back and stared at the night sky. The full white moon looked so close to earth, it seemed to be reaching out for him.

The phone wouldn't stop ringing. "Bloody hell," Armani muttered and stepped out of the hot tub. He wrapped a towel around his waist, walked to the bedroom and checked the phone. Of course, it was Rex. Armani silenced the phone. The last thing he felt like doing was talking to him.

Armani was halfway to the hot tub when he heard the doorbell ring. Agitated, he sighed and threw the towel on the bed and rummaged through the drawers for something to wear. He threw on a black sweat suit and slicked back his hair.

'Rex, why do you have to be so persistent?' He thought and rolled his eyes.

Armani stopped and stared at a picture of Simone and him hanging on the wall. His eyes moistened and his heart bled. It was taken at Manhattan Park a few months before the assault. They were standing in front of the large black horse sculpture. The sun shone through the blue sky and a fountain spurted water from behind the horse. Simone had a purple dress on that showed off her lovely toned legs. Her hair cascaded around her shoulders to her breasts. The smile on her face said she was the happiest lady in the world. Armani stood behind her, his arms wrapped around her waist. He studied the way she was gripping his hands and longed for her touch. "I would give my life to be able to hold and touch you again, my Simone. I am not complete without you." He said and caressed her cheek with his thumb. "I love you."

He wiped the tears and walked to the top of the stairs. He could throw himself over the railing and end all of this tragedy and heartbreak. The anger at the people who did this motivated him to continue his lonely desperate existence. The day he found out Simone died, he felt his heart, soul and mind die with her. He was just as dead as she was.

Armani jumped, lost in sorrow. Rex was beating on the door like a man gone mad. Brow furrowed, he made his way down the steps, not bothering to cover the deformed side of his face. He was too angry with Rex for his constant calling, the doorbell ringing, and now the beating on the door. The first thing Armani was going to say to Rex was to show some respect and learn patience.

Armani felt a chill and scanned the living room for an open window. Goose bumps peppered his arms and neck reminding him of the strange things he saw and felt at the funeral home.

Bang, bang, bang. Armani reached for the doorknob as his inner voice told him not to open the door. The knob was cold as ice. He ignored his gut and opened the door. A tall man in a long black cape stood with his arms crossed, a coy smile on his face.

"Hello Armani," he said with a bow.

Armani couldn't take his eyes off him. This man had the same form as the shadow he had seen at the funeral home.

The man swung the black cape behind him with lightning speed. "Forgive my manners. I haven't properly introduced myself. My name is Donovan and I am a member of the Dark Ones." Extending his hand, he took hold of Armani's.

Donovan's cold touch sent shivers down Armani's spine. "Where are you from? Have I met you before?" Armani asked. He rubbed his hand on his sweats trying to warm it.

Donovan stared at Armani with cold black eyes. He gestured with his large skinny hand. "Are you going to invite me in? We have many things to discuss."

"Oh, yes. Please do come in," Armani said. Why was he letting this strange man in? The book, the hawk . . . What was he thinking? Armani felt helpless to tell this man no.

Donovan put his hands on Armani's shoulders and stared into his eyes. "I promise that by the time we're through with our meeting all of your questions will be answered. We will discuss all of those things on your mind and so much more, my friend." Releasing Armani from his hypnotic spell, he walked past him straight to the couch and sat.

Fear coursed through Armani's veins. He swallowed and offered Donovan a glass of wine. He poured two glasses full and sat down on the chair across from Donovan.

Donovan smiled his teeth white as snow. "Don't fear me. I am here to help you. Consider me your new ally." He leaned forward and tossed the book on Vampirism to Armani. "Let's get started, shall we?" He questioned but it was more of an order. "Time is of the essence and

must not be wasted. There are men who need to pay for their crimes."
He raised his wine glass and offered a toast, "To our new lifelong
friendship."

CHAPTER FOURTEEN

V ICTOR TURNED AND smiled at Katrina. "Here we are, my love." He pointed to his large black mansion. The mansion looked more like a haunted house in a horror movie. The brick was black and slightly rundown, the roof was shaped into a high steeple and the wind blew tattered white curtains in and out of the windows like ghosts dancing in the wind.

Katrina gripped Victor's hand hard. "Where are we, Victor?" She asked, confused. "I don't remember walking here." She swallowed hard and tried to suppress her anxiety as Victor led her up the steps to the large wooden door. Katrina noticed the silver head of a vampire on the knocker.

The door opened when they reached the top step. Katrina tried to look inside but Victor blocked her view.

Victor turned, leaned toward Katrina and kissed her lips. "Wipe the worry from your face, child. You no longer have anything or anyone to fear." He held her eye contact and wiped the tears from her cheeks. He held her hand and led her inside against her will.

Katrina screamed in rebellion. "I want to go home!" She dug her feet in to the wood floor and tried to break free from Victor's grip, wiggling and squirming like a worm on a fishhook.

Victor stopped and grabbed her shoulders, shaking her. "Now, Katrina, stop this childish behavior. It will do you no good and you made the choice to submit to me by accepting my date invitation." He grabbed her chin and tilted her head toward his face. "Come now, child. You are trying my patience." He said, his eyes, emotionless. He jerked her arm hard.

Katrina winced. His touch was like ice. Helpless to fight him, she succumbed and let him lead her inside.

The interior was the bipolar opposite of the exterior. It was the most beautiful home she had ever seen. The home consisted of one giant room with the kitchen, living room, family room and dining room in view from all angles. The entryway was adorned with beautiful paintings from Van Gogh to Picasso. A crystal chandelier hung from the ceiling and mirrors hung on every wall.

Victor watched her take in the splendor of his magnificent home. An odd sensation overtook him. His heart warmed and heat flowed through his veins like fire rolling through a forest. Could it be love? Not a chance. Love died the day his parents started brutally abusing him.

His heart was sealed off to love and the women he met, as beautiful as they were held no meaning to him except for his own personal gratification. Treating them like trash was easy. Numerous women had come into his home, but none of them lived to tell about it. But, oh Katrina was going to be different than the rest. She would be recycled over and over. This woman was such a beautiful trophy, one to have and hold forever.

Katrina crossed her arms and stared at Victor. "Why are you looking at me like that?" She asked, her voice sweet as sugar.

"Like what?" He asked and drew her to his chest. "I'm looking at you like you are the best thing that has happened to me in centuries. I can't help but feel attracted to you, Katrina." He held her tighter. "I will never let you go." And he meant that. Only death would separate them.

Katrina shivered. What did he mean? She gazed around the house looking for an escape route. This man seemed obsessed and dangerous. Her gut instinct told her to run like hell. A tear slid down her cheek.

Victor held her away from his chest and stared at her porcelain face. He wiped the tear from her cheek with his thumb, caressing her face as he did. What was happening to him? He would have to fight these feelings of love. Love played no service to his mission but Victor couldn't help but pretend Katrina loved him. Taking her hand he led her to a large full length mirror in the living room. "Turn around and look at the two of us."

Katrina turned and looked. Victor stood behind her with his arms enveloped around her petite frame. He kissed the top of her head and neck. His tongue swirled around her jugular vein, fighting the desire to pierce her soft skin with his fangs and drink her pure sweet innocent blood. "If I could turn you over right now, I would. I want to be one with you in so many ways. Take a look at how perfect we are together." He said and tilted her head toward the mirror.

Katrina froze when she saw his eyes reflecting in the mirror. They were glowing yellow like a cat's. "What are you?" She asked and turned her head in disgust.

Victor laughed. "I am a vampire, my dearest." Victor gazed at the two of them and noticed that the smallest spark of love in his eyes seconds ago was replaced with sheer evil. "You turned your head away from our reflection. Why must you reject what I offer?" Victor asked. He despised being rejected.

Katrina looked for a weapon, something to hit Victor with so she could make a run for it. A bronze candlestick sat on the oak table in front of the mirror where they stood. She hoped answering his question would distract him. "I didn't reject you. I don't know you yet and relationships take time to build." She paused and bit her lip. "I'm hoping that you and I will begin building our relationship right now." She said, cleared her throat loud and grabbed the candlestick. She saw that Victor was staring at the ground while she spoke and she gripped the candlestick harder, her palms sweating.

"You don't fool me, young one," Victor said pivoting to face away from her. "You're not ready for a relationship of this kind. Let me show you to your room. I'm sure you will be more than pleased. It's decorated and furnished with only the best." He took a few steps toward the winding staircase and stopped staring straight ahead. "Come on, Katrina. Don't make me drag you up here by force."

Katrina raised the candlestick above her head, ran toward Victor and slammed it on top of Victor's head with all her strength. Victor fell to the ground with a yell.

"You can't force me to do anything, you son of a bitch!" She screamed and bashed him one more time over the head. She threw the candlestick aside and ran out the door taking the steps two at a time her heart beating wildly in her chest.

She had no idea where she was and didn't care. Katrina sprinted to the entrance of the forest, paused for a second and entered the dark woods. The snow slowed her down and branches cut and scraped her legs. One thought kept her going and that was to get away from this madman turned vampire. If Victor caught her, he would kill her. Tears stung her eyes. She was lost with a vampire after her. How would she ever win this battle? It may be impossible but she hoped Victor would stay knocked out long enough for her to get to safety.

The darkness and coldness of the woods suffocated her. If only she knew a way out but she didn't so she ran straight ahead with no jacket, no gloves and no hat. She felt as hopeless as a sailor in the eye of a hurricane.

She was running so fast. 'I must escape', she kept telling herself over and over. Not paying attention to the forest floor, her foot tangled in a pile of brush unseen because of the snow and she fell like a tree cut down by a lumberjack.

"Damn it!" She couldn't move her left leg. She tried to push the brush and wood off her leg, but it was no use. Tears streamed down her face. She felt like a mouse in trap. She tried to twist her leg and cringed in pain. 'I have to fight. I can't give up,' she thought. But, it was hopeless. The more she wiggled, the tighter the branches seemed to hold her in their grip.

Katrina laid her head in her hands and sobbed. She felt light headed and dizzy. Death was now unavoidable. She would either die here or die at the hands of Victor. She lifted her head and screamed. "Help me! Somebody please hear me!"

Silence answered her screams. It was useless. No one would hear her.

Owls hooted in the distance. Tree branches danced and waved in the wind. Katrina blinked. The forest spun in circles in front of her eyes. She turned her head and vomited fighting to stay conscious.

Victor's head pounded. How dare she do this to him and try to run away from him and the life he had planned for the two of them. To think he felt a slight touch of love and light in his heart when he was with her. Foolish human feelings! That's why they couldn't play a part in his life. His heart was black and always would be until the day he decided to end his immortal life. Katrina would pay for what she had done. There would be no escaping again. What did she think? That she would get away from him. Victor snarled. The dear young naïve girl forgot that he's a vampire and a skilled hunter. Finding her would be easy.

Victor stood and rubbed the top of his head. Dried blood lay on the floor. Fortunately, The Dark One's healed just as quickly as they were injured. He was more shocked that he had trusted her enough to turn his back on her.

"Damn me for letting my defenses down and trying to open my heart." Victor seethed. "Katrina, your worst nightmare is coming for you. You are mine and always will be."

Victor rose and glided out of his house. He stood at the entrance of the forest and inhaled her scent. She was only a mile away. Victor lunged forward and flew above the tree line scanning the forest for Katrina. The Dark One's were gifted with the eyes of a hawk. He could see even the smallest insects from the sky. His heart beat faster when he heard Katrina whimpering ahead. Angry as he was with her, concern shrouded his face. Not genuine concern from his heart for her but a selfish concern that something beat him to her and stole the first infliction of pain that was his to distribute.

Victor spotted Katrina lying helpless on the forest floor rocking back and forth. He circled like a bird eyeing its prey. He pondered his attack. His lips turned upward into a wicked smile as he descended to the ground, black cape swirling behind him.

Victor landed silent as a mouse standing a few feet from Katrina and watched her. She was oblivious to his presence. He glided in in front of her and crossed his arms, willing himself not to strike her.

Katrina looked up at Victor, her eyes red and swollen. "Get away from me, Victor!" She screamed. Scared and helpless stared at his face. "Just kill me and get it over with." She hung her head waiting for her execution.

Victor shook his head. "Katrina, Katrina. You do not know me at all." He knelt beside her and placed his hand on the brush that held her leg hostage. He pushed hard. "I like to play with my victims." Laughing he grabbed Katrina's face and forced her to look into his evil penetrating eyes. "If you're in pain, don't hide it. That had to hurt."

The pain was excruciating. Katrina's eyes watered but she refused to give Victor the satisfaction of knowing how much pain she was in. "Just let me go. I promise to never speak of you to anyone." She lowered her eyes from his.

Rolling his head back Victor laughed. "Look at me. Do you think I'm going to let you go?" He asked grabbing her face once more forcing her to look at him. "You are mine to do with as I please and you will never tell me no, my dear." He hissed, his fangs glistening in the moonlight.

Seconds later he was on his feet. He bent over, picked up the brush and threw it aside. Victor gently picked up her foot and examined it. "It's just a sprain so it won't take too long to heal."

Katrina whimpered. "Please just take me to my own home. I need to see my dog." She twisted her hair with her index finger trying to look innocent. "I promise I will come back to you."

Victor bent over and picked her up, holding her close. "What reason do I have to trust your word?" He didn't wait for a response. "That's right, Ms. Katrina, I have no reason. Now please be quiet until we get home."

Katrina closed her eyes fighting the tears that threatened to fall like pouring rain. Helpless to fight Victor she let herself go limp in his arms.

Victor shot into the air like an arrow. The wind whipped Victor's cloak around the two of them as he soared through the sky with her cradled to his chest like an infant child. Something about Katrina made it impossible for his darkness to surface completely. That was not to say he wouldn't hesitate to force her into submission to him through violence. His heart wasn't that soft. 'Yet,' a silent voice told him. He ignored it.

Within mere moments he was standing outside of his home, Katrina still in his arms. He glided up the steps and the door opened. He walked inside his home and laid Katrina on the couch and covered her with a blanket.

"Oh, Katrina, you make me feel human again." He smiled and wiped a strand of hair from her cheek. "I will bring your dog here for you."

Katrina felt helpless and the best thing she could do was play Victor's game for a while. Thank God for the drama courses she took in high school and college. She smiled at Victor, took his hand and held it to her heart. "Thank you, Victor." She bit her lip and added, "Will you bring my other things here as well? Since I will be living with you, I'd like very much to have my possessions with me." Her voice cracked. How she hated to say that to the creature she found herself hating more with every minute that passed.

Victor leaned over and kissed her on the mouth. How sweet she tasted. Soon enough the taste of her blood would satisfy him. "Anything for you," he smiled. "I also have a request of you." He paused placing his hand on her neck. "You may not like this but it has to be done."

CHAPTER FIFTEEN

G ABE WAS NOT going to be told what to do. Some creature was trying to stand in his way of making money and that enraged him. A meeting needed to be held with two associates of his concerning this matter.

Driving on Interstate 196 was a battle tonight. One he didn't feel like contending with. Gabe was a man consumed with power and control. He demanded it from the musicians and bands he represented as well as from his peers and the public.

"Come on people, move out of my way!" Pounding the steering wheel he shook his head in frustration. The roads were slippery but not that bad, especially not for residents of Michigan who should be more than used to the slick roads. "You people are driving like Texan's when they get one inch of snow. Damn it!"

Gabe swerved to the left and saw what the problem was. A half mile ahead two cars had rolled and lay in the median. Driving too fast was as much of a problem as driving too slow. What a shame. Gabe hoped no one was hurt. "Well, at least not potential talent or someone with money and status." He said a wicked smile on his lips.

The row of cars inched closer to the scene. Red and white lights flashed from police cars, ambulances and fire trucks. A police officer directed traffic with a light stick, swinging it back and forth. Gabe sneered and peered past the accident noting the traffic sped up. Thank God because he was running late the minute he stepped out the door for his meeting and this only made it worse.

When Gabe was directly next to the accident scene he turned his head and stared at the over turned cars. A young woman on a gurney was being wheeled away from her car. His stomach flip flopped. She looked exactly like Simone. He shook his head, turned and stared at the cars taillights ahead of him, trying his hardest not to look again. But, something forced his head to turn and his eyes to focus on the scene of the accident. Gabe couldn't move his foot to accelerate or turn his head away. It was like he was in a trance. Unable to shift his gaze, he watched as the medics pushed the gurney to the waiting ambulance. Horns blasted but he was frozen in time. The woman stared at the sky, her hand extended to a black shadow that rose over top of her. Didn't these people see what he was seeing? Her soul was about to be taken from this earth.

Gabe slapped his face trying to break the spell he was under. What he saw next was horrific and the color drained from his face. The shadow held the woman's hand, turned its head and stared at Gabe with hatred and rage. It was the same creature that had assaulted him at Armani's house, except this one had long flowing white hair and piercing blue eyes that seemed to stare into his soul. Gabe tried to scream but nothing came out. The white haired vampire lifted its free arm and pointed a long finger at him and smiled.

"What are you? What do you want with me?" Gabe asked eyes glued to the light haired vampire and the woman who could've been Simone's twin sister.

The vampire turned away to face the woman lying on the gurney. Gabe saw a red tear fall from its eye.

The vampire faced Gabe again mouthed, 'You,' and licked its lips in a circular motion.

A large shadow approached the car window, knocking twice. Gabe jumped, looking directly into the eyes of a heavy cop. The cop motioned for him to roll down his window.

"Yes officer?" Gabe asked as if nothing was wrong but inside he was shaking like a nervous schoolgirl before her first kiss. "Can I help you?"

The cop gave him a crooked grin. "Yes, you can help me by moving your car and following traffic." He gestured to the line up behind Gabe's car, "Is there a problem? A reason you're gawking at the scene of this accident?" Folding his arms the cop waited for a response. Horns continued to honk. A few people shouted obscenities out their car windows.

Gabe cleared his throat. "Did anyone die?" He asked trying to peer around the large cop to see if the vampire was still there.

The cop placed his hands on the door and rolled his eyes. "What the hell kind of freak are you? I see you trying to look at the accident some more. Are you one of those people who gets off on seeing dead people or what?" He asked his voice thick with sarcasm. "It's really none of your God damn business, but yes, a young woman passed away." The cop tipped his hat. "We got here too late. God rest her soul."

"Did you see anything unusual?" Gabe asked pressing the issue further. He had to know if anyone saw what he had just seen.

The cop smirked. "Ah, you're a blasted reporter." He tapped the top of the car twice. "Nope, I didn't see anything unusual, just the typical accident scene and the drama that unfolds with it. Now, speed along. You're trying my patience and I'm ready to write a ticket." The cop turned and walked away.

Gabe accelerated wishing he could erase what he had seen and leave it all behind. He glanced in the rear view mirror and saw nothing. The vampire was gone. The deceased woman was loaded into the ambulance. He remembered seeing the red tear fall from the vampire's eye. Why was it crying? The vampire that threatened him at Armani's seemed like a cold, ruthless killer. What would make them feel sorrow? Traffic was still slow but the cars in front of him and behind him were welcome company giving him a sense of safety.

Gabe turned on the radio and channel surfed until he found a good rock station. 'Faded Cross' was playing one of their rock ballads. He tapped the steering wheel and bobbed his head to the melodic tune of Armani's voice.

Guilt for what he had done to Armani plagued him but it passed just as quickly. This madness would end soon. Armani refused to comply with him and his wishes for performing and appearing on national television. He knew he was losing his number one band due to Simone's death. Armani was a cold empty vessel with no desire to pursue his once successful career and more importantly, putting money in the management's pockets had ceased which angered Gabe. Armani would pay. Gabe's plan for fame, fortune, publicity and revenge had turned the tables on him and he wasn't pleased.

Gabe knew what had to be done. There was a coffin that needed a final nail and he held the hammer, ready and willing to execute.

Alex and Adam lived a few miles off the highway in a home with no neighbors and little traffic. It was peaceful, but Gabe imagined how boring it would be. At least he didn't have to worry about anyone knowing of their secret meeting.

Gabe was analyzing the could've would've and should've of what Adam, Alex and himself had done to Armani's life when a deer bolted out from the woods. Gabe slammed the brakes, his car skidding to the left and the right.

"Damn you, deer!" Gabe exclaimed when his car jerked to a stop barely missing a tree. With sweaty and shaking hands he shoved the car into drive, turned and drove the remaining mile in a foul mood, but at a slower pace.

A couple sharp turns on the road and he turned right into the driveway of Alex's home. The home sat at the end of a half mile long winding driveway. Alex's home was a large three story brick home. Who would have thought some one of such wealth would live in such seclusion. Most people wanted to show off their riches, but not Alex. He was a very private man.

Gabe parked in front of the three stall garage and stepped out of the car, smoothing his shirt as he walked toward the house.

Alex opened the door and greeted him, "Hello Gabe, you're late." Alex said and squeezed Gabe's hand hard.

Gabe squeezed back. "Due to matters out of my control I'm late." He looked at Alex in the eye. "So, do you have the rest of my money for this half-ass operation we conducted?"

Lines of anger spread over Alex's face like the earth cracking during an earthquake. "Spare me your charade, Gabe. Of course I do. It's not my fault things didn't go perfectly." Alex spat and put his hands in the air. "Maybe you should have left me in charge of the whole game plan instead of taking over. You always need to be in charge and in control, correct?" He shook his head and walked into the house. "I don't think it always works out in your best interest."

Gabe clenched his fists and followed. "I'll admit, it didn't, but I want the rest of my money and I want it tonight."

Alex smiled. "Adam, Gabe has finally arrived. It's time for our meeting." He shouted to his son.

Gabe sat on the brown leather sofa and put his feet on the table. "As you know, Armani is not interested in being in the band. What we thought was a good idea by killing Simone has backfired . . . ."

Alex shushed him with a wave of his hand. "Please wait until my son joins us to discuss the matter." He walked to the kitchen and returned with three glasses and a bottle of scotch. "Care for a drink?"

Gabe nodded. "Yes, please. The trip here was enough to make me want to drink the whole damn bottle." He scowled.

Adam walked in the room, hunched over. "Hi Gabe," Adam said and sat on the chair across from him. "Good to see you again."

"You too," Gabe stated. He didn't care about Adam. Alex was the one with the money and the one who pulled the strings. Adam served their purpose as a puppet in the scheme of things. Gabe knew that Alex was shrewd and if anything went wrong with their previous action and plan and they needed someone to take the fall, that man would be Adam. A smile pulled at Gabe's lips. If Adam only knew that he was just a pawn in his father's game.

Adam was the first to speak. "So, why are we having this meeting?" He asked. "We did what we planned to do and everyone got what they wanted out of it." He stated and cocked his head to the side waiting for an answer.

Gabe sipped his scotch and set the glass on the table a little too hard. "No, I did not get what I wanted and I'm here to collect the remaining money for assisting you. Remember, I'm the one who gave you Armani and Simone's location and hotel key the night you and your father killed her and scarred Armani for life after the bands concert." Gabe rose and stood in front of Adam. "Without my connection and identity as the manager of Armani and 'Faded Cross' you would never have been allowed access to the floor where their hotel suite was." Gabe arched his eyebrows and mockingly laughed at Adam. "It seems you're taking me and my services for granted and that makes me angry."

"Sit down," Alex ordered. "Let's discuss this like gentlemen, shall we?"

Gabe poured himself another glass of scotch and sat with a grunt, glaring at Adam.

Alex cleared his throat and looked at Gabe. "The plan in the beginning was for you to hire some friends from the Mafia, but instead I chose to go the route with you Gabe, since you're Armani's manager. I figured I may as well put the money where it belongs." Nodding his head at Gabe he continued. "And yes, I do have the rest of your money. I don't like how that bitch, Simone toyed with my son's heart and mind. And quite frankly, I hate the music Armani and his band puts out." He smiled at Gabe. "Sorry to tell you that."

"It doesn't matter what your tastes in music are, Alex. I was making good money thanks to Armani and his band and am making nothing now." Anger rose in his voice. "I'm not happy with how the whole thing turned out."

Alex glanced at Adam urging him to speak up. "Go ahead, son and tell Gabe what you got out of this." He smiled.

"Peace of mind." Adam answered and chuckled. "The last face Simone saw before she died was mine. It was such a victorious feeling having the ability to control her for once. I was in charge." He smirked. "Thanks, Gabe for allowing us to do the dirty work ourselves. I can't repay the rush of excitement I had killing her and torturing that rock star Ken Barbie Doll kind of guy." He sighed, his eyes glazed over like he had just had an orgasm. "I replay it in my mind everyday. It was the most beautiful thing making that bitch tell me she loved me before I choked the last breath out of her." He held his hands in the air, making a 'V' with two fingers. "I'd do it again if given the chance."

"Excuse me," Alex stood and walked to the kitchen. He slammed a cupboard door shut and returned with an envelope. He handed it to Gabe. "Here is the rest of your money. There's fifty thousand dollars and by all means feel free to count it if you must."

Gabe grabbed it like a child taking a cookie. "Thank you." He walked to the window and stared at the full moon. "There are some things I need to talk to you both about." He stated and pivoted to face them. "I have been seeing strange things lately and I believe we are in some sort of danger." Gabe proceeded to tell them about the strange things he had been seeing and the experience he had at Armani's house earlier. He talked for the next thirty minutes and realized his hands were shaking when he finished.

"Oh my, you have got to be kidding me?" Adam said laughing uncontrollably. "I think it's your guilt clouding reality." He rolled his eyes. "You need help, Gabe. A shrink may be a good place to start." He snorted. "I had fun doing the deed and I feel satisfied. No one will ever catch us."

Gabe could see that Alex thought he was crazy too. "So, you don't believe me?" He asked and gulped the remaining scotch in his glass. "Well, suit yourself, but don't say you weren't warned. They will appear to you, too."

Alex put his arms over his head. "I didn't say I thought you were crazy, but I think you need to stop thinking about what we did and the part you played in it and move on." He put his hands on his face and stroked his chin. "Guilt is a killer."

"It's not guilt. The things I've seen and experienced are real. Just ask Rex, the lead guitarist in Faded Cross. He was with me at Armani's." He stated matter-of-fact. "Now, I really must be going. I have a long drive home."

Alex walked to the door and opened it for Gabe. "Thank you for coming over and enlightening us with your spooky tales." He cocked his head to the side and said, "If we can ever be of help again, let us know."

Gabe shook his hand and left without a goodbye. He had his money and that was what he had come for. Adam and Alex were a thing of the past now. If they chose not to believe him then that was their problem.

Gabe slammed the car door shut and cursed himself for being part of the evil scheme. How did he know he could trust these two not to blackmail him? After all, they were con artists. Gabe regretted being part of this murderous scheme. He wasn't simply treading water anymore. He was in too deep and he feared the only way out was to drown.

CHAPTER SIXTEEN

ARMANI DIDN'T KNOW what to say to Donovan. He frowned and stood, crossing his arms. "I don't know you and to be quite honest, I don't want to know you." He said bitterly. He walked to the window and gazed at the night sky.

Donovan sipped wine and picked up the Vampirism book Armani had thrown at him. "Let me ask you something. Did you read the book I wrote?" He crossed his legs and stared at Armani's back.

"I skimmed through it for a few seconds. I have no interest in becoming a member of some cult." Armani said, placing his hands on the window. He glimpsed his reflection and shuddered. How had he forgotten to put a mask on before answering the door and letting this stranger inside. "Excuse me for a moment. I need to get something."

He took the steps two at a time, ran to his bedroom and picked up the mask. Pictures of Simone hung on his walls and pierced his heart deep every time he looked at them. He took a deep breath and walked downstairs with the mask in hand to talk with Donovan.

Donovan looked up when Armani walked in the room. "It hurts every time you look at the pictures of Simone. Especially the ones with the two of you so in love and so close. Am I correct? Why don't you take them down so you can heal?" He rubbed his chin and frowned. He had an agenda with that question. It was what Donovan referred to as bait. He studied Armani's face. A patient vampire by nature, he would take things slow with Armani, unlike Victor, who waited for no one.

Armani shot him a menacing look. "Who are you to come into my home and tell me what to do?" He asked, pacing the living room floor. Hurt clouded his face. "I loved and still love Simone. To take them down would be like removing what I have left of her in this home." He shook his head and added, "The pictures will never come down. Not until the men who killed her and destroyed my world die for what they did."

Donovan smiled. "My friend, that's my specialty. Revenge is one of the most beautiful things in this world when administered correctly." Donovan rose and held his hand out to Armani. "Take my hand. I want to show you something."

Armani shook his head. "I'm sorry, but I will not play your games. I don't know what you are or what you want." He leaned forward placing his head in his hands and wondered if this was just a dream.

"You are not dreaming. I'm the one you saw at the funeral home. That little girl died a horrific death and another member of the Dark Ones got revenge for her death." A tear fell from his eye. "It's sad, but killing her parents felt good for Victor." He sat and waited for Armani's reaction.

Startled, Armani stared at Donovan. Finally, Donovan knew he had his attention. Maybe this would be easier than he thought. It was always hard to convince someone to cross over, but once they did, it was a victory for the Dark Ones. They needed more vampires out there promoting justice for the people who died at the hands of malicious people. He knew he was running out of time so it was time to get to the point of his visit and hope that Armani would see things his way.

Armani's deep love for Simone and his need for revenge seemed to be enough fuel to convince Armani that crossing over and becoming a vampire was how he would avenge her death.

"What the hell are you talking about?" Armani asked. "You must be a fiction writer. So, that's why you dropped off this book. You're looking for someone famous, such as myself," he said pointing, "to give you a critique. A five star rating or something." He tilted his head back and laughed.

That was the first time Donovan saw him laugh since he arrived. The poor man was such a hurting desperate soul. Emptiness lay vacant in Armani's eyes, even when he laughed.

"Well, give me a chance to read your novel and I will let you know what I think. Thank you for stopping by." Armani said and walked toward the front door to say good-bye to Donovan.

"Not so fast Armani." Donovan ordered evil lurking in his eyes. He was in front of him in a second, his black cape swirling. "I am not done here. Now, sit down and let me finish before you decide your own fate because when I leave, you are no longer safe." 'And my friend, that's a promise, not a threat.' A voice in his head told him.

Armani's blood ran cold. Donovan's eyes glowed red like the creature he had seen at the funeral home. He hadn't imagined seeing a vampire there after all. His whole body shook but he managed to walk to the chair, preparing himself for what was coming. It amazed him how fast Donovan moved and with such fluid grace. Donovan seated himself on the couch before Armani had a chance to sit.

"I was in your shoes at one point in my life. The love of my life was taken from me at the hands of a very cruel man. Her uncle killed her while I was away at work. I had no idea who had murdered her, but when I came home I found her lifeless bloody body in a heap on the bedroom floor." Donovan's face paled and his eyes watered while he spoke of his memories. "There is not a day that goes by that I don't remember that tragedy. Suicidal thoughts entertained me daily when I was human." Donovan paused and drank a long sip of his wine and wiped his mouth with a napkin. "I had the noose ready. All I had to do was jump and end it all. The suffering was too much for me to bear and so I thought this was the only way out. I was saved within a minute of killing myself and ending all the pain and torment so I could be with my Darla."

Armani listened, intrigued. "What made you change your mind?" He asked. "Thoughts of revenge or knowing you would die and the murderer was still out there? Did someone save you?" Armani asked his attention devoted to Donovan. His heart hurt for the vampire. Maybe he and Donovan had more in common than he had initially thought. "I'm sorry for interrupting. Please continue."

Donovan smiled weakly. "Yes, you could say someone saved me. His name is Victor and he is the master of the Dark Ones. A vampire not to reckon with, that's for sure, a ruthless killer with a dark, jaded past. Revenge is his vendetta and not only for the torture he endured, but also for those who are brutally beaten and living the abuse of his past." Donovan paused briefly and studied the architecture of Armani's home. The man had expensive taste. The home was breathtaking, a beauty to behold.

Armani wondered if this was the way for him to avenge Simone's death. Was Donovan here to give him the answers, even possibly help him cross over as the vampires say? He was ready to do whatever it took to kill the men who killed Simone and his soul. Whoever was responsible for this deserved the just punishment of an eternity in Hell. "I have a question. So, this Victor, what torment did he go through? How did he cross over and become a Master?"

"You must have read my mind. I was getting to that point," he said and smiled. "Victor was abused and tortured as a child in horrific ways beyond comprehension. His parents had images of his bruised and beaten body painted so they could hang them on the walls of their home."

Armani's face twisted in disgust. "What the hell kind of sick people were his parents to do this to him?"

"Sick beyond a shadow of a doubt, my friend. They are dead now and rightfully so." Donovan smiled a wicked gleam in his eye. "And a brutal death his parents faced when Victor got his revenge. Gruesome and full of torture as it should have been. Someday when you meet Victor, he will inform you of what he did to his parents and how he continues to kill the abusers of children in the same manner."

Chills ran up and down Armani's spine. "So, what does any of this have to do with me? I want revenge for Simone's death, but I have no desire to cross over and become a vampire to make this happen." He placed his hand on the left side of his face and winced in pain. It felt like someone had taken a cattle prod and pierced the side of his face. He needed his pain medication and now. "Please excuse me, Donovan. I must get a pain pill. This cursed side of my face feels like it's on fire."

Donovan eyed him like a hunter stalking its prey. "Be my guest and when you return I have two choices for you." He folded his hands and said, "And you will be making a choice tonight."

Armani wished he had never let Donovan into his home. He wanted revenge for Simone's death, but the price he had to pay seemed much too steep for him. Crossing over was not something you just did. Hell, people took more time to decide on the purchase of a car. This was his life Donovan was talking about and not something you could return if you didn't like the way it felt. 'Curse the day I had thoughts of revenge,' Armani thought. Maybe those thoughts somehow reached the undead and now he was going to get what he asked for. Would it be possible for Donovan to get revenge on the guilty while he watched? He would have to remember to ask him that.

Armani walked upstairs and into the bathroom. He opened the cabinet and took twisted the pill bottle open. He threw two pills in his mouth and chased them down with water. Armani walked to the bed and sat on the edge, his eyes moved to the picture of Simone sitting on the end table. He picked it up and stared into her eyes.

"I wish you were here, my love. Daylight has died in my heart since your death. I'm so sorry I couldn't have saved you." Armani said and wiped tears from his cheeks. He set the picture on the table. "There is not a day that goes by that I don't hope that you will be here when I return home. When I hear a knock on the door I can't help but hope it's you on the other side. But, it's a fool's dream to keep believing you will show up when I know you are dead and gone." He wept. "Hope fills the heart and fades away, my Simone."

Armani slowly made his way back downstairs and returned to the living room where Donovan sat on the sofa waiting for him.

"I feel your pain, Armani. I was in your shoes once. Believe me, crossing over was the best thing I ever did for myself. Victor helped me pick the pieces up and move on." His unblinking eyes never left Armani's face. "Revenge, closure and an end to the pain is worth the price of becoming a vampire and saying good bye to your mortal life." Donovan said.

"I want revenge more than anything in the world, but it won't bring Simone back." Armani said, sadly. "But, I'll feel better knowing the guilty people who killed her and did this to me," he said pointing to his face, "are dead."

Donovan floated to his feet. "Let me give you your two choices, Armani. A choice is to be made tonight." He said. "Your first choice is to cross over and become a vampire. You will get revenge on the people who killed Simone and murdered your soul. Being a part of the Dark Ones means you will have eternal life as an immortal. You will never die, at least not by physical means." He paced to the window and stared outside. Hunger pains seized him. He needed the energizing life blood of a mortal but time was of the essence and Victor would be checking on his progress soon. He smiled and put two fingers in the air. "Option number two is what we call a temporary cross over."

Armani looked at him skeptically. "What do you mean a temporary cross over? I've never heard of such a thing." He shook his head and snorted. "Hell, I've never heard of crossing over. Let alone the fact that vampires do exist."

Donovan knew telling Armani about the temporary crossover was a lie but it had to be done. Donovan feared for Armani's life and convincing him to cross over of his own free will was only going to lead to a dead end. In time he would explain why he had to manipulate him and Armani may hate him but in time he would accept being a vampire and understand why Donovan had to lie to him.

"A temporary cross over means that you become a vampire, but only for a short time and die once you have gotten your revenge on the people who did this to you and Simone." Donovan noticed Armani looked skeptical. He threw in another lie to motivate him to accept the offer. "You will have eternal life with Simone. The minute you torture and kill the guilty ones, Simone will be waiting for you when you die and the two of you will go onto eternal life, never to be separated again." He hoped he sounded convincing.

"I am an empty lifeless vessel, a hollow log. Will the pain ever subside? Slowly I die each day. What once was a life of color is now black and white." Armani quoted lyrics from a song he had recently written. "Life is hopeless. I am a sailor lost at sea, waves roll around me threatening to sink my ship. Hope dies each and everyday. Life is not worth living without the one who completed me . . . . ."

Donovan cleared his throat and interrupted Armani. "Those lyrics are beautiful. Your songs are filled with your heart and soul and I would like to hear more of them. But, right now I need you to make a decision. We don't have much time." He walked to the window. "Victor will be here soon to check on our progress and his temper is not something you or I want to reckon with." Pivoting, he floated to Armani and stood in front of him. He offered his hand and asked, "Have you made your decision?"

Armani knew he had to make a decision. "I have a question first."

"Go ahead and ask anything you want," Donovan nodded his head. He understood how confusing and hard it was to make such a life changing decision having been in the situation himself long ago. But, time was running out. Some questions would have to remain unanswered until the transition.

Armani stood and stared into Donovan's eyes. "Is there any way you can get revenge for me and I help you? Only I stay a mortal and not have to crossover."

The hopelessness in Armani's eyes pained Donovan's heart and soul. Guilt tore at his insides knowing he had lied about the temporary cross over. But he kept telling himself he had no choice.

"Armani, I'm sorry, but no I cannot get revenge for you. Only you can do it," Donovan said and shifted his feet. Donovan placed his hands on Armani's shoulders and said, "You must decide between the two choices I gave you or Victor will come and kill us both. A decision must be made right now." The hunger pains would not subside. He wished he had time to feed on human blood, but time was ticking and every second counted.

Armani walked hunched over to the bar a few feet away and poured himself a tall glass of scotch. He gulped half of it down in a second. "Ok, Donovan, I have made my decision. I want to temporarily cross over." He swallowed the remaining scotch and sat on a bar stool and wallowed while allowing the scotch to do its job. "The men who did this will pay for their crime. Death is too easy for them. They need to suffer as I have suffered. I am ready." He said and stumbled toward Donovan.

Donovan watched him. Armani was about to cross over and become a vampire, an immortal forever. Donovan tried to tell himself that Armani would forgive him in time for his deceit, but he wasn't entirely sure about that. Donovan took Armani's hand, steadied him and led him to the couch. "Lie down and make yourself comfortable. Let us begin."

CHAPTER SEVENTEEN

Katrina pulled the blanket up to her chin. The couch was comfortable enough, but what Victor said to her made her uncomfortable. What kind of request could a vampire possibly ask of her? A human couldn't do much for a vampire except offer an endless supply of blood or worse, be the one meal before death. Well, she supposed she could end up being his 'feeding tank'. The thought of being food for a vampire's existence sent chills down her spine. Maybe he thought of her as something to remind him what it felt like to be human. An accessory, just like furniture, was that what he wanted of her? She was scared to ask him what his request was. He had such a wicked gleam in his eye when he mentioned having a request of her.

Victor watched her from the kitchen. Such a beautiful woman, and she fit perfectly in his life right now. He decided to act as a vampire of chivalry. After all, he forced her to move in and chivalry was by no means an act of love.

"Katrina, would you like something to eat or drink?"

Fear seized her. Was he going to feed her blood? What type of foods could a vampire have stored in his refrigerator or freezer? "No thank you. I'm not hungry or thirsty." She said and pulled the blanket up to her nose trying to hide from what was happening. Katrina wished that she could disappear under the blankets and wake up in her bed realizing this was all just a bad dream. Curiosity was killing her. "What do you have that a human could eat or drink, Victor?" She asked. Fury at the situation drove her to sit up and face the kitchen where Victor stood. "Are you going to offer me a glass of blood? You will never make me taste blood, Victor!" She screamed and clenched her fists.

Victor watched her, aroused by her feistiness. "I would never make you drink blood, my dear. I was offering to cook food for you or offer you a beverage of your choice. Not blood. Would you like a glass of wine or a cocktail?" He asked, smiling inside. Katrina wasn't afraid to speak her mind and he loved that about her already. "For dinner I was thinking steak or lobster." He crossed his arms and stared at her, a warm expression on his face. Mere moments ago he had been ready to kill her, but something about her had calmed him. The monster within was at bay when he was in her presence, but it didn't mean the monster didn't exist. Unfortunately, it did and always would.

Victor thought of Donovan. He was with Armani convincing him to cross over. Armani would be a perfect fit for the Dark Ones. Donovan knew his life depended on a successful cross over. Once he had Katrina settled in he was headed over to Armani's home to check on things and make sure that every thing went as planned. If not, God have mercy on Armani and Donovan's souls. They would both be destroyed. Victor didn't have a soft heart when it came to his followers. But, the woman on the couch made his heart feel things it hadn't in many centuries.

Katrina smiled at Victor reminding herself to play nice. She may have lost the first battle but she would win the war. "You know what. I am a bit hungry, Victor. I'd love a hamburger with onion and mayo only, please. And a glass of red wine sounds wonderful. I could use it after tonight." She said. "Maybe it will help ease some of this pain in my ankle."

Victor sensed she was in more pain than she lead him to believe. "Let me get you some ice for the swelling. That will help the pain a little bit as well." He disappeared and a moment later he was at Katrina's side with ice wrapped in a towel. He placed it on her ankle. Katrina was lying back staring at the ceiling. Her beauty would never cease to amaze him. "You know what?" He asked. "You are the most beautiful creature I have ever seen." He whispered.

Katrina winced. He called her a creature? What man would ever call a woman that? It sounded ridiculous and absurd. She snickered. "I'd like to think of myself as more than just a creature, thank you very much." She lifted her head and gazed at her ankle, letting out a deep breath. The cold ice chilled her from head to toe. "Could I have another blanket, Victor?"

A blanket appeared out of nowhere and Victor covered her with it and brushed her cheek with his palm. "I would do anything for you." He smiled.

It was the first real smile Katrina had seen and the first time he seemed happy. Katrina laid her head back, closed her eyes and tried not to think about where she was and how she got here. Let alone, how the hell she was going to get herself out of this situation.

"Don't worry you will learn to love me and your new home." Victor said.

Forgetting he had the ability to read her mind, she chastised herself. Many of her thoughts needed to be kept at bay so he wouldn't eavesdrop on her private thoughts and motives. "I have to ask. How you do that?" She asked.

"Do what, Katrina?" Victor asked his lips turned upward in a crooked smile. "Read your mind?" He laughed. "It's easy, really, especially for an old vampire such as me." He walked to the kitchen, stopped and placed his hands on each side of the doorway. "Would you like to learn?" He asked, moving his head from side to side.

"Yes, if it means I get to read your mind." She stated matter of fact.

Victor faced her, a cold hungry look in his eyes. "I don't allow people or other vampires to read my mind. That will never happen. I am much too powerful and strong. Even when I find my mate and share blood with her my mind will not be open to her."

Katrina sat up again. She had so many questions. "You said when you find your mate and share blood with her, your mind and thoughts will remain closed to her. Is it true, then what they say in books about sharing blood with a vampire that it forms an unbreakable bond and connection with the ability to read each others minds?" She asked a puzzled look on her face.

Victor smiled. Katrina was such an innocent mortal. "Yes, that fact is true, but many things they say about us are not true. Fiction, as you know tends to be the imagination of an author. Some facts and reality is mixed in with what the author wants to make up about vampires. Most of the facts written in fiction books that involve vampires are taken from the very first vampire book titled, Dracula. I'm sure you've read that one." Victor ran his hands through his black hair. "I have much to teach you, but right now I want to prepare you a meal. My queen needs to eat and rest." Victor turned and walked into the kitchen.

Katrina didn't say a word. The sounds of clanging dishes and Victor whistling reminded her of home. She closed her eyes and imagined she was lying on her own couch.

A kiss on her nose awoke her. Katrina jumped. Victor kneeled beside her, a smile on his face. What if he had decided to pierce her neck with his sharp fangs instead? After all, she assumed death would be the final end result in her stay here. "How long was I sleeping?" She yawned.

Victor stood and held his hand out to her. "Only about thirty minutes. Come with me. Dinner is ready for the two of us."

Katrina sat up and rubbed the sleep out of her eyes. "It sure smells good." Her stomach growled. "I guess I'm hungrier than I thought," she grinned and placed her hand in Victor's and he helped her to her feet.

"How does your ankle feel when you put weight on it?" He asked.

"Much better than I thought it would," she said amazed it didn't pain her more.

"Come, dinner is ready," He said leading her to the kitchen.

She stood in awe and stared at Victor's kitchen. It was the biggest one she had ever seen in her life. It didn't even compare to the ones in magazines. The walls were a pale gray, the shiny marble floor was black and red checkered. It was a bit dizzying, but pretty and rich all the same. Three large stainless steel refrigerators lined one wall. A large oven and grill stove sat next to the sink. Two silver dining room tables were placed on each end of the kitchen. A bar sat next to the walk out patio with ten black bar stools surrounding the table. Katrina noticed that there was enough alcohol to stock a small bar.

"Do you drink a lot?" She asked and pointed the bar.

Victor set the food on the table and smiled. "No, my dear, I tend to stay away from alcohol. Once in awhile a glass of wine suits me well." He gestured for her to sit down. "The bar is for looks and entertainment purposes."

Katrina walked toward a chair and smiled when she saw a dozen roses in the center of the table. "The flowers are beautiful." She leaned over and smelled them. She touched the glass vase and noticed how expensive it was. "My God, this is a Tiffany vase."

Victor stood behind her and pulled the chair out for her to take a seat. "I have expensive tastes and always have."

Katrina sat and Victor pushed the chair in. "Thank you. You sure are a gentleman, and believe me they are hard to find these days." She said, unfolded a napkin and placed it on her lap.

"You are most welcome." Victor hummed while prepping her plate. He floated to the table and set her plate down in front of her. "Enjoy." He said and sat across from her.

"Aren't you going to eat? I don't want to eat alone."

Victor shook his head. "I'm saving my appetite. I have plans later tonight and will eat then." The smug expression on his face told her Victor was talking about feeding on a human and drinking blood.

"Ok. I don't want to hear about it." Katrina said. Here she was sitting at the dinner table with a vampire. How crazy was this? How crazy was she? She dismissed her thoughts and picked up the burger and took a big bite. "Delicious." The burger was gone in less than five minutes. She knew it was probably bad manners to eat so fast, but she couldn't help herself. This would give her strength and help her heal quicker in order to make her escape in the near future. She sipped her wine and stared at Victor. He sat sideways in his chair, looking out the window at the full moon, a hard menacing look on his face.

"Yes, Katrina. Do you have a question?" His expression softened when he returned her gaze.

"You look a thousand miles away. What's on your mind?" She asked.

Victor shifted in his chair. "I have business to attend to this evening, so I will be leaving you here alone." He stared at her and added, "So don't try to escape and run away from me. There's no way out. The doors and windows will not open for you." He said an evil glint sparkled in his eye. "Get that thought out of your mind immediately."

Katrina blushed. "That's not on my mind. Stop being so paranoid, Victor." She said with a wave of her hand. "I mean, really, did everyone in your past leave you or something?" She figured she might as well try to get to know him and that started with his past.

Victor's gaze was cold as ice. "No, not everyone in my past left me, my dear. I left quite a few people myself," he paused and placed his hands on the table, "dead." He laughed, his fangs showing. "My past does not concern you. I want you to get to know the 'me' that is before you, not the 'me' I left behind." He said. Victor knew it was time to change the subject. One thing he knew was that women, in general were persistent on topics. They wanted answers and wouldn't stop asking questions until they were satisfied with the specific answer they were searching for. That would be deadly for Katrina and Victor didn't want to hurt or kill her, so it was best for the subject to change. And fast. "Would you like some more to eat?"

Katrina got the message. "No thanks. I'm stuffed. Maybe later I'll find something sweet to eat." She smiled. "What am I supposed to do while you're gone?" She asked. The thought of being locked up in some small room like a caged animal made her angry. She hoped he would let her roam about the house freely, but she wasn't sure he would after her last escape attempt. How could she have been so stupid? Waiting until daylight would have made more sense. She shook her head and cursed herself for acting on impulse.

Victor held his hand out to her. "Come with me. I have a wonderful entertainment room that I'm sure you will find amusing." He said and led her through the house to the basement stairwell.

Awestruck, Katrina followed holding Victor's cold hand. Every time she walked through the house, she was amazed at the beauty. It was dark with a gothic twist, but so elegant and rich at the same time.

She stopped and looked up. "I love the chandelier," she said. It was black with red crystal shimmering throughout. The bulbs were placed under small white lampshades that illuminated the walkway with an eerie red color but it was breathtaking.

Victor smiled and allowed her to admire it. "Thank you. I purchased it in England on one of my many trips. It reminded me of Count Dracula." He laughed. "It was an impulse buy. I knew I had to have it when I saw it." He tugged her hand and led her toward the basement.

A few minutes later they stood in front of a closed door with a sign posted to it that read, 'Enter at Your Own Risk.' Katrina wondered why in the world anyone would put a sign up like that on a door in there own home. She glanced at Victor. Ah yes, a vampire would. But, no one in their right mind would roam through his home. Victor would sense the presence of an intruder and that poor soul wouldn't live to see another day.

"Why in the world do you have that sign on the door?" She asked puzzled.

Victor pointed at the sign and smiled. "Think about it for a moment. Why do you think I would put that on there?" He asked and studied her face waiting for an answer.

Katrina had no clue. "I asked you the question. If I knew the answer I wouldn't have asked."

The door opened and a cold breeze swept over Katrina, covering her body with goose bumps. She rubbed her arms. What the hell was Victor planning on doing to her?

"Magic," Victor said and placed his cloak around Katrina's shoulders. "I suppose you want me to explain the sign." Katrina nodded. "I'm a careful vampire, but there are always the curious who come upon my home and decide it's their God given right to enter and take a self-guided tour. The sign is to keep them from coming downstairs and forcing me to kill them." He said and turned the lights on in the basement. "This is where my lair is. Where I sleep and no one is to disturb me. Besides, what would they do if they found me? That's easy. They wouldn't hesitate to kill me." Victor stated answering his own question.

Katrina was confused. "Why do you think they would kill you?" She assumed they would be more scared and run like hell to get away from the house.

"They would because I sleep in a black coffin." He said. "Either that or they would have every cop in town here and I'd be on the news and have more people after me than you or I could ever dream of." He dismissed the conversation and took her hand. "Come now."

She followed but hadn't forgotten the sign. "Victor, tell me the truth about why the sign is up."

Victor floated down the stairs, his feet never touching one step. "I'm not a bad vampire." He said knowing this was not entirely true. Evil dwelt in his heart and soul. It was possible that Katrina could change him, but he didn't think so. He had answered the question the way he knew she would want to hear it but it was not the whole truth. Victor liked to pick his victims, not the other way around. "I wouldn't want to kill someone just because they were in the wrong place at the wrong time, such as my lair. How fair would that be for that innocent soul?" There were humans he didn't consider innocent and those were the ones he delighted in torturing and killing. The people he considered animals that abused children in horrible ways and deserved the deaths he dealt them.

Katrina swallowed hard. Victor's eyes glowed red. She turned from him trying not to look scared. He talked about killing like people talked about the weather, as though it was just normal everyday conversation. Regaining her composure she faced him. "That's nice of you to want to spare the innocent souls. So what do you like doing to the guilty souls?"

This woman was too smart for her own good and much too inquisitive. "Dear Katrina, let's discuss this another time. I told you at dinner that I don't want to share my past with you yet." He smiled and pulled her into his embrace. How easy it would be for him to kill her. She was a small frail woman and he was hungry and thirsty for human blood. The sooner he got out of here and to Armani's the better off they would both be. He was a powerful vampire and his powers knew no end.

Katrina forgot about their recent conversation and walked around the entertainment room.

"This is amazing. I love it. Do you play pool?" She asked and rubbed the felt green surface.

"Not much. Most of the things in my home are for decoration. I entertain myself in other ways. You're free to do anything. Let's just say everything in here is yours now." He studied Katrina and tried to remember what it was like to be human. It was so many centuries ago and his childhood memories were all painful. Maybe he chose not to remember. When he became a vampire, it suited him well. Loss and sadness were replaced with rage and hate. The older he got the colder his heart and soul became.

Katrina walked around and stopped at a large door. "What's in here?" She asked and slowly opened the door.

"Seek and ye shall find," Victor replied.

Being cautious, she peeked inside and gasped. "You must be so wealthy. This is awesome!" She exclaimed. The room had a large swimming pool with a diving board and slide. Patio furniture sat around the pool along with a wet bar. "Do you have a suit I can wear?" She asked and realized what a stupid question that was. Why would any single man just happen to have a woman's bathing suit lying around the house? Let alone a vampire. She laughed and added, "That was a dumb question."

"No question is ever dumb. Asking questions is how one learns. Only the foolish people assume they know the answers." He said and smiled. "I'm sorry but I don't have a woman's swimsuit. I guess you'll just have to swim naked." He winked and motioned for her to follow him. "I have one more entertainment room to show you."

Katrina was shocked. It sure was some entertainment room. Movie posters from all eras hung on the walls and candles were everywhere. There were even two old video game machines that looked like they came straight from the eighties. Katrina grinned, picturing Victor playing a video game. 'Just for show', she remembered him saying. He was the type who went out and created his own game. The hairs on the back of her neck rose and she shuddered.

"Come," Victor ordered. "This is the movie theatre. It's small but I like it because it gives you the feel that you're really sitting in a public theatre."

Katrina stared. Five rows of ten seats each sat before a large movie screen. Two aisles with steps lined the outsides just like at the theatre. He wasn't kidding. There was even the booth above everyone in the center where the employees put the movies in the reel. Well, not by reel anymore in this day and age. Most of the movies were by satellite.

"Wow. That's all I can say." Katrina said. "I'm sure I'll have no issues with boredom while I'm down here."

"No, you won't. The only rule I have and ask that you follow is this. You are not to go into the room with the black steel door." Victor said his eyes black as midnight.

Katrina assumed that was the room he called his lair. "What if I do?"

Victor hovered over her, grabbed her face and pinched her cheeks hard. "You won't live to tell about it." He pinched harder. "Everyone needs space and you are not to invade my space, my place of rest. Do I make myself clear?" Spittle flew from his mouth landing on hers.

Katrina flinched. Her cheeks hurt. She thought of spitting in his face but she knew better than to do that. Victor's emotional mood swings shocked her. "Yes, I understand." At least part of her understood. Damn her curious nature. The truth was she had a feeling she would have to take a look around in Victor's lair. Curiosity already had the best of her.

Victor backed away never losing eye contact with her. "Curiosity killed the cat, Katrina and it may end up getting you killed as well. Think twice before you act on impulse." He said and wagged his finger at her. "I must leave now."

"What do you have to do?"

The questions from her would be the life of him. It was starting to drive him mad. "It's none of your business. This is a personal matter. I will be at a friend's home and that's all you need to know."

"Can I still go upstairs in case I get hungry or am I a prisoner of the basement?" She asked.

Victor handed her a key. "You are free to roam the whole house. Just make sure when you come upstairs that you lock the basement door behind you." He kissed her cheek. He walked toward the staircase and stopped to face her. "Also, I have cast a spell around the house, doors and windows. There is no possible way for you to try and escape." He laughed. It was an evil laugh that made the room temperature feel like it dropped twenty degrees. "Good night, Katrina." He said and vanished.

Katrina stood staring at the spot where he stood only a moment before. A voice inside told her to check out his lair but she hushed it and headed for the pool room instead. How the hell would she ever get out of this house and away from Victor? Any hope of getting her normal life back was fading fast. Would she always be a prisoner of Victor's? Questions flooded her mind. She stood at the pool's edge, screamed, tore off her clothes and jumped into the pool, wishing she would drown and put an end to the madness.

Victor stood outside and cast a spell on his home. He heard Katrina's desperate thoughts. She was correct, she would never escape and the more Victor thought about it the more he felt he could love her and make her love him in return. She would be the end to his loneliness.

Victor walked into the night, his black cape swayed behind him. He smiled. "Yes, Katrina. You will always be my prisoner. There is no escape."

With a leap, Victor ascended into the sky soaring higher and higher. He gazed at the forest beneath him seeing things only the human eye could wish to see from such a distance. The enhanced vision was one of the many things he loved about being a vampire. The senses were heightened to exciting degrees.

Victor would be at Armani's home within a few minutes, but he had to feed first. Blood lust beckoned to him and he felt the need to give Armani and Donovan more time. Was Katrina having a positive effect on him? Never in his years of being a vampire would he dream of giving someone time to complete a task he ordered to be done. Patience was not a virtue he had.

He soared higher and saw the prey he had to have. He could hear the blood flowing through her veins. She was a pretty red head strolling through Manhattan Park with headphones on, ponytail swaying back and forth. Victor inhaled. She had such a sweet aroma. Women were like flowers in that they served a purpose and once the beauty of their blood nourished him they were as good as dead.

Victor descended in front of her. The girl stopped and stared at him.

"Excuse me, you're in my way. Don't you know it's rude to stop and stand in front of someone?" She asked, trying to get around him.

Victor laughed. For her lack of manners, she would die.

"Well, well Madam, you sure aren't very polite and for that you will pay." He exposed his fangs, grabbed her ponytail and pulled her into the woods nearby. The girl screamed. "Shut up, Red. I'm hungry and I believe you should make sure you're right with God." He slapped her face and thrust her onto the snow.

The girl trembled. "Please just let me go." She clawed the dirt and tried to escape but Victor had a hold of her ankles. "Help!" She screeched.

Victor pounced on her. "You must've never paid attention in school in the education of animals." He seethed, his face inches from hers, eyes blazing red. "I smell your fear and it excites me. It drives me to want to kill you even more."

Tears rolled down her cheeks. Eyes as big as saucers, she stared him in the eyes and spit in his face. "Do it then."

Victor swore and wiped the spit from his face. "Oh, I will you bitch." He punched her in the gut. "You will feel every second of this pain." Victor's fangs protruded and he tore into her neck, drinking slowly. He stopped, lifted his head and watched the girl struggle for her life. What satisfaction.

"You shouldn't have spit in my face, you worthless piece of meat," Victor yelled. He cleared his throat and spit her blood in her face and in her eyes.

Unable to move, the girl stared at Victor, her eyes pleading for him to have mercy on her soul.

"No mercy, sweetheart." He said, and bit a piece of her arm off like a lion tearing apart a zebra.

The girl's skin turned ashen gray and felt clammy to the touch. No turning back now. Victor grabbed her ponytail shoved her neck to his mouth, but before he drained her of all the blood in her body, he stopped to look into her eyes one last time. Her eyes were full of emptiness, sadness and hopelessness. "Good bye, my dear." He said and sank his fangs deep into her neck and sucked whatever blood was left in her body.

He stood and felt a renewed strength. He picked up the dead woman's body, raised her over his head and threw her into the bushes. "May you rest in peace my dearest." He licked his lips, wiped his hands on his black cape and leapt into the sky and flew toward Armani's home to hopefully welcome Armani to the Dark Ones.

CHAPTER EIGHTEEN

Armani stared at the ceiling and wondered if he was making the right decision to become a vampire. Well, the good news was that it was a temporary thing and once he avenged Simone's death, he would die and be with her forever. That was the only reason he agreed to such a ludicrous idea.

"It is the right decision, Armani." Donovan said while lighting the black candles. "When we are done with the ceremony you will need much rest. The cross over will drain you both physically and mentally." Donovan paused and looked at Armani's face. The charred flesh on the left side of his face would always remain, even after becoming a vampire. The men who did this to him deserved the vengeance that Armani would deal them. "Not that you asked, but I will be with you when you avenge Simone's death."

"When I become a vampire, can we kill these people right away?" Armani asked. "I don't want to waste another minute on earth living such a tortured life." He said with a choked voice. "The sooner it's done, the sooner I'm with Simone." He wiped the tears and looked at Donovan. "Thank you for giving me hope."

Donovan cringed. Guilt pierced his heart like a double-edged sword. He had given Armani hope, but it was false hope. Maybe he should just tell Armani the truth and let Victor come and kill both of them. At least Armani would be with Simone then. 'What a wicked web we weave when we deceive.' That quote rang in Donovan's ears. Lying was something he never liked to do, but felt he had no choice with Armani. The man was stubborn and wouldn't agree to cross over if he hadn't lied to him. But, Armani still deserved the truth. Good men always did. Donovan swallowed hard. "I have to tell you something important. You deserve the truth . . . . . . " Donovan began.

Armani interrupted him. "Let's hurry and do this before I change my mind. One small request first." He said and closed his eyes. "Would you get a photo of Simone for me to hold while we do this?"

A tap on the door startled Donovan. Could it be Victor?

"Yes, I will do that for you." He said and walked to the door. Fear filled him as he turned the knob.

He opened the door and saw the black hawk stare at him, its gaze cold and menacing. "Curse you," Donovan scolded.

"Who is it?" Armani asked. He hoped it was Rex or someone he knew so he could think more about this whole crossing over thing. Was he making the wrong decision? 'No,' he thought. This was the right thing to do for Simone and for himself. What a pleasure it would be when he was able to look the killers' in the eyes as he slowly killed them and sent them to Hell for eternity for what they did.

"A friend," Donovan replied. He reached toward the hawk and took the note from the hawk's sharp beak and read it.

> 'Donovan,
>   I'm informing you that I'm on my way to Armani's home.
> I hope you are there and have completed the task I asked of
> you. The Dark One's need more strong men like Armani. If the

task has not been completed, you and Armani will die a slow horrific death at my hands. Be prepared.

Sincerely,
Victor, Master of the Dark Ones.

The hawk shrieked and bowed.

Chills ran up and down Donovan's spine. He was a strong vampire, but not nearly as powerful as Victor. Age made a vampire acquire strength and skills that younger ones were no match for in a battle.

"Thank you, my friend. Don't worry, it will be done soon." Donovan said.

The hawk spread its long wings and flew high into the sky. Donovan watched as the hawk circled in the dark sky before landing in a high tree. The hawk was a gift to him from Victor when he crossed over. The hawk taught him valuable lessons on survival as a vampire. The black hawk was a companion and fierce protector as well as his eyes and ears. Donovan liked to think of the hawk as a dog for a vampire. Humans had dogs for the same reason he had the hawk.

"That was my hawk. The one you have been seeing for years. We've had our eye on you." Donovan said and realized that was a stupid thing to say. And he didn't have time to answer any more questions. Victor was well on his way. "I'm going to get the picture of Simone."

Armani was silent. What the hell? Was this a dream? Would he wake up from this horrible nightmare? Of course, he knew it wasn't. This was reality. Soon his emptiness would be gone. He would feel again and be in Simone's arms for all of eternity.

Donovan returned with a beautiful picture of Simone standing in front of the yacht where Armani first met her. He handed it to Armani and said, "We must begin. Time is of the essence and we don't have much of it. Victor is on his way."

Armani held the picture in front of his face and stared at Simone. Tears welled in his eyes. He lost control and let the dam break, tears streaming down his cheeks. "I will be with you soon, my love. I am going to avenge our misfortune and will see you after that." He kissed the picture and placed it on his chest. Warmth flowed through him as if she were lying on top of him.

Donovan placed a blanket on Armani covering him from the waist down. "Lay your head back, Armani. I'm going to recite some rituals before I pierce you with my fangs."

Armani's face turned white. Reality set in. The thought of dying to be reborn as a vampire frightened him. He wished he could drink some more of the scotch he had earlier. "What all is involved in this procedure anyway?" He asked, afraid to hear the answer, but needed to know.

Donovan gave him a reassuring smile. "It's fast, but I won't lie to you. It's painful, but it only hurts just once. You will drift into a deep sleep when I am finished and wake the next day as a vampire." Donovan glanced around the room once more before continuing. "I will bite you and drain you of your blood to the point of death. Immediately following that, I will slice my own wrist and you will drink blood from me, which will bring you back to life." Donovan picked up a glass of water and drank. "And upon drinking my blood you will become a vampire." He squeezed Armani's shoulder. "When you feel pain think of Simone and she will give you the strength to fight. You must fight. Don't give up. Resist death."

"What happens after that?" Armani asked. "I sleep for a long time, wake up and . . . ." His voice trailed off.

"I will become your teacher. You will learn from me the skills and magic I know of being a vampire." He snapped his fingers, dimming the lights in the room. "Like that. You will learn magic. The most important lesson is not the vengeance of the guilty ones who did this to you. That comes natural to humans as well as vampires. The most important lesson you will learn from me is how to mesmerize and hypnotize people to come to you when it's time to feed and to drink their blood without taking too much and killing them." He cleared his throat and said, "Let's proceed."

"Promise me I'll live," Armani pleaded and grabbed hold of Donovan's cloak, his face etched with desperation.

"My friend, I cannot promise that which I have no control over. That fate lies in your hands." He said and squeezed Armani's hand. "But, I can tell you this. You are a strong man who loves Simone and wants revenge. That thought alone will aid you in surviving. I firmly believe you will live and I promise to do everything to see to it that you do."

Armani closed his eyes and focused on breathing while Donovan recited rituals involving sacrifice, blood, death, new life and vampirism.

"I am now going to take the breath out of you and be the death of you." Donovan said and leaned over Armani. "Please lie still and keep your eyes closed."

Armani winced as Donovan's fangs sank into the flesh of his neck. Images of Simone and him flashed through his mind. Dizziness swept over him and he felt sick to his stomach. Donovan sucked the blood out of him like a ravenous animal. The noises would forever haunt him.

Armani stared at the ceiling and saw Simone standing surrounded by a bright light, arms extended out to him. 'Don't do this, Armani. Please. Stop him while you still can.' Simone whispered with the voice of an angel.

Armani tried to resist, but he was too weak and too close to death to fight what had already begun.

"Simone!" Armani screamed. Weakened by the loss of blood, Simone was the last person he remembered seeing or hearing before black darkness enveloped him.

"You must fight. Don't let death defeat you." Donovan ordered, shaking Armani. "Armani, drink now, damn it!" Donovan sliced his wrist with a sharp nail and blood dripped from the wound. He held his wrist to Armani's mouth. "Take from me and have eternal life." Donovan willed him to drink by force.

Armani pressed his lips to Donovan's wrist and drank. When Donovan was sure he had enough for survival, he pulled his wrist away and sealed the wrist wound with a lick of his tongue.

"Welcome to the family of the Dark Ones, my friend. We are now brothers." Donovan laid his hand on Armani's forehead and quoted a mantra for full recovery and healing. "It is finished."

Donovan covered Armani with an extra blanket, walked to a chair and sat staring at Armani. Would Armani regret his decision when he woke up? Of course he would. Donovan had deceived him in the worst possible way. Armani would forever be a vampire. Not temporarily, as Donovan had made him believe. It pained Donovan. He wondered if he lied to Armani to protect him or to save his own soul from death at the hands of Victor. Was he so selfish that he put his own needs before thinking of Armani's?

Now was not the time for self-doubt. Victor would arrive soon and Donovan knew his Master would be pleased. The thought of Victor filled him with hate and anger. He didn't know why, but forcing someone to cross over was not what he ever imagined he would have to do. He laid the blame on Victor.

Donovan jumped, chilled to the bone. A strong wind rattled the windows. The hawk shrieked signaling that Victor had arrived. Thunder boomed. A bright bolt of lightning flashed past the window. Donovan closed his eyes sending out a silent prayer to any higher being in the universe who would listen. He was sure God was out of the question.

Donovan rose and glanced at Armani. Armani was in the state of deep coma like sleep. His face was pasty and ash white. Armani was the picture of death. What did Donovan expect? He had witnessed and been a part of aiding humans in crossing over many times in the past but every time he saw them after the transformation process it shocked him. Reasoning reminded him that yes, the humans who became vampires did actually die, only to re-born. A day or two of rest and Armani would wake more alive than he had ever been in his short lifetime, and with powers and abilities that were indescribable. Donovan smiled and hoped the feeling of complete power would enable Armani to forgive him for his deceit.

Donovan faced the door. Lightning flashed furiously outside, thunder boomed louder and louder as Victor neared the door. He hated to think of the future battle for Armani and himself but he knew in time the two of them would have to destroy Victor. Victor's heart was cold, black and empty. Empathy and love were a fading wind. The only emotions Victor felt anymore were hate, anger and revenge. Victor's kills had gone from justice killing to thrill killing. He killed for survival and it didn't matter who he murdered. Innocent, helpless people were dying at the hands of Victor because he had lost self-control. Victor drank their blood and longed to feel them begging for their lives. Donovan heard from other members of the Dark Ones that many a vampire had to be destroyed because their hearts grew cold and the need to kill overpowered them. Drinking blood from a human to the point of death was like a high from drugs. It was a rush that some vampires got addicted to and most, being of strong will didn't want to stop. The only option for the other vampires was to destroy them.

A loud scream sounded behind the door. What the hell was going on? It was a human and the voice yelling sounded too familiar to him. Within a second Donovan stood in front of the window and peered into the darkness, seeing as clearly as if it were broad daylight. Vampires all possessed night vision.

"Lord, have mercy on your soul, Gabe." Donovan muttered. "I warned you not to come around here and you refused to obey." Donovan stared at Victor and knew Gabe's death would be swift.

Victor must have just killed because he had a murderous look of satisfaction in his eyes.

Victor gazed at the window and smiled at Donovan, his eyes crimson red. There was no denying Victor was drunk on blood and unfortunately the blood of an innocent. Donovan forced a smile hiding his disgust and disapproval.

Gabe cocked his head to the side, placed his hands on his hips and glared at Victor. "You think you scare me, you freak!" He laughed. "Armani is my client and is going to listen to me. So, move on and trick or treat at someone else's home and let me handle my business." He said and waved his arms in the air in a 'get out of my way' motion. Gabe pivoted and walked to the front door shouting profanities over his shoulder. At the top of the stairs to the entry of Armani's home, he paused. "Oh, and by the way you're a couple months late for Halloween." He chuckled and rang the doorbell.

Donovan was shocked that Victor allowed Gabe to disrespect like that.

A bony finger tapped Donovan's shoulder.

"Hello, my friend." Victor said. "Well done. Armani is now a part of the Dark Ones and I am very pleased with you." He rubbed his chin and smiled. "Truth be told, I had my doubts that you could follow through with the mission, so to speak."

Donovan didn't take his eyes off Gabe. "Why did you let him disrespect you like he just did? That's not your typical behavior."

"Ever hear of playing cat and mouse?" Victor asked mockingly. "Gabe is the mouse and I'm the big cat who is going to attack and kill, but I want to play with him first."

Victor had a sneaking suspicion Katrina walking into his life was a big part of the reason for his changed behavior, especially dealing with someone as despicable as Gabe. But he wasn't going to tell Donovan that, at least not yet.

"Sounds like fun," Donovan replied standing in front of the door. "Gabe deserves to die. He set up the whole plan of torturing Armani and killing Simone. Justice will be served tonight." A feeling of satisfaction rolled over him like waves in the sea. The vigilante side of the Dark Ones was what he enjoyed most about being a vampire. He smiled at Victor and twisted the doorknob. "Now, it's time for this worthless piece of humanity to walk the 'Green Mile' as Stephen King would say."

Victor grinned, fangs gleaming. "Yes, my son now is the time. You and I are the executors." Victor crouched to the left. "Let him in and let the games begin."

CHAPTER NINETEEN

R EX HAD NEVER been as angry as he was right now. Insomnia allowed him little sleep after Gabe dropped him off. The run in with some creature named Donovan gave him relentless nightmares. Worry plagued him and questions of why Armani refused to answer his one hundred or so calls.

Rex rubbed the sleep out of his eyes and jumped out of bed. He picked up the phone and checked the time, only five in the morning.

"When I see you Armani there is an ass kicking to be had by you." Rex said to no one. He pushed Armani's number and Armani's phone rang five or six times and went to voicemail. What had Rex expected? He had a nagging suspicion something was going on and it wasn't good.

Rex walked into the bathroom and stared at himself in the mirror. Brownish-black bags hung under his eyes like a drug addicted junky. "You look like hell, Rex," he told himself and pushed the bags as if that would somehow make them disappear. Time was ticking and he needed to get to Armani's house and the sooner the better. He hoped he would be able to sleep once and for all after his visit was over.

He turned on the shower and inviting steam rose from behind the curtain. He had one foot in the shower when he heard his phone ring. Hope filled his heart. He ran to the bedroom naked. A frown creased his brow. It wasn't Armani. A number he didn't recognize flashed on the phone's screen. He let the caller go to voicemail and walked to the bathroom like a dog with its tail between its legs. He stepped into the shower allowing him self the pleasure of relaxing. He had no idea what awaited him when he arrived at Armani's house later. One thing he was sure of though was that it wouldn't be anything good. Gut instinct, he supposed. He drowned out his thoughts and tipped his head back sighing as the water rolled on his body and bounced off him like rubber balls on a sidewalk.

Chapter Twenty

THE HAWK LEFT Armani's home when Victor arrived. He had flown to Adam and Alex's home and watched them from a distance. The hawk shrieked. Hatred filled the hawk's core being. Soon, the hawk would have the pleasure of watching these two men die at the hands of Armani. The hawk had grown fond of Armani over the years. So fond in fact he could feel the pain, loneliness and despair in Armani's soul that was turning into hatred day by day.

Perched on the branch of a high oak tree, the hawk watched Adam and Alex walk out of their house. Alex, always a bit paranoid and rightfully so made sure to check that the door was locked three times. The hawk cocked its head to the right its yellow eyes never leaving Alex's face. The hawk gripped the branch tight with sharp claws like talons. The hawk had to control itself from flying high into the dark sky, swooping down like a torpedo and gouging both of their eyes out. What a delight that would be. Unfortunately the hawk knew the consequences of that act: swift death at the hands of Victor. It wouldn't be worth losing his life over. Donovan already promised him the eyes of these two fools on a platter once Armani and Donovan had destroyed them. Donovan was a vampire of his word and good things came to those that wait, even hawks. The hawk must always obey his Master and now that Armani had become a vampire, he had three Masters he would give his life for. Just as a seeing eye dog was for the blind, the hawk was the eyes of his master and showed Donovan what he saw and relayed it to him through the crystal globes the vampire's used to see what the hawk viewed in real time.

Adam stumbled and fell flat on his face. If the hawk had the capability to grin, it would have won an award for the world's largest grin.

"Damn it all to hell!" Adam hollered. Alex stepped over him like a pile of trash. He didn't even bother to ask him if he was ok.

"Maybe that will straighten out your face, son," Alex said without a backward glance. "Get in the car." He ordered and jerked open the car door.

The hawk found them to be quite entertaining to say the least. One thing the hawk was allowed to do was scare the enemies, and now seemed to be the perfect opportunity.

The hawk spread his large wings and took flight soaring high into the sky. The crisp cold breeze swept over him. He circled and watched Adam slowly get to his feet. 'Let him get his balance.' The hawk thought. 'More fun that way.' The hawk screeched and circled once more before it dove headfirst toward the car.

Alex saw the hawk headed straight for his car and jumped in slamming his door. "What the hell?" He heard a thud on top of the car. Alex glanced at Adam who was bent over re-tying his shoes and oblivious to the hawk. His son was a few watts short of a sixty-watt light bulb.

The hawk stared at Adam. What a weak human. Venomous hatred burned holes through the hawk's heart, its eyes glowed bright yellow. The hawk extended its sleek black wings and used its large sharp claws and scratched the hood of the car sounding like someone raking their nails on a chalkboard.

Goosebumps covered Alex's flesh and he covered his ears. "My beautiful car," he muttered. "Damn that bird to hell." Guilt washed over him like a passing rain. His only son stood outside with this rabid creature on top of his car. No telling what it might do to Adam. Alex rolled down his window as far as he dared and hollered at Adam. In order to save his car from more wreckage, Adam had to either shit or get off the pot, so they could drive away with his Cadillac in tact.

"Get in the car!" Alex hollered.

Adam looked at his dad, a glazed expression in his eyes. "Oh my God, what is that thing?" He asked and craned his neck to look at the hawk. He couldn't move. It was like his feet were cemented to the pavement.

Alex rolled his eyes and screamed, "What does it look like?" If his son couldn't figure out it was a hawk, maybe he should just drive off and leave him to fend for himself. But, he knew Adam lacked the ability and knowledge to think clearly. He wasn't smart enough to run back into the house. His son would more than likely run into the street and let the hawk chase him. God, Alex wondered how such a stupid excuse for a human being could come from his seed? What had he done wrong? Ah, nothing. It was the mother's fault. She was about as smart as a box of rocks. "Dead and gone since Adam's birth, and for the better," Alex said and smiled. A scowl replaced the smile when he heard the hawk clawing the hood of his Cadillac again. The cost of a new paint job wreaked havoc on his mind. And there stood Adam, immovable. Frustrated, he honked the horn numerous times.

Adam jumped and fell backwards landing on his butt.

The hawk hated the horn and it fueled the flames of anger. The hawk spread its wings flew into the air and descended at light speed using its strong sharp beak as a weapon. It slammed into the middle of the windshield making a large circular chip.

Alex, his face red as a ruby cursed and watched the crack grow eleven arms and spread from the top to the bottom of the windshield.

Anger boiled his blood. Cursed be his stupid son.

Adam hobbled to the car like a man with a gimp knee. The hawk struck him and Adam dropped to his knees and cradled his head.

"Dad, help me!" He screamed.

The hawk flew a few feet away, turned and aimed for Adam again. He hit him and knocked him onto his back. The hawk stood on Adam's chest and stared into Adam's soul, eyes yellow and hateful.

Adam turned his head and closed his eyes hoping when he opened them the hawk would be gone.

Alex pushed the garage door opener, stepped out of the car and ran into the garage. He needed a weapon to whack this creature with.

The hawk dug its claws into Adam's stomach. Adam cried out in agony.

Alex ran toward them with a shovel raised over his head, "Now you're going to die, you miserable bird," Alex seethed. "The first hit will be for ruining my car. Prepare to die!"

'Get out of there.' The hawk heard Donovan say. The hawk pierced Adam's cheek with its beak and tore off a small piece of flesh.

Adam screamed a blood curdling scream. Alex was steps away with the shovel in hand. The hawk lifted its head, the flesh hung from its beak and swayed in the breeze. Victory in its cold yellow eyes as it stared at Alex.

The shovel came down, but not before the hawk ascended and flew high to the angels. 'Close call,' the hawk thought. He felt the wind from the shovel skim his feathers.

The hawk circled above and watched in amusement as the shovel came down hard, hitting Adam's stomach and ribs.

"Dad!" Adam screamed in pain and agony. He curled in the fetal position and cradled his ribs and stomach.

The hawk sat in a tree satisfied with the torment it had caused. It flung the flesh from its beak disgusted at the evil it tasted in Adam's blood.

Alex threw the shovel aside and dropped to his knees beside Adam. "I'm so sorry, son. I didn't mean to hit you."

Adam kept his face turned so his tears would go unnoticed. A sign of weakness he wasn't about to let his father see. For all he knew, he'd be hit with the shovel again for that. His father said he was sorry but to Adam they were empty words.

Alex stood and looked into the sky. The hawk appeared to be gone. "Get up. Let's get you to the hospital." He extended his hand and took hold of Adam's, helping him to his feet. "Come, we have much to do."

Adam cringed and tears filled his eyes. Adam stumbled to the car, one hand on his cheek and the other holding his ribs. At least his dad had opened the door for him. He slowly maneuvered himself into the passenger seat.

"Put this on your cheek," Alex said and opened the glove compartment handing him a few tissues. "It will stop the bleeding. I don't want blood getting on the interior of my car." He slammed the car door and walked fast around the front of the car to the driver's side.

Before getting in the car Alex scanned the hood of the car and cussed like a drunken sailor. It was ruined and a new paint job was on his to do list now. He plopped in the car, glanced at Adam and shut his door.

"Can you drive fast to the hospital?" Adam asked. "I'm in so much pain."

Alex nodded. "Yes, I sure can. We're going to make a visit later to Simone's grave. We need to pay our condolences." He tipped his head back and laughed the most God awful wicked laugh Adam had ever heard.

Adam shivered. "I thought of something. Remember Gabe telling us about the things he has been seeing?" He questioned.

"Yes, I do. But, this is just a coincidence." He said matter-of-fact. "It's nothing more and nothing less."

Adam didn't believe his father. "He told us of this exact same hawk attacking him with a creature or vampire or something." He paused and watched the trees flash by the window as they sped to the hospital. "I don't think it's a coincidence."

Alex coughed, lit a cigarette and cracked the window. "Close your eyes and rest. I don't want to hear anymore about Gabe and his silly stories." He ordered. "Understood?"

Adam nodded his head. "Yes." He couldn't have disagreed more.

CHAPTER TWENTY-ONE

REX STEPPED OUT of his house, keys dangling in hand. He needed to get to Armani's as soon as possible. He slicked his wet hair from his face and got into his car and revved the engine of his sleek red Ford Mustang.

He pulled out of the driveway and gazed at the sunrise. They always reminded him of Armani and the better days. Armani loved sunrises. It was the hope for a new day.

The neighborhood slept. Drapes were pulled and lights were out. The people in the homes didn't realize just how lucky they were to have a peaceful night's sleep. Rex envied that more than anything. Sleep robbed him like a thief in the night. The past few weeks Rex felt like he was in a trance, walking with his eyes open, watching himself but not feeling anything that was happening.

His cell phone rang. He checked the number and sighed. It wasn't Armani. It was the same number that had been repeatedly calling him since he got in the shower. He assumed it was a salesman so he avoided answering. He threw the phone aside and stopped for a red light.

A shadow flew over top of the car. Rex leaned forward and stared at a black hawk. What the hell was going on? He looked closer and saw the white spot on its chest. He shook his head and rubbed his eyes. Could it be the same hawk he had seen at Armani's?

Determination etched the lines of his face like a sculpted statue. He gripped the steering wheel, vowing to get to the bottom of things and end the madness plaguing him. His recent dreams were all too real. Vampires, wolves, hawks and two people always present with them, only they were not entirely men. Rex was ready to admit himself to a mental hospital. Enough of entertaining the idea, maybe he should just drive there, but no, not without Armani in tow. His best friend needed help.

The phone ringing cut into his thoughts and broke his silent questions.

Rex looked and saw same number on the caller ID screen. He swallowed hard and answered, "Hello."

"Hello, Rex." A deep voice said.

The voice sounded familiar and chills ran down his spine. "Who are you? Why do you keep calling me?" Rex asked confused.

Laughter on the other end of the line filled the silent gap.

"I don't have time to play games with you. Give me your damn name and what business you have calling me," Rex ordered, making a sharp right turn onto the highway.

"My friend, this is Donovan."

Rex shook his head. Was this another dream? He rolled down the window to get some fresh air.

"What's going on? What do you want?" Rex asked confusion thick as honey in his voice.

"Rex, I don't want to hurt you and I have no intention of hurting Armani." He paused, hoping Rex would hear the sincerity in his voice. "Let me advise you to stay away from Armani for awhile. There are matters being taken care of and I'm afraid if you show up, you won't live to see your best friend again." Donovan thought of Victor. Rex would be killed in an instant if he set foot on Armani's property. Victor's sympathy and reasoning were gone with the wind as of late. Donovan knew the master of the Dark One's would view Rex as an obstacle and obstacles never stood in the way of Victor's plans.

Rex gulped, palms sweating. "What are you talking about? I deserve an explanation." He ordered. "Armani is my best friend, my brother. You must understand this." Rex pleaded with Donovan.

Donovan's heart went out to Rex. Some things he wasn't allowed to disclose yet. It would be up to Armani to share with Rex the transformation and his decision to cross over and become a vampire. Donovan would be as honest with Rex as was possible.

"My dear friend, Armani is undergoing a treatment as we speak. Please, I beg of you, do not come to his house right now." Donovan stated his voice soothing.

Anger flushed Rex's cheeks. "Who are you to tell me to stay away from his home? I will not listen to you, so go to hell."

Donovan understood denial. The sad fact was that Donovan was already in hell and had been since his lover had been killed centuries ago at the hands of her uncle.

"Damn you!" Rex screamed. "Prepare for a battle then. I am on my way."

"Please Rex. I beg of you to stay away for a short time. You will see your friend in due time. He is safe with me and no harm will come his way. I promise."

Rex snorted and laughed. "Ha. You are trying to scare me and give me your word of honor that he is safe with you? Ridiculous! If that's true and I can trust you then I see no problem with showing up at Armani's house. See you soon." Rex hollered into the receiver holding the phone in front of his face. He hung up and threw the phone on the floor.

Nothing was going to stop Rex from going to Armani's house, especially not now. Empty threats made by some carnival freak dressed like a vampire with a hawk as its sideshow. Screw this. He stepped on the accelerator, sped up and prayed he wouldn't get pulled over for going forty miles per hour over the speed limit.

Donovan hung up, his brow creased with concern and worry. He couldn't let anything happen to Rex. Armani would never forgive him if any harm came to his best friend. A still small voice told him forgiveness would be hard to come by for deceiving Armani in order to convince him to cross over. He didn't need one more thing plaguing his already guilty conscious. What would Victor do when Rex showed up at the door? This question plagued his mind. Time would tell.

CHAPTER TWENTY-TWO

K ATRINA SLICKED HER wet hair from her face. The pool was relaxing and just what she needed. Well, except for her beloved dog. When was Victor going to come through on his promise to bring her dog and all of her things to his house? Why wouldn't he just let her go? Because Victor had plans in store for her and she knew it.

Panic washed over her, making her head spin. She sat in a poolside chair and placed her head between her knees and cried. How would she get out of here? There was nowhere to go that would allow her to escape Victor. 'I will always find you no matter where you go. And that means anywhere in the world.' Those were Victor's exact words to her. She shuddered wrapping the towel tightly around her shoulders. His refusal to answer her many questions bothered her. Why in the hell should she trust someone who refuses to share their storyline with her? How in God's name did he become a vampire? He was as silent as a mouse when she asked him these questions. Would he kill her? Katrina knew the answer. Yes, he would and it wouldn't even bother him in the least.

She held out her hands and saw they were shaking like a crack addicts after a hit. She shook her hands violently and clapped them.

Damn it. They wouldn't stop shaking. What sort of power did this vampire have over her? Would Victor expect her to cross over and become a vampire too? He had been referring to her as his queen and from reading vampire novels, she assumed that was what the male vampire called his chosen wife. She would rather die than become a vampire.

Katrina stood and the towel dropped exposing her naked body. She picked up her clothes, slipping them on and left the poolroom. The door slammed hard behind her. She jumped, her heart skipping a beat.

Head pounding she walked to Victor's lair and stared at the steel door. She placed her hands on the door and winced. It was stone cold. She squatted and checked if there was a crack under the door. No luck. It was sealed tight like a vault. She knew there was a black coffin in the room, but there had to be things even more precious that lye behind the door and Katrina had to know what they were. It would help her put together the pieces of the puzzle named 'Victor'.

Katrina looked around the basement. She had that feeling of being watched. An old eighties song played in her head. 'I always feel like somebody's watching me.' Katrina chuckled realizing she was humming the chorus.

"Get a grip, Katrina," she ordered and blinked. She was having a discussion with herself. "As long as I don't answer myself I guess I'm not crazy." Locked up in Victor's home made her feel like craziness ascended upon her like a fog on the sea in the early morning hours.

She faced the door and placed her hands on the large circular vault opener, resembling the doors of a bank's safe. Boy, Victor sure was worried about his safety.

Katrina grunted trying to turn the handle but it wouldn't budge.

"Curiosity killed the cat, right Victor? Well, I'm not your cat and never will be!" She screamed. "I will find a way out."

Katrina leaned her back against the door, slid down and sat in front of Victor's lair. She had to figure out a way to get inside and start putting this mystery together. It was detrimental that she learned about Victor. Would it soften her heart towards him? It was a possibility but she could never love a vampire. That was insane. Victor was a very handsome vampire. But, there was more to love than just the outer appearances. The inside and who the person or vampire was mattered more in the end.

'Vampire's don't age,' a voice whispered to her. It sounded like Victor.

That was true. So what? Victor would always be handsome, but that didn't answer the questions she had about the colors of his heart and soul. Those were eternal too.

She wrapped her arms around herself, picked up the key and walked to the stairs. She needed to get out of the basements atmosphere. The feeling of being watched suffocated and nauseated her. She needed and wanted food.

Taking the steps two at a time she reached the top and gasped for air. She shot a glance backwards to see if something was chasing her. She wiped her forehead and turned fumbling with the key. Katrina breathed trying to slow her heart rate. She shoved the key in the keyhole, pushed the door open and stepped into the main floor. Katrina shut the door hard and double checked to see it was locked and skipped toward the kitchen.

She pulled the refrigerator's door open. It was stocked with the best food money could buy. Katrina decided to warm up a left over hamburger. It was simple and quick. She wanted to get back in the basement and figure out a way into Victor's lair. Ignoring Victor's advice may be the biggest mistake of her life but it was a risk she was willing to take. After all, she assumed she would die here anyway. Why not know the truth before she died? That made more sense than to die not knowing, she reasoned. Curiosity, reasoning and justification were a few of her greatest weaknesses. It was an impulsive thing. Her father always told her that one day her curiosity would get her in such a heap of trouble that there would be no way out.

"Well, dad you may be right this time, but honestly I see no way out of here as it is." Her dad had been dead since she was a young girl but she still talked to him as if he were alive and present with her wherever she was. If only she could call him to help her out of this mess. A tear trickled down her cheek and she brushed it away. She didn't have time to reminisce. She had her life to do that. Well, maybe depending on Victor's intentions with her.

She warmed a hamburger in the microwave, threw on a few toppings and ate it in less than a minute. Scanning the cupboards she realized there wasn't much healthy food in the house. Must be Victor's way of fattening her up for the feast or maybe all the junk food would make her blood taste sweeter. So be it, she thought and grabbed a bag of Doritos and ripped the bag open, shoving a handful in her mouth. She clicked open a can of Coke. The air spurted and the soda welcomed her with the fizzy noise. She gulped half the can and belched. She laughed out loud. What would Victor think if he saw her act so unladylike? She pictured his handsome face twisted in disgust at such inappropriate and improper behavior.

She left the kitchen and walked down a winding hallway. The walls were covered with eerie strange pictures. The pictures were dark, scary, gothic, painful and morbid. Katrina stopped, placed her hands on her hips and tipped her head to the side. The first was a painting of a little bruised and beaten boy huddled in a corner. His knees were drawn to his chest and he peeked from around his leg. She looked closer at his eyes. They showed fear like a cornered animal ready to be killed.

"What happened to you?" She asked and touched the boy in the picture. "And why in the world would Victor hang this type of art on his walls?" The room's temperature turned to ice. She shivered and walked further down the hall willing herself not to look at the other pictures. Her peripheral vision failed her. She looked at the other pictures and saw they were all of abused children and the boy in the first picture stared at her from each picture as if begging her to rescue him from pain and torture.

"Look closer, Katrina. Study the pictures. What do they say?" A familiar voice said.

"I can't!" She screamed. "It hurts too much."

"It's supposed to hurt, Katrina. These pictures are my life." Victor whispered.

She winced and turned in a circle searching for Victor. The hallway was empty.

"How can such sick disgusting pictures be your life? You have terrible taste." She grimaced. "Picasso or VanGogh, yes, I can see those expensive pieces being your life, but these?" Disgusted she walked to the end of the hall and saw steep steps leading to upstairs. She gripped the railing and walked to the top.

"I don't have time for your questions right now, but in time you will understand what I mean. They are my life, the blueprint that makes me what I am. Think about it." Victor said.

Katrina's stomach flip-flopped. She felt sick. She didn't want to and wasn't going to think about it. It was sick. To delight in the torture of humans, especially children and hang that art on your walls was despicable. "I hate you, Victor." She seethed and stepped into the upstairs hallway.

The upstairs consisted of four bedrooms, each with its own bathroom. The rooms were decorated almost alike. A large bed, a couple dressers and bedside stands. 'How boring,' Katrina thought. The only thing that made them different was the variation in colors of paint and carpet. She walked into the first and inhaled a flowery smell. It surprised her since it didn't look as though it had been cleaned in years. She swiped a finger across the dresser and picked up an inch of dust.

Having seen enough of the upstairs Katrina inhaled and stared down the long hallway willing her self to keep her eyes straight ahead. 'One step at a time,' she ordered. That lasted all of a minute. Running at light speed and practically falling down the stairs she made it to the bottom.

Katrina walked to the kitchen and opened the drawer. Placing her hands on the knives she caressed them and stopped when she found the biggest sharpest butcher knife. She picked it up and held it close. She refused to die without a fight in case things got ugly when Victor arrived home. Slanting her eyes, determination on her face, she walked to the basement door, unlocked it and walked down the stairs two at a time.

Five minutes later she stood in front of the steel door protecting Victor's lair. Wiping her brow, she fumbled with the handle and tried to pry it open. Uttering profanities she stepped away from the door and paced the basement floor, twirling her long hair around her fingers. She scanned the entire basement looking for something that she could use to open the door. She needed to think like Victor for a change. Getting the door open may prove to be an impossible task but she had to try. What would Victor do? How would Victor secure such a secretive lair?

Victor was proud of his age and the fact that vampire's had such extraordinary powers, like magic. She had to figure out what magical spell was protecting his lair.

Katrina walked to the lair's door and wondered if this was a test to see if she'd be obedient to Victor.

"Think," she commanded. "There's a way in. I just have to figure it out."

She had to figure it out. 'Think like Victor,' she thought again. Victor's age, possibly? The handle on the door resembled a safe so it made sense that it would be opened with a combination.

She grasped the circular door handle like a sixteen year old in driver's education class with her hands at ten and two and used his age as the combination. Victor told her he was four hundred ninety one years old. It was the only thing she knew about him numerically.

She turned the handle four times to the right, nine times to the left and one time to the right. She paused, palms sweating and slowly pushed the steel door open. An ice cold draft blew on her face. She pushed it all the way open and stood for a minute allowing the light from outside the lair to let her see into the darkness.

It was dark and cold. She sniffed. A musty smell hung in the air. Katrina squinted and saw the black coffin against the far wall, the lid open. Chills ran up and down her spine. Craning her neck, she glanced to the right and saw an old rickety rocking chair and a small coffee table with a few candles sitting on top.

Katrina's heart pounded wildly. She swallowed hard and stepped into Victor's lair.

She stood by the coffee table and stared at the coffin. How disgusting. Why did vampires insist on sleeping in a coffin when a bed would fit just fine in the lair? She shook her head, hair falling in her face and marched toward the coffin. It was so cold. Katrina cursed herself for not being smart and bringing a blanket with her.

Halfway to Victor's coffin, Katrina heard a creaking noise and turned her head. The door was slowly closing or was it just an illusion in the semi-darkness? A sinking feeling in her gut told her this wasn't good. She ran toward the door but the closer she got, the faster the steel door seemed to close.

Katrina sped up and was inches from the door when it closed in her face. From the other side of the door she heard a clicking sound. Did someone lock her in?

She screamed. There was no way out. Helpless, she ran in circles hitting the door and banging the walls like an animal in a hunter's trap. It was useless. She leaned her back against the door, rubbed the sides of her head and screamed at the top of her lungs.

Exhausted, she slid against the door, landing hard on her butt and placed her head in her hands and cried. She was in prison and had just executed her own death penalty. Victor would kill her when he returned. All she could do now was wait and hope he would forgive her.

CHAPTER TWENTY-THREE

"Hey freak show contestants. Let me in now or I'll call the police!" Gabe screamed. He banged the door with his fists. "You have two minutes to open this door." He ordered.

Victor snarled. "Let that piece of shit in. Who does he think he is trying to make the rules of our game?" Pointing at Donovan, Victor motioned for him to open the door. "We are never told what to do, how to do it or when to do it. I've heard enough of this man's voice to last me an eternity."

Donovan smiled. He felt the same way and opened the door.

"Please do come in," Donovan said smiling at Gabe.

"Damn you, you freak!" Gabe screamed throwing a punch at Donovan.

Victor was on top of Gabe in an instant and hurled him to the ground. "Listen hear you sorry piece of shit. Your sins have found you out." He said his face inches from Gabe's.

Gabe, lay on the floor wriggling his arms and legs like a fish out of water, trying to break free. "What in God's name are you talking about? My sins," he chuckled.

"Allow me to show you," Victor said. "Stand up."

Gabe twisted his nose. "No. I will not be told what to do by the likes of you." He said jutting out his jaw and sulked like a defiant child.

Donovan winced. "Not a good choice, Gabe." An evil smile crossed his lips. "Shall we?" He asked Victor.

Victor grabbed Gabe by the throat and placed him on his feet. "I'd like to introduce you to the new and improved Armani." Victor dragged Gabe to the couch and pointed at Armani. "You did this to him."

Gabe gasped. "You killed him. How could you?"

Victor and Donovan laughed. Gabe stared at both of them wondering why they found what he said so amusing.

"I'm reporting you two to the police when I leave here." Gabe said matter of fact.

Victor grabbed Gabe's face with one hand and pointed at Armani with the other. "No, you did this to him. You killed him when you set up to have Simone killed and then you left him scarred for life both internally and externally. How could you?" Victor asked his eyes never leaving Gabe's face.

Donovan interjected. "I know why he did it. It was out of greed, plain and simple." He said disgusted. "Isn't that right Gabe?"

"N-n-n-no," Gabe stuttered, his face red.

Victor slapped Gabe's face hard. "Stop stuttering, you fool. A sure sign you're lying. I punish people who lie to me."

"We have given Armani life again, eternal life." Donovan said.

Gabe rubbed the cheek Victor slapped. "See, you crazies killed him," Gabe said turning his head to face Donovan. "I knew it."

Victor looked at Donovan. "This guy isn't too bright. He doesn't seem to understand the fact that we already know he did it with the help of two accomplices." Victor paused and turned his attention to Gabe. "And you're going to help us find them, Gabey. Armani will see justice served."

"What are you talking about?" Gabe asked, puzzled. "Armani's dead. Look at him."

Victor smiled baring his fangs at Gabe. "He was dead and is now reborn."

Gabe opened his mouth to speak but nothing came out.

"What's the matter, Gabe? Cat got your tongue?" Donovan asked sarcastically. "Armani is very much alive. He is merely resting."

"The sleep of the undead, you idiot," Victor chimed in. "He's a vampire now."

Gabe shook his head no. "Impossible. What kind of drugs are you guys on?"

"No drugs I can assure you," Victor stated. With a strong grip on Gabe's wrist, he said, "Go ahead, feel his pulse." Squeezing his wrist harder Victor added, "And if you try anything stupid I will snap your neck in two."

Gabe swallowed hard staring at Armani's pale almost blue face. He looked peaceful, but dead. Didn't the dead always look peaceful? These two guys were nuts and probably the type that got off on this sort of thing. Could they be serial killers who prey on criminals who commit crimes of a similar nature? With apprehension Gabe reached down and touched Armani's wrist. Sure enough, he felt a faint slow heartbeat. The color drained from Gabe's face.

"What's the matter?" Victor asked. "Did you think either Donovan or I would deceive you? Now you know the truth and we know the truth about you as well." He nodded his head at Gabe, "And the truth shall set us all free."

"Ok, you're right. I set it all up but what do you want from me?" He asked lips quivering.

"Don't cry, big boy," Donovan said handing him a tissue. "You are officially on death row, so don't think about freedom or escaping ever. You're a day late and a buck short for that."

"Do the crime, do the time," Victor snarled at Gabe. "Picture yourself in a courtroom, Gabe. Armani is the judge and we are the jury." Placing his finger to his lips he added, "Do you think we will find you guilty?"

"Hell no, you forced me to admit what I did." Gabe said. "That's not fair."

"You sound like a baby," Donovan stated. "You will die at the hands of Armani. The Dark One's believe in an eye for an eye, son." Donovan winked at Gabe, giving him a devilish grin.

"Let me go now! I demand you free me from this house. Do what you want with Armani but I want no part of this Satanic ritualistic behavior!" Gabe screamed trying to break free of Victor's grip.

Thunder boomed and lightning illuminated the living room where they stood. Rain pelted the roof like pebbles falling from Heaven. The Rottweiler's whined running in circles.

Donovan drifted to the window and gazed outside. "It looks like a bad storm is headed our way. I say we let the dogs in and tie up Mr. Nice Guy here on a leash and treat him like the wild rabid dog he is." He turned to face Victor and Gabe. In his hands he held a shock collar. "Let the torture begin."

Gabe shook with fear. These guys were sick. There was no way out and it appeared they were going to torture him for a while before ending his misery.

"Where in the hell did you get that collar from?" Gabe asked. "Armani would never put one of those on his beloved dogs. They are like his children."

"It appeared magically. Vampires have many powers. Haven't you ever educated yourself about the undead?" Donovan asked. "Now come here and sit." Donovan ordered using hypnosis forcing Gabe to obey.

Victor released his grip on Gabe and watched in amusement. Gabe squatted on his haunches, crawling like an obedient dog and sat before

Donovan. Donovan slipped the collar around Gabe's neck tightening it just enough to make it uncomfortable but not deadly. They didn't want him choking himself to death. What fun would that be?

"Are you going to make him shake next?" Victor asked a smirk on his face.

Donovan laughed and shook his head no. He couldn't believe the sense of humor Victor had. It was unusual for him to have a funny bone in his body. Today for whatever reason Donovan saw a different, more likable side of Victor. Maybe he was changing and light was beginning to shine in his dark vacant evil soul. Donovan released Gabe from the trance and watched as Gabe tried relentlessly to remove the collar. Bad move on Gabe's part. Donovan pushed a button and both vampires watched Gabe land on his back screaming in pain.

"Friend," Victor began, "your pain was self chosen. Think about it. The more you struggle or disobey the more times we have to push the button and cause you pain. Please be an obedient dog because we will take great pleasure in treating you like a disobedient dog that gets beat." Victor said with great satisfaction.

Gabe stood, his hands gripping the thick black collar. A small compartment was attached to it that reminded him of the barrel on a St. Bernard's collar. Only this one wasn't to help, it was to hurt.

"Please, show me mercy and let me go," Gabe begged on the verge of tears. Desperation filled his voice. "I won't tell anyone. I promise."

Victor's head rolled back. Laughing he said, "Tell anyone? What in the world are you talking about? We are the servants of justice here, not you. The Dark Ones avenge the wrongs committed by people, such as your self. You more than likely would have gotten away with this. You would be just another guilty man who slips through the cracks. Well, consider your luck to have run out." Victor hooked a leash onto the collar, kicked Gabe in the ribs and jerked the leash hard making Gabe's head fly forward. "Don't worry you will be given water and minimal food. Although I haven't decided what kind of food I'll feed you yet." Victor smiled and walked toward the door, black cape flowing behind him and led Gabe into the early morning light.

Donovan watched. Victor had a way of putting fear into people with the simple fluctuations of his voice. He smiled and walked to where Armani slept looking so peaceful. He had cast a spell on him so that he would sleep until this evening. Having gone through the emotional turmoil Armani had endured the past few months, waking up and adjusting to this would prove to be a hard task. The truth of the transformation was a topic to be brought up at another time and place. Donovan rationalized that he would teach Armani the ways of the Dark One's and give him time to adjust to his new life as a vampire and allow him to avenge Simone's death before dropping the bomb. Armani would be angry when he heard the truth about the transformation. He hoped it wouldn't turn Armani's heart stone cold and dark letting the demons of hatred and anger that dwelt inside everyone, human and vampire alike loose.

"Come here Gabe." Victor ordered snapping his fingers.

Gabe swallowed hard. "I refuse to get in that dog kennel." Standing his ground, he crossed his arms. "I'm a human. Not a damn dog that you can control."

Victor laughed and pressed the shock collars button. Amused, he said, "Oh really now. I just made you lie down so I would dare say that yes indeed, I can and do control you." Staring at Gabe, he sneered. "Now get over here or I will do something worse than push this button and give you a shock." Victor stated his eyes black as a starless night's sky.

Gabe knew he would be a fool not to listen at this point. He felt like a mouse trapped in a maze with no way out. He took one step at a time wishing the walk to Victor were miles away. He stopped a few inches from him. He didn't know why he always felt so cold when he was near him.

Victor grabbed Gabe's arm and dragged him the rest of the way to the kennel, stopping in front of the large silver door. He smiled wickedly at Gabe. "Welcome to your new home. Of course, it's temporary." Victor sensed Gabe's fear and pulled him close. He grabbed a handful of Gabe's hair and jerked his head back exposing his neck. Victor watched the blood pulse through Gabe's arteries, his mouth wet with saliva. His stomach growled, loud enough for Gabe to hear.

Bile rose in Gabe's throat. "Oh God, help me. Don't do this to me. Don't bite me and drink my blood." Gabe stammered and closed his eyes waiting for the pain of Victor's sharp fangs to tear into his neck.

Victor thrust Gabe's head forward and threw him in the cage. Gabe fell hard on the cement floor. He rubbed his head and looked up at Victor. The kennel door shut with enough force to break it.

Victor pointed at him and laughed. "You were worried about me feasting on you?" He questioned not waiting for an answer. "First of all I don't drink tainted blood and the taste of your blood would sicken me. Secondly, I find it quite amusing that someone like you mentions God asking Him to help your sorry ass." Victor chuckled, slicked his jet black hair back and stared at Gabe. "The reality of this situation is that only God could save you, but I'm afraid you and Him aren't on good terms. That's just a guess. Oh, and welcome to Death Row and I hope you enjoy your stay." Victor gave him a polite bow and disappeared.

Gabe, feeling like a helpless child curled up in a ball and cried for the first time in years. He couldn't remember the last time he shed a tear. He hung his head in shame when he realized what a selfish person he truly was, for the tears he cried were for himself and no one else, not even Armani.

Donovan stood beside the couch staring at Armani lost in thought when Victor tapped his shoulder. He flinched. It still amazed him how powerful they, as vampires were. They could enter a room silent as a mouse and sneak up on anyone. Hunting was always easy. The person never expected or heard them coming.

Victor's brow creased. "I'm afraid I must be going and I'm not sure when I will be back." He said and rested his gaze on Armani. "There is a problem at my home and I need to go take care of it."

Donovan looked at him. "Don't you want to be here when Armani wakes?" He asked.

"I most certainly do, but there is a situation I need to take care of that takes precedence over this." He stated with no emotion in his voice and hatred written all over his face. "I trust you have this under control. I am pleased with you." He said trying to smile but failed miserably. 'Katrina, on the other hand, I am not pleased with. She will be punished for disobeying my one simple order. How dare she defy me?' Victor thought. Rage surged through his veins.

"What's troubling you? You have that look." Donovan asked concerned. He had seen that murderous look many times throughout the centuries. His concern was not for Victor, he could take care of himself. He worried about the innocent victim who would fall prey to Victor.

Victor walked to the bar and picked up a sparkling crystal champagne glass, holding it up to the light. "Our new member of the Dark Ones has excellent taste, I must say. This is real crystal." Victor whistled and set it down. "I think I'll treat myself to a glass of wine before I leave." He poured red wine into a glass, sipped and swirled the rich wine in his mouth before swallowing. "Delicious." He said satisfied. Victor hoped the wine would aid in taming the monster within before he confronted Katrina. He didn't want to kill her, but he was afraid he would end up doing just that. His lack of control when angry was frightening, even to himself.

Donovan knew Victor was trying to calm himself down, but why? It wasn't his typical behavior. Victor was a man of action and if angry he dealt with the issue immediately and in his own way. Donovan cocked his head to the side. He was witnessing a different, more patient Victor. A likable vampire, like the Victor he remembered first meeting. That was the time when Donovan viewed Victor as a father.

"Please Donovan, stop thinking and analyzing so much." Victor said. "Join me for a glass of wine." He raised his glass in a toast and said, "To the Dark Ones and our friendship."

Donovan took off his cloak, laid it over a chair and joined Victor. Pouring wine into the glass, he raised it and made his own toast. "To the Dark Ones, us and our newest member, Armani." Their glasses clinked and Donovan and Victor drank in silence.

Victor stood. "Thank you for staying with Armani. I must be going now." Victor said and gave Donovan a firm hug.

Donovan stood open-mouthed staring at Victor as he walked toward the door. What was going on with the Master of The Dark Ones?

Victor laughed. "Don't worry. I still have evil in me." 'God have mercy on Katrina's soul if she doesn't cooperate when I get home.' Victor thought. His lair was his private sanctuary and no one was allowed to enter it. Not even the other vampires saw the inside of it. And they never would, unless they wanted a swift death penalty.

A fly landed on his hand. Slapping it hard he watched the blood splatter. "Damn fly," he said in disgust. "By the way, if our friend, Gabe gets out of hand and starts acting wild, feel free to punish him in any way you desire. We don't need him acting obnoxious and drawing attention to the house." The door creaked open. "Good bye, Donovan. I shall return soon."

The door closed and Victor was gone. Donovan sat at the bar sipping his wine. It helped calm his nerves. He remembered Rex and his heart rate quickened. How would he explain this to Armani's best friend? He poured another glass of wine, took a sip and walked to the window. Gabe was in the dog kennel curled up in a ball sleeping. Well, at least that was one less thing he had to worry about. There were other pressing issues at hand. Staring at the snow covered ground and the fountains Donovan's heart went out to Armani. He once had such a beautiful life and that pitiful excuse of a human being took it all away from him. Frowning he tipped the glass of wine to his lips and drank what remained. He walked to the bar setting the glass on the counter and decided to give himself a tour of Armani's home and a grand home it was.

Donovan's home was much smaller, but he preferred that. It was the feeling of safety that came from knowing what was going on in each room. His lair was tucked away below the basement of his house. A carpeted trapdoor covered the entrance to his resting place. A vampire could never be too cautious or careful. There were quite a few instances where members of The Dark Ones were killed during their rest. And true to the old tales, they were either be-headed or staked through the heart. A lot of times it was the younger ones who had just become vampires. The sensory skills took time to develop, but even older and more powerful vampires had been killed during their slumbering time.

A jolt from the couch put the self-guided tour to a halt. He ran to Armani's side and crouched beside him. Armani boxed the air, his lips quivering and twisting. He was trying to speak but nothing came out. Donovan grabbed both Armani's hands and pinned them to the couch so he wouldn't hurt himself. Donovan stared at Armani's pale face. His eyes were closed, but rapidly twitching. Armani wouldn't wake from his deep sleep until that evening.

"Armani, you must relax. It's just a nightmare. Please." Donovan said gripping Armani's strong hands with more pressure. "It's O.K. Whatever it is you're seeing is not real, my friend. Be calm and rest now." Donovan ordered. "You must not waste your energy." Donovan silently prayed Armani would stop and be at peace. His heart broke when he saw a tear trickle down Armani's cheek.

Armani felt like a prisoner trapped in his own body. Why couldn't he wake up? What he was seeing was real. Simone needed him right now. He had to get to the cemetery. He had to kill these two men who were there destroying her resting place. How dare they do this! Their deaths would not be swift, but painful and slow. Donovan must know there is something wrong. Why couldn't he read his mind right now? He seemed to have no problem doing it when he was human. His whole body felt deathly cold.

"Armani, please help me," Simone begged.

Armani's body shook. He tried everything in his power to wake up but it was useless. Anger seized his soul, as he lay helpless.

'Please hold on and wait for me, Simone.' Armani thought. A silent tear rolled down his cheek. 'I will be with you soon, my love. The men who did this to us will pay with their lives. I promise you that.'

Simone's voice sounded a million miles away. "They're hurting me all over again. Please Armani."

Armani screamed. "Can't anyone hear me cry for help?" He had never felt as hopeless as he did at this moment. "Donovan! You son of a bitch, wake me from this sleep!"

Armani heard Simone crying and he wept. He was like a worm in a cocoon and wouldn't be able to come out of this sleep of the undead until it was time and the butterfly he was to become emerged.

"Armani, you have been deceived. You and I will not be together soon, if ever. You are going to be a vampire forever. You sold your soul to the Dark Ones when you made the choice to cross over . . . . ." Simone's voice trailed off.

Armani's heart pounded so hard, it hurt. What did she mean?

"Simone, please don't leave me. What do you mean?"

A long silence followed. Those were the last words Armani heard before his world turned to darkness.

Donovan released his grip on Armani's hands. His eyes had stopped fluttering and he was sleeping peacefully again.

"You're alright, my friend. When you wake I will explain everything to you," Donovan said and patted Armani's shoulder. "Be at peace now." Donovan sat on the floor next to the couch and held Armani's hand. He silently prayed for the forgiveness of his deceit.

CHAPTER TWENTY-FOUR

A LEX DROVE THE scratched up Cadillac away from the hospital peering through the cracked windshield, an irritated expression on his face.

"This is going to cost me a pretty penny." Alex said.

Adam looked at his dad. "I'll pay my own hospital bill so don't worry about it." He said, clutching his bandaged broken ribs and cringed. "I hope these heal fast." He averted his gaze to the window and watched the people walking along the streets downtown. "Everyone's in a hurry. What's with all the rushing around these days?" He chuckled, but even that hurt.

"I see nothing funny about this situation." Alex said matter-of-fact and picked up the cup of coffee he took from the waiting room. He sipped, rolled down his window and spit out the contents. "Why in God's name do institutions insist on making coffee extra strong? And for your information I wasn't talking about your hospital bill. I'm talking about how much it's going to cost me to repair the damage done to this car by that damn rabid hawk."

Adam should've known. Of course his father was more concerned about his car than his own son.

He pounded the steering wheel in frustration and swore. "When I see that bird again I am going to put a bullet right through its eyes."

"Dad, can we stop and pick up my pain meds on the way to the cemetery?" Adam asked. "I'm in a lot of pain." Adam knew the answer by the expression on Alex's face.

"Absolutely not, son. Work before pleasure and you know that."

Adam rolled his eyes and touched the stitches in his face. "My face hurts like hell. My ribs feel like they're trying to protrude through my flesh," Adam paused and continued, "like knives stabbing me."

Alex discussed the importance of revenge for a few minutes. "You know doing some damage to her grave is well deserved at this point. I wouldn't put it past that stupid rock musician, Armani to have trained that damn hawk. All he has is time on his hands." Adam stated holding up his hands. "Agree?"

Adam shook his head. "No, I don't. He doesn't know we did it so why in God's name would the hawk attack us? That doesn't make any sense, dad."

Alex smiled. It was the first real smile Adam had seen in a long time. "You seem to be getting smarter." He laughed and added, "Maybe hitting you with that shovel knocked some sense into you. I've waited a life time to hear you talk like you have some sort of clock ticking in that thick skull of yours."

Adam ignored his dad and focused on the passing scenery for the rest of the drive. If he were silent his dad wouldn't ask questions or try to start a conversation, which was better for both of them.

CHAPTER TWENTY-FIVE

DONOVAN LEANED OVER Armani and checked his vitals. Armani's heart rate slowed down and his breathing was shallow. Armani's nightmare was over. Donovan was frightened because he had never dealt with a mortal having problems of such magnitude during the rest after crossing over. Calling Victor to help with the situation wouldn't have been the most pleasant experience. He had a sneaking suspicion that Victor was hiding something, but what? He didn't have a clue. But whatever it was seemed to be a positive influence on him.

Donovan stood and stretched his legs and arms. He was sore and hungry but didn't dare leave Armani's side. Armani was like a helpless infant and Donovan had to protect him like a father would his son. He picked up the picture of Armani and Simone and smiled. They were a beautiful couple. He wished he had known Armani when he had so much light in his life. His face shone bright like the golden rays of Heaven. Donovan scratched his head with his free hand and placed the picture on Armani's chest. He pulled the blanket to Armani's chin and walked toward the kitchen.

A cars engine roaring and the screech of tires stopped him dead in his tracks. He had a feeling he knew who it was. Rex was here. "You're a lucky man, Rex. Victor had to leave for an undisclosed reason or you may not live to get out of your car." Rex said. Talking to him self was the norm. Anyone who knew him realized this. Donovan trotted to the door and peered out the window. Sure enough, it was Rex and he didn't look the least bit happy. Donovan watched him to see what he'd do.

Rex stared at the house, his face flushed red. He heard someone grunt and scream in the distance. His jaw dropped when he saw Gabe with a large collar around his neck lying inside the dog's kennel. Gabe stared back, his eyes large and filled with fear. What the hell was going on here? Rex ran to the kennel and placed his hands on the cold silver fence.

"Gabe!" Rex exclaimed. "What in God's name is going on? Let's get you out of there." Rex said trying to release the door's latch. "It's stuck. Who did this to you?" Rex asked looking down at Gabe. "Your face is bruised."

Gabe's eyes pleaded with Rex. "Get out of here if you value your life!" He shouted. "I can't escape. They won't let me and if I do they will find me."

"Who are you talking about?" Rex asked confused. He tried to unlock the latch a few more times but it proved pointless. He kicked the fence and said, "I can't leave you here to die." He walked in a full circle, stopped in front of the fence, hitting it with both fists. "I refuse to leave until I get you out of here!" He shouted. "Who did this to you?"

Gabe squirmed like an inch worm to the side of the fence, shimmying himself to a sitting position and pushed against the metal. Using his legs, he managed to push himself to stand up. "You must remember the freak and his hawk that dragged me into the woods where you found me. They did it." He stated. "The guy is a God damn vampire." Staring at the house, fear written all over his face he said, "Leave now, Rex or he will come out here and either kill you or even worse, lock you up in here with me."

Rex reached his boiling point. "We saw a vampire?" He questioned looking at Gabe like he had lost his mind. "You've got to be kidding." He said only half believing the words that came out of his mouth. A nagging voice told him before that this was the case and Gabe had been warned not to come near Armani's home. "The creature or vampire as you call it told you to stay away. So why did you even come here?" Rex asked turning his head to gaze at the house. Red eyes stared back at him.

Gabe followed Rex's gaze. "I told you. He's watching us right now. The predator is ready to attack his prey." Gabe said fearful. "The worst part is there are two of them." Clearing his throat, Gabe stated, "and daylight doesn't affect them in the least. The vampire who is the leader dragged me out here with a leash attached to this collar. He walked into the daylight without so much as flinching." Gabe said.

"Well, I'm going inside to handle this," Rex said. "My best friend is in there." He turned toward the house.

Gabe pleaded with him not to go. "You're making a big mistake, Rex."

"So be it." Rex said flatly.

Gabe beat his head on the fence. "Rex, before you go in there would you do me a favor and untie these ropes on my wrists?" He asked and placed his hands against the fence.

Rex faced Gabe and reached for the rope. "Yes, I will. While I'm in there why don't you try and free yourself. For whatever reason, I can't get the latch unlocked." Rex quickly untied the rope. There was nothing to it. Whoever tied it had used the magnus hitch method, the easiest knot to untie, but the hardest to undo if you were the one tied up.

"God speed to you, Rex." Gabe stated flatly.

Anger burned inside Rex ready to explode like molten lava from a volcano. He watched Gabe rub his hands together and scowled.

"I'll be back and you will be freed. I promise." Rex no sooner had the words out of his mouth when he heard a familiar voice.

"I'm afraid you're mistaken, Rex. This man, if you can call him that will never be free." Donovan said. "I'll be honest with you. He's going to die."

Rex watched Gabe huddle into the farthest corner of the kennel, his hands shaking. "Run Rex!" He screamed, panic stricken.

Rex turned, facing Donovan. It was the man on the cover of the book and the same creature he saw on top of Gabe in the woods. He was too angry to be scared. "Who are you? What are you doing to my friends?" Rex asked, his eyes never leaving Donovan's face.

Donovan smiled extending his hand toward Rex. "Take my hand."

"What? You're crazy!" Rex said sticking his hands in his coat pockets.

Donovan pointed at Gabe. "If you call that your friend, I'd hate to meet your enemies." Taking off his cloak he draped it over his elbow. "Go ahead, Gabe, tell your friend here what you've done." He stared at Rex and said, "I'm sure you'll change your mind about Gabe's current situation when you find out exactly what he's done. Armani is your true friend and as I told you on the phone, he is in good hands."

Gabe stared at Donovan then looked at Rex. He opened his mouth but nothing came out. This was insane. Should he call the police?

Donovan used his mind to shock Rex with the collar. A bolt of electricity flowed through Gabe making him shake and tremble on the floor like he was having a seizure.

"Stop that," Rex ordered. "You'll kill him."

Donovan laughed. "It won't kill dogs, my friend. It only puts them into submission. No worries. We won't kill Gabe." He paused and chuckled. "That's Armani's job."

"What are you talking about? Armani wouldn't kill anyone." Rex spat. He knew he should've brought his gun but he was so angry when he left his house that all he could think about was getting here and making sure Armani was not in danger.

Donovan sneered. "I dare say you will be ready to kill Gabe once he tells you what he's done." Averting his cold dead eyes to Gabe he ordered, "Speak Gabe. Tell Rex why you're in the dog kennel."

Rex stared in disbelief at Donovan. "You're a crazy lunatic." Rex walked past Donovan bumping his shoulder hard and walked to the house. "Go to Hell." He said over his shoulder.

"Stop right there!" Donovan ordered. Rex walked faster and at the speed of light Donovan stood in front of Rex.

"How did you get in front of me so fast?" Rex asked feeling frightened for the first time since he had arrived.

Donovan loomed over Rex staring at him. "Magic," he laughed. "I'm afraid I have not properly introduced myself." He paused and extended his hand to Rex. "I am Donovan, a member of the Dark Ones. We are a group of vampire's who act as vigilantes on the behalf of the dead. Our job is to seek and destroy those who escape the long arm of the law. We avenge the deaths of the innocent." He smiled, fangs sparkling in the sun and released Rex's hand. "It is a pleasure to meet you, Armani's best friend, band mate and in a sense his brother."

Rex stared in disbelief.

"I understand it's a lot to take in at once but in time you will learn to like me." Donovan reassured him.

Rex stammered. "I-I-I'm afraid I don't have to like you nor do I want to try and like you. I want to see Armani. That's why I'm here and so help you God if you've hurt him." He said clenching his fists, his anger resurfacing.

Donovan took Rex's elbow leading him to the dog kennel. "I want you to hear Gabe's confession and maybe you won't think I'm such a bad guy after all."

They stopped in front of the kennel door and it opened like an automatic door at a grocery store. Donovan entered first and motioned for Rex to follow. "Come and listen."

Rex did as told. Donovan walked to where Gabe lye on the cement. "Stand up, Gabe. This will be your first confession to a mortal."

Donovan called me a mortal? Rex shook his head, appalled. He was a human, for God's sake, not some mortal.

Gabe stood and screamed. "You did it! You and that other vampire admitted you gave Armani eternal life." He lowered his head and put his hands behind his back. He would pay for that comment.

Rex stared at Donovan. "Is that true? You killed Armani." Rex balled his fists, drew his arm back ready to hit Donovan.

Donovan grabbed Rex's fist squeezing hard. "Put your hand down or I shall punish you as well." He ordered.

"Gabe what does that mean? Did these vampires kill Armani?" Rex asked.

Gabe smiled. He had nothing to lose and when you've got nothing, you have nothing to lose. "They sure did, Rex."

Donovan jumped on Gabe and choked him. He then picked up his head and smashed it into the cement.

Rex jumped on Donovan's back and hit and kicked him. "Leave Gabe alone, you monster, you'll kill him!"

Donovan punched Gabe's face and blood splattered. Donovan reared backward throwing Rex into the corner of the kennel. Rex yelped in pain. Donovan stood and glared at both men.

"If you both insist on acting like mean dogs I shall take great pleasure in treating you that way." Donovan said brushing off his black clothes. He walked to Gabe, picked him up by the head and stood him on his feet. "Now Gabe shall tell you exactly what is going on here and what role he played in the fate of Armani and Simone."

Donovan led Gabe to the corner of the kennel where Rex sat rubbing his elbow. "By the way, I apologize for my indecent behavior, Rex but you left me no choice." He paused and cleared his throat. "I don't take people disrespecting me well. Let that be a lesson to you both." He stared at Gabe and said, "I believe Gabe would like to share the truth with you now." The look in Donovan's eyes dared Gabe to act out or lie again. Donovan was ready to kill him and if pushed far enough he would.

Rex stared in disbelief at Donovan. The vampire had an unpleasant aura about him. That was for sure. "Why are you doing this to us?" Rex asked.

"I'm doing nothing to you. Gabe is the one who is going to pay with his life for what he did to Simone and Armani. Now tell them Gabe lest I have to physically force you once again." He squeezed the back of Gabe's neck forcing him to look at Rex.

Gabe swallowed hard. "I set up the whole incident to have Simone killed and Armani tortured." He blurted out. "Are you happy now?" He asked Donovan, his face red as a tomato.

Donovan activated Gabe's shock collar. Gabe fell, his whole body jerked and shook. He curled into the fetal position too scared to speak or move.

"Tell Rex why you did it Gabe," Donovan ordered. He sympathized with Rex. The news was shocking and he knew it was slowly registering in Rex's mind. In mere minutes, he knew Gabe would take a beating from Rex and Donovan would allow it. Gabe was a selfish man and deserved it. "Hurry up. You are trying my patience." Donovan instructed.

Gabe stared at Rex. "I did it for money, publicity and more fame, plain and simple." Gabe said with pride. "We needed more attention so I thought this would fix that problem and it would have if that dim wit depressed lead singer friend of yours would have continued singing and touring. But no, he was too depressed. Waahh, a big baby!" Gabe shouted, angry lines creasing his forehead.

Rex gritted his teeth. "You son of a bitch!" He screamed. "I'm going to kill you." Rex lunged at Gabe, landing on him and hit and beat him. "How could you? You are a filthy excuse for a human."

Rex stood and stared at Gabe. Rex kicked Gabe several times. "This one is for Armani and Simone, you bastard," Rex said. He brought his leg back as far as it would go and kicked with all his might, his foot landing in the center of Gabe's gut.

Gabe cried out in pain. "Stop, please." He begged between ragged breaths.

Rex snorted. "I bet Simone and Armani begged you to stop too." Rex kicked him once more. Rex laid Gabe flat on his back and pinned him down with his knees. He balled his fists and punched Gabe's face several times before wrapping his hands around Gabe's neck until his face turned blue. Rex gritted his teeth and asked, "How does that feel?" Rex wanted to kill him.

Donovan grabbed Rex's hands. "That's enough." He said, pulling him off Gabe. "Come with me. We have much to discuss."

Despite the wintry cold, sweat beads covered Rex's face. Wiping them away he got to his feet, not taking his eyes off Gabe once. Gabe's tongue hung out of his mouth like a dog's after a long run. Panting and breathing heavy, Gabe rolled onto his side gripping his neck. Blood pooled from his mouth and eyes and his nose was crooked. "It looks like he might die." Rex stated satisfied.

Donovan smiled. "Looks can be deceiving, my friend." Taking Rex's hand he shook it. "Well done, my friend."

Reluctantly, he took Donovan's hand. "Thank you but I'm not sure I'm thrilled to meet you, I must say. Please tell me what's going on here."

The kennel door shut and locked. Rex turned and stared at the door. "How did you do that?" He asked, startled.

"Why must you mortals always ask such silly questions? Vampires can do that and so much more." The idea of having Rex cross over entertained him, but only for a moment. He wouldn't wish this curse on anyone.

It was both a blessing and a curse. A blessing in order to escape the realities of pain in your life, but a curse to know you could never be human ever again. Donovan longed for companionship, a lover, a wife and children. But, that would never happen. It was one of the negatives of crossing over. You were told these things only after you had crossed over and were a vampire. Had he known this before, his decision may have been different. 291 years ago, he would have just ended his human life and rested in peace forever with his beloved.

"Well, I want answers Donovan."

A hawk cawed in the distance. Large black wings flapped in the sky. Rex stared at the giant bird. The hawk descended and landed on top of the kennel. Sitting upright, head held high, it looked like a king on its throne. Its gaze pierced through Rex's soul. Rex shuddered, rubbed his arms and lowered his gaze.

Donovan smiled wickedly fangs protruding. "Hello, my dear friend, keep watch over Gabe for me." He pivoted and walked toward the house. "Come Rex, time is of the essence."

Rex was too shocked to speak but followed like a baby duck following its mother, staying close to Donovan. He couldn't explain it but the hawk scared him more than Donovan.

CHAPTER TWENTY-SIX

"WAKE UP, ADAM." Alex ordered. "We're at the cemetery."
Adam opened his eyes and saw the Blakesley Cemetary sign at the entrance. The ground was covered in snow, tall oak trees scattered throughout and a few large pine trees. What would be beautiful rose bushes in the spring and summer lined the outer skirts. Lined in neat rows were tombstones where people's loved ones rested in peace. The wind gusted and the car jostled.

Alex lit a cigarette and rolled down the window. He shivered and turned the heat up a notch.

Adam grimaced in pain. "That was quick."

Alex smacked Adam's head. "Of course it was quick. You were sleeping and it's really not that far from the hospital."

Adam fought the urge to punch his dad in the face.

"Let's see, according to the Google directions Simone's grave is in the back of the cemetery. Perfect place for that little princess," he said laughing. "Her tombstone should say, 'Spoiled little rich girl lies dead here.' Gut laughter exploded from him.

Adam laughed. "You got that right." He and Simone had been childhood friends and when they got older he tried his best to persuade her to date him but she was never interested. She always told him, 'Let's just be friends. I don't want a romantic relationship with you.' Adam had heard that enough and when the opportunity arose for his father and him to do Gabe's bidding, he was more than happy to volunteer. A grim smile spread across his lips. It was the best feeling in the world knowing the last face Simone saw was his. She begged and pleaded with Adam to let her live just as he had begged and pleaded for her to be his lover. It was such satisfaction. Karma was a wicked thing at times.

"Wipe that smug look off your face, boy." Alex ordered. Scanning the tombstones one by one he drove to the back of the cemetery. "You certainly can tell who has money and who doesn't by the type of stone at the gravesite."

"For sure," Adam agreed nodding his head being careful not to twist or turn his body much. His ribs hurt like hell.

"Ah, there it is, son. Simone's grave and no expense spared to give her a beautiful tombstone." He said pointing.

Adam stared, awestruck. The tombstone was black marble and sparkled and twinkled in the winter sun. The archangel sitting on top of the stone had large eyes that stared straight ahead, her wings pointed to the Heavens and in her arms she held a harp close to her chest. The angel wore a long flowing robe that appeared to be blowing in the wind. Adam's gaze lowered to the inscription below the angel's crossed feet, but he couldn't read it from the car.

Alex opened the car door. "Well, come on, let's pay our regards." Taking one last puff of his cigarette, he threw it on the ground and put his gloves on.

Adam took a deep breath and slowly got out of the car, trying to baby his ribs. He stood for a minute but the throbbing pain in his head made him fall to his knees.

"You've got to read what our friend, Armani had inscribed on her tombstone." Alex said and chuckled. "What a joke." He stared at the vase filled with multi-colored roses and cringed. "Son, get over here."

Adam scowled, cursing under his breath. Couldn't his dad see he was in a lot of pain? Using the car for leverage, he rose to his feet and walked hunched over to where his dad stood.

Adam read the inscription aloud. "Simone Richards. My Angel In The Night." Disgusted, he spit on the ground where Simone lay six feet under. "My angel in the night, what the hell kind of thing is that to put on a tombstone?" He asked, his face as red as a beet. He noticed the vase of roses and picked up the note that was attached. "I'm going to be sick." He said and handed the poem to his father. "Our musical genius, Armani wrote this to his beloved dead Simone."

Alex snatched the note from Adam like a starving man taking food. "You know what to do. Break the vase of roses." He ordered.

Adam picked up the vase, raised it over his head and threw it at the angel's face. It landed hard smashing into a hundred pieces. He held his ribs and laughed, staring at the angel's face.

"What could possibly be funny?" Alex asked staring at his son.

Adam pointed at the angel. "I chipped her nose." He couldn't stop laughing even though it felt like someone was jumping up and down on his ribcage. He felt like he was hurting Simone all over again and that felt good.

"Yes, you did. Who cares?"

Adam stared back at his dad as if he were some creature from another planet. He refused to say a word knowing what the consequences of that would be. Adam was unpredictable and always had been. There was no telling what his dad would do if he opened his mouth with a reply, even if what he said made sense.

The dead rose's lye scattered on the snow covering Simone's grave. Alex stomped on the flowers, twisting his feet and grinding them into the snow. "I hope she can feel the hatred." He said and spit on the marble platform the angel stood on.

Adam smiled. "Did you bring the spray paint?" He held out his hand and waited for his dad to give it to him. He wanted the honors of putting a proper inscription on her grave marker.

Alex reached into the duffel bag and pulled out a can of red paint. "This will show up wonderfully. Black and red always have been a great contrast to one another." He said and threw the can to Adam, a wicked smile on his face.

Shaking the can a few times, Adam pulled off the cap. He stood close to the marble stone, held the can upright and painted the word 'WHORE' in large letters over the inscription.

Adam laughed. "Well, Simone you now have your name written on here for the world to see." He said. He took a few steps back and stopped where he assumed her chest would be lying in the coffin and fell to his knees. He put his face as close to the earth as possible. "Simone, you whore, how do you like me now? I hope you're burning in hell." He stated and raised his hand to Alex. "Help me up."

Alex took his sons hand and hoisted him to his feet. "Let's get out of here before we get caught." He rubbed his chin and said, "It probably wasn't the smartest thing in the world to do this during the day."

"You're right." Adam agreed.

They walked toward the car. A cold wind blew bending the trees. The branches made an eerie creaking and cracking noise like an old rocking chair on a wood floor.

Alex zipped his jacket to his chin and folded his arms to keep warm. "It feels like it dropped ten degrees out here."

"I know. I feel chilled to the bone." Adam said. Something didn't feel right. He had a strange feeling they were being watched. He turned and saw nothing. The slamming car door brought him back to reality.

Alex motioned for him to get in the car. Adam slowly eased himself into the passenger seat and cradled his ribs as he did. He tried to shake off the feeling of being watched but it was hopeless. Something or someone was out there. Maybe Gabe wasn't lying and something was after them.

Alex started the car. "What's on your mind?" He asked and lit a cigarette.

Adam dismissed the question with a shrug. "Oh, nothing I'm just thinking." He looked out the window and watched the giant oak trees sway, their branches like skeletal hands reaching out to the car. Goosebumps prickled his arms. He rubbed his arms trying to forget the stories Gabe told them a couple nights ago.

Alex shifted the car into drive. "Bid Simone farewell." He said saluting with his middle finger. "I did this for you, son." He smiled and squeezed Adam's cheek. "No one rejects my son."

'Except you,' Adam thought. He grimaced and looked at Simone's gravesite as they drove away.

Adam's jaw dropped. The angel's eyes glowed red and she was staring at him. He blinked twice and looked again, not wanting to believe what he saw. He watched in horror as she smiled. Fangs like a vampire's protruded from her mouth. The angel held the harp in one hand and pointed to him with the other and mouthed 'you' to him.

Adam sat forward, breathing rapidly and put his head in his hands. 'This did not just happen,' he told himself.

Alex stopped the car. "Is something wrong? You look like you just saw a ghost." He pounded the steering wheel and repeated the question.

There was no way he would tell his dad what he had seen. "No, I'm fine," he said flatly. "I think the pain is getting to my head, that's all." He lifted his head and stared straight ahead. "Let's get out of here now." He wished he were driving so he could press the accelerator and speed like a bat out of hell.

Alex drove to the cemetery exit. "Well, we're headed to the pharmacy next." He laughed and added, "then the gun store. I need more bullets and I'm thinking I'll buy a special gold one to shoot that hawk when I see it on our property."

Adam and his father were gone. Simone heard and felt every insult they did to her and her grave. She had reached out to Armani and pleaded with him to help her but he was in a deep sleep. He would wake to become a vampire. He thought it was temporary but it was forever. She knew because her spirit was connected to his, even in death.

Simone's heart ached. She was dead but her spirit was not at rest. Why did Adam hate her so much? The night he killed her was etched in her memory; the stone cold look on his face, the hatred blazing in his eyes and the way he talked to her, calling her a whore. Why would he say these things? He had always been her friend since childhood. They would play games like make believe for hours on end and share secrets.

Deep in her soul she knew the reason. Adam fell in love with her and she didn't share those feelings with him. Jealousy and anger were a deadly combination. He never failed to announce his hatred of Armani. Even when she and Armani would visit Adam, he was never civil towards Armani, only cold and rude.

She should've seen the warning signs but she never would have believed in a hundred years that Adam and his father would end up killing her and torturing Armani.

Oh, how she missed Armani. She felt his presence when he visited her at the cemetery. Her heart ached to reach out to him, touch him and hold him one last time. Raised to believe in life after death and your soul going to Heaven or Hell, she found it odd that she was stuck somewhere in the middle. Dead, but her soul lived. She wished her soul could roam the streets like they do in movies. 'The Crow' came to mind. He came back to settle the score and get revenge on the men who killed his fiancée. Why couldn't that happen with her? What was stopping her soul from rising from this grave and making things right? She could see Armani again. He may not know she's near him, but she would be able to sleep next to him, hold him and love him.

Could it be that she needed to believe and have faith that this could happen? Really believe it. The mind has power to do the unimaginable if only the person has one hundred percent faith in what they believe they can make happen. That was it. She needed to focus her attention on rising from this dark cold grave. It would be a process. The ability to move her limbs did not exist. Her eyes could open and close but she assumed this was because the eyes are the windows of the soul and her soul was very much alive. She looked up and the only thing she saw was darkness and the outline of the frilly material within her casket. She needed to be with Armani.

A tear slid down her cheek. Maybe The Dark Ones could take a dead mortal person and make them a vampire. Was it possible? She closed her eyes and prayed that miracles did happen.

CHAPTER TWENTY-SEVEN

FILLED WITH RAGE Victor soared high above the city lights and busy streets filled with fresh blood calling out to him to drink to his content. Feasting on human's wasn't an option right then. Katrina dare defy him and his one rule. No one dare do this to the Master of The Dark One's. Trust in people was something he never had, even as a mortal. His parents forsake him and anyone he reached out to as a young boy just turned their heads.

Almost five hundred years ago people didn't want to hear stories of a young boy being tortured and abused. From the church to his school they would all say the same thing, 'Come on now young Victor. These things don't happen to children and especially not you. Your parents would never do such a thing. They are pillars of this community,' they always told him. Once he crossed over and was a vampire oh, how he enjoyed killing his parents and everyone who had ignored his cries for help over the years. Now, he feared he would have to destroy Katrina, the only person who listened to him and who had sparked a flame of hope about mankind within his soul.

Reliving his childhood memories drained what hope was left. Katrina had been a glimpse of hope but not anymore. He couldn't trust her and for that she would be severely punished, even killed. It would be a shame because she would have been a perfect companion for him as he planned on turning her to a vampire and making her his beautiful Queen.

He saw his house in the distance, his keen sense of sight allowing him to see that all the lights were on. Vampires had the eyes of a hawk seeing things with microscopic definition, color and sharpness. Keen ears were also a blessing. Victor was a mile from his home and could hear Katrina's heavy breathing coming from his lair, her heartbeat rapid. He smelled her fear and it excited him along with fueling the fire of his anger. He wanted to kill her, to drain the lifeblood out of her while she screamed for mercy.

He was raging and he was home. The front door opened the same time his feet touched the ground. He smiled, tracing his fangs with his long tongue. Katrina was in for a surprise. He wasn't going to let her manipulate her way out of this one. If he let her do that it would show that he didn't mean what he said and wasn't a vampire of his word. He wouldn't allow that to happen. Never had he done that in his lifetime and he wasn't about to start now.

"Honey, I'm home!" Victor boomed, chuckling at his sense of humor. That seemed to be what mortals said to their lovers when they returned home. He had seen it many times on TV and even heard it said by the despicable child abusers he took great pleasure in killing. He chuckled remembered a time when a young couple, too young for a child of two years old, would say this to each other upon arriving at their home. They were so sweet to each other but not the poor helpless child they had accidentally brought into this world. 'Our son is a mistake, an accident,' they would tell each other. His ears rang every time he heard them say this when describing their son. Many nights Victor spent time in the young boy's nursery singing lullabies to him.

The little boy lay beaten and bruised, his sweet eyes vacant with emptiness and the longing to be loved.

Victor cursed, face red with anger. He should've killed those two parents sooner than he had but he was a new vampire then and didn't know any better. His moment came to kill them and the pleasure was all his.

The young father had come home from work and said the three words Victor had grown to hate, 'Honey, I'm home.' When he said this Victor appeared from the shadows, smiling.

"Really honey, you're home. That's going to prove to be quite a shame." Victor seethed.

Fear was written all over the man's face. "W-w-who are you? What do you want?" He stuttered and stammered. "Get out of my house." He said pointing to the door, fingers shaking.

Victor waved a finger at the man. "Tsk-tsk, you shouldn't be so rude to a guest. Your wife invited me in, my friend." He smiled whipping his black cape behind him with one powerful sweep of his hand. "By the way, your son is beautiful. He's such a nice child. You're lucky to have him."

The man charged Victor. Grabbing him by the throat Victor threw him into the wall. "Now that wasn't nice. You should really think of the consequences of your actions before doing them."

The man glared at Victor. "If you harm a hair on my sons head I will kill you, man. You hear me. Where's my wife? Where's my son?" Rising to his feet he rubbed the back of his head.

"Did that hurt? Please, forgive me." Victor seethed. "I enjoyed it very much." He winked and added, "I bet your son hates getting his head banged against the wall, too."

The man tried to walk past Victor but Victor grabbed his arm, jerking him to a halt. "Not so fast. I will show you your wife and son. They are safe and resting peacefully."

Jerking his arm out of Victor's grip he stared at him. "You're crazy. Be gone now or I'll call the police."

"I am the police. Justice for all is my motto," Victor smiled baring his fangs. "Now shut-up and come with me."

Victor floated up the steps, dragging the man behind him.

They reached the top of the stairs and Victor faced the man. "Does anyone respect people who bully, beat and dominate others?" Victor asked. "Do you respect me?"

The man stared at Victor too frightened to utter a word.

"I didn't think so." He turned the knob to the toddler's room and said, "Let's see what junior is up to, shall we?"

The man swallowed hard. He despised his son but no one was supposed to know. Who was this man, this creature? He shuddered when he remembered the fangs and evil gleam in his eyes. Did he know he beat his son? That his wife was involved as well?

The door creaked open. Victor smiled seeing the little boy sleeping in the crib. Over the past few weeks he had grown attached to the boy. That sweet boy would never be abused again once Victor was through with his mission.

Pulling the man into the room he forced him to look at his sleeping son.

The man sighed, relieved his son was OK. "Alright, so are you going to leave us in peace now?"

Victor rolled his head back and laughed. He straightened his cloak, faced the man and grabbed his shoulders squeezing hard. "You amuse me. What's the story, you piece of shit? Let me guess, you want to be the only one who hurts him?" He asked pointing to the sleeping child. "Does it give you some sort of thrill, a rush? God forbid, some sort of high?"

The man stared into Victor's eyes and cringed. "I don't hurt him."

Victor wrapped his hands around the man's throat. "Don't you dare look me in the eyes and lie to my face. I've seen what you do and

I'm here to avenge justice for the innocent child. In time you would eventually kill him, so today I'm killing you." A satisfied smile crossed his lips. "Say your prayers buddy." He tightened his grip on the man's throat.

The man gasped for air his eyes bulging like two boiled eggs. "Where's my wife?" He asked when Victor let go of his throat.

Victor wiped his hands on his cloak and said, "Glad you asked. Come with me." He ordered. "We're going to the basement for this one. I think she may be doing some canning or something."

The man tried to be friendly, as if that would save him. "It's too damn late to be friendly to me." Victor spat. He was not a vampire of second chances. He had a mission and accomplished it. It was as plain and simple as that.

"My wife makes the best homemade strawberry jam and I bet she'll even give you a few jars to take home." He said faking a smile.

"Wipe that sick smile off your disgusting face," Victor said and slapped the man's face with his backhand. "You should've been kind to your son when you had the opportunity from his birth. I regret not finding you sooner." He said through gritted teeth.

"If you hurt my wife I'll . . . ." The man began.

Victor laughed. "You'll what? Kill me? Come on now, we both know that today is your Judgement Day. I'm your executioner." Pushing the man in front of him he shoved him down the steps. The man toppled over a couple times and landed with a thud. The fall wasn't enough to kill him but it inflicted pain. "Next time go a little faster. I am not a being of patience and I have none for the likes of you." Eyes blazing red he stared at the man and drifted down the steps. "Your wife is waiting and I really don't think it's polite to keep her waiting." Victor said and picked up the man by the arms.

The man screeched in pain. "You broke my bones, you bastard."

"That's not very nice," Victor said. "Look, I see a light on in the canning room. I do have a preference for sustenance of the color red." He smiled.

Walking toward the door, dragging the man behind him, Victor called out. "Honey, I'm home." He kicked the door open and set the man on his feet. "There she is." Victor was pleased with his work. It was art at its finest.

The man stared. "What have you done?" He asked, the color draining from his face.

His wife sat in a chair, her neck slashed, her head slanted to the left hanging by a thread. Blood pooled from her wound. In her hands she held two cans of strawberry jam.

"What does it look like I did?" Victor asked walking to the woman and taking the two jars out of her hands. "I guess these are mine to take, correct?"

"You bastard, I'm going to kill you!" The man screamed, tears falling. "Why?"

"Why not is a better question, don't you think?" He grabbed the jars and stood in front of the man. "I guess I'll let you keep these since your wife won't be around to make any more jam. Take them." He ordered.

The man grabbed the jars with shaky hands, tempted to throw them at Victor.

"If you do that I will kill you," Victor said reading his mind. "Open them." He ordered.

Victor smiled like a child watching his playmate open a box of Cracker Jack's wondering what surprise would be in the box. "Hurry," Victor said impatiently. "Consider it my departing gift to you."

The man's hands shook like a hanging picture during an earthquake. He twisted the cap, opening the first jar and then the second. He looked inside and saw his wife's big brown eyes jiggling like Jell-O lying on top of the strawberry jam. He dropped the jars, turned his head and puked. "You sick son of a bitch!" The man screamed.

Victor crossed his arms. "Now why did you do that? I thought you and I would take the jam upstairs and make some toast." He smirked and laughed.

The man barreled himself at Victor, hitting him hard. Victor staggered backward and toppled onto the man's wife knocking her bloody corpse off the chair.

Victor looked at the man. How dare he attack the most feared vampire of all time? "Why in the world would you do that? Have you no respect for the dead?" He asked and stood. "I used to be an excellent soccer player. Watch this." Victor said laughing.

Raising his foot he kicked the woman's head tearing it from her body. It flew across the room, hit the wall with a smack and rolled forward a couple inches. Victor stared at the man, eyes red, fangs bared and asked, "Do you want to play a game with me?"

The man turned to run but not before Victor grabbed him by the neck. "Let's make this quick. You've already wasted enough of my time." His face inches from the man's face, he inhaled. "I smell blood mixed with fear."

"I won't tell anyone. Leave now. Please." The man begged.

"Just like you thought your son would never tell anyone. Am I right?" Victor asked. "By the way, I am not a vampire who forgives." Victor tilted the man's head back. The man screamed.

Victor's fangs pierced the man's flesh and Victor used his sharp fangs to tear the man's neck from one end to the other barely missing his jugular.

The man coughed and gagged trying to breathe. Victor sat him up in the same chair his wife had died in. "I'll remember you and see you in Hell." Victor pierced the man's eye with his long sharp nail and held the nerve behind the eye.

The man screamed in agony. "Stop!"

Victor pulled the man's eye and it snapped like a rubber band when it breaks and held it in front of the man's face. "They say the eyes are the windows of the soul and evil should be plucked from a man." He paused, looking at the ceiling and tapped his finger on his cheek. He placed his hands on the dying man's chair and stared into his remaining eye. "And when I looked in your eyes I saw pure evil, my friend, so I'm removing them before you pass on to eternal damnation." He raised his hand and shoved his sharp nail into the man's eye and ripped it out. The man leaned over and threw up. "You're close to death. I'll be kind and help you get there a little faster. Sit back and try to relax."

The man opened his mouth and tried to scream but nothing came out. Death was knocking on his door and it wouldn't be long. Victor knew he had to kill him soon but first he wanted to make sure the abuser would remember his name in the afterlife.

"Peek-a-boo," Victor said. "I've seen you play that with your son, you monster. Now it's my turn to play it with you." Victor's voice dropped a few octaves. "My name is Victor Ramirez and I am a vampire. I am a member of the Dark One's, a strong and growing army of vampire's who invoke justice on people who go unnoticed or slip through the cracks of the justice system. Revenge is our specialty and now death is your final destination. You have abused your son long enough and I won't stand to see your son suffer through another day." Victor pulled a knife out of his pocket and playfully poked the man's chest.

The man jerked his head back. "Please . . ." he coughed spitting blood from his mouth.

"No need for manners. My will be done." Victor said and plunged the knife forward penetrating deep into the man's heart. The man's head rolled back and came forward. He was dead. Victor withdrew the knife, wiped it off on his cloak and threw it aside.

Mission accomplished. Next was to get the boy to a safe haven. He flew to the bedroom where the boy slept in a trance. Victor released him from the spell and picked him up. The boy smiled at Victor. Victor smiled back holding the boy to his chest in a protective embrace. "Let's get you out of here."

Victor opened the bedroom window and took flight. The boy squeeled and shrieked with delight as Victor flew through the air with him in his arms. Moments later they were at a large cathedral with a gold dome atop. Victor landed and stood holding the boy outside of the great building. He used his powers and summoned a nun to answer the door. He also embedded the story of this little boy and his abuse into the nun's mind. He didn't want to be seen. The nuns and priest's sensed the evil in vampires as the undead were considered 'Spawns of Satan'. Victor was in no mood to get bathed in holy water tonight. Not on his first assignment. He had to please his master, Julius, the vampire who saved his life.

Leaning over Victor kissed the boy's cheek. "Everything will be fine. You are safe now."

The little boy looked at Victor with big brown eyes and smiled. Victor heard the nun's footsteps coming from down the hall and he ascended into a high tree.

He watched the nun pick up the little boy cradling him to her large bosom. A tear slid down Victor's cheek. It felt good to see bad things have a good ending knowing he helped make the difference. He knew the boy would be safe and everything would be OK for him. He smiled and flew into the night sky.

That was when his heart was full of love and goodness, but over time his heart had grown cold and black. Love couldn't win when love was dead.

Victor paced back and forth upstairs reliving his first justice kill and remembering that sweet little boy he saved.

Katrina heard Victor pacing and her heartbeat quickened. What was going through his mind? What was he thinking about? She huddled into the corner trying to hide. She slicked her hair back telling herself to relax. Maybe Victor would just give her a good scolding and not hurt or kill her.

The basement door slammed into the wall. Katrina jumped and folded her arms trying to protect herself. Shaking, she squeezed her knees to her chest, tears flowing. 'I'm going to die,' she thought. She unfolded her shaking arms, making a cross over her chest saying a quick Hail Mary. There were un-confessed sins in her life and with no priest around she had to trust that the Virgin Mary would confess them to God for her.

The steel door rattled. The room grew colder making her blood feel like ice running through her veins. She counted and tried to control her breathing. She would need her wits about her when dealing with Victor.

The door creaked open. Katrina looked up and saw Victor standing with his arms crossed, eyes red and his fangs protruding. She squeezed her eyes shut and lowered her head.

Victor stared at her. Mortals were such cowards. Did she really think she could hide from him?

"Well, well Ms. Katrina what have you done?" He asked his voice low and monotone. "Didn't I tell you to stay out of my lair? One simple request and you defy me. Shame on you," Victor stated taking slow steps to where she sat huddled in the corner.

Katrina held her arms out. "Stay away from me, Victor."

"Shut-up," Victor spat. "Why should I listen to you? You failed to listen to me. It's an eye for an eye in my world, my dear." He laughed. Evil echoed off the cold dark walls of the lair.

Katrina screamed and tried to stand but her foot slipped on the damp floor and she lost her balance falling hard on the cement. Victor took pleasure in watching her wince in pain. He stopped walking and stared at her.

"Look at me, Katrina." He ordered. "I want to see your pain, fear and anguish."

Katrina looked at him, tears blurring her vision. "Please don't kill me." She lowered her head and said, "I'm sorry I didn't obey you."

Cocking his head to the side Victor studied her and in the blink of an eye he picked her up and threw her against the wall. "You're not sorry. Don't underestimate my intelligence by lying to me."

Katrina howled in pain and curled into the fetal position. "Please have mercy on me," She pleaded.

"I don't believe in mercy. That's for people of the religious mind." Victor picked Katrina up by the shoulders and pinned her to the wall. "And in case you haven't noticed I am not a religious being." Victor stated angrily.

Katrina was forced to look in his cold, empty black eyes. She shuddered. Those eyes would haunt her to her death. It was like looking into an empty abyss of nothingness. "Please don't hurt me. Please." She begged her face as white as a blank sheet of paper.

Laughter erupted from Victor like a volcano. This kill was going to be fun. Cat and mouse was especially wonderful when the victim was cornered with no way out and thought they could change the killer's mind with gibberish talk. "You're a foolish girl. I'm not going to kill you right away." He placed her on her feet and walked to the lair's entrance. "Come with me. Let's play a game." His black cape danced behind him like a dark shadow or ghost come to life. "Now, Katrina. I lack patience for humans." He turned and stared at her, hatred burning in his eyes. "Especially ones who dare defy me."

Katrina's knees wobbled. Feeling weak and dizzy, she slowly put one foot in front of the other focusing on the light outside of the dark lair. What did Victor mean by playing a game? It couldn't be anything good. She scolded herself for not being stronger. Where was the knife she had brought with her? The plan had been to attack Victor and fight if he caught her in the lair. There was no possible way she could fight him without a weapon.

Victor stood in front of the couch his arms folded. He was angry but he had to admit that Katrina was still beautiful even though she looked a mess. She must've really thrown herself around once locked in the lair. It even looked like she had ripped some of her hair out. But, that's what happens when a person or animal feels trapped and helpless.

Fear, anxiety and anger take over and make them act uncontrollably, and most times to the point of harming themselves. He smirked and chuckled.

Katrina glared at him before sitting on the couch. Strange as it was, she felt a sense of security being outside of the lair. "What are you so happy about?" She asked. Courage returned. Damn the knife she dropped and lost in the lair. If she had it right now she would fight for her life.

"Happy? Dear Katrina, I wouldn't say I'm happy. Humans are just amusing to me." He said pacing like a zoo animal trapped in a cage.

"What game are we going to play?" Katrina asked trying to avoid Victor's piercing gaze. "Shall we play a quick game of chess?" She couldn't help being a smart ass. It was her nature.

Victor smiled. She was a brave girl but there was a time and place for it and now was not it. "Sure, why not? Look at me." He ordered his voice filled with hatred.

Katrina slowly lifted her head and stared at Victor. She tried to dodge the blow Victor dealt her but her reflexes weren't quick enough. He slapped her face hard. His lightning quick speed was amazing. Tears stung her eyes and she rubbed her cheek.

"Learn self control. It will get you places." Victor spat and stared at her. Katrina lowered her head and cried. The slightest bit of pity pulled at Victor but was replaced with hatred for her disrespect and disobedience. "Now it's time for the game, my dear."

Katrina flinched when Victor grabbed her face, forcing her to look at him as he spoke. A fresh rainfall of tears cascaded down her cheeks. She wiped them away and stared at Victor.

"It's kind of like a married couple's game." He said. He let go of her face and walked to the door that led to the upstairs. "You're going to sit there and we're going to role play."

"What do you mean by role play?" Katrina asked thinking about the possible meanings of this. Rape? Abuse? What thoughts were swirling around in Victor's evil mind?

"Nothing like what you're thinking. It's far better and much more fun." He said and smiled. 'At least for me,' he thought wickedly. "Ready?" He asked. Now you are my wife." He saw the confused look on her face. "Don't worry, it's part of the game and it won't take long."

Katrina cleared her throat. "Do I speak? What am I supposed to do? Pretend to have dinner ready? What?" She asked not able to hide the nervous inflections in her voice. She looked up and saw that Victor had disappeared. A fine mist was all that remained where he had been standing only a second ago.

Fumbling with her hands and trying to get the shaking under control she sat up straight. Her gut instinct told her this wasn't going to be a good game and she wouldn't win. For once she hoped it was just pure paranoia. She found it hard to sit still but didn't dare get off the couch. Her heart sank when a loud knock sounded from the other side of the door.

The door opened and Victor walked in smiling brightly. "Honey, I'm home!" He boomed. Katrina's fear woke the predator within. The game had just begun.

CHAPTER TWENTY-EIGHT

REX FROWNED AND stared at Armani shocked by his deathly appearance.

Donovan was at his side in a matter of seconds. "I know you fear for your friend but please believe that this is for the best." He said.

Fury swept through Rex. He turned and faced Donovan. "How can you be so sure? What do you really know about Armani?" Kneeling beside Armani he took his friends cold clammy hand into his own and squeezed hard willing him to wake from his slumber.

"I am confident in what I have done to help him cross over. That is why I am so sure, Rex." He said sternly.

Rex let go of Armani's lifeless hand, stood and paced from one end of the living room to the other, his face creased with worry.

"Damn you, Donovan. I want answers. Why? Why pick Armani to join your ridiculous cult?" He faced Donovan. "I demand to know right now."

Donovan checked Armani's vitals before facing Rex. "First of all, I am not part of a cult and the Dark One's are most assuredly not cult related. We are a group of vampire's who are dedicated to justice being served where it has been overlooked." Smiling at Rex he drifted to the bar and poured himself a glass of chardonnay. "Care for some?" He asked, tipping the bottle toward Rex.

"No." Rex stated. "Don't avoid my questions."

Donovan sipped the chardonnay and licked his lips. "Let's get back to the subject at hand. I'll sum it up for you in the simplest form so that you may understand and see that we are a good group of vampires." Donovan sat near Armani and explained in detail what had happened to Victor and himself and how they ended up becoming vampires.

Rex nodded wanting to understand but he doubted the integrity of Donovan. Trust was earned.

"How did you convince Armani to cross over?" Rex asked gesturing with his hands. "He is slow to trust. For him to do something like this so suddenly is amazing to me." He placed his hands on his temples and added, "I don't believe you were honest with him."

Donovan rose from the chair, walked to Rex and placed his hands on Rex's shoulders. "Let me make myself clear. Never and I mean never call me a liar." He said, his eyes illuminating evil. "I should kill you but I'm not vengeful to the innocent ones." He shrugged and said, "But Victor on the other hand wouldn't hesitate to kill you."

Rex snorted backing away from Donovan. "Lucky me," he said and cocked his head resisting the urge to knock Donovan out with a punch.

Rex and Donovan jerked their heads toward the couch when they heard and saw movement.

"He's waking from his rest to his new life!" Donovan exclaimed and ran to the couch. Leaning beside Armani he motioned for Rex to sit down. "Please sit and be still."

Rex heard groaning, heavy breathing and a low growl. What the hell kind of creature would Armani be now? He was a tortured hurting soul with vengeance on his mind. Rex worried that anger and revenge would fuel Armani's will to live. Not to mention the fact that being a vampire would afford him incredible new powers that could be used for good or evil. Would Armani choose to let hate or love rule him? Rex feared the creature that Armani would become. "What have you done Donovan?" He whispered barely audible.

Donovan heard him. "I've done what's right. Please silence yourself or I will be forced to put you in a deep sleep." He said as he gripped Armani's hands in his own.

Rex craned his neck to see beyond Donovan's frame. It was hopeless. He tipped his head back and closed his eyes saying a prayer for Armani.

Armani opened his eyes and focused on Donovan's face. His stomach rumbled. Feeling weak and dizzy he sat up and looked around the room. "How long have I been out?" He asked. Sadness played on his face like a bagpipe at a funeral. "I saw Simone. She came and talked to me in a vision." He said his speech quick and eyes moist. "Why didn't you wake me? Something has happened at the cemetery. I must leave now." Throwing off the blanket he tried to stand but Donovan restrained him with his powerful hands.

"It was an illusion," Donovan began, "these things happen while you undergo the transition of crossing over and become a vampire." He shook his head and pointed to Rex. He had to change the subject. "Your friend is here. I'm sure you'll be pleased to see him." Moving to the side he allowed Armani to see Rex seated in a chair.

Smiling, Armani focused on Rex's face. "Rex, what are you doing here?"

Rex shot him an icy look. "What am I doing here?" He laughed. "What the hell is your problem? I tried to call you numerous times and you wouldn't answer so I came to check on you." He folded his arms across his chest and said, "I got here and found the Shrine Circus beat me to you."

Donovan shot him a wicked glare. "Watch your mouth, Rex," he warned. "I'm not going to tell you again that Victor, who is our leader, will kill you if you show even the slightest amount of disrespect to him, Armani or me." He turned and faced Armani. He picked up a glass of water sitting on the end table. "Drink this before you try to stand."

Armani drank the water like a man stranded in the desert. "Thank you." Wiping his mouth he said, "I feel so hungry. May I eat?"

Donovan sat in a chair across from Rex. "No."

Armani swung his legs over the couch and prepared himself to stand. He had never felt so weak and drained of life. He rubbed his head, closed his eyes and moaned. "The pain is too unbearable. I can't do this."

Rex's heart went out to his friend. Armani was so pale and white like one of the walking dead. What would happen next? "Shall I help him?" He asked Donovan.

Donovan stared at Rex. "No."

Armani slowly stood, his legs shaking and twitching. Lines of concentration creased his face. Taking a step he stumbled and fell to his knees, grabbing his head. "I feel like a monster!" He screamed in agony. "Stop this!" Sobs wretched his body and tears fell from his eyes. "What have I done?"

Donovan went to his side. "You have done the right thing. Vengeance shall be yours and so much more, my friend." He said. He took Armani's hand and helped him stand. "Focus on one step at a time. You're like a newborn baby. Concentrate on putting one foot in front of the other." He repeated. Shuffling his feet inch by inch he guided Armani.

Rex was impressed at the affection Donovan displayed to Armani. "Is there anything I can do Donovan?" He asked. He uncrossed his legs and stood ready to help in any way he could.

Donovan gazed at Rex and smiled. It was the first sincere smile Rex had seen from him. "Thank you kindly, Rex. How about you prepare something for Armani to eat? That would be wonderful." Averting his gaze to Armani he said, "I am going to be your teacher and in time you will learn all you need to be a powerful vampire and that you shall be. It's why you were chosen."

What did that mean? Armani questioned. He stopped and stared Donovan in the eyes. "I was chosen by you and Victor, correct?" He asked.

"Yes, you were." Donovan answered avoiding eye contact. "It takes time to learn and apply all the powers necessary to kill."

"I only want to kill the people who did this to Simone and me." Armani stated. "A second ago you stated that you chose me which means that you picked me of your choice, not because of the circumstances of my life." Armani paused, cocked his head and glared at Donovan. "Realistically I chose for you to choose me due to needing to get revenge on my enemies." Armani thought of the black hawk he and Simone had seen near his property for years. Did Donovan know that these this would happen and why didn't he stop it? The truth that Donovan deceived him pissed him off. He shoved Donovan and ran to the kitchen in search of Rex.

Donovan fell backwards, his head barely missing the corner of the end table. "Damn you, Armani!" He cried out. "You will not treat me in such a disrespectful way. Not in our immortal lifetime." He rose filled with rage and flew to the kitchen faster than a speeding bullet.

Armani grabbed Rex by the shoulders and shook him. "Get out of here and never come back. Leave or you will die."

He heard Donovan enter the kitchen and pivoted to face him. "Come on, Donovan. I dare you to try and kill me." He said and lunged at Donovan, arms outstretched, ready to choke the life out of him. "You fooled and deceived me. I'm a vampire forever now, not temporarily like you said." Armani wrapped his hands around Donovan's throat and squeezed hard. "I'm going to kill you." He seethed.

Donovan stared into Armani's eyes. A minute later Armani was thrown across the room. Armani hit the wall and collapsed to the floor.

Rex stared in shock and backed into a corner. How did he do that without physical contact?

"Never and I mean never disrespect your elders dear Armani. I will love you like a brother and protect you to my death but you must never defy me in any way." Kneeling in front of Armani he shook him. "I'm going to give you some advice and please, for the love of God if there is a God, adhere to what I say." He waited to make sure Armani was listening. "Do not ever in your lifetime treat Victor the way you have treated me. He is not kind and will not hesitate to do away with you." Standing, he paced back and forth, hands clenching into fists. "He will torture you in the cruelest ways known to mankind and then watch with delight as you take your final breath."

Armani swallowed hard. "I thought The Dark Ones were good immortals who served justice to the evil people in the world. Isn't that what you told me?" Armani looked at Rex who was huddled in a corner and gave him a sheepish grin. "I'm sorry, Rex that you have been brought into this mess because of me. Please forgive me."

Rex nodded accepting his apology unable to speak. His tongue felt like a mouse caught in a trap.

Donovan apologized to Rex as well. "Don't fear me Rex. I will not hurt you and that I promise you." Extending his hand to Rex, he shook with a firm but soft grip. "My advice applies to you too. Victor would kill you as well. I am 291 years old and have seen many things. Some disturbing, some miraculous and through it all I have learned a great deal."

Armani rose to his feet. "I don't forgive you for deceiving me. Once I have destroyed the evil ones who killed Simone and destroyed me I want to die so I may be with my Simone. You told me this was temporary and I want it to be temporary. I refuse to live an eternal life of solitude without Simone." Tears stung his eyes. "It was hard enough as a human. I can't even fathom what it will be like as one of the living dead." He said his voice frail, "and to live a life of eternity forever feeling as I do. I cannot." He shuddered and walked past Donovan into the living room. "I must go visit Simone. There was a disturbance at her gravesite. She appeared to me in a vision and needs my help. It was not an illusion, Donovan. It was real. I'm leaving now and no one will stop me."

Donovan extended his hand in a 'be my guest gesture.' "Allow me to send my hawk with you. He will watch over you in case you need my assistance."

"That won't be necessary." Armani said and paused at the front door. "How would you see me anyway?"

"That's simple, Armani. I see through the eyes of the hawk." He said, placing his hands on the doorway, he smiled at Armani. "In your darkest hour I have seen you and sympathized with you, sharing your pain. I too have endured a great loss when I was human, one that made it impossible for me to live. I became a vampire of my own choosing and I will say at first, I hated it, but in time I have grown to love what I am and what I stand for." He lowered his head and whispered, "My hope is that one day you will feel the same."

Armani was silent. He had nothing to say to Donovan. He wanted to visit Simone and see if she would speak to him again. His heart longed to hear her voice, even if only in his mind.

Rex ran toward the living room. "I'm coming with you." He stated breathless. "I'm not sitting here helpless waiting for you." He was halted at the door with Donovan's long strong arm. Gulping in air, he stopped.

"You are going nowhere." Donovan stated. It was an order. "You have seen and heard too much."

Armani rushed to his friend's side. "You are not crossing him over to a life of damnation and eternal hell." His voice rose. He and Donovan stood toe to toe like two dogs ready to fight for the alpha rank.

"Have no fear. I have no intention of doing so," Donovan said. Lifting his arm, he placed it around Rex's shoulder. "He deserves an explanation of everything that has happened past, present and also what the future holds." He smiled at Armani and gestured toward the door. "Be on your way, my friend."

Armani grabbed his jacket sliding into it with ease, grabbed his car keys and hustled out the door into the cold winter morning.

Rex watched with an aching heart as Armani left. Gabe was locked up in the dog kennel. He tried to move but his feet felt like they were cemented to the floor.

"What about Gabe, Donovan?" Rex asked. Armani's going to wonder what the hell our manager is doing locked up."

Donovan smiled. "Don't worry, that's been taken care of." Drifting to the window, he looked out at the morning sun sparkling on the white snow. His eyes skimmed to the kennel. Gabe was inside the doghouse trying to keep warm. "There's not a chance in hell he will see Gabe." He faced Rex and held up a finger. "Number one, Gabe is in the doghouse." He held a second finger in the air and said, "And number two, I have cast a spell on the kennel so even if Armani were to go inside the doghouse, Gabe will be invisible to him."

Rex nodded his approval, walked to the couch and gathered up the blankets and began folding them.

"Come Rex, sit down. I believe I owe you an explanation." Donovan floated to the bar and picked up two glasses. "Do you have a preference on a drink, my friend?" He asked over his shoulder, his long hair swaying like the North wind had swept through.

"Brandy sounds like a wonderful drink to discuss serious issues over. Thank you." Rex said.

Donovan returned with two glasses of brandy. He handed one to Rex and sat across from him. "It's a good brandy. I hope you're pleased." Donovan lifted his glass to his mouth and swallowed, licking his lips. Rex noticed how long his fingers were. Chilled, he drank faster hoping the Brandy would warm him. When he had Rex's full attention Donovan stated, "Let's start from the beginning." Donovan told the story from centuries ago when the Dark One's began their reign on earth.

CHAPTER TWENTY-NINE

A RMANI SPED DOWN the road faster than a race car driver. He shook
his head and tried to figure out why he was seeing everything so
clearly. His vision was beyond perfect. He turned his head and looked
out the window. He saw deep into the forest, not just the trees. Maybe
that's what they mean about seeing the forest for the trees, he thought.

He cursed realizing he had forgotten his ski mask at home. He
didn't want anyone to see his face like this. He was a vampire now, but
unfortunately crossing over didn't correct physical scars and ailments.
He leaned into the steering wheel, perched himself forward and gazed
at his reflection in the mirror. His face stared back at him. Were the
tales about vampire's only myths? He assumed you weren't able to see
your reflection. Guess that theory was wrong.

"You're a pathetic creature!" He shouted at the face staring back.
The left side of his face was ugly. What he wouldn't give to have a
normal face, the face that Simone fell in love with years ago. He turned
his head to the undamaged side of his face and smiled. He had to
admit, he was a handsome man. It would be impossible to count how
many women wanted to hook up with him after shows, but he had

more integrity than that. Once he met Simone he only had eyes for her and no other woman in the world would ever compare to her perfection.

He slammed his fist on the steering wheel and turned into the cemetery. Never again would he see her perfect face and the way her eyes lit up when she smiled.

Driving to Simone's grave he scanned the tombstones reading the names and inscriptions. He hoped they were resting in peace. Knowing other people mourned the loss of loved ones was a comfort to him. It was a sense of not being alone and being the only one with a bleeding heart.

He stared into the distance. Rage filled his heart and soul. He accelerated and reached Simone's gravesite. He parked the car and ran to his beloved's grave.

"Who did this? Why would someone do this to my Simone's place of rest?" He asked staring at the sky as if expecting God to give him an answer.

He slowly lowered his eyes, stopping when he reached the angels face. Her nose was chipped. What the hell happened here? He wondered.

The roses he bought lye scattered on the snow, the vase shattered into a hundred pieces. Dropping to his knees, he placed his head in his hands and wept. Why was the snow turning red? He wiped his cheeks and looked at his hand. He was crying tears of blood. He tilted his head and saw the word, 'whore' in red spray paint covering Simone's inscription. Rage flowed through his veins. He screamed and ran to the nearest tree kicking and hitting it.

"I will kill whoever did this!"

He flinched. Out of his peripheral vision he could see a car with lights flashing headed his way. The car pulled up beside him and the driver rolled down the window.

"Sir, is there a problem?" The security guard asked.

Armani's face hid no emotion. "Yes, there is a slight problem." He said pointing at Simone's grave. "Let me ask you something. Do you know how to do your job?"

The security guard looked shocked. "Of course I do. Who are you to ask me such a question?"

"I am your worst nightmare," he said, eyes red. It felt good to put fear in a human. He viewed this man as his enemy. Security should've prevented this from happening. If this cop wanna be was doing his job, that is.

The man looked scared. "Sir, have you been drinking? Your eyes are red."

"I wish I could say that I was." Armani's tongue slid over his teeth. Two of them felt sharp and pointy. They were growing. What was he supposed to do about this? Regret filled his heart. He should've listened to Donovan about having some training about being a vampire before venturing out on his own.

The security guard stared at the gravesite and stone. "Sir, I am so sorry about this vandalism. Would you like me to call the police for you and have them come out and file a report?"

A hawk flew in the distance distracting Armani. It was the black hawk. Donovan's eyes and fierce protector he had been told. He averted his gaze to the security guard. If the hawk sensed fear, anger or hatred it may attack the security guard and Armani didn't want that on his conscience.

"Forgive my rudeness." He apologized. "I'm just rather upset about what someone did to my lovely Simone's gravesite." He apologized.

The security guard smiled. "I understand and it's not a problem." He stepped out of the car and walked toward the tombstone. He chuckled. "Believe me, in this line of work I deal with people much more angry than you and without a reason for it." He shrugged. "It's a damn shame this is what people resort to doing."

Armani followed him. "Yes, it certainly is." He cleared his throat grateful his fangs had disappeared. "And thanks for the offer to call the police, but I'll pass." He knew he'd figure out who did this and the luxury would be his to destroy them. Make them suffer as he had suffered the last few months.

The security guard bent over and started picking up the pieces of the vase in haste. "Ouch!" He exclaimed wincing in pain. "I got one hell of a cut." He said staring at his hand.

Armani smelled the blood before the man announced he had been cut. Cursing, he wondered why it made him hungry. The fangs grew again. "Damn it." He said and jogged to his car pulling out an extra shirt. "Here, wrap this around the cut," he said and threw the shirt to the guard, keeping his distance.

"Thank you, sir," he said wrapping his hand in the cloth, bright red blood seeping through the white cotton. "You never did tell me your name?"

"Armani Belvedere and you are?"

"Charlie, but my friends call me Chuck." He said while tending to his wound. "I've got to ask you a personal question if that's OK?"

Armani wondered what Stan would ask but assured him that it was fine.

"What happened to the left side of your face?" Color flushed his cheeks.

"It was burned in a tragic accident of sorts." Armani stated, hatred filling his soul. "That's as personal as I'm going to get with my answer. I'm sorry."

Stan studied Armani for what seemed like hours. "I understand."

'People and all there stupid questions,' Armani thought. Couldn't they all just leave well enough alone? Maybe this is why Victor chose to let evil rule him after so many years of being a vampire. Armani sighed. He was ready for Stan to be on his way.

Armani looked up and saw the hawk sitting high atop an oak tree. It made eye contact and shrieked as if waiting to see what would happen next.

"Do you need help cleaning this up?" Stan asked clasping his arm. "I'd be more than happy to help."

Armani put his hand up. "No thanks. This is something I'd rather do by myself. I need to be alone and you should go get that cut checked out by a doctor. You may need stitches. " He turned his back on Stan, crouched on all fours and started picking up the pieces of the vase and roses. "It was nice to meet you." He said over his shoulder hoping Stan would take the hint before he lost his patience or even worse, unleashed the monster within aching to get out. The smell of blood brought out a predatory instinct and he didn't know how to handle this yet. He had many questions for Donovan.

"Have a good day, sir." Stan said and walked to his car.

The car door slammed and the engine roared to life. Peace at last.

"Simone, can you hear me?" Armani asked. "You came to me while I was sleeping the rest of the undead. Please talk to me again. I need you." He placed his hands on the ground wishing he could somehow warm Simone's cold dead body with his touch.

He listened. No sound but the wind. Maybe Donovan was right and it was just an illusion he had while undergoing the transformation. He would give anything to hear her sweet angelic voice one more time.

"Simone, I've done something I don't think you'll be too pleased with," he said. "I'm going to get right to the point. I'm a vampire now and have plans to kill the people who did this to you, to me, to us." Armani's voice broke. He held his head in his hands and wept bitterly. His life was ripped apart in that one fateful night. Simone would never be a part of his life and the world he knew was gone forever. He was no longer human. Yes, on the outside he had every resemblance of who he used to be. That too was an illusion because he was now a soulless vampire seeking revenge. Armani was sure he was an abomination to be sent straight to hell upon his death.

"Oh, Simone, what have I done? I've sold my soul to the devil."

Helpless, he stood, staring at the blue sky while snowflakes fell from the like powder sprinkled from Heaven.

"What's the matter, Donovan?" Rex asked. "You look puzzled."

Donovan stared into his crystal ball. He was observing Armani through the eyes of his black hawk. "I don't think I made the right choice by allowing Armani to venture off on his own." He said and stared into space, lines of worry etched on his pale face. He focused on Rex and said, "Armani will be a strong vampire, probably one of the most powerful forces in The Dark Ones, and I should've trained him before letting him go out into the world solo." He held up the ball, turning his head this way and that while observing Armani.

"We can go get him." Rex stated. "Can't we?"

"He will come back to us soon." He said and set the ball on the table. "I want him to know and believe that I trust him." Hoisting himself off the chair he paced the room. "If we were to go to him, he would feel I don't have faith in him and that could prove to be detrimental to his growth as a vampire."

Rex looked puzzled. "I don't understand what you mean."

"Rex, you have much to learn just as Armani does." He said and walked to the window. "We are highly intelligent beings with powers you can't even imagine." He said. "When I first turned, it was baffling to me all of these new things I had to learn. Victor was a wonderful teacher. He became my friend and my father. He created me and never once abandoned me." Donovan turned away from the window to face Rex. "Most importantly, he loved me and trusted me. He showed me this by letting me experiment things on my own, venture out into the world, explore my newfound life," he said, making a circle with his hands. "The world is a different place for vampires than humans. When a mortal is turned, they are similar to a newborn baby. You would never expect a newborn to take care of itself and understand this world we live in without his or her parents."

Rex nodded in agreement.

"Just as a new vampire cannot possibly learn all there is to know without a teacher, a parent. I've seen many new vampires destroyed because the one that turned them abandoned them in their time of need."

"Why would they have to be destroyed?" Rex asked folding his arms across his chest. "That doesn't make sense to me."

"Left to their own devices, they turn evil." Donovan said. "We promote justice and only allow justice kills. The ones we destroy kill for the thrill of the chase and the adrenaline rush from killing innocent people." He said and licked his lips. "The blood of pure innocent humans does taste sweet. It's a daily fight for us all not to kill for the thrill. And once a vampire turns evil he becomes like a drug addict and must have more and more blood from the innocent to satisfy the urge. Once they are addicted to the taste and the rush, they must be destroyed." A cold look in his eyes sent chills down Rex's spine. "We don't care who the vampire was as a human or who he is as a vampire, we kill them. No questions asked." Removing his cloak he said, "Even if it's Armani who becomes this way. He will be put to death."

"Armani would never turn that way. I know him too well." Rex said, shaking his head no. "How would you know if a vampire is doing these things? You can't possibly keep track of every single one."

Donovan sat down and stretched his hands over his head. "Good point, Rex. The young new vampire's make it easy. They lack the ability to disguise their actions. The older and more ancient the vampire the harder it is to see through the mask of good." He folded his hands in his lap and stared at them. "In fact it's almost impossible. One must watch for the subtle hints and clues. If an ancient vampire is becoming evil, the aura will unveil itself in time. Just as in human behavior, there will be a shift in their personality, the way they carry themselves, the look in their eyes. It's a look that would chill any human to the bone."

Rex had heard enough for now. Changing the subject he asked, "What's Armani doing now?"

Donovan commanded the crystal ball to come to him. Rex watched amazed as the ball floated like a feather to Donovan. Donovan grasped the ball and held it to his face and frowned. "He's crying."

Simone heard every teardrop from Armani's eyes fall on her grave like raindrops from Heaven. The desire to reach out to him was intense but she found herself too tired to communicate. She tried numerous times since Armani arrived. His pleading with her to speak to him broke her heart. Was it something she could only do once in a while? Why couldn't she do it at will? So many unanswered questions plagued her. Armani's wails and cries were more than she could bear. Never in her life had she heard such sounds of pain and anguish. Squeezing her eyes shut, she said a prayer for Armani. Wishing for death was futile. She was already dead, stuck in a universe between Heaven and Hell. Lying in a cold coffin she wondered why God would punish her like this. She believed in God once but now doubted her faith. Her eyes opened wide. Armani screamed a loud gut wrenching painful scream. That scream would haunt her for as long as she lay six feet under the earth.

CHAPTER THIRTY

KATRINA'S BLOOD FLOWED cold as ice through her veins. Victor strode up to her with such an air of confidence it numbed her. What in the hell did this vampire want her to do? What was this game?

"Victor, are you going to kill me?" Katrina managed to ask. She closed her eyes and waited for him to strike her dead. "Just do it then. Let's get it over with."

Victor laughed and scoffed. "Little lady, have you forgotten that I call the shots around here? You will not tell me what to do or when to do it." He stated, patting her head like she was his pet dog.

Katrina flinched. His touch was cold. "Ok. So, you said, 'honey, I'm home.' What am I supposed to do?"

"I happen to take a great pleasure in creative people." He said and tilted her chin forcing her to look into his eyes. "Think of a response. You seem to have no problem coming up with some quick witted things." He finished letting his finger slide under her chin.

Katrina felt sick. His touch repulsed her. "Ok." She cleared her throat and said, "Yeah, I see you're home. Fix your own glass of blood." A sly smile played on her lips.

Victor took delight in her attitude but he refused to let it soften his heart. That wasn't going to happen. Not after what she did. He raised his hand and slapped her hard across the face.

Katrina's head rolled back. She saw stars like fireworks flash in front of her eyes. Her lip curled and she cried.

"That's not the right answer but it doesn't matter. I have brought a guest to play with us." Victor turned toward the door, motioned with his hand and said, "Come to me."

Katrina opened her eyes, blinked twice and saw a man of forty years old walk in. "Who is that?" She asked and rubbed her cheek.

"He's part of your punishment, my dear," Victor smiled at Katrina. "He and I are going to act out what The Dark One's do." He placed his finger on his lips. "Shhh, this is a private show and I don't want anyone to ever know what went on here." He winked and turned toward the skinny brown haired man standing before him. "Speak, you fool." He ordered releasing the man from the spell he had put him under.

The man screamed and ran in circles around the room. "What are you?" he demanded when he stopped and faced Victor. His eyes caught sight of Katrina and he asked her the same question.

Katrina looked at the man with sympathy. What sort of sick game was Victor playing with them? "I'm not a 'what.'" Katrina said. "I'm a person. A hostage held by him." She said pointing at Victor, venom in her eyes.

"You mortals are so amusing." Victor stated. "To answer your question, sir, I am a vampire. The Master of The Dark Ones."

The man laughed. "What sort of cult are you in and what drugs are you on? You're tripping on acid." He said, matter-of-fact.

Victor jumped him. "You dare call me a liar!" He shrieked. "Then what do you call these?" He asked baring his fangs at the man. "Look into my eyes and tell me I'm human."

The man lay under Victor as helpless as a mouse in a cat's death grip. "Shit, I call them eyes." The man stared at Victor's red evil eyes, the hatred illuminating where human eyes should be. Swallowing hard he said, "You're an evil monster. I want to leave this place."

Victor choked the man.

Katrina ran to where Victor had the man pinned down and pulled on Victor's arms. "Let him go! You're going to kill him."

Victor released his grip on the man's throat and smiled. "Ah, yes, Katrina I have every intention of doing that." Shoving her backward he stood and picked the man up by the neck, throwing him next to Katrina. "This is the game you created by defying me. You are going to watch me kill him and if you dare interfere in anyway, I will kill you too. I bet you're blood tastes sweet, Katrina." He said licking his lips. His desire to drink blood was hard to control. More than anything he wanted to kill and feel the rush. An innocent like Katrina would be perfect and so satisfying. But, that wasn't part of his game. He was playing mind games with Katrina and teaching her a lesson at the same time.

"What in God's name did I ever do to you, Victor?" The man asked.

Victor rolled his eyes. "Oh, you have done nothing to me." Victor said and stood in front of where Katrina and the man lay on the floor, Victor peered down at them and sneered. "You shouldn't have to think too hard about why it is that you're here." Victor walked a few feet away, turned and ordered Katrina to come to him.

Katrina stood, crossed her arms and answered with a defiant no. "Why would I do such a stupid thing? If you're going to kill me then you should come to me." She looked at the man and shivered. "Why should he and I do as you say when we will ultimately die? Why the games? Just do it and be done with it, Victor." Setting her chin stubbornly, she stared Victor down.

The man nodded his head agreeing with Katrina. "She's right you know."

Victor had little patience for Katrina and none for the man. He drifted to where they were and stopped in front of Katrina. He hoisted her over his shoulder. She kicked, screamed and pulled his hair.

"You're insane you monster!" She hollered at the top of her lungs.

Victor ignored her and placed her on a chair. "Now you are going to sit here and be my audience." He took a set of handcuffs, clasping Katrina's hands together. He was impressed at the struggle she gave him but she was no match for him. A weak small frail human could never overpower him. He was the strongest and most fierce vampire to exist, except for his father, Julius. Julius rescued him from his parents and crossed him over to eternal life as a vampire. None of the members of The Dark Ones saw Julius anymore. He was a solitary vampire.

Katrina looked into Victor's eyes. "Why, Victor? Why?" She asked, tears brimming in her eyes, making their color stand out.

Victor's gaze softened as he stared into her eyes. What a beautiful creature she was. He could fall in love with this woman but he wasn't going to allow himself the pleasure or the softening of the heart.

"A better question to ask my dear is why not," he stated flatly, his eyes hard as stone once again.

Katrina stared at the man sitting across from her.

"Who are you anyway?" She asked him.

He stared at his hands, bending and twisting his fingers and ignored her question.

Victor stared at the man. "You heard the lady. Now answer her question." He ordered. "She deserves respect from a person of the likes of you."

Looking up he stared at Katrina. "I'm Gordon. Gordon Appleton. I have a wife and two children. I work full time as a computer tech at the local university. Why do you care who I am? We're going to die." He finished averting his gaze back to his hands.

'You forgot to add the part about you beating your children senseless for the smallest mistake.' Victor thought. He would make sure Gordon confessed his sins to Katrina before he gave him the final blow of death.

"You are right about one thing, Gordon," Victor said. "You got your name and information correct but apparently you left out a vital piece of information about who you really are and what you do behind closed doors which is the reason you are going to die." Victor smiled when Gordon stood and tried to run away.

"Victor!" Katrina screamed. Her body ached. She didn't think she could bear to watch Victor kill an innocent man. This poor mans death would leave a woman widowed with two children. "Victor, how dare you even think about killing him and leaving his family without a father and a husband. I hate you!" Her whole body shook with hate, fear and sorrow. How could anyone, even a vampire be so cruel and cunning?

Gordon ran to the door twisting and turning the knob. He shook it hard. Frustrated, he kicked the door. Victor watched amused.

"Going somewhere, Gordon?" He asked splaying his arms to the side like Jesus on the cross. "Why not just make this easier on you and me and come to me for your self crucifixion. You did this to yourself."

"You son of a bitch!" Gordon screamed. "Girl, help me!" He shrieked running toward Katrina.

Katrina stared at Gordon. She never saw so much fear on anyone's face in her lifetime. "There's nothing I can do." She said in a soft voice. "I'm sorry." She looked past Gordon and screamed, "Look out Gordon!"

Gordon whirled around and was met with a blow from Victor's fist. Gordon doubled over and held his stomach trying to catch his breath.

Victor picked Gordon up and threw him into a chair. "The first rule of the game is stay away from my woman. Don't speak to her unless I give you permission. Understood?" He asked his eyes filled with hatred.

Katrina was angry. "I'm not your woman and never will be."

Cocking his head to the side, Victor shushed Katrina. "Yes you are my woman forever. Accept your fate. It makes things a lot easier for you and for me." Facing Gordon he asked, "Have you figured out what important piece of information you left out when introducing yourself to Katrina?"

Gordon stared at Victor. "I left nothing out."

"Liar!" Victor yelled. "Katrina, this man isn't the man he wants you to think he is."

Gordon knew he was hiding the truth. He would joke to his wife that he was a computer technician by day and a raging alcoholic by night. It was his best-kept secret. His wife and children dared tell no one because they knew all to well what the consequences would be.

Victor interrupted his thoughts. "I am giving you one more chance to come clean, Gordon. Tell her what you do to your family behind closed doors." Pointing to Katrina he said, "She deserves to know the truth about why I have you down here."

Katrina spoke up. "You have him down here to prove just how evil and crazy you really are." She glared at Victor. "I think this man is telling me the truth."

Victor shot a venomous look at Katrina. "That, my dear is where you are dead wrong. When this is over you will know who The Dark Ones are and what we do. It's about justice." He looked at Gordon and smiled. "Isn't that right, Gordon?" He asked extending his arms and cracking his knuckles. "Something you managed to escape. Correct?"

"Victor, you're about murder. Cold blooded murder for the sheer thrill of it." Katrina said. "And just like Dracula, you suck innocent people's blood for your survival and then you kill them." Disgusted, she stuck her tongue out. "You do it for the fun of it all."

Gordon wished Katrina were right but she was wrong. Victor knows what he does at night and how he has tortured and beaten his wife and children for years. Why the game? Why make Katrina watch? "Can we just get this over with?" He asked Victor. "May I ask a favor?"

"It depends what kind of favor you ask." Victor stated impatiently.

Gordon stared at Katrina and managed to flash a reassuring smile. "I would like the lady to leave the room. She shouldn't be subject to see you murder me."

Victor stared at the ceiling and tapped the side of his head, pretending to think for a minute. "Request denied." He said and walked from one end of the basement to the other. "The reason for that is because she's here to learn a valuable lesson just like you. Katrina dare defy me and go against my wishes and for that she will be punished by having to watch you suffer and endure great pain." He said indicating the case was closed with a nod of his head.

Katrina snorted. "I'm learning a life lesson alright. It's that monsters and sick twisted people really do exist."

Victor smiled. "You learn quickly, Katrina. I'm more than impressed."

"Are you admitting that that's what you are?" She asked.

"Dear child, so innocent and naïve," he began, "the sick person and monster you talk about is sitting across from you." He finished pointing at Gordon.

"Whatever," Katrina replied with a shrug. There was no sense in arguing with Victor. She wasn't going to win anyway.

"Who would like some popcorn?" Victor asked looking at Katrina and then at Gordon. "We're going to watch a movie together for a few minutes." He smiled wickedly as his gaze bore into Gordon. "A home video made by yours truly," he said nodding to Gordon. "Isn't that right Gordon? What did you do? Jack off to these the day after you made them? Did it turn you on? Make you feel like a real big strong man?"

Gordon shifted in his chair and wet his lips with his tongue. "I don't know what you're talking about."

Katrina sat in silence wondering what would happen next. Too scared to look she closed her eyes. Her gut told her Gordon just gave Victor the wrong answer. She was right.

Victor punched Gordon's stomach a few times. Victor couldn't believe how stupid this man was. "Where were you when God handed out brains?" Victor snorted.

Gordon tried to scream but Victor shoved a sock in his mouth. "No one wants to hear a coward scream, especially not me or my woman."

Bile filled Katrina's mouth. The sickening sound of Victor saying she was his woman made her wish she could die instead of Gordon. She opened her eyes and saw Victor tying Gordon's hands to the chair with rope.

"I'll be right back." He said and shoved Gordon's head backwards.

Katrina stared at Victor. His fangs were extended and the hungry look in his eyes made every fiber in her body go numb and cold.

Victor stopped in front of Katrina and leaned toward her. She dodged him but not fast enough. He kissed her hard on the lips savoring her sweet taste.

"I'm going to make the popcorn so be prepared for an X-rated graphic true story." He said winking.

'Victor was a sick, sick vampire.' Katrina thought. But Victor wasn't just any normal vampire, he was a monster. She leaned over the end of the chair and spit. His kiss made her stomach turn.

Katrina stood, her hands handcuffed and walked to where Gordon sat. He looked like a decent man. Victor had to be wrong.

"Did you do these things that Victor said you did to your family?" She asked. Of course he couldn't answer and she wasn't about to pull the sock out of his mouth. Or should she? A cold hand wrapped around her neck gripping tightly.

"Katrina. Don't you dare take try to help that monster." Victor ordered his breath hot on her neck.

How did he sneak up on her without a sound? Her stomach growled. The popcorn smelled so good. She thought about better days when she hung out with friends at the local theatre.

Gordon's eyes widened. He was more afraid than he had ever been his whole life. Death was his penalty for what he had done in secret for years. How did this vampire find him? He managed to escape the long arm of the law and out of the blue this freak comes along and ruins his world.

Katrina faced Victor and tried her best to keep her wits about her.

His gaze bore into hers. "Come with me honey. I have a seat saved just for you." Victor took her by the arm and led her to the movie theatre. His loud laugh echoing off the walls. "I'm your evil angel but in a moment you will see that I'm a vampire of justice. I serve the good of humanity by taking out the trash and ridding the world of monsters." He saw the doubt in her eyes. "I promise you will love me after this."

Katrina scowled. How dare he mention love at a time such as this? "I will never love you." She spat and followed him into the theatre and up the steps.

Victor placed her in the center and led her to a chair in the middle. "This is a perfect viewing spot and to make sure you don't try to get up and leave I'm strapping cuffs on your ankles and securing you to the chair." He clamped them on her ankles roughly. "I'm sorry but you did this to yourself." He squeezed one of her cuffed hands.

Katrina watched disgusted as Victor floated down the aisle steps like he was riding on a cloud. It was amazing to watch him but she knew what he was about to do would prove to be too much for her to handle. She stared at what was in front of the movie screen and gulped. It was a hangman's ensemble; a chair stood under a rope and next to that were a bunch of shiny objects. She leaned forward as far as the cuffs would allow, squinted and saw there were knives, swords and a chain saw. A sour taste filled her mouth and her stomach churned. She leaned her head forward and puked. Feeling dizzy she closed her eyes wishing this day was over.

"Honey, we're home!" Victor boomed.

Katrina bolted upright. Speechless and scared, all she could do was watch and pray she could make it through this.

Gordon's body shook, his eyes filled with tears. Victor carried him to the spot where the noose ensemble stood and shoved him in a chair to the right of it.

"It's time for the movie." He stated. "Roll one."

Victor sat next to Gordon and held his face forcing him to watch the movie. Katrina sat as still as a stone statue unprepared for the things she saw. Shock, horror, terror, disgust and repulsion consumed her like a grease fire doused with water.

The video showed Gordon setting up a video camera, a can of beer in his hand. He smiled and waved into the camera. Katrina knew she would never forget what happened next. The wife walked in through the front door with their two children, both under five years old. The camera showed Gordon guzzling his beer and throwing the can at his wife. The wife screamed, and Gordon jumped on top of her and punches and hits her with the force of a madman. The children sit screaming and crying too afraid and too young to help.

"You sick son of a bitch!" Katrina screamed. "How dare you beat your wife in front of your children?"

Victor turned and shushed her. "Let's pay attention. Gordon is going to have a test of sorts on this movie. I want him to focus." He laughed squeezing Gordon's neck hard.

Katrina flinched and winced and watched in horror as Gordon picked up each of his tiny children and threw them on the ground, screaming profanities in their small little innocent ears. Tears stung her eyes when he slapped the face of the five-year old boy. The boy curled into the fetal position trying to hide and protect him self. Katrina watched shocked as the mother approached Gordon from behind only to have him turn and wrap his hands around her throat. The camera then flashed to the two boys holding each other crying. Their eyes were so full of fear it ripped Katrina's heart in two. Why? Why would this man do this?

Victor rose from his chair and the movie stopped. "I think we have all seen enough of this sickness." He turned to Katrina and apologized. "I'm sorry you had to see innocent lives shattered by this monster." He picked up Gordon and threw him over his shoulder like a sack of potatoes. He hoisted his kicking body onto the chair, wrapped the noose around his neck and secured the knot.

Gordon's body shook like a dog having a seizure. He stared at Victor and tried to kick him. Victor grabbed his ankle and snapped it like a twig. Katrina winced. The sound was sickening.

"Don't ever try to do that again." Victor warned. "Now the games will begin." Victor picked up a butcher knife and carved a hawk into the left side of Gordon's face. Blood spilled from the fresh wound. Gordon's muffled cries filled the room. Victor took the knife and carefully cut off Gordon's shirt. "I must warn you I'm not a surgeon but I'm going to try my hand at this." He stated picking up the chainsaw. "When you are about to die and go to Hell I'm going to hold your beating heart in the palm of my hand."

'God save your soul, Gordon,' Katrina thought.

Victor heard her thoughts, turned and laughed. "It's too late for that. His eternity is secure in Hell where he will burn in flames forever for the sins he committed against his wife and two beautiful children."

Katrina heard a touch of sorrow in Victor's voice when he said 'children.' She wondered why. He didn't seem to be a caring vampire in the least. And this would prove the level of monstrosity in Victor. There was no way she could get out of this room. Gordon was an evil despicable man but it didn't mean she wanted to watch this gruesome torture and murder.

Victor removed the sock from Gordon's mouth with a fierce tug and threw it on the ground. "I want to hear you scream in pain and agony." Victor rose so he was level with Gordon's ear and whispered, "It will be music to my ears, like a symphony."

Gordon cried out in pain. "My God, save me! Please stop this. I'll change, I promise." His eyes bulged.

"You're a funny man but I highly doubt that." He scoffed. Victor revved the chainsaw. "You are the violin and this is the bow." He said raising the chainsaw above his head. He pointed at himself and said, "I am the composer and conductor." Facing Katrina he said, "That beautiful woman is the audience we are playing for. Let us make beautiful music together." He held Katrina's gaze, the hatred left his eyes. Victor scolded himself. That woman was making him soft. Damn it all to hell. Katrina was making his heart feel things he didn't want it to feel. He turned back to Gordon and all the hatred and coldness returned to his heart.

"You won't get away with this." Gordon said. "They'll find you and make you pay for killing me." Tears streamed down his face. "Fuck you, Victor." Victor stared at Gordon. "No, I'm afraid they won't find me dear friend. I have been doing this for 491 years and not once have I even been a suspect in an investigation." Victor placed the chainsaw on Gordon's foot making a small cut.

"AAAHHHH! I'm going to bleed to death before you finish. Why don't you just do it quickly?" Gordon asked, his face ashen.

"Don't worry, I won't let that happen." Victor set the saw down and stood next to Gordon. "You're going to suffer for a time, but not too long because quite frankly I'm already sick of looking at your disgusting self." Victor reached up and tightened the rope around Gordon's neck making him wince and yelp. "Now tell Katrina what you did to your family." He ordered jerking the rope one more time.

Gordon caught his breath. Avoiding eye contact he told Katrina the movie was real and that he had in fact been beating all of them for years.

"Why? How could you do that to the people you're supposed to love more than anything in the world?" She asked horrified at his confession.

Victor punched his face. "Speak when spoken to. Answer her. I too would like to know what made you tick."

Gordon stuck his lower jaw out and moved it back and forth.

"Because I could, that's why and I loved every minute of it." Gordon responded, no emotion on his face.

Katrina balled her fists. If she weren't in handcuffs she would be up there inflicting pain on this monster. "You're sick. I hate you."

Victor was pleased with Katrina's response. Smiling at her he said, "Time for him to die, my love. You've seen enough for one day."

Taking the saw he started it up and waved it in front of Gordon's face. "Here we go." Eyes gleaming red, he plunged the saw deep into Gordon's chest sending pieces of flesh flying in all directions. Gordon screamed in agony, his face twisted. Victor was smart and didn't hit any major arteries. He pushed a button on his hang man's ensemble and hoisted Gordon into the air. A few seconds later he let him drop and his body jerked, plunging up and down like a yo-yo. "Don't worry my dear friend Gordon, the plunge wasn't enough to snap your neck, only cut off your air. You will die of asphyxiation." Victor revved the chainsaw and said, "But not before I do this." He placed saw at the center of Gordon's ribs and sawed his way in. Gordon's bones separated sounding like wood being cut. Gordon's face paled and he puked. Victor threw the saw to the side, reached into Gordon's chest cavity, ripped out his beating heart and held it in front of Gordon's face. "This is the last thing you shall see. Now die you sick son of a bitch." Victor shoved the heart into Gordon's mouth and walked away.

Katrina's blood ran cold. She sat silent afraid to talk, afraid to move. This would haunt her forever. Gordon deserved the fate Victor dealt him but why did Victor have to make it so torturous and gruesome? It would've been a lot easier to shoot Gordon, right?

She looked up and saw Victor standing in front of her with his hand extended. "I'm sorry you had to witness this." Katrina realized her handcuffs were gone. It must be more vampire magic. She didn't know what to do so she took his hand. His grip was cold and uncaring. "This is what The Dark One's do. Gordon was an evil man who escaped the justice system one too many times. We take it into our own hands and execute these kinds of people." Cocking his head he smiled. "His wife and children will now have peace. We give people peace."

Katrina huffed. "Why did I have to watch this?" She asked shaking her head disgusted.

"Katrina, you defied me and I told you there would be a punishment. Watching this execution was your punishment and it also gave you an understanding of what us vampire's stand for." He moved a stray piece of hair from her face and kissed her cheek. "I promise you will never have to go through this again." He stared into her soul. "As long as you never defy me or go against my wishes again. Promise me."

Katrina stared into his dark eyes. She didn't trust him. "I promise," she said. The smell of blood, death and decay made her feel dizzy. She looked away from Victor and stared at Gordon. His body was nothing but a tangled mess of flesh and blood with bits of bone scattered on the floor. His mouth was open and his heart lay at his feet. Heat and nausea swept over her and everything went black.

Victor bent down and gently picked her up in his strong arms holding her close to his chest. He stared at her pale face, his heart warming. He kissed the top of her head and drifted out of the theatre his black cape swirling behind him.

Chapter Thirty-One

A RMANI STOOD IN the cemetery watching a black hearse lead a group of cars to a burial site. The orange flags attached to the cars waved in the breeze as if saying good bye to the deceased one. Armani's excellent vision allowed him to clearly see the passenger in the first car. It was an older woman, more than likely the wife of the deceased. She held a tissue to her nose as tears fell. His heart broke in two for her and for himself. What he would have given to be able to attend Simone's funeral. But he had been trapped in a drug-induced coma lying in a hospital bed.

He balled his fists and stared at the sky asking God why He would do this to him. It wasn't fair. His mission was to find the ones who destroyed his life and reason for living and make them suffer. Death to them would be peace for him.

Armani watched the funeral procession again. "At least you people have a chance to say a final good-bye. God rest your loved ones soul." He said softly and did the Hail Mary.

A black shadow moved beside him. Armani looked and saw the black hawk standing, its head upright and face courageous like a guard dog protecting his master.

"Hello friend," Armani said amazed at the beauty of the hawk up close. Its sleek black coat covered its large frame. The hawk turned its head upward staring into Armani's eyes. The hawk's black eyes stared into his soul. The hawk averted its gaze back to the funeral procession standing in reverence like an English soldier protecting a castle. Armani shivered and shoved his hands into his coat pockets. The hawk's beak was long thick and sharp. It could easily tear someone to bits. No wonder Donovan chose this bird to be his eyes and protector.

Armani crouched to his knees not taking his eyes off the hawk. He held his hand out waiting for the hawk to notice and come to him.

The hawk twisted its head and stared at Armani.

"Come here fella," Armani said. "I won't hurt you. I just want to touch you. It seems I've seen you around my home for such a long time."

The hawk listened to no one except Donovan, his master. He was an intelligent hawk and was taught to trust no one, especially not a new vampire. The destiny of the new vampires remained a mystery for a time according to Donovan. The hawk had seen many newly born vampires choose evil instead of good. These new vampires who chose evil were killed but close encounters had almost cost the hawk his own life. The great and mighty black hawk was a gift to Donovan upon his cross over and the hawk's destruction would limit Donovan's powers and would leave him partially paralyzed. The hawk was fiercely loyal to Donovan. Victor promised the hawk eternal life as long as long as he obeyed Donovan and adhered to the cause of The Dark One's. Over time the hawk had developed a deep love and devotion to Donovan and he would do nothing to jeopardize their relationship.

Armani inched closer to the hawk. The hawk spread its large wings and flew away at light speed. Armani flinched and stared into the sky. The hawk circled high above. How did he fly so high and so fast?

Armani kissed his fingertips, placing them on Simone's tombstone. He closed his eyes, sighed and walked to his car.

"I love you, Simone." He whispered and wiped fresh tears that fell.

Simone longed to reach out to Armani. 'Please know I love you, too.' Simone mouthed, unable to speak.

"What's going on?" Rex asked concerned as he studied Donovan's face.

Donovan set the crystal ball down. "Rex, you really need to calm down. I understand your concern for your friend but I have everything under control." He said in an 'end of discussion' tone.

Rex cleared his throat. "Excuse me for being concerned."

Donovan turned to Rex. "You're excused. Let's go outside and check on Gabe," he said and walked toward the door. "Armani will be arriving shortly as well as Victor."

Rex stood and stretched his hands over his head. He followed Donovan. Hatred flowed through his veins like venom from a snakes bite. "Do I get the honors of torturing Gabe some more?" He asked and chuckled.

"You sure do, if that is what you desire." Donovan answered. Rex was the sort of man Donovan took a liking to immediately. Maybe one day Rex would agree to join The Dark One's. He would be an asset to them and their cause.

"Oh, believe me I more than desire it. I wish I could kill him."

Donovan smiled, holding the door open for him. "I always let the finest gentlemen go first." He said ushering him through with a wave of his hand.

"Thank you," Rex said. Stepping outside he shivered in the cold air. "Gosh, I think I need my jacket. I'll be right back."

"Here you are," Donovan said handing Rex his jacket. "Let's get moving before our friends arrive."

Rex stood open-mouthed, took his jacket and slipped it on grateful for the warmth it offered. "How did you do that?"

Donovan smiled. "Magic." He laughed. "You keep forgetting I'm a vampire and have many powers." He stated. "Hell, I could rob a bank for you and leave no trace of evidence."

Rex liked that idea. "Well, what are we waiting for? Let's go." Biting his lip he thought aloud. "It's not like Armani is going to tour with the band anymore so I'll need to make money somehow and that sounds like a perfectly logical idea."

Donovan and Rex walked slowly to the dog kennel. "Rex, you're a funny guy. Let's get this straight. The Dark One's do not commit crimes. We promote and deliver justice and only justice for the crimes people commit which they get away with."

Rex held his hands up. "O.K., O.K. I get your point." With a shake of his head he walked past Donovan calling out for Gabe as he neared the kennel.

Donovan watched Rex while listening for the sound of Armani's engine. "I know you get the point because I can hear your thoughts." Donovan laughed. "Gabe, come out of the doghouse. You have a visitor." He ordered.

Gabe crawled out on all fours, a distraught look on his face. "I'm hungry. Get me some food to eat or I will die out here." He stood swaying like a drunken sailor. "I'm so cold." He squelched wrapping his arms around himself.

Rex sneered. "Good. Allow me to warm you up a bit."

Donovan opened the kennel door allowing Rex to enter. "Gabe, consider this your refresher course. Let's call it Revenge 101."

Gabe looked confused. "What do you mean?"

Donovan's head rolled back, laughter escaped him. "You're really that stupid? Armani will have his revenge for what you did to him. This is the first class, so to speak. Don't worry, when this over you will have graduated to the 401 level and get your diploma in Hell, my friend."

Rex marched toward Gabe, fists clenched, filled with rage. "I'm your professor, Gabe. Let's begin our first lesson."

Gabe ran to the corner trying to escape. He dropped to his knees and held his hands in front of his face begging and pleading for Rex to have mercy. Rex punched and hit Gabe in the face a few times. It made him feel powerful and good.

The sound of a car racing toward the house halted Rex. It was Armani and he was driving like a bat out of hell.

Donovan smiled.

"Oh shit," Rex stated racing out of the dog kennel. "Why are you smiling?" He asked Donovan.

"I want Armani to see this."

Armani parked his car and saw Rex and Donovan in the doghouse. He gasped when he saw Gabe lying on the floor taking a beating. Armani didn't know what to think. Too many things he didn't understand were happening . . . and now this. Why in the world was Rex beating Gabe? Why was Gabe in the doghouse cooped up like an animal? Armani shoved the car into park and ran to where Donovan and Rex stood.

Armani grabbed Rex and shoved him to the ground. "What is wrong with you? Have you gone mad?" He asked, his voice boiling over with anger. He turned to Gabe and asked, "Are you alright? Gabe, what are you doing in my kennel?"

"Help me, Armani!" Gabe screamed his face swollen and bloody. "These men have gone mad."

Donovan and Rex laughed. "Mad? Are you kidding me, Gabe? You're the one who is mad." Rex stated flatly and stood. "Tell Armani what role you played in the death of Simone and his self-mutilation and then we'll discuss who's mad."

A confused look plagued Armani's face. "What is going on? Is someone going to explain this to me?" He asked. "Not to mention a thousand other questions I have for you Donovan."

The great black hawk flew overhead and circled the men. Donovan waved his hand and stretched his arm out like a tree branch. "Come, my faithful friend." Donovan ordered.

Rex and Armani watched in awe as the hawk descended, gently landing on Donovan's outstretched arm. The hawk's gaze pierced through the two men. Rex turned away. Something about the bird gave him the chills.

Donovan reached into his pocket with his free hand and pulled out a cracker. The hawk took the food in its sharp beak and flew toward the house landing by the front door. It watched them while eating its treat.

"I'm sorry but your hawk friend gives me the creeps." Rex said.

"You have nothing to worry about, my dear friend Rex. If you are a friend of mine, you are a friend of the hawks." Donovan said. "Now, come with me men. Victor will be here soon and I know Armani has many questions for me."

Armani didn't move. "I want Gabe to be released. It's insane to leave a man caged up like this," he said pointing at the kennel.

Rex walked beside Donovan and turned to see if Armani was following. "Come on, Armani. Let's go. You'll understand what 's going on soon."

Armani trusted Rex but was reluctant to follow.

"Armani, please don't leave me out here to die." Gabe begged.

Donovan silenced Gabe with a wave of his hand.

"Please Armani. You must trust Donovan and me." Rex said. "Listen to Donovan. If not for us, do it for Simone."

That hit a nerve in Armani. Just the mention of her name tore him apart. "I will follow." He said. He stared at Gabe and said, "I'm sorry, Gabe." He turned and marched to where Donovan and Rex stood.

'Not as sorry as that son of a bitch will be,' Rex thought. He knew in time Donovan would open Armani's eyes to the reality of the situation and why Gabe was locked up like the wild animal he was.

CHAPTER THIRTY-TWO

"CAN WE GO home now?" Adam asked popping a Vicodin in his mouth and chasing it down with water.

Alex laughed. "You sound like a toddler. Are we there yet? Are we there yet? I want to go home . . . ." Alex turned right onto a busy street in town. "Two more stops and then we'll go home."

Adam groaned and stared out the window.

"You knew full well the pharmacy was the first stop, son. Our next stop is the gun store." Alex smirked. "I'm going hunting when we get home. I don't care how long it takes to shoot that son of a bitch black hawk. I'll sit out in the woods and wait for a chance to kill it forever if I have to."

"Can't you let it go?" Adam asked. "It happened and now it is what it is."

Alex smacked his son's face. "Watch your tongue. Respect me and you may get respected in return."

Adam flinched and rubbed his face. His dad managed to miss the wound. Thank God for that.

"I'm thinking maybe I'll skip the body shop today. I can always have the car fixed tomorrow." Alex said.

Alex pulled the car in front of the gun shop, parked and jumped out. "Be right back." He hollered and slammed the door.

Adam rolled his eyes. He didn't care if his dictator dad ever came back. He could die for all he cared.

"Would you really want that now Adam?" A deep voice asked.

Chills ran up and down Adam's spine. He held his hands in front of him and they were shaking. Maybe it was the Vicodin causing him to shake, hallucinate and hear voices.

A tap on his shoulder proved his theory wrong.

"Turn around, Adam. I want to look into the eyes of a killer." Victor ordered. "I've been watching you for quite some time now and I must tell you that you and your father's work is sloppy, to say the least. I am not impressed."

Adam tried to scream but a forceful hand covered his mouth silencing him. He wiggled and fought but it did him no good. The man in the backseat was strong.

Victor leaned forward. "I will release you and uncover your mouth if you promise to be quiet." Victor whispered in his ear. "If you so much as make a peep I won't hesitate to snap your neck." Victor pulled Adam's head back by his hair hard with his free hand. "Nod if you understand."

Adam nodded, swallowing hard. He remembered what he saw at the cemetery when they had left earlier. Could this man have anything to do with the stone angel seeming to come to life?

Victor released him and leaned back. "Now do as I say and face me." He ordered his tone low and cruel.

Adam did as told. He was shocked at what he saw. This couldn't be a man. He looked too powerful, too strong . . . too evil. He lowered his head and tried not to look at his face. "Who are you and what do you want?" He asked. "I have money if that's what you want. Tell me how much and I'll give it . . ."

"This isn't about money, Adam." Victor said cutting him off. "This is about justice." Slicking his black hair back Victor said, "Has anyone ever told you that it's impolite to avoid eye contact when you meet someone and carry on a conversation?"

Adam still didn't look Victor in the eyes. "Yes, of course. It's just that you look familiar. It's your eyes. I've seen you somewhere. So who are you?" Adam gazed at the store entrance hoping his dad would walk out soon. It would be one of the few times he'd be relieved to see him.

"I am Victor, the Master of The Dark One's and I'd prefer if you call me sir until we get better acquainted on my terms." Victor smiled holding out his hand. "You are Adam, correct?" He asked cocking his head to the side.

Adam stammered and took Victor's hand. "Y-y-yes Sir." He knew he had to look at Victor's face as much as he didn't want to. "How do you know my name?" He asked.

Victor released Adam's hand. It appalled him to touch a murderous human, let alone interact with him and try to appear friendly before unleashing the monster within. But, he knew if he didn't befriend this stupid fool he'd be forced to chase him down in a busy area which would break one of the rules of The Dark Ones which was to never make a scene in public. The new vampires learned this immediately. Victor smiled, amused. Showtime was about to begin. Adam wasn't the brightest and it would be easy to lure him away with him.

"I've been watching you for awhile, dear boy." Victor said. "Look into my eyes and tell me where you've seen me before. I bet you'll get it right with the first guess."

Adam's blood ran cold. Victor stared at him with the same red eyes the stone angel had at the cemetery. He shook his head in disbelief and said, "This can't be real. Simone's tombstone, the angel, it had the same red eyes." He turned around and fumbled with the door handle trying to open it. "It's my medication. This isn't real." He pounded the door with his fist. It was locked. "Let me go!" He screamed.

Victor smiled, his fangs protruding. "You're a funny lad, you know that?" He asked. "This is as real as it gets. Look at me and tell me if the angel had the same sweet smile as mine?"

"You're insane!" Adam hollered. Against his own wishes he glanced at Victor's fangs. "You'll pay for this."

Victor grabbed Adam's head and jerked his head backward. "No, you're wrong. You will pay for this. Remember the angel mouthed 'you' and it was directed towards you not me." Pulling Adam's hair he said, "I believe you're the one with a debt to pay. Eye for an eye my dear friend."

Adam winced. His head throbbed. "What are you talking about?"

Victor hated when the guilty played dumb and innocent. As if he was just going to let them go and forget about the debt they owed.

"You know I do sympathize with you in the fact that you were abused by your father your whole life and still are but unfortunately you played a role in the murder of an innocent woman leaving her fiancée mentally tortured and dead inside. For that you will pay."

"I don't understand. You're trying to tell me something as evil as you is capable of sympathy?" Adam asked. "That's what you just told me."

Victor let go of Adam's hair and yawned. "You're boring me, Adam. Of course I have sympathy. Let me share with you where my heart lies." He said making sure he had Adam's full attention before continuing. "I love children. I love good people. I hate evil cruel people who abuse either of them, but especially children. Do you understand so far?"

Adam nodded. He didn't dare say a word.

"Good," Victor stated. "I am a vampire who is 491 years old and as a mortal child I was abused by my parents. The moral of the story is most of the abuser's get away with what they do and the poor children continue to get abused in the most horrific ways. That's where I come in. I find these people and kill them freeing the little ones to find true happiness."

Adam stared at Victor, a cocky smile on his face. "Well then, I'm free to go because I've never hurt a child."

"Wipe that grin off your face. You are not free to go anywhere. You are a murderer."

Adam's temper flared. He reached back and punched Victor's face.

"That's for the false accusation you crazy man, vampire or whatever you are. Now, let me go!" Adam screeched.

"Tsk, tsk. You are going to pay now." Victor leaned forward grabbing Adams hand in his. Adam tried to wriggle his hand free but to no avail. Victor squeezed Adams hand hard until bones creaked. "Respect me or next time I will show no mercy and snap your wrist in two." He said and shoved Adams hand away from himself. "It's time to go." Victor opened the car door and stepped out.

Adam opened the car door and stood beside Victor. He didn't dare try and escape unless he wanted broken bones. He looked at the gun shop hoping his dad would see him and wonder what he was doing out of the car.

Victor answered his thoughts. "He won't see you so lose the false illusion of hope. Your dad has one thing on his mind and that's getting a special bullet to try and kill my hawk." Victor held Adam's arm and led him down the sidewalk.

Adam tried making eye contact with passer-bys but no one noticed Victor and him. "What's going on? Can't these people see us?" Adam asked walking faster to keep up with Victor. He looked back to see his father walk out of the store. "Hey, there's my dad."

Victor kept walking, eyes forward. "No one can see us. In a moment we are going to take flight." He jerked Adam's arm hard, pulled him under his arms like a football and ran. "Don't worry, you will be reunited with your dad soon and believe me it won't feel so good like the old popular song says." Victor jumped and ascended toward the clouds and flew in the direction of Armani's house. The wind was exhilarating. Such a freedom to feel it whip around you and feel one with the white billowy clouds.

Adam screamed. He watched as the people and buildings below him got smaller until everything looked like it was part of a Lego village built by a child. He wiggled and kicked trying to fight against Victor's grip. He knew he was going to die either way but he'd prefer to die by falling instead of at the hands of this sadistic vampire.

Victor tightened his grip around Adams wrists. He wasn't about to let this cowardly boy fall to his death. He wanted Armani to enjoy the revenge killing. He felt Adam go limp in his arms. Victor smiled wickedly. This was going to be more fun than he thought.

Alex opened the car door and threw the bag of bullets onto the seat next to him. Letting him self fall into the car he realized Adam wasn't where he was told to stay.

"Now where did that boy go?" He asked aloud. "I tell him to stay in the car and do you think he has the mental ability to listen? No, he's too stupid. Always has been." Alex groaned.

A piece of white paper lying on the floor of the car caught his eye. Alex leaned over, grabbed it and unfolded it. "Someone has sloppy handwriting," he said squinting to read it.

> *Dear Mr. Alex,*
>
> *Please don't be alarmed. Your son is in good hands. But, I must warn you this will not be the case if you don't respond and act with much haste. I want you to meet me tonight, nine o'clock sharp at Manhattan Park. I will be waiting for you near the black horse statue. Bring me two hundred thousand dollars for the release of your son.*
>
> *Most sincerely yours,*
> *Victor Ramirez, Master of The Dark Ones.*

Alex cursed and threw the letter on the passenger seat. What kind of sick joke was this? How much more drama would he have to endure for his son? This was getting absurd.

"Master of The Dark Ones?" He questioned aloud, his brow furrowed. "What in God's name was that? Some sort of devil worshipping cult?" He slammed his fists against the steering wheel and sounded the horn. Several people turned to stare at him.

He rolled down the window and yelled, "What are you staring at? Mind your own God damn business!" He turned the key in the ignition, shoved it in drive, did a U-turn and sped toward the bank, leaving people staring after him with shocked expressions.

Alex laughed. He watched their expressions in the rear view mirror. "Well, Victor I will see you at nine o'clock with two things for you. The money and my gun loaded with special gold plated bullets." He stated smiling like he had just won the lottery. "I never lose."

Chapter Thirty-Three

Armani paced the living room floor pausing every couple minutes to glare at Donovan and Rex. "Is someone going to tell me just what the hell is going on here?" Armani asked. "Why is Gabe cooped up like a dog in my kennel? What the hell did I do to myself by crossing over?" He rubbed his face and continued pacing.

Rex spoke first. "Gabe was one of the men responsible for killing Simone and torturing you . . ." He blurted out only to be cut off by Donovan.

"Please Rex. There is a proper way to say these things." Donovan stated glaring at Rex. In the blink of an eye he was beside Armani restraining him.

"Let me go!" Armani ordered. "I'm going to kill him!"

Rex shivered. Armani's eyes were bright red, his face a mask of anger. He watched Armani lift his head and stare at the ceiling his fangs long and sharp ready to tear Gabe to shreds.

Donovan held him. "Armani," He ordered. "Calm yourself down."

Armani took a few deep breaths trying to relax. "I can't. I want to kill him now." He balled his fists tight, digging his sharp nails into his hands and blood dripped down his arms.

Donovan released Armani and led him to the sofa and forced him to take a seat. "Get a hold of yourself and your emotions. First of all, Gabe isn't the only one responsible. There are two other men." Donovan stated matter of fact.

A shocked expression on his face, Armani asked, "How do you know? Why have you done nothing to end their lives?" He was angrier than a thousand bees when their hive is disrupted. Thoughts of strangling Donovan entered his mind but left just as quickly. He forced himself to think logically. He knew if he tried to harm Donovan he wouldn't stand a chance against him. He saw the blood dripping down his arms and asked Rex to get him a box of tissues. "God knows I don't dare stand up for fear that Master Donovan will restrain me." He snickered and glared at Donovan.

"Very funny, Armani," Donovan retorted. "Please keep your smart ass comments and humor to yourself when Victor is present. He is not as patient as I."

Rex threw him the box of tissues and walked to the window. "I heard something." He said and pulled the curtains back and gazed out at the snow covered earth.

Donovan rushed beside Rex and peered out. "Armani, stay seated." He ordered. "It's Victor and he brought a guest with him."

Donovan shuffled nervously and splayed his fingers over and over in the same motion.

"Man Donovan for being a vampire I didn't think you got nervous." Rex said shocked.

Armani watched Rex and Donovan stare out the window like two little boys waiting for Santa Claus to bring gifts on Christmas morning.

"Do you recognize him?" Donovan asked Rex pointing to the man in Victor's grasp.

"Rex squinted shading his eyes from the sun with his hand. After a long pause he said, "No, I don't have any idea who that is. I've never seen him in my life."

Donovan knew it was one of two people. Either one of Gabe's associates in the killing of Simone or it could be a man Victor picked up that was slipping through the cracks of the justice system and Victor had brought him here as an example of how The Dark One's reacquainted guilty people with the law. He hoped it was the first. He didn't want Victor setting an example for Armani and showing him the ropes. Donovan shuddered. Victor let the torturing get out of hand and more blood was shed than necessary when ending the lives of the guilty.

Donovan and Rex watched Victor descend from the sky his black cape swirling behind him. Victor's feet touched the ground gracefully like a swans landing on water. He released his grip and threw Adam.

"Recognize this place, Adam?" Victor asked making a circle around the area with his arms. "I know you've been here a couple times with your dear daddy. Am I right?"

Adam gazed around the large property. "I don't know what you're talking about." He said quietly and lowered his head.

Victor picked him up and shook him. "You know exactly what I'm talking about. Fess up, son or I will kill you right here and now." He set him down, folded his arms and waited for a response.

Rex's jaw dropped. "What is he doing? You have to help that young kid." He waited a minute and walked toward the door. "If you're just going to stand there and let that monster you call the Master beat on some innocent boy then I'll go out and take matters into my own hands."

"You will do no such thing if you value your own life." Donovan ordered. "Victor would not bring him here if he wasn't guilty of something."

Victor uncrossed his arms and tapped his foot giving Adam one more chance to tell the truth. 'Coward,' he thought. "I'm going to count to five and if you don't tell me the truth I will snap your neck faster than you can blink." He stated holding up five fingers. He started the count. "One," he said pulling one finger down. "Two."

Adam stared at Victor and said, "O.K., O.K, I'll tell you the truth."

Victor grabbed Adam by the throat and held his face inches from his own and sneered. "Good boy. I knew you'd see things my way." He set him on his feet and added, "Honestly, you have nothing to lose now."

Adam wasn't sure what this Victor thing meant by that. It meant he would either live or die for telling the truth. In a shaky voice, Adam told Victor everything.

Gabe hollered from the dog kennel. "Shut your mouth, you coward!"

Victor rolled his eyes. "The only coward here is you, Gabe. You know you're going to die and can't even die like a real man. Maybe if you would've been honest, I'd be more kind to you." He took Adam's hand, leading him to the house. He stared at Adam and said, "For your honesty I am going to lock you up in the house, not this dog kennel."

"Why can't I just go home?" Adam asked. "I did what you said. I told you the truth with God as my witness." He held his free hand over his heart. "Please."

Victor knew Adam's heart was empty, ruthless and angry. The way he killed Simone and the pride he felt in having her stare into his eyes when she took her last breath. This boy was pushing Victor's patience and he was on the brink of exploding. "Yes, you told me the truth and no, you are not free to go. Think about what you did to Simone and the reason why. That, my friend, is why you're going to die."

Adam dragged his heels in the dirt. "No. I'm not going to die. Damn it! I told you the truth. Didn't you hear me?" He asked, desperate.

Victor tugged Adam hard making him yelp. "Adam in life every man needs to learn a lesson and the lesson here for you is that the truth will not set you free this time."

Gabe laughed. "We're going to die, little man. The only person missing is your old man . . . ." He trailed off.

Victor turned and stared at Gabe. "Shut your filthy mouth or I'll gut you like a deer right here and now."

Tears streamed down Adam's lion shaped face. "Oh God, what have I done? Just kill me now."

"That would be too easy." Victor replied. "Come along, let's get moving. I'm going to store you in the garage for your crocodile tears."

From inside the house Donovan and Rex watched in silence. Armani stood and stretched. This whole thing was more than he could bear.

"I'm going to take a shower and relax for a while. I need some time alone." He said and walked to the stairwell. "Please respect my wishes for complete solitude and privacy at this time."

"It is done." Donovan said and smiled sympathetically at Armani. "Be on your way." He watched Armani walk to the stairs with a pain swelling in his heart. Armani would never be the same. Happiness was but a dream for him that would never come true.

"He'll never be happy, will he?" Rex asked searching Donovan's face for any sign of hope.

Donovan wished he could lie to Rex and tell him everything would be OK, but he knew it would not. Avoiding eye contact he responded, "I will do everything in my power to make Armani happy." He slipped his cloak on motioning for Rex to come by his side. "Victor will be coming inside soon. Stand close to me for the introductions."

Rex didn't budge.

"Please." Donovan said. "It's for your own safety. I will not let any harm come to you."

Slow and steady footsteps approached the front door forcing Rex to obey Donovan. The handle twisted and the door slowly creaked open. Rex's face paled. He gripped a handful of Donovan's cloak in his palm squeezing hard. Beads of sweat perspired on his forehead.

Victor walked in with an aura that demanded respect. He eyed Rex with an evil gleam in his cold eyes and licked his lips.

"Victor," Donovan stated, "This is Rex, Armani's best friend and former band mate." He placed his arm around Rex's shoulder and scooted him towards Victor. "I've become quite fond of Rex as well, I might add." He smiled. "He is a wonderful and courageous man."

Victor took Rex's hand. "Nice to finally meet you face to face, Rex. Any friend of Donovan's is a friend of mine." He smiled warmly. "I trust his judgment of mortals and vampire's with all of my being."

Rex breathed, relieved. He was standing in a room with two very powerful vampires who could kill him in a second if they wished. What kind of mess has Armani gotten himself into? How did these two vampires find Armani and convince him to cross over? So many questions he knew might never get answered. Victor released his hand. Rex rubbed his hand on his side trying to warm it. Victor's touch was cold.

"Where's Armani?" Victor asked scanning the room. "We need to celebrate his transformation and give him a proper welcome into the family of The Dark Ones."

Donovan cleared his throat and replied, "He needed some time alone. He's upstairs relaxing."

"I shall go and speak to him myself then." Victor stated his tone bitter. "This is no way to celebrate new life."

"Wait . . ." Donovan said. But it was too late. Victor was halfway up the stairs and silenced Donovan with a wave of his hand.

Donovan and Rex stood staring as Victor's tall dark shadow dimmed into nothingness.

CHAPTER THIRTY-FOUR

K ATRINA WOKE WITH a jump. It took her a minute to remember where she was, Victors home. How would she get out of here? She closed her eyes trying desperately to hold back the tears. The only thing she could see was Gordon's mutilated body and the image of Victor wielding the chainsaw in his hands carving him like a pumpkin. She sat up and swung her legs over the bed. The large bedroom was decorated to perfection. Paintings by Picasso hung on the white walls and pretty pink flowers sat on two oak dressers.

"Impressive," Katrina said aloud. Most of the decoration in Victor's home was dark and dreary, including the pictures. She remembered the pictures that hung in the hallway on the fourth floor of abused and sad children. It was heartbreaking. Victor still hadn't told her what they meant or why he had them hanging in his house. What kind of morbid sick man or vampire in this case had those kinds of things hanging on their walls like a trophy? Sick.

She saw a full bath at the end of the bedroom. A hot bath sounded inviting. She stood and her legs felt weak. She slowly walked to the bathroom, stopping at the entrance. A large whirlpool bath welcomed her. She turned the water on and picked up the lavender scented bubble bath pouring a cap full in. Maybe this would help her feel human again. She scoffed. Here she was trapped in a vampire's home that seemed to be in love with her or something. She knew nothing about him except that he was the leader of some Dark Ones cult. "We promote Justice," Katrina said aloud repeating what Victor had told her. She laughed. There had to be a way out of this house and by God, after her bath she was going to find it.

Katrina stripped her clothes off, glanced in the mirror and shuddered. It looked like she had been hit by a few too many trains. Her hair was tousled in different directions, her eyes swollen and her lips were chapped. She leaned forward and touched the bags under her eyes. She pushed them in and watched in horror as they slowly popped out. "This is beyond gross." She stated sticking her tongue out. She saw a red envelope sitting on the counter and picked it up. Her name was written on it in perfect penmanship. She was almost scared to open it because she knew who it was from. She bit her lip and carefully opened it pulling out a white card.

> *My dear Katrina,*
>
> *I hope you had a peaceful rest. I apologize that I cannot be home with you right now but I will be soon. I must also apologize for the gruesome events you had to watch but it was important that you see what The Dark Ones stand for. There are a few things you may use for your personal hygiene in the bathroom. I'm new to having a woman in my home but in time I will learn everything about you and will strive to please you in all things. Please don't try to escape for you are all I have ever wanted in a woman. And if you leave I promise that I will hunt you down and find you no matter where you go. Much to discuss when I get home, including my request of you*
> *. . . . .*

Sincerely yours,
Victor, Master of The Dark Ones.

Katrina threw the letter on the counter. Creasing her brow, she shut the water off and pushed a button. Bubbles swarmed and circled in the large bathtub. The smell of lavender and vanilla mesmerized her. She put one leg in the tub and sighed. A taste of Heaven in a place called Hell. She swung her other leg into the tub and immersed her body letting the water envelope her. She closed her eyes and tried to relax but the letter kept invading her thoughts. 'I will hunt you down,' Victor had written. Chills ran down her spine. She wrapped her arms around herself trying to find comfort. She had to think logically. Something else troubled her about the letter. The request Victor had of her. What could that possibly be? He mentioned this when she was first in his home and she had a sinking feeling she didn't want to know. She leaned back drenching her hair in the water. No matter the request, Victor wouldn't take no for an answer. So, it would be more of a demand than a request. She'd have no choice but to agree, unless of course, she managed to escape.

What she thought would be a long bath turned out to be a ten minute dunk. Time was of the essence here. She wished she could stay in the bathtub forever but she had to get out, get dressed and devise a plan. Careful not to slip she stepped out of the tub wrapping her self in a large lush purple towel. It was soft and smelled like fresh linen straight off the clothesline. Savoring the scent for a minute a tear slipped from her eye. It reminded her of home. Her poor dog has been alone all this time. Could he be dead? Victor was selfish not to bring him to his home for her. She asked him several times and he acted like she was speaking a foreign language. This refueled her anger at Victor. She threw the towel over the door and ran into the bedroom ransacking the drawers for something to wear. Each drawer was full of clothes and ironically enough all of them were her size. She took slow steps to the closet and opened the door. She gasped. There were gorgeous ballroom dresses sparkling like diamonds in the sunlight, at least twenty pairs of shoes, sweaters, jackets, scarves, hats, gloves, boots and running shoes. She had never seen so many wonderful and expensive clothes except in the magazines or high end clothing stores. Places she didn't frequent.

She trotted to back to the drawers, rummaged through them and pulled out a pair of black sweats and a black hooded sweatshirt. She slid them on and grabbed a green Patagonia coat and a pair of running shoes. Checking the size she grinned. A size too big but that worked to her advantage. It was hard to run in boots and double socks would keep her feet warm. She had no intention of walking away from Victor's home. Hell no. Katrina was going to run like an inmate escaping prison. Hat, gloves and scarf on and she was ready to play detective determined to get out of this house and away from Victor forever. She wasn't going to let him intimidate her with his threats.

Where to start? The bedroom window was the place to start. One room at a time is how she would do it. Eventually she would find an escape route. She tried to open the window but it wouldn't even budge. Sighing she moved on and scolded herself. Of course Victor wouldn't allow anything in the bedroom to be a means of escape.

An hour later she gave up on the rooms upstairs. Katrina raced down the steps two at a time and ran to the front door. She twisted the knob and pulled. The door opened and a rush of cool air blew in. "This is way too easy." She said and looked behind her to see if anyone was waiting to lunge at her. The house was quiet and empty. Why would Victor leave the front door unlocked? He had to know she would leave if given the opportunity. Maybe he thought she would be too scared to try after reading the letter. No, that didn't make sense. She was a stubborn girl and already escaped once. She glanced at the grandfather clock sitting against the wall, four o' clock. There was still enough daylight to find her way through the forest surrounding Victor's home. She took a deep breath and walked down the steps holding the railing. At the bottom of the steps she turned and looked at Victor's home for what she hoped would be the last time and ran like hell into the forest.

Chapter Thirty-Five

"I HOPE ARMANI IS receptive to Victor for all our sakes." Donovan said looking at the clock. "Victor has an appointment at nine so he wants to make sure Armani learns all there is to know about The Dark Ones." He shrugged and said, "At least what he needs to know for the time being."

Rex coughed. "Do you think Victor will hurt him?"

"No. Not in a million years. The only reason he would is if Armani becomes an evil vampire and loses the vision of The Dark Ones and what we stand for. In that situation I cannot guarantee his safety." Donovan said like a professor giving a lecture. "I know for a fact he would be killed in a horrific manner. Why don't you go home and get some rest." Donovan said walking to the closet and pulling out Rex's coat. "You need it. I hate to say this but you look a frightful mess." He said and smiled sheepishly.

Rex ran his fingers through his hair. "Yeah, I'm sure I do but I don't care." He said rubbing his eyes. "I guess I am pretty tired." He took the coat from Donovan and stood. "Please take good care of my friend."

Donovan took Rex's hand and gave it a reassuring squeeze. "You have my word."

Rex made eye contact with Donovan and smiled. "Thank you, Donovan for being so kind and patient with Armani and me. I appreciate it more than you know." He slipped into his jacket, zipped it to his neck and walked to the door. With his hand on the door handle he said, "Keep in touch. You have my cell phone number."

"Will do," Donovan said. He drifted to the door and watched Rex walk to his car. He knew Rex had many unanswered questions and in time he would provide the answers. He closed the door and listened to the sounds of the house. Panic struck him. Victor was speaking in a loud tone which was never a good sign. Armani must be giving him a hard time. Something you don't do to the Master. Donovan heard Armani hollering at Victor.

"I refuse to drink anyone's blood, Victor!" Armani yelled. "It'll never happen. All I want is to avenge Simone's death and I'm out of here."

Victor paced back and forth in Armani's bedroom. "I'm afraid that's where you're wrong, my friend. 'Out of here' you say," he laughed. "That sounds like such a mortal's statement. You are not going to be 'out of here' as you say. You are now a member of The Dark Ones. We are family. Didn't Donovan explain things to you before you agreed to cross over?"

Armani didn't have a chance to answer. Donovan walked into the room apologizing to both Victor and Armani that indeed he deceived Armani in order to get him to cross over.

Victor wagged his finger at Donovan. "Shame, shame, you know better than to deceive a prospective new member."

"Since when do you care about morals, Victor?" Donovan shot back. "He's a vampire now and part of the strongest team of vigilante's around." Donovan crossed his arms standing a few feet from Victor.

Victor shot him a venomous glare. "You dare insult me in front of our new member." Victor paced the room and stopped at the window staring at the landscape. "I see the hawk is keeping guard of Gabe." He pivoted and faced Donovan and said, "At least one of us is doing their job around here."

Armani had enough. "Is someone going to explain to me what is going to happen to me? I want to die once I have avenged Simone's death. That is all." He said toying with his hands. "I find it a rather simple request."

Donovan gave Armani a sympathetic look. "I'm sorry, Armani. I have failed you."

Victor sat in an easy chair glaring at both vampires. "You both sound pathetic. Where's the longing for revenge? What happened to wanting to rid the world of sick men and women who escape the justice system? We are the only ones who can help save the innocent people being tortured by these fools that escape the hand of the law." He stared at Donovan and said, "You were like a son to me."

"I still am," Donovan shot back. "You and I are not the issue here. I believe we need to let Armani know every single detail about The Dark Ones. And by that I mean everything."

"How can I die once I have completed my task?" Armani asked. "Please tell me I can. I cannot bear to remain alive for all eternity without Simone. Killing the guilty men won't bring her back and will not fill the hole in my heart." A tear slipped from his eye. He quickly wiped it away with his shirt sleeve. "Pardon me." He apologized. "The pain of losing Simone is still very real and alive for me. It's as if it just happened yesterday."

This gesture softened Victor. He flew to Armani's side taking his hand in his. "No need to apologize to us, my friend. Donovan and I both know pain. That's why we are what we are. We have used the painful experiences in our lives in a positive way. Granted, you and Donovan were never abused as a child like I was, but you know deep excruciating pain, the type of pain that cuts deep into the heart." Victor's voice shook. He placed his fist over his heart. "It hurts. It will always hurt but the pain lessens in time. It's like a flesh wound. At first it's deep, it hurts and seems it will never heal but in time the pain subsides and sure, there's still a scar but it looks and feels better. Does that make sense to you, Armani?" Victor floated to Donovan and stood next to him. "This man lost the love of his life too. I saved him from killing himself. Tell me, Donovan, has the wound of losing your lover healed in time?"

Victor thought of Katrina. She could be the love of his life, should she choose to be his forever. He realized he couldn't force her to stay. That wouldn't be true love. He wanted her to love him for what he could be if given the chance. He left her a note but also left the door unlocked. He would know her choice when he arrived home. He realized that he too may be able to relate to losing someone. He didn't love Katrina but he knew he could love her in time.

Donovan nodded. "Yes, to a degree." He paused. "What I mean by that is that the memories of her don't make me want to die. They make me want to live. I kill people who are hurt the way my love was hurt by her uncle. For many years he tortured her emotionally, mentally and physically and the sad part is I never knew. Now I seek and destroy men who do this to their family members." He wrapped his cloak tighter around him and added, "It brings me peace. Every kill makes me feel like I'm putting a band-aid on the wound left after she died."

"Does that help?" Victor asked Armani staring deep into his eyes searching his soul.

Armani lowered his gaze. "I'm sorry but no it doesn't." What they said made sense but he had no desire to be a vampire and have eternal life. There had to be a way to kill yourself. Every piece of fiction he read about vampires, there was always a way they could be killed. It could be exposure to sunlight, beheading, garlic, holy water or spearing a cross through their heart. He had to find out what ended the life of a member of The Dark Ones. "May I ask a question? You promise to answer honestly?" Armani asked looking from Victor to Donovan.

Donovan cleared his throat, smiled and said yes. Not Victor. He was a savvy smart vampire, the fearless leader, the Alpha and always took precautions. With him trust was earned and never had he trusted an immortal or mortal until they proved they could be trusted.

Victor laughed. It sounded more like a growl. "Armani, the level of an honest answer depends on the question. I promise to listen to your question and answer it as honestly as I deem necessary." Victor pointed at Armani. "Ask your question. I don't have patience for beating around the bush types." He glanced at the clock and added, "I have an appointment at nine so let's make this quick." He ordered. Nodding, he waited.

Armani licked his lips and touched the burnt side of his face. "How do we die?" Glancing at Donovan he continued, "There has to be a way to terminate the vampires. It's in all the fiction novels and I know from what Donovan told me that many new vampires in The Dark Ones have to be terminated due to the evil permeating from within their souls and the bad choices they make." He waited for an answer. "Tell me the truth. Please."

Donovan kept his mouth shut. He wasn't about to tell Armani how to destroy himself. He knew that's what Armani planned to do once he avenged Simone's death. Armani would prove to be a key figure in The Dark Ones. They needed him.

Victor stood in front of Armani and took his face in his hands. "I will give you an honest answer and only because something has changed my way of thinking. I realize that everyone deserves free choice, not a person dictating them by telling them what to believe or what choices to make." He released Armani's face and walked away. With his back to Donovan and Armani he lifted a finger in the air and stated, "This is strictly confidential between the three of us." He faced Armani and a shocked Donovan, drew in a deep breath and said, "Fire destroys us."

"Why in the hell would you tell him that, Victor?" Donovan asked. "You know he wants to die after he kills the men who killed Simone and stole his soul." He shook his head in disbelief and stared at Victor. "You're going to be held responsible if any harm comes to Armani."

Victor shrugged slicking his jet-black hair off his face. His eyes showed no compassion. "That is something I am ready to face. I did the right thing and you know that."

"Thank you kindly, Victor." Armani said. "I appreciate your honesty and trusting me enough to share the darkest secret of The Dark Ones."

Donovan smirked at Armani. "It's a dark secret I hope you have no intention of fulfilling. Death by fire is a painful death and I cannot assure you that your soul will go to Heaven. You will die and be free from this world and your life as a vampire but there is no guarantee you will be with Simone." Donovan wondered if Armani would still feel grateful for the honesty now. Damn Victor for telling Armani this.

Armani's brow creased. "What do you mean? You don't know if I will be with Simone once I end my immortal life?" He asked rising to his feet, his face and eyes red with anger. He picked up a lamp and threw it at the wall smashing it into pieces. "Damn you both! You cursed me forever and for that I will never forgive you." He walked up to Donovan and spit in his face. "Fuck you!" He screamed. "My life is an eternal hell now. I feel like a minion of the Devil thanks to you both." He walked past Victor purposely bumping his shoulder with force. "Call me when the guilty men are all here." Armani ordered and stomped out of the room and down the stairs.

Donovan raced after Armani but was stopped by Victor at the doorway. "Let him go. Time is what he needs." Victor ordered.

"Time is what he needs?" Donovan questioned. "Have you lost your mind? He is on a quest to do two things: get revenge and commit suicide. You know that. Why would you tell him how to die?"

Victor grabbed Donovan's shoulders and shook him. "Have you forgotten I'm the Master? No one questions my motives, not even you." He released his grip and stared into Donovan's eyes. "My theory is that if Armani kills himself then he was never fit to be a member of The Dark Ones in the first place." Running his fingers across his cheekbones he traced his finger down to the tip of his chin. "I consider it a test of sorts."

"Do you care about anyone except yourself? You seem to have lost your mind." Donovan stated flatly.

Victor laughed. "You're a funny vampire telling me your assumptions of my actions." His face turned to stone and evil gleamed in his eyes. "Armani must ask himself a very simple question and that is 'do you really want to die?' He knows there is no guarantee that he will be with Simone. It's a risk I don't see him taking." Victor stated lighting a cigar. He inhaled and exhaled blowing smoke rings into the air. "He doesn't strike me as the tragic type. I don't see him playing Russian roulette with his existence now." Using his bony finger he speared the rings. "He lost Simone once. Armani won't risk losing the memory of Simone."

"Sir, with all due respect these are all just mere speculations." Donovan said. "Your theory of a man you really don't know."

"Ah, but I do know him. I've watched him for years. Long before I sent you to be his guardian." Victor smiled a crooked grin. "Also, he's not a man anymore, Donovan. He's a vampire now. Get it right."

The front door slammed followed by a blood-curdling scream from outside. Donovan and Victor ran to the bedroom window and saw Armani inside the dog kennel stabbing Gabe over and over. Blood splattered everywhere. Gabe's hands were in front of his face while pleading and begging for mercy.

"Oh God, no." Donovan stammered.

Victor grinned. "Oh God, yes. This is better than watching Sunday afternoon football."

Donovan faced Victor. "I didn't know you watched football." He stated, shocked.

"I don't. That's what mortals would say, correct?" Victor stared with delight at his newest vampire. "I love him already. Now this is entertainment for vampires, the merciless slaying of the guilty." Victor walked away from the window wrapping his cloak around him. "This reassures my thinking that Armani won't kill himself. He will have such a high, a rush from killing Gabe that he will want to continue in the works and mission of The Dark Ones."

"I hope you're right," Donovan said watching Armani tear Gabe to pieces.

"Have faith in me as you once did," Victor said. "I must go now to meet Alex at Manhattan Park."

The room was cold. Donovan turned to say something but Victor was gone. A mist like fog floated where he stood only a second ago.

Armani stared at what remained of Gabe. "Take that you son of a bitch!" He felt good. The floodgates of anger opened in his heart with each stab into Gabe's filthy body. "I hope you burn in Hell forever." He knew killing Gabe and the others wouldn't bring Simone back but it brought peace into his heart and soul. That is if he still had a soul. Donovan claimed he might not be with Simone if he killed himself. But there was a 50/50 chance he would. Was it worth the risk? Life as he knew it now was hell. What difference would it make?

He grasped the knife with both hands and held it high above his head. "This one's for Simone." Gritting his teeth he brought the knife down. Seconds before piercing Gabe's mutilated body a strong firm hand gripped his arm and squeezed like a python. The knife fell and Donovan kicked it to the side.

"That's enough, Armani." Donovan said. "You did what was necessary. He's dead. Let it go."

Armani stood tall and faced Donovan. "Let it go. Let it go, you say. I will never let it go."

"Come. It's dark and cold out here. You need to clean yourself up." Donovan said. "Gabe is dead. Why do you feel the need to stab an already dead man?" He questioned. "You must tame the rage or lose yourself to evil."

"The last stab was going to be for Simone."

"Wasn't every stab for Simone?" Donovan fired back.

Donovan stared at Armani eyes seeing nothing but darkness. Evil penetrated around them. He had to keep a closer watch over Armani. He feared Armani was susceptible to allowing evil to control and dominate him. Snapping his fingers in front of Armani's eyes he said, "You must learn when to turn the evil off. The only other vampire I've seen act as you have during a kill is Victor. You must never let the darkness control you. Once it does you become its prisoner and there's no escape."

Armani's eyes bore into Donovan. "What do you mean?"

Donovan took Armani's arm and led him to the house. "It's simple. Everyone has good and evil within them. We must control our emotions or they will control us. That applies to both humans as well as us vampires."

Armani looked confused. "If I kill as Victor does then why isn't Victor pure evil as you presume?" He stopped walking and faced Donovan.

Donovan stared straight ahead. "Victor is a four hundred ninety one year old vampire and has years of experience and control over himself. You are merely a day old in the vampire sense."

"What makes you so different from Victor?" Armani asked. He had so many questions and was prepared to ask Donovan each and every one tonight. The need to know everything about The Dark Ones weighed heavy on his heart.

"We are really no different, just as you are no different from us.

Age is our difference and that is all. Victor kills in torturous ways and enjoys each and every minute of it." Donovan said his lips turned down for a second. "I kill for justice and justice alone. It's not something I look forward to or enjoy doing. I'd much rather see the world as a peaceful place without evil people. But, wouldn't we all?" He questioned and shrugged. "But unfortunately we live in an imperfect world."

Armani nodded in agreement. Donovan always seemed to make sense when he spoke. He had respected him almost instantly. "Were you a professor at one point?" Armani couldn't help asking.

Donovan smiled. "Yes, I was." He answered. "You're very observant. How did you know, my dear friend?"

Armani shrugged. "You speak as an instructor does. I could see it right away in the professional way you carry yourself and in your manner of speaking." Armani stared at the house looking up at his bedroom window. He closed his eyes wishing when he opened them that Simone would be standing at the window waving at him. Armani opened his eyes, glanced at the window and lowered his head. A red teardrop splashed onto the baby powder white snow. He quickly shuffled his feet trying to cover it up. He was sick of having his weakness and pain on display all the time.

Donovan saw the teardrop. His heart went out to Armani. The poor soul was struggling each and every minute of the day. "Armani, remember I lost my love in the same manner as you. I know exactly what you're feeling and going through." He stopped to face Armani. "Look at me," he ordered. He waited until Armani's gaze locked with his. "You are not weak. You have every right to mourn the loss of Simone for as long as you need to. Pain, agony and suffering have to be dealt with and there is no time limit on how long a heart takes to heal. I still feel the pain of losing my fiancée."

Armani heard sincerity in Donovan's voice and saw it in his eyes. He wasn't alone after all. He knew Donovan would prove to be a true friend in the end. Victor, on the other hand, was not one Armani saw himself warming up to. He seemed to be more of a loner and happy being that way.

"Has Victor always been a loner?" Armani asked. "He just seems so cold and brash. Do you understand what I mean?"

Donovan laughed. "Of course I understand exactly what you mean and yes, Victor enjoys a solitary life. He's a vampire who has little need for relations of any kind. Although, I will say that Victor is devoted to The Dark Ones with all of his being. He would die for each and every one of us vampires." He took Armani's arm leading him to the house and continued to talk. "I already discussed Victor's childhood with you. It should give you an understanding of his issues with trust and love. I'm afraid he isn't capable of neither of those two things immediately. Give him time and he'll warm up to you. Contrary to what he displays, he does have much kindness and goodness in him." Donovan pointed to the black hawk perched high in an oak tree overlooking the house. "Look at him. He's my protector and my friend, a gift from Victor."

Armani stared at the hawk like a lamb in the presence of a lion.

Donovan sensed Armani's fear. "No need to fear him. He's harmless to vampires and people who are good." Donovan reassured him. "My point is that if Victor was cold and ruthless he wouldn't have sent a hawk to be my protector. Do you see what I'm saying? Does that make sense to you?" Donovan questioned.

Armani thought for a moment and nodded. "I understand. If Victor was only evil and selfish he never would've cared enough for your safety by giving you that hawk." He walked up the steps and opened the door. "Come on, it's cold and I'm a mess. I want to wash Gabe's blood off me." He finished disgusted.

"You will be getting a hawk as well." Donovan said once inside the house. "Don't say I told you, though."

Armani took his shirt off and threw it in the trash. "Do all the members of The Dark Ones have a hawk watching over them?" He asked.

"No, only a few of us do."

"Why is that? Doesn't Victor want all his vampires protected?" Armani asked a puzzled look on his face.

"He does want them all protected but he chooses a select few to have a hawk." Donovan stated and sat on the couch. "I'm going to tell you something if you can swear to secrecy."

Facing Donovan, Armani said, "Yes, I can. You can trust me." He folded his arms over his bare chest and waited.

"Victor likes you a lot. He thinks highly of you just as he does me. When I first crossed over, Victor referred to me as his son." Donovan paused and smiled. "He hasn't said it but I know he views you as a son, too."

Shrugging, Armani walked to the bar and poured two glasses of brandy on the rocks. "Is that supposed to make me feel better? To be honest it doesn't." He handed Donovan a glass and sat across from him.

"No, it's not supposed to make you feel better. Only you can make yourself feel better. But, it should give you some encouragement in your new life as a vampire. Victor chose you because he sees so much potential and has great respect for you. He's been watching you for years, my friend." Donovan said taking a sip of brandy and licking his lips. "Ah, now this hits the spot. Thank you kindly." He said raising his glass to Armani.

"If he has been watching me for years then why did he allow Simone to die? Why didn't he stop it?"

"Armani, first of all, Victor is not God and never will be. He is not omnipresent. You and Simone were attacked at a hotel, not at your home. Victor was not your personal bodyguard and was not there to stop the horrific and brutal attack on you both. Believe me, if he had been there those men would have been unrecognizable to the human eye."

"I guess I don't understand why he couldn't have stopped it before it happened then." Armani stated angrily and rubbed the burnt side of

his face. His face felt like it was on fire when he got angry. "Well . . . ."
He trailed off waiting for an answer.

"Armani, do you fully understand what we're about?" Donovan asked not waiting for a reply. "The Dark Ones are about serving justice where it has been overlooked, ignored or is just not known to anyone. We cannot avenge the deaths of anyone if they are living. Our code prohibits us from killing someone without a justifiable cause, which in our circle of vampires means the guilty ones have murdered or abused someone. Victor could not kill Gabe, Adam or Alex without them having committed a crime. He heard their conversations about what they wanted to do but as they say, it's only talk. As I'm sure you're aware, talk is cheap and actions speak louder than words. Talking of committing a crime is different than actually committing the crime. For all Victor knew, these men were full of shit and could have backed out of doing it in the end. That would make Victor a killer, a murderer. No worse than these men. We must never kill or avenge wrongdoings unless we see or witness the crime being done. Victor tends to target adults and people who abuse children and he witnesses the acts being done before he plans his attack. Believe me you never want to see Victor in action. He's ruthless in his technique. He makes his victims suffer but rightfully so."

"They should suffer. It's what they deserve. Don't you make your victims suffer for the crimes committed on innocent humans?" Armani asked. He set his glass down and stood.

Donovan thought for a second and answered. "Every member of The Dark Ones has their own technique. I make my kills swift and deliberate. I for one don't care to waste my time playing games with the scumbags of the human race. The less time I have to see them and hear them cry out their innocence the better for me. I target a wide range of people who commit crimes, but all are murderers."

Armani was silent allowing this new information to sink in.

Donovan smiled. All this questioning from Armani had to be a good sign. Why would he ask questions of this nature if he planned on killing himself once he avenged the death of Simone? He wouldn't. Relief flooded his soul. He changed the subject and suggested that Armani take a shower.

"That's a wonderful idea. I will be back in awhile." Armani said walking to the stairs. "You're welcome to use a bathroom and shower if you would like." Halfway up the stairs, Armani stopped and looked at Donovan. "By the way, I think you should know that suicide is still weighing heavily on my mind. I'm a curious man and ask many questions. Don't read into them and make assumptions." That being said he turned and took the rest of the steps two at a time.

Donovan frowned. He had to convince Armani that suicide was not the solution. Armani was not a coward and by God, he was going to do everything in his power to keep him from taking the easy way out. The road to recovery was a tough one but well worth it. Donovan knew the pains of losing the one special person you loved like no other.

He knew what he had to do when Armani finished showering. The same thing he did for himself so many centuries ago. He must convince Armani to live for those he lost and will lose along the way. It was going to prove to be difficult but he had to try with all his might before it was too late.

CHAPTER THIRTY-SIX

ALEX SAT ON a bench near the black horse statue in Manhattan Park. Where in God's name was this son of a bitch named Victor, The Master of The Dark Ones? Alex scoffed. What the hell kind of joke was this? Alex stroked the gun hidden in the inside pocket of his long brown trench coat. This guy would prove to be an easy kill for him. He was probably on all sorts of drugs. Gazing at the seat beside him he patted the black briefcase full of money. He had no intention of losing this money. Not today and not for his son. To his surprise there were still people walking through the park at this time of night. Victor sure wasn't too smart when it came to picking a spot to meet. This was a public place, not an abandon old building or someplace he would've chosen for a meeting of this nature.

A woman passed, glanced at him and smiled. Alex returned the smile. She sure was a pretty little thing dressed in a black sweat suit, jogging boots and a pink hat on her head. Long auburn hair flowed behind her back. He checked his watch, a few minutes before nine. Why not get this fine young woman's number? Once this meeting was done he could call her and take her out for a victory celebration. Only she wouldn't know what the celebration was about. He waved her over to him and stood waiting for her to jog his way.

"Hello. My name is Alex and you are?" He asked extending his hand.

"Michelle. It's nice to meet you." She said smiling sweetly. "What are you doing in the park at night?" She asked.

Michelle was a bit too nosy for Alex's taste. It was none of her business what he was doing here. He had a right to be at the park just like anyone else. However one look in her eyes changed his mind. She was a beauty, a trophy for him and he planned to have his way with her tonight once he was finished meeting with the nutcase who claimed to have his son held hostage. Fuck his son. He'd kill Victor, get his son, beat the shit out of him and lock him up in the garage. His reward would be picking up this beauty, taking her out and bringing her home so he could make sweet love to her all night long.

"I come here to relax after a long days work at the office." He stated smiling warmly at her.

Michelle eyed him up and down. "I assumed you had been working. You're dressed in business attire." She chuckled and cocked her head to the side. "It's funny I've never seen you here before."

Alex dismissed her comment with a wave of his hand. "I don't work late every night and I most certainly don't come to the park every time I'm stressed. A lot of times I prefer the local bar and a nice cold drink for relaxation."

"That's understandable." Michelle said. "I best get going. I have one more mile to run."

Alex pulled a business card out of his pocket careful not to expose the gun. Handing it to her he smiled and asked, "Could I interest you in a drink with me later tonight?"

Michelle smiled. "Sure, that would be lovely." She reached into her coat pocket and sighed frustrated. "I guess I didn't bring my business cards with me. Do you have a pen?"

"Sure do." Alex said handing her a pen and another business card. "Just write your number on the back. Either you call me or I'll call you and we can either meet somewhere or I can pick you up, whichever you prefer."

Victor watched from a few feet away and growled in disgust. Who did this Alex think he was? "Sorry buddy you're not going to live to see the break of dawn." He smirked. "Your day of judgement is about to begin. He swirled his cloak behind him with a sweep of his hand and approached the two deep in conversation.

"Excuse me folks I'm afraid I have to break up this happy occasion." Victor stated not taking his eyes off Alex. Hatred filled him.

"Who are you?" Michelle asked staring at Victor smitten by him.

Victor extended his hand. "Pardon my rudeness, my dear beauty. I am Victor Ramirez. And you are . . . ?"

"M-M-Michelle," she stammered taking his hand in hers. She couldn't stop staring at Victor's eyes. For the first time in years she was speechless.

Alex glared at Victor. He dare interrupt his conversation. "Excuse me, sir. I'm afraid neither of us know you so do you mind giving us a moment?" He asked with an authoritative tone.

Victor averted his gaze to Alex and smiled a wicked smile. "By all means I sincerely apologize for my rudeness." He motioned with his hand and said, "Carry on, my dears." Cold evil eyes bore into Alex's. "But first let me remind you of our meeting." He pointed to the clock in the park and said, "Tick-tock, tick-tock, it's nine o'clock. I don't like to wait."

"I'm sorry, Victor." Michelle said. "I'm going to scoot so you two can have your meeting." She said and slid Alex's number in her pocket.

Alex dismissed Victor with a wave of his hand. "Don't rush on account of him. He's nobody to me. We're having a quick meeting and I'll be giving you a call when we're finished." He smiled at Michelle.

Victor rolled his eyes, his fangs growing. He wished he could kill Alex instead of bringing him to Armani's home but it was closure for Armani and a necessary step in the healing process. Armani had to kill Alex and Adam. Self-control would have to be of the utmost priority. It didn't mean Victor had to refrain from a little abuse. Alex had it coming for his lack of respect. Victor floated next to Michelle and placed his arm around her shoulder. He silently put her in a trance. He could wait no longer to deal with Alex.

"Take your arm off her you freak!" Alex ordered lunging toward Victor.

"Stop while you're ahead you filthy excuse of a human being." Victor shoved Alex in midair forcing him to fall down. "Stay seated there and be a gentleman for once in your pathetic life. That is if you care an ounce about your son's life." He pointed at Alex and continued his rant. "I have no problem leaving right now and killing your son. I don't need your money."

"What are you going to do to Michelle?" Alex asked.

"I am going to do nothing, absolutely nothing. She's an innocent lady who happens to be in the wrong place at the wrong time. We are going to bid her farewell like gentlemen and then do our business." Victor said making sure Alex understood before releasing Michelle from the trance. "Nod if you are in agreement with me." He ordered. "And for God's sake, stand up. You look like a cowardly fool sitting in the snow." Victor chuckled.

Alex bit his tongue and glared at Victor. He couldn't wait to put a gold bullet straight into this lunatic's heart. He stood and wiped the snow off his butt. "Let's get this show on the road."

"I call the shots here, Alex. Not you. Get that through your head and things will go much smoother." Victor said. "I'm the Master, not you."

Placing his hand in his coat pocket Alex gripped the gun. Good, still in place. He couldn't wait to use it. What a fun evening this was going to be.

Victor snapped his fingers in front of Michelle's face.

"That was odd," she said. "I felt like I blacked out for a minute. Pardon me," she apologized.

"No apology needed my dear." Victor said kissing the top of her hand. "Alex and I must have our meeting so if you'll please excuse us."

"Oh, by all means," she blushed smiling at Victor. "Good bye, Alex. Give me a call when you're finished." Waving to both of them she jogged out of sight.

"Now, where were we, Alex?" Victor asked rubbing his chin with his index finger and thumb. "Ah, I remember. You were going to pull your gun out and try to shoot me." He pointed at Alex. "Correct me if I'm wrong."

"No, you're right." Alex said and reached for his gun. "Today is your day to die." He pulled it out and aimed it at Victor, his hands shaking. How did Victor know he planned on shooting him?

Victor looked around the park. "Have you gone mad? There are still a few people here. You could accidentally shoot and kill an innocent bystander."

"I guess that would mean they were in the wrong place at the wrong time." Alex laughed like he was the funniest man on the planet. He lowered the gun. "Before I kill you tell me where my son is." Alex ordered.

Victor was losing his patience with this fool. Cat and mouse was something he had no time for. He would love nothing more than to play predator and prey with this Alex but only if he would be the one to kill him. Alex was Armani's kill and that changed everything.

"I'll do even better than that. I'll take you to him." Victor said trying to sound stupid so Alex would agree.

Alex thought for a minute but it was a minute too long for Victor. He was on top of him in a second and punched him in the jaw. "This game is going to be played my way or no way. Do you understand?" Victor asked baring his fangs at Alex.

Alex tried to scream but Victor covered his mouth with his hand. The gun was gone. Realizing he must've dropped it he panicked and started kicking Victor.

"That wasn't nice, Alex." Victor said. He reached back, grabbed Alex's leg and twisted it.

Alex tried to signal to people walking past but they ignored him like he was an invisible ghost. Victor moved his hand from Alex's mouth and laughed at him.

"Why are you laughing? One of these people will help me." Alex said. He turned and hollered at a young couple.

"You could try all night to get help but guess what? They can't see or hear you. You don't exist to them thanks to me." Victor said pointing at himself. "Now, stand up and I shall take you to your son."

Fear was written all over Alex's face. "What do you mean they can't see me?" He asked. "Of course they can. They're just choosing to ignore me."

Victor forced Alex to stare into his glowing red eyes. "Tell me, what do you see?" He asked.

"I see the eyes of a drug addict." Alex shot back.

Victor laughed. "Good one, Einstein." He stopped laughing. "Now what do you see?" He asked baring his fangs.

Alex laughed. "I see a left over prop from Halloween." Rolling his eyes he picked up the briefcase. He had no intention of losing his precious money.

Victor grabbed his face and squeezed. "What you see is the face of a vampire and tonight you are going to die, plain and simple." He released Alex's face and tapped his temples. "A thought just came to me. I know you don't want to lose your precious money so how about I teach you a lesson on generosity before we go to your place of execution."

"What the hell are you talking about?" Alex asked confused. He glanced from the left to right looking for his gun. No luck. It couldn't have gone far. Damn him for not holding it tighter. No way was he going to give his money away.

Victor held the gun and asked, "Looking for this?"

"Give me my gun!" He shouted. "That's mine."

Victor laughed so hard he thought his insides would fall out. "My, my you sound like a child. That proves to me that you do need a lesson on giving and sharing."

"I need no such thing. That's Adams ransom money. If you're going to kill me at least leave it for my son." He pleaded with Victor.

"No need for that. Your son is going to die with you." Victor grabbed Alex's arm forcing him to walk beside him. "Keep up with me."

"What do you mean? We have done nothing to deserve this."

"Say that again and I will be forced to hurt you." Victor said picking up the pace. "You know what you did and so do I."

"I did nothing." Alex replied. "We did nothing. I want you to leave me alone. Let me go." He said struggling to break free of Victor's grip.

"You and Adam both wiggle like weak worms. You're both such spineless humans. You won't escape me now so stop fighting. Your destiny is in my hands now." Victor faced Alex, putting both of his hands around Alex's neck and lifted him off the ground. "I can either crush your windpipe right this second or you can confess to me the crime you committed." He held him for a few more seconds and threw him on the ground. "We both know what you did so don't try to lie to me."

Alex looked up, a scowl on his face. "I didn't kill Simone. My son, Adam did it. The whole thing was set up by Gabe Davis, Armani's band manager." He stood and held his hands in the air. "You got your confession. Am I free to go now?" He asked and smoothed his trench coat. "This is sickening and a waste of my time."

"Not so fast slick." Victor said. "You left an important detail out about that fateful night." He stood with his arms crossed waiting for

Alex to speak. "You may as well come clean. You're going to die for being an accomplice at this point anyway."

Frustrated, Alex slicked his hair back. "I don't know what you're talking about. I wasn't in that hotel room with Adam when he killed Simone."

Victor pointed his finger at Alex. "Who said they were in a hotel room when she died?" He smiled at Alex but he was not happy. "We both know your son isn't capable of carrying out an execution on his own." Victor patted his head and said, "He lacks the mental ability to handle such a responsibility. What do mortals say?" He asked. "Oh, I know," he stated snapping his finger. "He's twenty three crayons short of a full box and I'm talking about a box of twenty four crayons." Victor laughed.

Alex laughed. That was the wrong thing to do. Victor stared at him. This man had no compassion. He was willing to let him son take the fall for both of their actions. For that Victor decided he'd have to inflict pain. Alex could've at least acted like he gave a damn.

"You're not too bright yourself, Alex because if you were you would confess and be done with it. Now I will have to hurt you." Victor stated walking toward Alex.

Alex tried to run but Victor grabbed his trench coat ripping it in two. Alex fell forward and Victor grabbed a handful of hair, jerking his head back.

"Stop this! Please!" Alex begged.

"Stop what, Alex. You did this to yourself. Didn't your mother teach you that every action has a consequence? You should have thought of this before agreeing to the plan Gabey devised." Victor pulled Alex's hair harder.

"Ahh. Gee, that hurts." Alex cried. "What do you want from me?"

Victor put his lips next to Alex's ear and whispered, "A confession."

"No way." Alex said defiantly. "Never."

"Excuse me I don't think I heard you correctly." Victor seethed jerking Alex's head back even farther and ripping out a handful of hair. He shoved Alex's head into the snow. "Are you ready to confess now?"

Blood oozed from Alex's head turning the snow red. He covered the back of his scalp and rolled onto his back looking up at Victor, tears in his eyes.

Victor stared at him. "Well? Please don't try my patience." Victor knew Alex would confess. After all he was crying, something Victor thought he was incapable of. Was Alex a sociopath? It was a huge possibility, but Victor wasn't here to play shrink. He was here to bring Alex to justice at the hands of Armani.

"Ok, ok, I'll tell you the truth." Alex said his voice shaky. "I was a part of it. I didn't kill Simone but I tortured Armani in horrible ways, even burned half of his face." He finished and closed his eyes.

"Stand up now." Victor ordered. "I appreciate the honesty but it will not save you. You will be executed tonight."

Alex stood, his shirt saturated with blood. Victor grabbed his arm and the briefcase. "We've got a delivery to make before going to Armani's house." He walked fast forcing Alex to keep up with him.

"Where are we going?" Alex asked. "I'm cold."

"Deal with it, Alex. You'd still have your jacket if you were smarter. One must never try to outrun the long arm of the law." Victor stated. "And for your information we are going to a woman's home who was recently widowed and has been left to raise two young children ages five and three alone."

"Why do you care about this woman and her children?" Alex asked. Vampires didn't seem the types to care about anything but blood lust.

"You're wrong. I'm a vigilante and I am in the profession of serving justice where it has been overlooked." Victor slowed his steps tightening his grip on Alex's arm. "I care deeply about this woman and her children. I killed her husband. His name was Gordon Appleton, computer tech by day, alcoholic by night. For your information I didn't kill him for his love of the bottle. I killed him because he was beating his wife and children every night when he'd arrive home from work drunk off his ass. The worst part is he videotaped each and every one of these sick beating sessions. He was proud of what he did and he thought no one knew." Victor paused and smiled. "But I knew and I ended it."

"Good for you." Alex blurted. "See, my crime wasn't so bad."

Victor backhanded Alex's face. "As a matter of fact it was. I view all criminals with the same disgust and contempt. All of you are equals in my eyes." Victor grabbed Alex by the arms and took flight. "Shut up and enjoy the flight. Our next stop is the Appleton residence."

Alex closed his eyes, his heartbeat quickened. He was afraid of heights and he hoped Victor wouldn't drop him to his death. The cold wind beating on his face and body chilled him to the bone. Victor's grip was strong and cold, his long nails digging into his flesh. Now that he thought about it Victor reminded him of a hawk, a dark deadly hawk.

"How fast are we going?" Alex asked, his voice booming.

Victor scowled. The man didn't need to holler at him. His hearing was keen. He could hear mice running through the forest below them. But, besides that he didn't like to be bothered while flying. It was when he felt peace, a peace he lost so long ago as a young beaten boy.

"Not fast enough," Victor replied. All he wanted to do was deliver the money and give Alex to Armani and allow closure to this mess.

Ten minutes later they landed in front of a small suburban home. 'Appleton' was written in large thick black letters on the mailbox. Victor handed Alex his cloak and demanded he put it on.

Alex grimaced. "Why do you want me to wear this? Is this a peace offering or a gesture of kindness because I'm so cold?" He slipped it on quickly wrapping himself in the long black cape like a baby swaddled in a blanket.

Victor glared at him. "It's none of the above." Alex made him sick. Kindness was the last thing Victor would ever show him. "As you may recall your shirt is full of blood. I don't want Ms. Appleton to see that. She's been through enough with the death of her bastard husband." Victor held the briefcase in his right hand, in his left he gripped Alex's arm. "One wrong move or wrong word out of that mouth of yours and I will kill you." Victor led Alex up the sidewalk to the front door. He set the briefcase down and rang the doorbell. "We're here to show kindness, caring and sharing. I wish I could say it would be a life lesson for you, but unfortunately for you it's not."

The door opened and a woman of forty five smiled at them. "Hello. Can I help you?" She asked.

Victor eyed her up and down. He was surprised a woman with her looks would marry Gordon. Her red hair was tied back in a ponytail, her physique perfect and she had legs miles long. Staring into her large swollen green eyes, Victor grimaced. He'd never forget how old they looked, how much pain they hid. It was heartbreaking.

Victor extended his hand. "Hello ma'am. I'm Victor and this is my associate Alex. We are here on behalf of your deceased husband."

She looked confused and shook Victor's hand. "I don't understand."

Alex opened his mouth to speak but Victor shushed him. "We would like to extend our sympathies and condolences to you and your children." He smiled a warm friendly smile.

She blushed. "No need for that but I thank you just the same. He wasn't always an easy man to live with but it's still hard without him." A tear trickled down her cheek. She wiped it, avoiding eye contact with Victor and Alex. "Well, I should be going. I've got a long list of things I need to get done. Thank you for taking the time to stop." She stepped back and tried to shut the door but was stopped by Victor.

"Wait." Victor said picking up the briefcase. "This is for you and your children." He smiled and handed it to her. She was almost as beautiful as Katrina. But no one would fill his heart with such love and hope as Katrina had done in such a short period of time. "I hope this helps."

She took the briefcase and opened it. Her eyes bulged and she cried, hugging Victor and thanking him over and over. "Why would you do this for us?"

Victor held her a moment before letting her go. "It was Alex's idea." He said and turned to Alex. "Isn't that right?" His gaze told Alex to cooperate.

Alex cringed and muffled a yes. He folded his arms and glared at Victor. "Let's go now, shall we?" He waited for Victor to agree.

"Ms. Appleton, I know things won't be easy for you but this will help. Your husband was not who everyone thought he was. I know what he did. Take comfort in the fact that you are free of him and his abuse." Victor winked. "Take care now. If you ever need anything don't hesitate to call." He said handing her a business card.

"Thank you so much, both of you." She said looking from one to the other. She held the briefcase to her chest, turned and shut the door behind her.

"That was exhilarating. To know I made a difference in someone's life." Victor stated leading Alex toward the road.

"Yup," Alex responded unenthused. "I didn't know vampires had business cards."

"We don't. It's a mortal friend of mine. If she were to need anything she'd call him and I'd get the message." Once at a safe distance from civilization Victor took his cape from Alex. "Now, it's time for us to go." He slipped his cape on, grabbed Alex and ascended into the sky with Alex dangling in his grasp.

Chapter Thirty-Seven

Armani stepped out of the shower feeling better than he had a few hours ago. He wiped the steam from the mirror and stared at himself.

"I need some peace of mind," he stated aloud. Frowning, he placed his hand over the burnt side of his face. It sickened him to think he had the capability to kill without remorse but he felt nothing. Why should remorse be an issue? Gabe and the other two men felt nothing but excitement when they killed Simone and brutally tortured him. Armani knew he'd be better off dead than cursed to be an unwilling member of The Dark Ones for all of eternity.

One look around the bathroom and he realized he needed his employees back on duty. His home was a treacherous mess. Simone would've cringed at the sight of it. He cursed himself for letting himself and things go. Towels lye scattered on the marble slate, the bathtub had the God-awful yellow ring around the drain. The toilet was an issue all in itself. Armani peered into the toilet and cringed. No time to worry about that right now. His time to serve justice was just around the corner. Armani smiled. Gabe was dead, a man was caged in the garage and Victor was in route with Armani's last kill. "Paybacks are a bitch." He seethed.

He shut the bathroom door surprised to see clothes set out for him on the bed. He picked them up and scowled. What in the hell kind of clothing was this? He loved black but this was extreme Goth attire. A long black cloak with black fur around the collar lay on top of a skin tight pair of black pants, a black turtleneck and a pair of black army boots. Armani laughed and threw the cloak to the side. What would Simone think of his new 'chosen' taste in clothes? She'd probably think he lost his mind. Sure, the band sang dark songs but they were in no way a Gothic rock-n-roll band.

"Donovan!" Armani hollered. He walked to the bedroom doorway and waited for Donovan to come upstairs with an explanation.

A second later Donovan appeared and smiled at Armani.

"Please wipe that smug smile off your face." Armani ordered. Pointing to the clothing he asked, "What the hell are these doing set out on my bed?"

Donovan shook his head trying hard not to show his amusement. "That's what you're wearing for the kill." He stated walking into the bedroom picking up the cloak. "You will look splendid in this." He beamed. "Try it on."

"Does being a vampire automatically mean you have to wear the long black Dracula cape?" He asked sarcastically and rolled his eyes. "That's such a stereotype."

Donovan threw the cape to Armani and said, "It's more than a stereotype. The cape is a source of power. You have no choice but to wear it and wear it proudly, my friend." He watched Armani catch it. His speed and reaction time was impressive. "Good catch," he added with a wink.

"Ok. I can understand that but not the tight black pants." He stated disgusted. "I was a rock musician turned vampire, but I am not gay. With all due respect I'm telling you I refuse to wear the pants."

"So be it," Donovan said. "Now get yourself ready. Victor will be here soon with the unsub, so to speak. The guilty will pay for their crimes tonight at your hand." Donovan walked slowly toward the door and stopped. "If I may make a suggestion to you I think it would be beneficial for you to relax and do something you enjoy before all of this takes place."

Confused, Armani asked, "Shouldn't I be getting myself pumped up like a boxer in the ring?" He thought the adrenaline should be flowing through his veins.

"No. This is your new life, not some sport. A calm spirit and cool mind are of the utmost importance when it comes to being a vigilante vampire or you risk losing yourself to the evil forces." He placed his hands on his hips and faced Armani. "Once evil takes hold and rules you I cannot guarantee your future." That being said, he left the room.

Armani thought about what Donovan told him. Music was the answer. He dressed, even tugged on the tight pants to his dismay, and slipped the cloak on last. A tingling sensation ran down his spine. He felt strong, capable, warm and magical with the cloak on. The cloak comforted him like someone's arms wrapped around him in a protective embrace.

Armani stood in front of the full-length mirror and smiled. "You look like a fierce predator in that cloak, you handsome devil," he joked. He saw his first real smile staring back at him since Simone's death.

He whirled around and walked to the music room, his cloak flowing behind him. Armani picked up a few sheets of music, sat at the piano, pounded out melodies and sang with all of his heart and soul.

Donovan sat at the bar sipping brandy. He listened to Armani play the piano and sing. For the first time since Simone's death Armani sounded happy. His hope was that this would last and drown out Armani's thoughts of suicide. Armani was in a dark place away from the sun. He needed to rise above the darkness and come to the light.

How could he help him once he killed the guilty men? Armani must live as a vampire forever. Donovan was lost in his thoughts when he heard screams from outside.

"What in God's name?" Donovan asked shoving his chair back.

The door was kicked open and Victor walked in dragging Alex by the arm.

"Honey, we're home!" He boomed laughing hysterically. "Where's my newest vampire?"

Donovan shot Alex a hateful glance. "Armani's upstairs in the music room and I must say he's quite the talented artist. His voice is hypnotic." He eyed Alex noting bruises on his face. It appeared Victor had some fun with him. "How could you kill Simone and torture Armani?" He asked Alex.

Alex knew he was going to die so he assumed there was no point in being polite. "How could I not?" He shot back. "For money I would do anything." A coy smile played on his lips. "You know if this has worked out smoothly I would have gotten a twenty percent cut from Gabe for all the money Armani and the band 'Faded Cross' would have brought in."

Donovan folded his arms over his chest. "So you're saying you're willing to die for money because that's what this has come down to." He paused briefly waiting for a reaction and got none. Alex really was heartless.

Alex looked from Victor to Donovan. "You bet. It's worth the risk." He looked around Armani's house. "This is an impressive home for such a pathetic man." He scoffed. "Pour me a drink you bastards." He ordered making eye contact with Donovan. "I'd like to die a gentleman."

Victor laughed, his head rolling back. "How can you die as a gentleman when you never were one to begin with? You'd be better off asking for a Bible or a Priest. This may be my own speculation but I'm thinking you have some wrongs to make right with the big guy in the sky."

Donovan agreed. "How about you get on your knees and say a few prayers. I make a really excellent priest." He joked.

"You can both go to Hell." Alex shot back. "I'm leaving now. Enjoy your day." Placing his hand on the doorknob, he said, "Give my son my regards."

Victor watched, allowing Alex to enjoy the delusion that he was in control. "You say you want a drink? Allow me to make you a cocktail."

He grabbed Alex's arm and threw him down. "Hand me the handcuffs, Donovan." Victor ordered.

"Allow me the honors," Donovan said cuffing Alex's hands behind his back. "I'll pour him some whiskey."

"Take these off!" Alex screamed.

"Victor picked him up and lifted him to the level of his eyes. "Consider yourself pardoned by me. I wanted to break your hand for touching the doorknob." He placed him on his feet and ordered him to walk to the bar. "Sit. I will get your dearly beloved son to join us for the celebration." Victor spat and raised his hand slapping the smile off Alex's face. Alex spit blood, a tooth landing on the bar table.

"Keep him company," Victor said. Donovan nodded and sat next to Alex.

Silence surrounded them like the calm before the storm.

Donovan sipped brandy and found it amusing to watch Alex lean forward and sip whiskey thru a straw.

Alex cleared his throat. "I've got a question for you."

"Yes. What is it?"

"If you're a vampire then why are you drinking brandy instead of blood? Why aren't you drinking my blood to be exact?"

"You're a fool, Alex. You must be one of the mortals who believe everything they read. Some vampire's can drink and eat other things besides blood and The Dark Ones can." Donovan's red eyes bore into Alex's. "Let me answer your question about why I'm not drinking your blood. To me, it's tainted. It would be like drinking a bottle of poison.

Why would I do that to myself?"

Alex shivered, scared for the first time. Donovan's eyes would haunt him to the grave. "I-I-don't know. I didn't think vampire's even existed. I assumed you guys were just the product of artists and author's wild imaginations." He leaned forward, wrapped his lips around the straw and drank like a baby suckling its mother's breast.

Donovan poured him another glass. "It's a shame you won't live to write a memoir on how you survived 'The Attack of the Vampire's,' so to speak." He laughed. "Just think of all the money you'd have, Alex. You'd be on television giving interviews and getting paid big bucks to testify your sightings of us and I'm sure the book would bring in a lot of money for you, too. People love stories about the supernatural and would read it out of simple curiosity." He shook his head, a crooked grin on his face. "Drink up. It'll ease some of the pain that's due to you." Donovan stated. It was all he could do not to beat Alex to his death but that was Armani's job. Armani was the surgeon and Donovan's job was to prep Alex for the operation.

Donovan listened to Armani singing songs of hope and love lost. It broke his heart.

Donovan and Alex stared at Victor when he came in the door. Alex was nursing his second glass of whiskey when he laid eyes on his son standing behind Victor.

Adam looked at the ground, afraid to see his father.

"Alex, you're pathetic. Your son is more afraid of you than us right now." He pushed Adam in front of him. "Your old man can't hurt you anymore, Adam." Victor stated. "It's quite poetic because you're going to die together. How would you like to watch your father die?" Victor asked. "It would be healing for you to see him suffer and breathe his last breath." Victor walked around Adam like a cat circling a mouse and said, "Maybe Armani will even let you wrap your hands around his neck and assist in ending his life." He tapped Adam's nose with his long finger and smiled, fangs glistening like sharp knives.

"That's a wonderful idea," Donovan chimed. "How does that sound, Alex?" He asked.

"I think this whole thing is pathetic." Alex said his face red. "I hate all of you, especially you Adam. If it weren't for you we wouldn't be here right now."

Victor stood in front of Alex. "That's where you're dead wrong. I knew what you did and would have caught you. I just wanted to make it more interesting so I took your son first and found out just how stupid you truly are. Meeting me with ransom money for the release of Adam?" He grunted. "Honestly Alex, I think you're the stupid one."

"Adam, tell them you're the stupid one." Alex ordered his son.

Adam was silent and stared at the ground.

"Mute fuck," he muttered glaring at Adam. "He was never able to stand up for himself. He's a coward and the world will be a better place to be rid of him." Alex said, his eyes shifting from Victor to Donovan. "Agree?"

Donovan nodded at Victor, who returned the gesture. Donovan left the room in search of Armani.

Victor glared at Alex. "Wrong, Alex. The world will be a better place to be rid of you both." He grabbed both of the men's arms and led them to the kitchen like lambs to the slaughter. "I believe it's time for your last meal." Victor laughed. "Prisoner's get this casualty on death row so guess what? Each of you gets to pick your favorite meal prepared by yours truly." He said, let go of their arms and mockingly bowed. "Your wishes are my command."

Adam was silent while Alex screamed profanities at Victor fighting him with each step. Victor gripped Alex's arm hard squeezing tighter and tighter like a blood pressure cuff that should be on recall notice.

"Pick a meal," Victor demanded placing Alex and Adam across from each other at the large table. "You are not going to escape so face your fate with dignity. I'm cuffing you both to the chairs." He smiled dangling a set of handcuffs in front of them.

Adam was cooperative. Victor appreciated it although he would never tell him so. He was still a despicable murderer and he had no patience for the likes of evil men.

"How are we supposed to eat with handcuffs on?" Alex asked. "And to think you called me stupid." He coughed and sneered at Victor.

Victor took slow, deliberate steps toward Alex. "Why can't you be as cooperative as your son?" He asked. "To answer your question, you will eat with your mouth." Victor said baring his fangs at Alex. When he reached him he locked Alex's already cuffed hands to the chair.

Alex screamed. "Are you trying to pull my arms off or what?"

"Believe me, if I wanted to I would." Victor floated to the counter, opened the drawer and pulled out a sharp butcher knife. He held it to the light and smiled. "This knife looks like the ones they use in the Horror movies to slice and dice people with, don't you think?" He asked.

Adam remained silent not looking at Victor or his father. Tears dampened his cheeks. He tried to wipe them on his shirt but to no avail. He was guilty of killing Simone and there was nothing he could do about it now. Death was his punishment and he accepted his fate hours ago while tied up in the garage. Waging war with himself he accepted the fact that this was where it would end. He felt regret and remorse, but it was too late. He chose his own fate when he committed his crime.

Alex glared at Victor. "You won't get away with this." His eyes fell on the knife. It gleamed like a predator's sharp teeth in the light. Victor swooped behind him. "What do you think you're doing?" Alex asked his eyes huge and face pale. He twisted his head to look.

"This," Victor answered pulling Alex's head back and placing the cold blade against his throat.

Alex swallowed hard, his Adam's apple making the knife rise and fall.

Victor removed the knife from Alex's throat and set it on the table. "I would dare say I caused your heart rate to increase." He laughed casting a glance at Adam, whose head was still down. "Cheer up Adam. It's not so bad. You and your father will be together in paradise tonight but the bad news is I won't be there to protect you from your old man."

Adam snorted.

"You're crazy," Alex said.

Victor backed away from Alex and held his finger to his chin. "Excuse me. I don't believe I heard you correctly. I don't see a mirror in here." He opened the refrigerator door and said, "Alright men, what would you like to eat?"

"Who cares," Alex said not amused.

"Then I shall surprise you." Victor said flatly and pulled two steaks out of the refrigerator. "Let the festivities begin." Laughing he added, "Welcome to my restaurant, 'Ode to Death.'" Victor said, turned his back on the two and whistled while preparing the meal.

CHAPTER THIRTY-EIGHT

ARMANI SAT AT the piano engrossed in his music. It was the first time since Simone's death that he felt the music with such passion and electricity. Lost in his own world he didn't hear Donovan enter the music room.

Donovan stood in the doorway watching Armani's hands move over the piano's keyboard. It amazed him how artists got so into their work that they lost themselves in another world. Armani's body shifted with the beats of the piano, swaying back and forth, his voice melodic and soothing. Donovan folded his arms across his chest waiting for Armani to finish.

The song ended and Donovan cleared his throat.

Armani spun around on the piano bench and stared at Donovan. His eyes held more pain than one should ever have to. "This is the only time I feel any sort of peace. Killing these men won't mend my broken heart." He stood the black cloak swirling behind him like a curtain in the wind.

"You must give yourself time to heal." Donovan said. "Of course it won't mend your broken heart and hurting soul but it's the first step in the healing process." He pointed at himself and said, "I'm living proof of this."

Armani rolled his eyes. "I get that. You keep shoving your experience down my throat and so much so that it tastes like bile." He raised his hands in a helpless gesture. "I'm sick of this. All I want to do is kill these men and be gone and done with all this."

"Life shall come." Donovan retorted. "You've got to believe in yourself. If you kill yourself after you kill these men, in essence they have won."

Armani laughed. "That doesn't make a damn bit of sense."

"Think about it logically. You may have won the battle by avenging Simone's death, but if you kill yourself then they have won the war. The battle against evil and malicious men and women will never end but we must continue on and pursue ridding the world of them one at a time. Someday in the future there will be enough vampires in The Dark Ones to fight and win the war." Donovan paused staring straight ahead. "But that cannot happen if our new members seek out justice for only their losses and end their lives. Do you understand so far?"

He nodded, not sure he understood the logic Donovan preached but went along with it. "I have a question for you if I may ask."

"You may ask me anything." Donovan smiled. "Questions are how one learns."

There was no mistaking Donovan had been an excellent professor at one time.

"How many strong are we?" Armani asked and rephrased the question. "I mean, how many vampires are members of The Dark Ones?"

"I'll answer honestly, not all that many."

Armani was impatient. "Do you have an estimate?"

"I would say twenty or so." Donovan motioned for Armani to follow him. "We can discuss this later. Right now there are two men downstairs waiting for you." He turned and walked into the hallway.

Armani let out a slow breath. "My time has come."

"Is the meal to your liking?" Victor asked watching Alex crane his neck and lap up the steak, corn and potatoes like a dog eating from a bowl. He noticed Adam hadn't touched his meal. "What's the matter, Adam? Not hungry?"

Adam looked up. "I have no appetite, sir." He said in a feeble voice. His eyes returned to the full plate of food.

"I'll eat his rations," Alex said his mouth full. "I've got nothing to lose now. I may as well die with a full stomach." He laughed and stuck his face into the plate, his stout pink tongue licking it clean.

Victor couldn't believe how disgusting Alex was. No manners. Even without silverware surely one could still eat with dignity. The thought of pulling Alex's tongue out of his mouth and choking him with it made him laugh out loud.

Alex grimaced. Victor's laugh sounded like it came from the bowels of Hell.

"Time's up," Victor said gathering the plates. "I think we have company."

Donovan and Armani entered the kitchen side by side, their black capes gracefully dancing in unison behind them like two ballerinas in the Nutcracker.

"Hello Alex and Adam. Are you ready to meet your maker?" Donovan asked. He tapped his head and said, "Excuse me, I mean your executioner."

Victor watched Armani and Donovan and smiled like a proud father.

"Ah, the time has finally come. This will be all over soon." Victor said stepping back. "One is stuffed full of food and both are ready for slaughter."

Alex glared at Armani. "I should've killed you instead of injuring you." He chuckled and said, "So, tell me one thing. How does your face feel? Does it hurt both physically and emotionally? I bet every time you look in the mirror you are reminded of Simone." Alex gave him a challenging stare. "Well?"

Armani lunged at Alex but Donovan grabbed his arm stopping him. "Don't let this coward take the easy way out. Never listen to them." He released his grip and gave Victor a glance. Victor was enjoying all of this.

"If I may offer a suggestion . . . ." Victor trailed off before continuing. "Cut this coward's tongue out of his mouth." He picked up the knife and swung it in front of Alex's face like a pendulum. "It'd be in your best interest to keep your mouth shut from this point on and if you can't I'll tape that filthy hole of yours shut."

Armani looked at Adam shocked. "Why? How could you kill Simone?" He asked. "Why?!" He screamed.

Armani's question was answered with silence.

Victor set the knife down and walked behind Adam's chair bending to the level of his ear. "Answer him or I will inflict pain so severe on you that you will beg for death." He slapped the back of Adam's head.

Adam's head lunged forward. He stared at his father and said, "We did it for money. Gabe set the whole operation up. My dad wanted the money and I wanted to make you both suffer. I loved Simone since childhood and she didn't love me back . . . ."His voice trailed off. His face turned red, a tear ran down his cheek. "I'm sorry. I killed her because I didn't want anyone to have her but me."

"You son of a bitch!" Armani screamed. "I thought she was your friend. Simone would've done anything for you." He paced wiping the sweat from his face. "You've ruined my life. I loved and still love her more than anything in the world." Armani raised his hands to the Heavens and cried out.

Donovan and Victor watched. They knew he needed closure and the opportunity to have the 'whys' of this answered before the killings commenced.

"I found it quite heroic of my son to kill that bitch." Alex said a smug smile on his face. "He finally took action and did something for himself for once."

"Y-y-you thought I was a hero, dad?" Adam asked pleased.

Victor was beside Alex in a flash. "Didn't I tell you to keep quiet?" He picked up the knife and made a small incision in Alex's cheek. "Now, you are going to shut the hell up." He ripped off two large pieces of duct tape securing them over Alex's mouth. He wiped his hands in front of Alex's face and for good measure punched him square in the right eye. He winked at Adam. "You're next if you speak without being spoken to."

Armani's body shook with rage, anger and hate. He didn't know how to handle this. These two took away his reason for living.

"Sit down, Armani." Donovan said pulling a chair out for him.

Armani couldn't get to the chair quick enough. He felt weak and dizzy.

"We need to know how you want to kill these two. Victor will get all the necessary tools and set everything up for you in the backyard."

That question didn't require much thought. He had imagined killing whoever was responsible for quite some time. "I want to burn them alive at the stake. Burn them as they have burned my face, my heart and my soul. I want them to suffer as I have suffered."

"So be it." Donovan said. He stood and patted Armani's shoulder. "Stay seated. Victor will get everything we need. Tonight is victory for you, my friend."

Ten minutes later Victor had a list. He smiled at Armani and Donovan. "I want the two of you to have a little fun with the Double A team until I return." He said and closed the door.

Donovan offered Armani his hand. "Come. Let's inflict pain on the men who destroyed you and your world."

Adam and Alex exchanged fearful glances. "We're going to die, dad." Adam said. "I don't want to die . . . . ."

"I suppose you should've thought of the consequences before acting, correct?" Donovan asked unlocking Adam's handcuffs. "Try anything and I chop off that dirty hand of yours."

Armani didn't hesitate. He wrapped his hand around Adams hand. "Is this the hand you choked the life out of Simone with? Answer me!" He screamed in his ear.

Donovan walked out of the kitchen. He remembered he promised his hawk a taste of these men. He smiled. His faithful black hawk loved eyeballs like people love desserts. Alex would look better with one eye, he reasoned. He laughed heartily and opened the front door.

What he saw made him sick. The hawk was pecking at Gabe's mutilated dead body. One of the rules was not to eat meat from the ones they killed unless it was given to him. He whistled. The hawk jumped like a child caught stealing cookies from a cookie jar.

"Come to me," he ordered holding his arm out. The hawk obediently flew to his master landing on his arm. "You know better than to do that." Donovan chastised him but was cut short by a scream in the kitchen. "Armani better keep his wits about him," he told the hawk. He ran into the kitchen.

"What in God's name is going on?" Donovan asked. The hawk cocked its head to the side and flew toward the table landing in front of Alex.

Alex's mumbles and groans from his duct taped mouth were barely audible. He stared at the hawk frozen in fear.

Adam was underneath Armani kicking and screaming like a spoiled child. Armani's hands were wrapped around Adam's throat and Adam's hand looked dislocated. Donovan pulled Armani off Adam and shoved him into the wall.

"What did you do that for?" Armani asked. He glared at Adam who lay on the floor trying to catch his breath and holding his broken hand against his chest. "I felt the bones in his hand and fingers crackle and it was music to my ears. I want to kill him now. I don't see it as a problem since they're both going to die anyway."

Donovan picked Adam up and set him in the chair. He stared at Armani and said, "Get under control, Armani." He ordered. "Hate and anger can never under any circumstance take over your emotions during a kill."

"Is it not true that hate and anger are the sticks of dynamite that ignite the revenge within the soul?" He asked Donovan and walked to where Adam sat. "You're lucky to be alive." Leaning toward Adam, he placed his hands on the arms of the chair. "But you won't be for long." He smiled releasing the chair with a thrust.

"That's enough." Donovan ordered. He stared at Alex who had the fear of Jesus in him. He laughed.

"What could possibly be funny?" Armani asked. He followed Donovan's gaze and saw the black hawk perched on the table staring at Alex with pure hatred. "Alex doesn't need a guard, you know."

"I know that. I made a promise to my friend that I intend to keep."

"And what is that?" Armani questioned folding his arms over his chest.

He walked up to the hawk and ran his hand down the hawk's body. "He gets to gouge out and eat one of Alex's eyes." He stated. He smiled at the hawk and asked, "Isn't that right my faithful companion?"

The hawk nodded obediently never taking its eyes off Alex.

Alex muffled a cry. His face paled and he shut his eyes.

"It's nice to see such a hot shot cocky man feeling the fear, wouldn't you say, Armani?"

"Sure is." Armani agreed. He checked the time. "When is Victor going to be back?"

"He will be here soon. Sometimes it takes a while to gather all the tools necessary for the kill. You want these men to burn at the stake and that requires a few more tools and accessories than normal." Donovan walked to the window peering into the darkness. "Be patient. Our Master will be here soon."

CHAPTER THIRTY-NINE

VICTOR HAD THE tools needed for Armani's kills but a burning desire to stop at his home was impossible to avoid. He had to know if Katrina was there. He drummed his fingers on the steering wheel waiting for the person in front of him to turn right. He would've been home an hour ago but had to take Donovan's truck and trailer to haul the supplies needed for Armani's kill.

Victor honked the horn pressing on it for a minute. The person in front of him sat idle at the stop. Victor saw the man was talking on the phone. He honked again. The car didn't move and the driver held his middle finger in the air. Victor was rabid. He had places to be and things to do. No one dare stand or park in his way.

Victor stepped out of the truck, walked to the man's car and tapped the window.

The red haired man rolled down the window, an irritated look on his face. "Let me call you right back," he said to the person he was talking to. He stared up at Victor. "Dude, what's your problem? I'm trying to settle an argument with my girlfriend here." His eyes wandered from Victor's head to his feet. "And what's with the crazy black get up?" He chuckled.

Victor had no tolerance for this man. "The problem, red, is that you are sitting at a stop sign holding up traffic and I have places to go. And as for my outfit, it's what vampire's wear." Victor gave him a look daring him to make a sarcastic remark. "Are you going to move now or shall I move you?" He asked. "Your fate lies in your own hands."

The red haired man laughed uncontrollably. "Man, you're hilarious!" He boomed. "'It's what vampire's wear . . . '" He scoffed repeating Victor's words. "Now that is too much." He picked up the phone and started dialing a number. "If you'll excuse me I have to call my woman back." He said waving a hand at Victor. He rolled the window up but Victor stopped it halfway and grabbed the cell phone snapping it in two like a twig.

"You just chose your own fate by ignoring me. I guess I have to move you myself." Victor said, opening the door and pulling the man out. "So be it."

"What the hell dude. Settle down," he said, eyes large and a shocked expression on his face. Victor wrapped his hands around reds throat. "Please," he screeched. "I'll move," he was losing air.

Victor threw him to the ground. "Listen and listen close, boy." He waited until he had his attention. "Believe it or not I am a vampire. Care for proof?" Victor asked and bared his fangs. He paced in front of red. His predatory lust for blood was too much to bear coupled with his feeling that Katrina wouldn't be at his house. He stopped pacing and stared at red with gleaming hungry eyes.

Red stood and ran. "You're a freak!" He shouted over his shoulder.

"Have it your way, big red." Victor stated. "Ready or not here I come!" He boomed. His house was only a few miles from here so the probability of someone being around was highly unlikely. "Red must not be familiar with these parts," Victor said with a Southern accent and laughed. It was time to eat, drink and be merry. Victor ran after

Red for a few city blocks and watched his prey turn his head this way and that looking for an escape route. Red slowed down. No one ever escaped Victor when he was on the hunt.

Red glanced over his shoulder, his breathing labored. Victor ascended and flew in circles above him like a hawk circling a rabbit. Red stopped, bent over and put his hands on his knees trying to catch his breath.

"Up here!" Victor yelled. Red looked, his mouth open. "Believe in vampires yet?" He asked and descended on top of Red knocking him to the ground. Victor made Red look into his eyes. "If only you would've moved your car we wouldn't be in this predicament right now."

Red tried to scream but Victor covered his mouth with a cold hand. "Don't beg for your life. It's no use. No one will hear you. Normally I only kill murderers but today I'm making an exception. The blood of the innocent is so much sweeter." He raised his head, bared his fangs and lowered his head to Red's throat.

"Stop, please. I did nothing wrong. I'm not a criminal." Red pleaded when Victor uncovered his mouth.

Victor stopped, looked at Red and smiled. "But you did do something wrong. You are guilty of a traffic violation and for ignoring me when I gave you a chance. You chose this."

Red argued but Victor covered his mouth again, lowered his head to Red's throat, sunk his sharp fangs into his neck and drank until Red was dead. Victor stood and wiped his mouth. "No more fights between you and your girlfriend anymore." He chuckled and walked away.

Five minutes later he was at Donovan's truck but he had one more thing to do before going to his house. Victor used his powers and forced Red's car to hit a tree making it look like a high-speed head on collision. The police would suspect the coyote's dragged Red's body into the wilderness. Victor smiled, satisfied with himself. He was beginning to enjoy being evil more than being good. That was a problem but only if any of other vampires in The Dark Ones were to find out, which they would not.

Satisfied, Victor got in the truck and accelerated. He turned onto the road leading to his house and hoped Katrina would be there. He gave her a choice to stay or leave by leaving the front door open. If she were looking for a way out then it showed she wanted to leave. It shocked Victor knowing he did this. Why did he allow her to have freewill? He asked himself this question half a dozen times already.

He turned into his driveway lined with pine trees on both sides. Nothing but beautiful forest surrounded his home. He would have it no other way. Here he had seclusion, peace and a sense of security. The truck and trailer were making it slightly difficult to steer along the winding drive. "Flying is so much easier." Victor said, cursing Armani for his choice of torture and the tools it required.

His heart sank when he saw the front door open. He should've known Katrina would leave. He hoped that maybe she would be inside.

Victor parked the truck and walked up the steps. He entered his cold house. His senses told him she was gone as he drifted from room to room, scanning corners and closets looking for her but to no avail.

His heart ached and a crooked smile lit his face. "I still have a heart and emotions." He said aloud. 'Not for long, Victor, it's too late for you. You've made it clear your true happiness lies in the dark wicked deeds of the most evil vampire's in the world.' An inner voice told him. "Must be the Devil speaking to me." Victor whispered.

"Shut-up," Victor told his inner voice. "I don't need to hear from you right now."

Victor walked into the kitchen and opened the refrigerator and pulled out a bottle of wine. He didn't bother to pour it in a glass. He tipped the bottle to his mouth gulping it down until he couldn't breathe. A piece of paper lying on the kitchen table caught his eye. It was from Katrina. He picked it up and held it to his heart. Breathing in he smelled lavender vanilla. 'At least she used the bath bubbles I bought for her,' he mused.

Dear Victor,

I'm sorry but I cannot stay here with you. I assume you left the door open as a choice for me to stay or leave. I will not be with a vampire by force. Many questions I had for you remained unanswered and still do like those disturbing paintings hanging on the wall in the hall on the fourth floor of the little battered and abused boy. You told me they were your life. What did that mean? Please forgive me for the choice I have made. I will not tell anyone about you if you promise to leave me alone forever.

Sincerely,
Katrina.

Victor crumpled the letter and threw it on the floor.

"What did the pictures mean? She asks. I told you they were my life because they were the life I lived as that young boy and those events made me what I am. They are my life then and now." Victor stated, walking out of the kitchen. "All Katrina had to do was use logic and put the pieces of that puzzle together."

It was late and he needed to get back to Armani's. He didn't have time to analyze and think about what he could've or should've done differently. He turned off the lights and locked the front door.

Victor sat in the truck and stared at his house before leaving. How he wished he would see lights on in the house. While Katrina was in his house, he felt hope and a possibility to love and be loved. Something wet ran down his cheek. He wiped it away and saw it was blood, a tear.

His heart ached with loss and sadness. He placed his head in his hands and for the first time in four centuries, he wept.

His body was cold. Rage, anger and hatred swelled inside him like a flood drowning what little love he had left.

Victor gripped the steering wheel, his knuckles turning white. He gritted his teeth and screamed. He pulled down the visor and saw his cold black hollow eyes staring at him as if they weren't his own. His face streaked with red bloody tears.

"Love and hope are illusions! From this day forth I will make all of mankind, the guilty and the innocent suffer as I have endured suffering my entire existence." He shoved the visor in place and sped down the driveway, the truck trailer bouncing and swerving behind him. "Madness has taken over and it shall now be my Master." He laughed shrill and evil. A wolf howled in the distance, birds scattered in a rush and the wind blew hard making the trees bend and twist like a hurricane had struck. "My reign is about to begin."

CHAPTER FORTY

THE BLACK HAWK spread its wings, puffing out its white chest, reared its head and screamed.

Donovan jumped. He was staring at the darkness that surrounded Armani's home.

Armani stopped pacing to look at the hawk. "What's the matter with him?" He asked lines of concern on his face. "Is he sick?"

Donovan faced Armani. "No, he is not sick. Something is wrong. The hawk can sense these things."

Adam had his head on the table cradling his broken hand, rocking back and forth. He didn't bother to see what the hawk was doing. Alex stared at the hawk, his eyes bulging out of his head. A trickle of urine ran down his leg pooling underneath the chair. The sounds of his mmm, mmm, mmm were all he could say thanks to the duct tape.

"What could possibly be wrong?" Armani asked. "Everything seems to be going as planned so far. As long as Victor doesn't take much longer, that is."

Donovan stared hard at Armani. "That may be the problem." He pivoted, staring out the window again. He couldn't tell Armani his fears about Victor turning evil.

"You can't just make a statement like that and turn away without an explanation." Armani said. "Tell me what the hell is going on." He demanded.

"Now is not the time or place for this discussion, Armani." He said in a case closed tone. "Ah, I see headlights in the distance. Prepare yourself. The games are about to begin."

The hawk screeched its eyes glued on Alex.

"I'm glad. I have seen enough of these two men and I am more than ready to kill them." Armani said and impatiently tapped his foot.

Victor walked through the door. "Honey's I'm home!" He yelled and laughed. He barged into the kitchen and slapped Adam upside the head on his way to the refrigerator. "I got all the tools necessary for the revenge kill." He snapped open a beer and guzzled it before turning around. "Yeah, you're welcome."

"Thank-you," Armani said. "Are you going to help me set it up?"

Victor whirled around, his cape whipped behind him. "Naturally I will as well as Donovan. Isn't that right Donovan?" He asked. "I want the kill to be successful. Not some botch up half ass job."

"Are you saying that I may not do it right?" Armani asked.

"That's exactly what I'm saying." Victor replied eyes black and full of hatred. "When this is all said and done I'm leaving you in Donovan's hands. I have a few private matters to attend to." Victor hummed. "And don't ask what it is because quite frankly, it's none of your business." He retorted glaring at Donovan expecting him to be nosy.

"Armani, if you'll excuse me a moment." Donovan stated flatly. "I need to use the restroom."

Armani nodded and focused his attention on Alex and Adam. The hawk sat like a stone statue glaring at Alex. Armani supposed it was waiting for the command to eat Alex's eye. "A few minutes, buddy and you can have your treat."

Victor held two glass jars out to Armani. "Take this."

"What is it?" Armani asked, confused. He took the jars and stared inside.

"It's acid and you're going to throw it on the left side of both Alex and Adam's faces." He said. Walking toward Alex he said, "Burn them as they burned you." He smoothed his hand over Alex's cheek and bent down to stare into his eyes. "You're going to love your new look. And to think you thought the damage to your precious Cadillac was bad." Victor patted the hawk's head. "Well done damaging his vehicle by the way." The hawk nodded. "Go ahead and feast." Victor commanded.

Alex tried to push the chair away from the table tipping it over instead. The hawk was on top of him in a flash. Alex turned his head to the left and right trying to scream but all that came out was hmmm, mmm, hmmm.

"Thank God for the tape. No one wants to hear a coward scream." Victor laughed. "Watch and learn Armani. You will get a hawk as well that you must train."

The hawk used its powerful sharp beak and gouged it into Alex's eye. Alex's legs kicked like he was riding a bike. The hawk cocked its head, pushing its beak in further. Alex kicked harder moaning and groaning. The hawk grasped the eye, wriggling its head, pulled back and with a snap the nerve severed and the eye pulled from the socket. Blood gushed from Alex's vacant eye socket. The hawk flew off Alex back onto the table and chomped the eye like it was an exquisite delicacy.

Armani cringed. This was the sort of thing he saw in horror movies, not his kitchen. What would Simone think? Had he gone mad? Was he a sociopath now? No, he wasn't. Damn it, this was revenge and it felt good.

"Armani, stop thinking, set that damn acid on the counter and get a towel." Victor ordered, leaning over Alex. "We must stop the bleeding. I don't want him dying from blood loss."

Armani threw Victor a towel and watched him shove it into the hole where Alex's eye used to be. "There, there, Alex. It's Ok. This is just an intro to the pain and torture you have coming that you deserve." He mockingly patted his head like a man would his dog.

Alex muttered and moaned, cuffed to the chair and rolled side to side on his back like a beetle that can't turn over and knows it's going to die.

"Why must you put us through the torture?" Adam asked. The first few words he spoke in awhile. "Just kill us already." He said and rolled his eyes. "This is sadistic."

Victor grabbed Adam's throat, squeezing hard. "Eye for an eye, Adam and I mean that literally this time, as you saw," he seethed pointing at Alex. Lifting his leg, he kicked Adam's chair over.

Adam groaned. "Why did you do that?" He asked. Staring at the ceiling, he prayed aloud this would end soon.

"Oh Adam, it's too late for prayers." Victor straddled Adam's chair. "God doesn't want to hear from you." He smiled. "Armani, it's time to dowse this boy with acid." Glaring at Adam he asked, "Why did you kill Simone?" He snapped his fingers and said, "I know why, because you couldn't have her."

Adams face turned red and he screamed. "Fuck you! Fuck you both!"

Victor punched him. "Tell me why boy," He ordered.

Adam spit. "Because I could and my face was the last thing she saw before she died. That was satisfaction for me." A smug smile was plastered on his face. "How do you like that answer?"

Victor stepped aside and smiled.

Armani heard enough. Rage ran through his veins. He grabbed the jar of acid, leaned over Adam and poured it on the left side of his face. "How do you like that response to your answer?" Armani asked.

Adam screamed, closed his eyes and begged for mercy while the skin on his face sizzled like popcorn in oil. He turned his head trying to rub his burning face on the floor.

"Did Simone beg for her life?" Armani asked. "I bet she did." He kicked him in the ribs over and over. "It's just like you're begging the floor to wipe the acid off your face." He laughed hard. "It's too late asshole." Armani stared at Adam.

Victor shoved a mirror in Adams face. "Take a look, son. How do you like it?"

Adam tried to avoid looking in the mirror. Armani grabbed his face forcing him see his reflection. "Do you like what you see?"

Half of Adam's face sizzled and purple and red sores protruded out of what used to be flesh. Tears formed in the corners of his eyes. "Stop this. Please." He begged.

Victor raised his arms. "The only time we will stop is when you're dead." He set Adams chair back in its proper place and released the cuffs. "Stand up next to me, boy." Victor ordered. "I believe it's time for Alex to enjoy an acid bath." He nodded at Armani. "How about we have Adam pour it on his old mans face?" He asked.

Victor enjoyed poetic justice. He firmly believed in spicing up the kills, making them more fun, interesting and mentally torturing. With Victor it all depended on his mood at the time of a kill. Some were swift and some were slow and deliberate.

"Pardon me," Donovan poked his head into the kitchen. "I wanted to let you know that I'll be outside preparing the kill zone." He didn't wait for a reply.

Adam dug his heels in the marble floor trying with all his might to resist Victor. "Stop fighting me or I will inflict more pain on you." He gripped his arm tight, digging his nails into Adam's arm. Drops of blood dripped on the floor like raindrops. "Understand."

Adam nodded.

Armani handed Adam the glass of acid. "Do it." He ordered.

Alex lay on his back staring at Adam with his remaining eye. He tried to squirm and wiggle away but Armani stomped on the chair securing it in place. Adam's hand shook as he lifted the glass, turned his head and poured the acid on his dads face. "I'm sorry dad." Adam whispered.

Alex shook his head to the left and right like a child telling their dad and mom no. Muffled sounds of agony came from his mouth.

Victor picked Adam up and congratulated him. "Let's get the party started. Come." He said leaving the kitchen.

Armani lifted Alex's chair into a sitting position and unlocked the handcuffs. He grabbed Alex's arm dragging him behind and followed Victor. The monster within had been released. Evil, hate and revenge filled his heart, soul and mind. The end was near for these men. Armani vowed to visit Simone when this was all said and done for closure for them both.

Tears fell from Simone's eyes. What was happening? Armani hadn't visited her in days and she missed his voice. Violence and dark thoughts plagued her. Her gut instinct told her something wasn't right. Either Armani was in some sort of trouble or he had gone mad.

Six feet under and trapped in a coffin, her love was strong for him. She was dead but her soul lived on. She longed for God to take her to Heaven where she would be reunited with loved ones and sing with the angels. Why was God keeping her here? Why wouldn't He just take her to eternal rest? Unable to move because her body was dead, her soul cried out for mercy.

"God, why are you torturing me? I can see, hear and think. Why?!" She screamed feeling like a patient with advanced MS.

God was silent. Simone rolled her eyes. This was not the afterlife she had imagined or been taught about while growing up. "I'm dead! Take me already!" She cried. Her body lay motionless in the small coffin, her hands folded over her chest in eternal prayer. Anguish rolled over her like waves on the ocean. She was in constant and never ending torment. How much more could she endure?

"What will happen to me? What will happen to Armani?" Simone asked. She stared at the black cloth that lined the coffin lid. If she were granted one wish, she would wish for mobility so she could fight her way out of this coffin. But even if wishes came true, she was dead and no one would see her. She'd be a ghost. She closed her eyes and cried. Gut wrenching sobs filled the dark coffin.

There had to be a reason for this. She thought about the movies she had seen over the years and remembered seeing how souls roamed the earth until justice was served to avenge the death of an innocent. She was murdered. Was Armani going to avenge her death? Would he kill Adam and Alex, allowing her soul the freedom to leave her body and go to Heaven? Opening her eyes, she had a new hope and prayed that this was the answer to her unrest.

CHAPTER FORTY-ONE

ARMANI AND VICTOR walked side by side like soldiers marching to war, black capes flowing in unison, jaws set and no emotion on their faces. Adam and Alex followed like puppets on a string.

Gusty winds blew and heavy snow fell. Armani stopped and stared at the fountain in his yard reminding him of the happy days he once shared with Simone. What was once beautiful was now covered in snow and ice like his heart. He was dead inside and for that these two men would pay the price. He was broken and hated what he had become.

Victor shoved Adam and Alex toward Donovan. "Hold them." He ordered. "Armani, come to me." Victor stated. "The time has come. Vengeance is yours, my dearly beloved son."

Armani glanced at Victor and looked to the right of him at the stakes lying on the ground.

"Beautiful, isn't it?" Victor asked, wiping a snowflake off his face and gazing at it.

Armani smiled. "Yes. I've always loved snow." He bent over and picked up a handful of snow examining it. "They say each snowflake has its own unique design."

Victor smirked. "I'm not talking about snow or snowflakes. Do I look like a sentimental vampire to you?" He asked.

"No." Armani shot back. "But the snow is still beautiful."

"Now, that's beautiful." Victor said. He pointed at the shrine Donovan set up for the burning at the stake ceremony. "Who's ready for a pig roast?" Victor asked and laughed loud.

Donovan laughed. Alex fell to his knees and pleaded for forgiveness. Adam stood still and stared at the stakes. "Oh, God no." He mumbled.

"I must admit. This is set up exactly as they used to do it back in the days when they burned witches at the stake." Armani said. "Impressive."

Victor agreed. "Well done, Donovan. Thank you kindly." He wrapped his cloak around himself. "Shall we get started? It's getting cold and the fire will warm us."

"Let it begin." Donovan said. He walked to Armani and led him to the wooden stakes lying on the ground.

Armani cocked his head. "That's odd. These stakes resemble a cross." He couldn't take his eyes off them for some unexplainable reason.

"Why certainly," Donovan stated with a wave of his hand. "These men are paying for their sins. Correct?" He smirked proud of himself. "It's poetry in motion."

Victor laughed. Armani grunted and studied the place of execution. There was bundle of rope, a couple gas containers, a large hammer, nails and a few railroad stakes. Armani assumed they were to pierce the men's forearms in order to insure they stayed up on the stakes.

The snow was cleared around the place of execution. Piles of wood surrounded the area like the set up for a bonfire. In the center stood what looked like a large wooden teepee pointing to the Heavens.

"Once we have them secured firmly to the stakes we place them in the middle of the standing triangular wood," Donovan explained pointing. "Then Armani, you light the fire and torch these two miserable creatures." He said and turned to glare at Adam and Alex who were crouched like cowards in the snow.

"Please, I beg you to let us go." Adam whimpered staring at the stakes.

Victor walked to where Adam and Alex were huddled together and picked them up with swiftness dragging them to the stakes. "Let's begin, shall we?" He shook Adam and Alex and threw them. "I don't think I can bear to hear one more desperate cry for mercy." He kicked snow in their faces, folded his arms and waited for Donovan and Armani.

Donovan held his hand out to Armani and asked, "Are you ready, my dear friend?" He gave him a reassuring smile like a father teaching his son to ride a bike for the first time.

"More than ready," Armani responded taking Donovan's hand. He clasped it for a moment, let go and walked to stand beside Victor.

The hawk flew above, eyes focused on the group. Satisfaction flooded its soul. What made humans become so evil and vile? Why did they want to hurt their own kind? The hawk circled once more before landing on a tree branch. Armani was a good man and now would make an excellent vampire. Donovan told him so and the hawk trusted Donovan. The hawk cocked its head, staring affectionately at Donovan, his forever Master.

Donovan gazed at the hawk and smiled. This was the moment the two of them had been waiting for.

Victor picked up Alex and thrust him on the stake. "Bind him." He said spreading Alex's arms out and holding him down. "Make haste Armani." Victor ordered. Victor had his own agenda to take care of once this was over and the sooner the better.

Armani grabbed the rope, tied it around Alex's waist and wrapped it up his body ending at his outstretched arms. "This reminds me of Jesus on the cross," Armani remarked.

"Is that so?" Victor asked scoffing. "I would've said the thief to the left of Christ myself." He laughed in Alex's face. "We do have a humorous side." Victor ripped the duct tape off Alex's mouth. "I want to hear you scream. It will make me feel better."

Alex flinched. It didn't hurt nearly as bad as his eye being gouged out by that pathetic bird. The socket where his eye had been throbbed and his face burned. Death would be a welcome end from this torment and pain.

"Hand me the rail road ties Armani." Victor ordered.

Armani handed them to Victor watching as he placed them on Alex's forearms. Victor looked at Armani and smiled. "They have to be placed here because if they were placed through the hands the weight of their bodies wouldn't be supported." He snapped his fingers. "All that would happen is a tearing of the hands and they would fall to the ground." Victor held the railroad ties waiting for Armani to pound them in. "Do it."

Armani stared into Alex's eyes and seethed, "This is for Simone, you son of a bitch."

Alex spit in his face. "You'll never get away with this."

"Oh, but we will." Victor retorted. "I'm an expert and have been getting away with this for over four hundred years." He stared at Armani waiting for him to strike.

Raising the sledge hammer above his head Armani tightened his grip and brought the hammer down with force. It met the railroad tie with a loud metallic thud.

"My God!" Alex screamed his face etched with excruciating pain. Blood flowed out of his hand like a river when the dam is released.

"He's going to bleed to death." Armani stated.

"That is exactly why we must move with speed and deliberation." Victor responded. "Now pierce the other hand. Donovan will place the stake in the center of the wood pile when you finish." Victor flicked his head in Donovan's direction. "Start the fire."

"Yes sir." Donovan replied. He walked to the large circle, spread gasoline on the wood and set the can aside. Lighting a match, he threw it on the wood and watched it burst into red and orange flames that danced in the wind waiting to be fed.

Armani pierced Alex's other hand while Victor placed a kicking and screaming Adam on the second stake. Armani rushed to the second stake and hammered the railroad ties into Adam's arms. Adam clenched his fists each time the hammer hit the railroad tie. "How does it feel to have your life taken from you?" Armani asked.

"About as good as it felt when I took the life from you that should've been mine," Adam said, his voice barely audible. Adam raised his head, opened his mouth and shrieked like a crying baby.

Armani slapped him. "I'll tell you a secret, Adam." He waited until Adam was silent. "Simone cherished you as a friend and you killed her, you pathetic bastard." He stood, raised his foot and stomped on the railroad tie shoving it further into Adam's hand. "For your crimes you will pay." He folded his arms and stared into Adam's eyes. "And I must say I feel damn good right now for the first time in months so thank you for this." He spit on Adam and walked away.

Adam wiggled like a mouse caught in a trap. Alex screamed profanities at the vampires. "You sick demented creatures! I'll see you in Hell." Alex said, blood pooling out of his mouth.

Donovan flew above and laughed. "Welcome to the Dark Airlines. We are pleased to announce that today you will be traveling to Hell in first class seats." He dove down and grabbed Alex's stake. Victor followed suit and plucked Adams stake from the ground. Armani watched with anticipation. He hoped this would heal his wounds and bring him closure.

"This is for you, Simone." He said softly, tears escaping his eyes. "I love you and may you now rest in peace." Wiping the tears away he watched as Victor and Donovan descended, stakes in their powerful grasps, each setting a stake in the middle of the fire. Victor and Donovan secured the stakes in place, ascended into the sky and descended to stand next to Armani. Victor waved his hand and the fire erupted like lava from a volcano. Donovan smiled, draping his arm over Armani's shoulder.

"This is the moment you've been waiting for, my friend." Donovan said. "Watch closely, think of Simone and let go of the hurt. This is avenging her death. Release and let go of the pain and allow the closure to take hold of you and your heart."

Victor stood in silence, his face like stone, eyes black as a starless midnight sky and full of hate.

Armani watched the flames dance around Alex and Adam like a predator toying with its prey. Alex and Adam screamed trying to wriggle out of the way of the flames lapping at their ankles.

"How long does this last?" Armani asked. He assumed they would die within a matter of minutes.

Victor answered the question. He had lived for over four centuries and had witnessed many executions of this style. "It all depends. More than likely they will burn for some time before death takes them, either by heatstroke, shock, loss of blood or thermal decomposition of body parts. Some people die from suffocation and they are the lucky ones, I'd say." He paused and watched as Alex and Adam's calves and thighs caught fire. "The fire is starting to devour them." He said and rubbed his hands together like a child anticipating a gift. Victor turned to look at Armani. "Pardon me," he said, "The longest I've seen someone suffer is two hours."

Armani nodded and watched Adam and Alex suffer. The pain they were going through was unbearable. Adam stared at Armani screaming and moaning. He tried to move but it was no use. Armani smiled at him, his fangs protruding. He was trapped, a prisoner of the flames of Hell now. Alex's face turned blue and his breaths were labored. His mouth opened to scream but nothing came out. His torso burst into flames. He moved his head from side to side a few times, his body shook and his head went limp.

"Alex just passed away." Victor stated. He looked at Armani and then to Donovan. "He was what I referred to as one of the lucky ones." He averted his gaze back to Adam.

Adam called out to his father but it was no use. "You killed my dad!" He screamed his bound body bouncing on the stake. Adam's forearms were in flames. His body buckled, his face wet with sweat. He looked at Armani. "Please. Help me!" He shrieked. His eyes grew large as the flames lapped at his face. Donovan, Armani and Victor watched as Adam's face crinkled and sizzled like steak, turned black and melted off his body. He was dead in seconds. They continued to watch the flames engulf the dead men burning them to nothing but ashes.

"Ashes to ashes, dust to dust may you two burn in Hell forever." Victor prayed and did the Hail Mary. "Well done, my sons. It is finished." He shook Donovan's hand and turned to face Armani. "Congratulations on your first kill. This one was for the purpose of revenge. You have avenged the death of your one and only true love." He placed his hand on Armani's shoulder. "The Dark Ones stand for justice and peace as you know. From this day forward your kills will be for justice alone. You are a vigilante vampire, shining a light into the darkness by ridding the world of evil and wicked people." He paused allowing Armani time to process the information. "Do you understand?" He asked.

Armani nodded. "Yes, I understand."

"Good." Victor replied. He bent over and wiped his hands in the snow. "Donovan will be your guide for a time." He stood and stared at the fire still burning strong. He slicked back his jet-black hair and secured his cloak. "Donovan will help you clean up the ashes when the fire is out. The evidence will be burned away so no need to worry." He reached out to Armani and embraced him. "I'm proud of you, my son.

Welcome to my family, The Dark Ones." He released Armani and stepped back. "If you'll both excuse me I'm famished and have some business to attend to." He bowed and was gone.

Donovan glanced at Armani. "Are you doing alright?" He asked, concerned.

Armani shrugged. "Yes. No. I don't know." He replied staring at the fire, his heart pounding out of his chest. He felt relieved, happy, sad, empty and guilty. He had so many different emotions swirling inside him like a blue sea that he thought he would drown. "I just need a moment of silence."

"I understand." Donovan said. "I'm going in the house. Once the fire is out I'll take care of the clean up." He rubbed Armani's back in a soothing manner. "Take all the time you need. Let go of the negative emotions. You did the right thing. All vampires experience the guilt you're feeling. Don't be hard on yourself. You, my friend made yourself and the world a better place." He smiled and walked toward the house stopping at the door to look at the branch the hawk was perched on. "Watch over him, my guardian and friend." He whispered. The hawk nodded in acknowledgement.

The fire crackled and snapped. Armani watched the fire, amazed that just a while ago there were two men burning in the middle of it. The fire warmed his cold body but not his heart and soul. He closed his eyes praying to a God he knew would never forgive him for his transgressions.

A gust of wind blew over the fire making it dance in circles. Armani watched his eyes wide. What was happening? A surge of energy swept through the trees and they waved and danced in the wind like people celebrating a new life. The fire beckoned him to come near. Armani looked from left to right and walked toward the fire. He watched as the fire took on a life form. It twisted in a circle forming a spike at the top, flames flying rampantly around it. A human rose from the flames with outstretched arms. Armani squinted holding his hands above his eyes.

Who was this? He wondered. It was a woman. A bright white light illuminated around her beautiful curves, her long brown hair blew in the wind. Simone. Armani held his arms out to her. "Simone . . . ." He whispered his cheeks damp from tears.

Simone was three feet above the fire staring at Armani with love in her eyes. "Armani, I have missed you." She said. A tear fell from her eye.

Armani was breathless. Simone was the most angelic beautiful woman he had ever seen. "Now that it's over, I just want to hold you. Please come to me, Simone."

Simone smiled. "We will be together in another lifetime. When it's your time I'll be waiting for you in Heaven." The light surrounding her grew brighter and two angels appeared to the left and right of her. "You have set me free and for that I am grateful. I love you, Armani."

Armani tried to smile but his face cringed and he couldn't stop crying. "Please don't take her from me. Give her to me." He looked from one angel to the other.

Both angels were silent.

Simone put her finger to her lips and blew a kiss to Armani. "Good bye Armani. I'll see you on the other side." She whispered. The bright light surrounding Simone dimmed like a flickering candle being blown about in the wind.

Armani reached out to her wanting to touch her, longing to hold her and never let go. He smiled, red tears falling from his eyes like a downpour of rain. His heart ached. Armani watched as Simone held hands with each angel. She smiled and they ascended to the Heavens.

Armani watched until they were a speck in the sky. Placing his head in his hands Armani dropped to his knees and wept. He lifted his head to the Heavens, grabbed a handful of hair and screamed. "God, why did you take her from me? Why did you let this happen?" Desperation washed over him. "I can't live with this pain and agony!" He sobbed. Armani sat and stared at the place where Simone had just been. He had freed Simone by avenging her death but he didn't feel closure. He felt empty and alone and always would without Simone in his life. "I can't live with the choices I've made." Armani said watching the fire burn out. "We will be together soon, Simone." He whispered, wiping the tears from his eyes. Armani stood, wrapped his cloak around himself and turned to look at the house he used to call a home. He knew what he had to do next and nothing and no one was going to stop him.

CHAPTER FORTY-TWO

D ONOVAN WAS LYING on the couch when Armani walked in. Armani paused and looked around his house. It amazed him how something so majestic and glorious could feel so cold and empty. He grasped the necklace around his neck and rolled the engagement ring between his fingers. Putting the ring to his lips he tenderly kissed it and placed it against his heart. How he ached for Simone. Killing Adam, Alex and Gabe brought no peace. Revenge only made his pain worse. He could not live as a vampire with these feelings for all of eternity. Armani thought about waking Donovan but decided against it.

He slipped quietly passed Donovan and glided up the spiral staircase stopping at the top to meditate. Seeing Simone was magnificent but served only as a knife stabbing deeper into his heart. How can one have closure when you're not willing to let go of the past? Surely avenging Simone's death was to bring him this idealistic term thrown about so easily by humans. 'All you need is closure and the pain will be healed.' Armani thought and swore. What did they know? People appeared to know nothing. Death was closure, not the mere righting of a wrong. Being a vampire in The Dark One's was not the life Armani wanted or needed.

He walked into the bedroom filled with rage and hate. He pulled the sheets off the bed heaving them into a corner. Why did the angels take her away from him? They were capable of performing miracles if God allowed. Why did He deny him the one thing he wanted most in this world? Armani was afraid he knew the answer.

'The Lord gives and the Lord takes away,' a voice whispered.

"Shut-Up!" Armani screamed his face red. His body convulsed and he fell to the floor. Turning his head aside, he vomited. "He's taken from me for the last time." Armani said through gritted teeth.

Armani rolled on his back and stared at the burgundy ceiling. It reminded him of better times when he and Simone would lay in bed talking about their future. Now, here he lay staring at the same ceiling thinking of what could've been.

Hours past and Armani stirred, sitting up to look out the window. It was dark. "Damn it all to Hell." He cursed himself for falling asleep. He raced to the bathroom with the speed of a gazelle.

Ten minutes later he was showered and dressed. Hunger pained him but that was the least of his worries. Armani slipped on his black cape and adjusted the collar. He stared at his reflection in the mirror. Cold, dead and empty eyes stared back.

"I'm a monster and I must save myself from what I've become." Armani said. He grabbed his mask and placed it on the left side of his face. He slipped on his black gloves and stepped into the hallway. What he heard stopped him in his tracks.

A violin, it's majestic and glorious sound soothed him like a mother's lullaby. Whoever was playing was a master of the instrument. The music grew louder as he walked in the direction of the music room. He peeked around the corner and saw Donovan sitting in a chair, violin held to his chin, bow in hand erratically and lovingly playing his violin. Donovan's body moved with the music with such passion it brought a tear to Armani's eye. He knew too well how music had the power to move your soul. Armani was tempted to compliment Donovan but didn't. Instead he turned, floated down the stairs and stopped at the front door. He clutched the door knob and bid his home and Donovan a silent farewell.

CHAPTER FORTY-THREE

ARMANI TAPPED HIS foot while waiting in line at the grocery store. Didn't these people sleep? It was the middle of the night and there were scores of people shopping. He was on a mission and lacked for patience.

"Long line, huh?" A man in front of him asked.

Armani agreed and gazed at the basket of groceries the man was carrying. Milk, eggs, cereal, microwave meals . . . simple bachelor foods. The tall lanky man noticed and chuckled.

"Yep, I'm living the single life." He smiled. "It's hard to cook for one." He cocked his head. "What's up with the mask covering half of your face?"

Armani wanted to beat this man senseless. Some people seemed to lack in the privacy department. What kind of question was that? "Does it matter to you?" Armani shot back.

The man shifted the basket to his other hand. "It doesn't. Sorry I asked."

'You should be,' Armani thought. "You're forgiven." He stated flatly. "The burn unit at the hospital is a bitch. Enough said. Do you understand now?"

The man turned his back on Armani, placing his groceries on the conveyor belt. The cashier smiled at him and Armani.

"You know who that is, don't you?" She asked the man.

"No." The man replied.

"What cave have you been living in?" She asked. "That's Armani Belvedere, the lead singer of the band, 'Faded Cross.'" She gushed and smiled a thousand watt smile at Armani.

"Ah, ok." The man responded. "That's wonderful but unfortunately I don't listen to rock. Country music for this boy," he laughed.

Armani wanted to leave. He had what he needed and wanted nothing more than to get the hell out of here. "Correction, madam, I was the lead singer of 'Faded Cross.' Those days are over. The band is dead to me now." 'My life was over and soon will be.' He thought.

The cashier didn't respond. The tall lanky man quickly paid for his groceries and bustled out of the store without a backward glance.

"Forgive him," she said scanning his purchases. "He's a regular customer here and quite odd, I might add." Picking up the dozen roses she inhaled. "Who's the lucky lady?" She closed her eyes enjoying the fragrance.

"That would be my fiancée. Now if you'll please hurry I have places to go." It took all of his willpower not to scream.

"Yes sir." She responded. "These are odd things to buy." She stated scanning the price of the roses.

Armani was sure the things seemed a rather odd combination: a gas container, roses, a card, a large box of matches and coal.

"I suppose so but when the furnace is broke at your house one must do what you gotta do to keep warm." Armani knew that would shut her up. He was trying his best to be polite but if she kept asking questions he would snap.

She didn't say another word and bagged his items handing him the roses. "I don't want to crush them." She smiled. "Have a nice day, Armani and reconsider singing. Your voice is Heavenly."

"Not in this lifetime." Armani smiled, thanked her and rushed out the door to his Navigator. Blakesley Cemetery was his next stop.

The ten minute drive to the cemetery he managed to do on auto pilot.

The cemetery was dark, cold and dreary. Lamp posts lit the first couple rows of tombstones.

Armani pulled up to Simone's tombstone. The angel had been repaired and he thought he saw the stone lips smile at him when he exited the car while cradling the dozen roses like a delicate newborn.

Armani walked to where Simone's body lay six feet under. Her soul was free and at peace singing with the angels in Heaven but he felt like a failure. If only he had been alert he could've saved her from the attackers and none of this would've happened. But dwelling on would've, should've and could've wouldn't change what happened. He had been drugged and was helpless to protect her in her time of need. It was time for him to lose the shackles and escape his own private insane asylum.

He stared at the angel admiring what a glorious majestic being she was and wondered if this is what the angels looked like who took Simone to Heaven.

Armani dropped to his knees, wiped the snow away, kissed the ground and set the roses against the marble stone, fresh tears falling like a waterfall.

"Simone, I miss you and I can't live without you. You are everything to me and you are free now. But, the choices I made are too much for me to bear." He paused and took a breath looking around the cemetery. Avenging her death and saying good-bye wasn't closure for him. He knew what he was going to do to obtain closure and in the end he would be with Simone forever.

"I am coming home, my sweet Simone." Armani said and rubbed the marble stone. "All I want is to hold you in my arms. I am dead inside and only you can bring me to life." He stared at the roses and wept. Armani pulled off his white mask and wiped the tears. Life as he had known it was over and the life he now lived was soon to end. He set the card next to the roses. He stood and stared at the stone angels face. A peace comforted him like a warm blanket on a cold winter's day.

Armani turned and walked away from the grave. Before getting in the Navigator he glanced at Simone's grave and smiled. He would see her soon.

The black hawk flew overhead watching Armani. He sensed that something wasn't right. His needed to make haste and warn Donovan of Armani's pending plans before it was too late.

The hawk's eyes glowed yellow and he flew fast zigzagging up and down in the air like a man on a roller coaster. Time was of the essence and he needed to alert his master of what he had seen and heard so Donovan could stop Armani from sealing his own fate.

CHAPTER FORTY-FOUR

ARMANI EXITED THE highway in search of the abandoned warehouse he had researched online. It was the perfect place to end his life. All he wanted was to die and be with Simone and not live a pathetic existence for all eternity as a vampire. He had been deceived into crossing over with the promise that once he avenged Simone's death he would be reunited with her and that was far from the truth. Donovan had told him that to force him to comply with the request to become a member of The Dark Ones. As far as Armani was concerned, Donovan and Victor were both self-serving vampires only looking out for the good of them selves first and foremost and The Dark Ones second.

Armani pulled into the parking lot of the large abandoned warehouse. Chills ran up and down his spine. The McKeller Furniture sign stood at the entrance. The old warehouse was dark and eerie reminding Armani of the haunted attractions in horror and thriller movies. Armani parked and stepped out of the Navigator wrapping his cloak tight around him. He pulled the coal, matches and full gas can out of the backseat.

"Perfect," he said staring at the roof of the warehouse. The fall was far enough to kill him as long as the pool of fire he was jumping into burned with intensity. With his jaw set stubbornly he walked to the center of the building where he'd build the fire.

He spread the coal in a large circle and placed wood on top. Armani walked around the circle, a crooked grin on his lips. What would Donovan think when he couldn't find him? Armani will have won in the end. He would not live his life being something he didn't want to be. What would Victor think? He'd be upset but he was the type that would get over it and replace Armani with a new recruit. What of Rex? Armani sighed. His best friend would be devastated but time would heal his wounds and his best friend would move on and live a productive life. Armani smiled. Everything he owned was willed to Rex. Armani was a wise man and had met with an attorney making sure his riches went to Rex when he died. He left no loose ends upon his death.

Armani shuddered. His keen ears heard a rustling in the bushes a few feet away followed by a low growl. The hairs on his neck stood. He turned, shocked to see a large man, head held high with long flowing gray hair walking towards him.

"Who are you and what do you want?" Armani asked in a demanding tone.

The man's black cape swished around him and he raised his hands in the air. Long bony fingers with nails three inches long protruded. He got closer and Armani saw his eyes were glowing bright blue like the sky on a clear summer's day.

"Do not be afraid, Armani." The vampire said his voice low. "I am here to bid you farewell." He stopped in front of Armani and gazed down at him.

Armani swallowed and looked up into the vampire's eyes. "Who are you?"

"I am Julius, the founder of The Dark Ones." He smiled and stepped back. "No, we have never met but I've seen and heard of many a vampire such as yourself who are turned against their choosing and I want to applaud you for the strength and courage to choose your own destiny." He turned and stared at the old building. "Good spot for a suicide." He stated. He fixed his eyes on Armani. "If I were you I'd make haste and complete your mission." He paused. "If that's what you really want to do."

Armani picked up the gas can and poured it on the coal and wood. "That's what I'm trying to do but I keep getting interruptions." He said hinting for Julius to leave him. "Why are you so concerned with me fulfilling this quickly?"

"That's easy," Julius said. "Donovan will be here soon to stop you. That damn hawk of his had his eyes on you at the cemetery and surely rushed to your home to warn Donovan of your intentions."

Armani took off his mask and threw it aside. "I realize that but how do you know so much?" He asked confused.

Julius smiled. "I am five hundred thirty one years old." He paused for a moment before continuing. "Didn't Victor tell you that I am the one who found him as a helpless beaten child?" He asked. "I rescued him from his despair and turned Victor into a vampire."

"I think he may have mentioned something like that. I don't really remember." Armani stated not hiding the irritation in his voice.

"Yes, that is me." Julius said like a proud father. "The problem is that Victor needs to be destroyed. He has chosen evil and we need you to help defeat him."

Armani shrugged. "That's not my problem, Mr. Julius. You can take care of that problem with Donovan. He's a good vampire. You don't need me. After all, I didn't choose to be a vampire. I was deceived and I am choosing to end my life tonight."

Armani rubbed a match on the box and threw it on the gas covered coal and wood. Small flames licked and lapped and within minutes the fire exploded into massive flames.

"Get to the top of that building and do what you have to do." Julius ordered.

Armani grasped Simone's engagement ring attached to the necklace and placed it inside his shirt. He stared at Julius. It was odd that he was so intent on him killing himself. "Why are you so interested in my death?" He asked.

"Quite frankly, Armani, I'm not." He said walking away from Armani. "I'm not staying to watch. I was sent by an angel of God to try to persuade you to choose life." He turned one last time. "And you don't have much time. If you fail, Victor will curse you and make it impossible for you to ever die. You will forever be a vampire with no hope of escape and the memories of Simone will haunt your aching heart forever." He raised his arms and said, "You can join me in the fight for good or you can kill yourself. It's your choice, Armani." Julius closed his eyes and ascended to the stars, his black cape and long gray hair flowing behind him.

Armani shook his head. What next? He stared at the fire roaring before him. He was ready to finish this once and for all. He ran toward the door and floated to the top of the stairwell counting thirty flights of stairs. If he were still a human he'd be too drained to throw himself off the building and was thankful for the first time to be a vampire.

Armani clutched his cloak, walked to the edge of the building and stared out at the forest surrounding the warehouse. A cool breeze blew on his face. He inhaled the fresh air and smiled. It was time. Steadying himself he looked down at the massive fire frolicking to and fro waiting to be fed. Armani was pleased with his work.

"Soon," Armani whispered. He stepped away from the ledge, dropped to his knees and clutched the necklace. He kissed the ring and tucked it inside his shirt next to his heart. "Now and forever we will be together my sweet Simone."

Armani raised his head to the Heavens and screamed, his body shaking with sobs. He hoped he would be reunited with Simone. Julius' visit troubled him. He was having second thoughts about suicide but then again Victor and Donovan had lied to him to make him cross over. Why should he be faithful to the ones who lied to him? That made no sense. And for all he knew Julius could be lying to him too.

Armani stared straight ahead and saw a vision of Simone dancing in a beautiful lacy white dress. "Oh, my love I am coming home to you this night." Armani said and stretched out his arms trying to grasp her but she disappeared. Armani wanted to hold Simone more than anything in the world. His heart ached like a parents at the death of a child.

"I've struggled long enough with this existence. Life will never be the same without Simone!" Armani hollered into the empty dark sky. "I will wake a new man reunited with my beloved." He slowly walked and stopped at the buildings ledge. Tears cascaded down his cheeks. "God, forgive me for the choices I have made." He sincerely prayed.

Armani closed his eyes and saw Simone and the way her beautiful angelic smile lit up her whole face. He saw the two of them on the boat when they first met and danced together and her true excitement and glee upon his marriage proposal a couple years after. He felt the longing the two of them had to start a family once they were married.

He opened his eyes and thrust his cape behind him with force lining his toes along the buildings ledge.

"I rebuke the darkness that has imprisoned me for too long. It is time for me to take my last breath and fall out." He looked toward the Heavens. "God, surely you understand that no man can live with the pain, agony and loneliness that I have endured these past few months without Simone." He sighed, closed his eyes and whispered, "Forgive me."

CHAPTER FORTY-FIVE

T HE HAWK WILDLY beat its body against Armani's front door with no response from Donovan. Where was his master? He flew to the side of the house landing on the windows ledge. Cocking its head to the side he saw Donovan sleeping the rest of the undead. What careless behavior on his master's part. Why would he allow himself to fall into that type of sleep in an insecure environment? The hawk screeched and beat its head on the window. Donovan rustled but didn't wake.

The hawk soared high above the house, did a three sixty in the air, eyed the window and flew toward it at light speed. He smashed the window, shattering the glass into bits and pieces. The hawk landed beside the couch with the grace and agility of a gymnast.

"Who's there?" Donovan asked startled. He rubbed the sleep out of his eyes and sat up. He saw the hawk standing before him, with wings outstretched and eyes as yellow as the sun. "What is it? Where's Armani?" He asked looking around the room half expecting Armani to appear. "Shit." Donovan jumped off the couch and threw his cloak on. "What's happened?" He asked feeling panicked.

The hawk led Donovan to the crystal ball, focused and replayed Armani's visit to the cemetery.

"What have I done?" Donovan asked. He set the crystal ball aside. "We must get to him before he commits suicide." Donovan cursed himself for not paying closer attention to Armani. Such a new vampire filled with so much pain. He should've never left him alone. Victor would make him pay for his neglect of Armani. But, that was the least of his concerns right now. He had to save Armani from his fate.

"Come, we must go." He said. "We don't have a second to waste." He ran to the door, pushed it open and looked at the hawk standing beside him. "Where is he? You must know my friend. Take me to him."

The hawk screeched, spread its shiny black wings and took flight. Donovan followed suit. The cold wind slapped his face like an angry wife upon finding out her husband cheated. He kept his eyes glued to the hawk hoping its senses were on target with Armani's location and prayed they wouldn't be too late.

Armani's heart beat like a drum in his chest. He swallowed the lump in his throat and looked at the starless sky. He hated being a vampire and felt like a monster. This was the end. Armani wiped the sweat from his face and stared at the red and orange flames dancing in the wind waiting to devour him.

Armani blinked twice and rubbed his eyes. He couldn't believe what he was seeing. Dressed in a white wedding dress, Simone appeared next to the fire staring up at him. Her long hair blew in the breeze, a sympathetic smile on her face and compassion in her eyes. She stretched her arms out to him and whispered, "I understand why you killed those men and you're not a monster."

A red tear trickled down Armani's cheek and he tried to smile. Simone brought him the peace and courage he needed to follow this through to the end. Armani took a deep breath, closed his eyes and mouthed, 'Simone.' He spread his arms like an eagle ready to take flight. "It is finished." He whispered.

From afar Donovan saw Armani standing on the ledge, ready to fall to his death. The hawk dipped up and down in the sky trying with all its might to get Armani's attention. It was no use. Armani was focused on something below and nothing and no one was going to stop him from completing what he had set out to do.

Donovan cursed the fire waiting to envelope his friend. He and the hawk were two hundred yards away when he saw Armani free fall from the building's ledge descending like a torpedo toward the fire.

"Armani, lift yourself up!" Donovan screamed. "Fly Armani!"

Donovan cried out in anguish. They were too late. Armani was going to die.

Armani fell into the middle of the fire and screamed in pain. A loud explosion filled the night sky and balls of fire rolled toward the Heavens.

Donovan and the hawk were thrown backward.

Donovan wiped the debris off his face, lifting his head to stare at the place where Armani ended his immortal life. "God rest your soul, my friend." He placed his head in his hands and wept bitterly. "I have failed."

The hawk bowed its head in reverence and patiently waited for his master.

Filled with anger, sorrow and regret Donovan wiped his eyes and rose to his feet. "Come, my faithful guardian, we must report to Victor what has happened." He held out his shaking arm. "The Dark Ones must continue their work."

The hawk nodded and flew onto Donovan's outstretched arm.

Donovan glanced at the fire and lowered his head praying to a God he hoped would have mercy on Armani's soul. He exhaled and walked from the abandoned warehouse without a backward glance at the fire burning like the forces of hell devouring what remained of Armani.

Julius hid behind the bushes watching Donovan walk away and disappear like the setting sun. Julius's heart went out to his old friend but he had plans of great proportion and in the end The Dark Ones would prevail.

www.ingramcontent.com/pod-product-compliance
Lightning Source LLC
Chambersburg PA
CBHW020640030726
47498CB00002B/298